THE BROKEN CROSS SERIES

BOOKS 1-3

BRI BLACKWOOD

BRETAGEY PRESS

SAVAGE EMPIRE

NOTE FROM THE AUTHOR

Hello!

Thank you for taking the time to read this book. This trilogy is a dark billionaire enemies-to-lovers romance. It is not recommended for minors and contain situations that are dubious and could be triggering.

Chapter Twenty-One of Steel Empire might be triggering to some who have a sensitivity to guns. If you do, please skip or skim the chapter.

BLURB

He's a savage

Damien Cross treats New York City as if it's his personal playground.

He sees.

He touches.

He conquers.

He holds the fate of my family in his hands

And makes a deal with me I can't refuse.

He'll forgive my father's debt if he can have something in exchange: me.

I promised myself I wouldn't get addicted, but nothing is guaranteed when you make a deal with a savage.

Now this debt is my cross to bear.

PLAYLIST

What I've Done - Linkin Park
bad guy - Billie Eilish
I Hate Everything About You - Three Days Grace
Hate Me (with Juice WRLD) - Ellie Goulding
Monster In Me - Little Mix
Bad At Love - Halsey
ocean eyes - Billie Eilish
Paralyzer - Finger Eleven
Dance With The Devil - Breaking Benjamin
Panic Room - Au/Ra
everything i wanted - Billie Eilish
Love Is Madness (feat. Halsey) - Thirty Seconds To Mars

The playlist can be found on Spotify.

1

ANAIS

"Anais?"

I looked up from the document I was reading and smiled at the man standing at the door, but he didn't return it. I waited to see if he would walk into my office, but he stayed where he was. "Hey, Dad. What's up?"

He cleared his throat. "Are you still coming home tonight? I need to talk to you."

I almost missed his question because I was more concerned with the dark circles under his green eyes, the eyes we shared. It seemed as if he had aged overnight. A myriad of emotions crossed his face when he uttered those words, and a feeling of dread came over me that had nothing to do with his question. The expression that settled on his face was one of worry. *What is going on and what does he need to talk to me about?*

I racked my brain for a moment, trying to remember if I said I would go to my parents' home tonight. "My mind is drawing a blank. Was I?" I picked up my phone and checked the group text message I had with my family. I confirmed my father was right and sighed. The stress had to be getting to me.

"Does eight still work for you?"

I nodded, closed my eyes, and placed my index fingers on my temples. I wished the building tension away while my father remained at the door. Part of me wanted to postpone dinner and crawl into bed after work, but it was clear that Dad needed to talk to me about something important and I wanted to be there for him.

"Anais, are you okay?" I could hear him move closer to me.

"Yeah, Dad. I'm fine. Just had a long day. I'll be there tonight." I opened my eyes to find him just to the left of me. He leaned down to give me a warm hug and patted my back. My father was the CEO of Monroe Media Agency and I worked as the social media director. Our company was established over twenty-five years ago and we took care of just about everything that a company might need for their public image. I was the lead on the social media team and that included managing a few people who helped oversee the online presence of our clients.

"Don't work too hard, kiddo."

I spared him a small smile as he took a step back. "I won't. Is everything okay with you?"

He nodded his head, but it wasn't hard for me to notice his hesitation.

I debated whether to ask but refrained because I didn't know how that conversation would go. He might be more willing to talk at home. "Okay. I'll see you tonight."

Dad finally returned my smile with a small one of his own and left, closing my office door behind him. The air in the room shifted dramatically once he left. Before I could analyze the interaction further, my office phone rang.

"Monroe Media Agency, Anais speaking."

"Anais? Hi. This is Edward from CASTRA."

I held the phone away from my ear and sighed before I could stop myself. As if I didn't recognize his voice because Edward and I had talked multiple times a week about CASTRA and how to help them with their social media accounts. Even though I was the senior director of public relations and social media and managed a couple of employees who had taken on the CASTRA account, Edward still preferred to call me, no matter how many times I asked that he didn't. Since CASTRA was one of our biggest clients, I bit my tongue to stop myself from asking him once more.

"What can I help you with today?"

He rattled off a couple of issues, which could have easily been sent to me in an email and hung up the phone. I placed it back down on the hook and groaned. A quick glance at my laptop told me I had a couple more hours before I could go home and prepare for dinner with my parents.

A long day of work meant by the time I left the office it was already dark outside. It didn't help that it was December in New York City. The sun set earlier, the temperatures were colder, and people were preparing to celebrate holidays. That made a long day in the office feel even longer. I zipped up my thick, insulated winter coat, pulling it tighter around my neck as I steeled myself to brave the cooler temperature outside.

I left the office and headed to the subway. Thankfully, it took no time to get there because the closest station wasn't too far. Sometimes having a car in New York City was helpful.

Sitting in a traffic jam in the driver's seat wasn't, which was why I didn't have one. When I needed a car, I would rent one.

The familiar smells of the subway greeted me. If someone were to ask me what those smells were, I'd tell them it was a combination of many things and leave it at that. I checked my phone to see what time it was when I reached the platform, somewhat patiently waiting for the train. I had about ninety minutes to get to my parents' home, but I was going to stop by my apartment first. I didn't have to wait long for the train to come into the station, screeching to a halt. The conductor opened the doors, and I quickly stepped inside, making my way toward a vacant seat.

I kept my eyes focused on the window once the train pulled out of the station. As the train moved closer and closer to my destination, I was glad I only had to take one train to get to and from work, making my commute easy. Unless there was some sort of incident that screwed up the trains' schedule. About twenty minutes later, I walked over to a set of doors on the left side of the car. Once the train stopped, I jumped off, not paying attention to all the other people who had followed suit. It took almost no time for me to exit the station and start walking down the street. My normal stroll turned into a fast-paced gait because I wanted to escape the cold and get home. I mentally made a list of things I needed to do, like change my clothes, before I headed out to my parents'. I was caught up in my own world when I felt something brush up against me, causing me to jump back.

"Sorry," I said as I realized I had bumped into someone who was walking in the opposite direction. When I heard nothing back, I looked over my shoulder and found a man. The way the streetlights bounced off of his face hid some of his features, but exaggerated others, painting a sinister picture.

"Watch yourself," was all he said. His voice was rough, like how I imagined someone with vocal cords wrapped in sandpaper would sound.

I didn't give him a chance to say or do anything else. I started walking backward down the street, trying my best to keep him in view, in case he tried to do something. Instead, he continued in the opposite direction, not once bothering to turn around to give me a second look. Alarms went off in my head and I became more aware that there weren't any people nearby.

I switched back around as I reached into my purse to grab my keys and my phone, hoping the former was enough of a weapon to buy me time in case I needed to get away. I walked even faster down the street, not caring how silly I looked because I knew I had to get home.

When I could see my building, I said a silent prayer, thankful that I was almost home, and I was pretty sure that the man hadn't followed me. When I crossed the threshold into my apartment building, I breathed a sigh of relief. I was safely in my lobby where there were other people wandering about, and the warmth from the heated building wrapped around me like I had just taken a sip of hot chocolate on a cold winter day.

I made it up to my apartment in record time and whipped off the coat and blazer. A quick call out to see if Ellie Winters, my roommate and best friend, was home confirmed she wasn't. It took longer than normal to unwrap the bun I had placed my hair in that morning, but once the pins were on the table, I could feel the tension easing from my head. But it

soon came back with a vengeance when I replayed the scene
that had unfolded with my father earlier.

If I knew my father as well as I thought I did, I knew
something had to be wrong. Throughout my life, he had been
this pillar of strength, never one to sway much in any circum-
stance. If anyone had a problem and wanted help to solve it,
he was there to lend a hand. There wasn't a time I could think
of that I'd ever seen him rattled until today. Although he tried
to put on a brave face, it did little to prevent his actual feelings from showing through the cracks.

I somewhat dreaded dinner at my parents' house tonight,
although it had been a while since we'd had dinner together,
just the three of us. If I had to be honest with myself, that was
something I missed, but with being so busy it had become a
lower priority. I was still feeling weird about the encounter
with the strange man and all I wanted to do was put on my
pj's and go to bed. But I vowed there was no way I was going
to do that. I needed to find out what was going on with Dad.
Before I got too lost in thought, my phone chimed, and I
placed the creepy incident behind me.

Ellie: *Do you want to go to a gala with me?*

I closed my eyes and groaned before my fingers flew
across my keyboard.

Me: *You know how I feel about those types of things, El.*

Ellie: *I think you'll like this one. It's a fundraiser for Project
Adoption.*

Project Adoption was a nonprofit created to support the
rescue of cats, dogs, and other animals, and to help them find
their forever homes. Now I had another reason to go. Besides,
Ellie would have dangled my not going over my head for the
rest of my life. Ellie's love for animals was one reason her

parents supported Project Adoption, so I knew she was dying to go.

Me: *Fine. I'll go.*

Ellie: *Awesome! We can even go dress shopping.*

Me: *I might have something here, but I'll never turn down the excuse to go shopping. Would Thursday work for you?*

Ellie: *Yes, it would. I'm so excited!*

I put my phone in my pocket, determined to finish getting ready for dinner at my parents.

"Dinner was superb as usual, Mom." I leaned back in my chair, debating whether or not it would be proper to loosen the belt I had on. It might not be out in public, but hell, I was home anyway.

"Thanks, dear. I'm glad you liked it." The grin she gave me didn't quite reach her eyes, reaffirming my belief that something was wrong. My mother and I were very open with each other when it came to a multitude of things, and I knew when something was up. Or so I thought. My mom and I shared the same pale skin and long, dark brown hair. I also inherited her thin, fit body type and we shared a love of fitness.

"Anais is right. You really outdid yourself tonight. Thanks, honey." The roasted chicken, broccoli, and crispy potatoes hit all the right spots when it came to a wonderful, comforting meal.

Mom's gaze turned to my father, and she beamed.

Although my parents had enough money to hire people to help them around the house, my mom enjoyed cooking.

Heck, sometimes we would cook together, which had always been fun.

"Anais, can we talk for a moment?"

Dad's words stopped my thoughts. I nodded my head and sat back. "Thanks for dinner, Mom."

"You're welcome. Why don't we take this to the living room?"

"That's a good idea, Ilaria. I'll put the dishes in the sink and then I'll join you in there."

"I can help."

"Don't worry about it. Go relax with your mom while I do this." Dad stood up first and walked over to Mom and rested a hand on her shoulder. He held his hand out and she placed her hand in his and they both stood up. I stood up as well and my mom and I walked together into the living room as Dad was taking the dirty dishes into the kitchen.

I almost asked Mom what was going on, but it was clear that this was something they wanted to tell me together. After we sat down on the couch, Mom reached over and squeezed my hand, telepathically telling me that things were going to be okay. That made me feel worse.

Dad soon joined us and sat next to Mom. He glanced at me but said nothing.

"What is going on? Are you both okay? Is someone sick?"

Mom nodded her head as Dad said, "We're both fine and no one is sick. It's related to work."

I could have fallen back on the couch as relief came over me at the news that no one was sick. Dread trickled in at what he could possibly want to talk to me about regarding work. There was no way he was retiring yet because we'd talked about that briefly earlier this year. I was somewhat shocked he didn't want to talk about this in his office, a place with which I was all too familiar. I remembered being allowed to play on the floor in front of his desk while he spoke on the phone with a client. Then once he'd finished with his calls, he would pull me into his lap and tell me about what he was doing and how he was helping communicate their company's vision with the world. I would say that, without a doubt, he inspired me to go into the field, and I hoped one day when he retired, I would be next in line to run Monroe Media Agency.

"Dad, you're making me nervous. What's up?"

He took a deep breath, and I waited. The weariness I had seen in his eyes earlier that day returned, causing my stomach to shift. Was I even ready to hear what he had to say? If it had something to do with work, was he going to fire me?

"Kiddo, you know how much I appreciate everything you do at Monroe. I don't know where we would be without you and the work you've done over the last five years."

I'm getting fired. I said nothing, but I knew he must have interpreted the look I was giving him correctly: rip off the Band-Aid and tell me what this is all about. I was scared shitless.

It took a second for me to calm my anxieties down when I told myself that he had no reason to fire me. I had done nothing to warrant losing my job. Another idea floated into my mind that shook me even harder: Was Monroe Media Agency going under?

He sighed and Mom said, "Monroe Media Agency isn't doing well."

"What do you mean not doing well?" This was worse than me getting fired.

This time Dad spoke up. "We are losing a lot of money. In fact, it's been happening for a while."

This was the last thing I'd expected my father to say. "Does anyone else know about this?"

He ran a hand through his hair. "A few people do. We kept it secret because we thought we might turn it around quickly, but business hasn't picked up."

I nodded, wrapping my head around what he was saying. "Is there anything I can do to help? Recruit more clients?"

My father reached across my mother and patted my knee, before pulling Mom's hand into his. "You've been doing an amazing job. You and the social media team have been doing a phenomenal job and are the one component keeping Monroe Media Agency alive."

"But that's not enough."

He shook his head. "No. It's not enough, unfortunately. A series of poor investments have hurt us financially, but I'm taking full responsibility because everything stops with me. I'm doing my best to save the company, but we wanted to tell you personally. We didn't want you to hear about it through the rumor mill or potentially from someone else. We will give everyone plenty of notice if they need to find new jobs. We know how much this company means to you."

I didn't know I had cried until a tear landed on my hand resting in my lap. Mom grabbed a tissue from the coffee table and handed it to me. I dabbed at my eyes and sniffled.

"Thanks for telling me."

My mom leaned over and pulled me into her arms, enveloping me in her warmth. How I wished I could stay in her arms and have my problems drift away, much like they did when I was a child.

"Your mother knows what's going on with the company, because I never want to lie to her, and she knows I'm trying to fix everything. And I have a couple of things in the works that might pan out, but nothing is concrete."

"Is there any way I can help?"

"Not right now, kiddo, but I'll let you know if things change."

The desire to tell my parents about the encounter with the man who gave me terrible vibes was shoved to the edges of my mind. His words ran through my mind once more and a sense of unease overtook me, but I assumed my father's news was playing a role as well. After all, we had bigger problems to deal with.

I tried to block the thoughts racing through my mind, because I knew if I didn't, I wouldn't be able to stop crying. My father, the man I had always known to be indestructible, was barely hanging on by a thread. We all rose slowly. Dad took a step around my mother and pulled me into his embrace, and it was something I didn't know I'd needed. I appreciated him coming to me with this issue. Not just as one of his employees, but as his daughter. He knew how much the company meant to me and how one of my own goals was to take it over one day once he retired. Now that dream was hanging in the balance. In an attempt to not go down a rabbit hole of emotions, I took that moment to feel the comfort my father's loving arms brought me.

2

ANAIS

"You look tense."

"And that's why I'm here. Well, outside of seeing you." I loosened my coat as I walked farther into Devotional Spa. Ellie had been working at the spa for the last couple of years.

"I'm glad you clarified that comment." Ellie's smirk was ever present, much to my chagrin.

"Are you giving me a massage or what?"

"You won't let me have any fun, huh?" she asked as she stood up. She headed toward the door, and I followed behind her. "You know the drill. I'll see you in my usual room."

"Thanks." I paused. "Also, thanks for letting me come in at the last minute."

"Not a problem. You know I'm here whenever you need me. You sounded pretty upset, and I had no more appointments, so it was fine."

I stopped to look at her. Her long brown hair was pulled back into a low ponytail and mischief was shining in her brown eyes. She was a couple inches shorter than me, even more so because of me wearing heels to work today. "You have no more appointments because you're supposed to be closed."

"Semantics," she said with a shrug. "How about you get ready, and I'll meet you in the other room? Then maybe we can go out for a drink?"

"That sounds heavenly. You are literally an angel."

"Or a devil in disguise," she told me with a snort. "See you in a second." With that, she left me in the changing room. They designed the brightly lit room in neutral colors and had a couple rows of lockers for people to put their stuff in. There were some neatly folded towels set up on a small counter near a row of sinks for patrons to grab if they needed it. I walked to the row of lockers that I usually went to and placed my valuables inside. It didn't take me long to change out of the clothes I was in, put a robe on, and lock my things up. I then headed to the room that Ellie used for most of the sessions we had together.

The lights in the room were more mellow than the ones in the locker room, creating a warmer and more relaxed atmosphere. Light music was playing in the background and I took off my robe and lay down on the massage table. Once I was settled, Ellie knocked on the door and entered the room. She said nothing as she began the massage. My body relaxed almost immediately, and the stressors of the day flowed from my mind. I knew if Ellie would let me, I would stay on this table forever because it would prevent me from having to face any of the issues that I needed to deal with. Work had been taking a toll on me recently because of longer working hours balancing the clients we had and doing my part to recruit new ones. That, plus a lack of sleep and always being on the go was leading to some of the heightened anxiety I was feeling.

"Relax," she said.

That's when I realized I had tensed up once more. I did my best to think of tranquil and peaceful ideas versus the thoughts that had been raging in my mind for the last couple of weeks. The Swedish massage that I normally received, and that Ellie was giving to me now, helped to relieve the tension and stress that I was feeling. The kneading and circular motions that she was performing worked wonders on my back and I felt some of the troubles from work melt away.

It was time I left work at work and focused on relaxing. I might have nodded off because by the time I came to, Ellie was softly tapping me on the shoulder. I squinted briefly and realized she was standing with her feet crossed, leaning on one of the counters. I closed my eyes once more, not really wanting to move from my position.

"You can head down to the sauna if you want to," she said.

I groaned as I moved my muscles a bit. "That felt amazing, but I think I'm ready for that glass of wine."

"Okay, well, I have a few things to finish up here, but they shouldn't take long. I'll meet you out front."

"Sounds good." I opened one eye to watch her leave the room. I sighed, and it took a couple of seconds for me to convince myself that I need to move in order to get what I desired most right then: wine. I extracted my limp body from the table, grabbed my robe, and headed into the locker room to change back into my work clothes.

Reclothed in my brown dress and black heels, I threw my long brown strands into a quick ponytail. I smiled at my reflection in the mirror, because for the first time in a long time, my pale skin glowed while my green eyes had taken on new life after the massage. I snatched my purse off the bench in the locker room, put on my coat, and walked back into the hallway toward the front desk.

Ellie exited out of another room. "Ready?"

"Yup," I said as I fixed the strap of my bag. "I think that massage made me look twenty-nine again."

Ellie chuckled. "It doesn't hurt that you're only thirty. I just need to say goodbye to Jill at the front desk, and we can be on our way. Are you cool with just heading back to the apartment?"

"Do we even have wine in the apartment?" The idea sounded heavenly. I could take off these shoes for a short while and ride in a car versus the subway.

"Now what type of question is that?" Ellie smirked at me and turned her attention back to the front desk. "Do you need anything from me, Jill?"

Jill smiled. "Nope. Everything is wonderful here. I'll lock things up. I'll see you tomorrow."

"See you tomorrow." Ellie walked over to a side door and held it open for me. "I drove today, so the car's parked in the garage."

"I'm so glad you went into massage therapy."

"Is that because it's beneficial for you?" The sly look on Ellie's face told me she was kidding.

"No, because you're so good at it. Well, I guess it's on a selfish level, because I do directly benefit from it."

"I will let Mom and Dad know. Another point in the win column for me," Ellie said. She was alluding to the fact her parents disapproved of her chosen career path, but she wasn't willing to change her profession to fit their desires.

I nodded as we started down the brightly lit hall. The clacking of my heels echoed off the walls and floor, and soon we reached a huge white door at the end of the corridor. Ellie pushed the door open and held it for me as I walked through. It opened into a smaller hallway with two elevators.

Ellie pressed the down button and turned her head to look at me. "When was the last time we hung out?"

I tried to think. "Has it been about a month? Although we've lived together for years, it has been a while since we saw each other because of work or other obligations."

"Whoa," she said. "I can't believe it's been that long."

"Is this why you wanted to invite me to the gala?"

She shook her head. "It was very last minute and I'm only going because my parents can't go."

"Ah, okay."

"Don't sound so enthusiastic about it."

I chuckled at her sarcasm. I wasn't thrilled about going to an event because when it came to the things that Ellie's parents attended, the people were stuck up, but I wanted to help Ellie out if I could. Throwing on a pretty dress and some makeup was fine, but sometimes schmoozing with other people got tiring.

"I have the invitation at home, so I'll show you when we get there. I know this isn't exactly your scene, but I know you have several fancy dresses or like I said we could go shopping. It would be an opportunity for us to hang out."

"I'm shocked you didn't want to bring one of the guys you're dating."

She shrugged. "I probably could. I want to invite you. Because it's way easier than having to ditch somebody at the end of the night."

That got my attention. Ellie never had a problem securing a date, but never did anything serious. I, on the other hand, hadn't dated in at least six months, and preferred it that way. "Don't you usually have an understanding with the people you date?"

"Yes and no. It's complicated."

"Sounds like it." But I didn't prod any further because the elevator had arrived. We stepped inside and waited as it took us to the garage.

Once the door opened, I stepped out and looked around. "I didn't know there was another way to get down here."

"I know many things about this place and this town."

Although she finished her comment with a wink, I knew she wasn't kidding. I had seen her knowledge in action, and it impressed and terrified me. The random things she retained were both useful and scary.

It wasn't long before we were driving down the New York City streets on the way to our apartment. I watched as the glow from the streetlights bounced off the cars crowding the street. Although it was evening, traffic was still pretty heavy in the "City That Never Sleeps." The low, airy, and soothing music that played at the spa served as the soundtrack for the light conversation we were having to pass the time. The ride home was swift, all things considered, and I sighed and closed my eyes when my back hit the soft cushion of our couch.

"Here you go."

I opened one eye and found a glass of wine staring back at me. "Thanks. Is this Merlot?"

"Yes, it is, and don't worry about it. Also, here's the invitation."

I took the thick ivory-colored card out of her hand and read it over. "Pretty invitation and an open bar."

"Happy to be going now? Plus, what else were you going to do on a Friday evening?"

"Bury myself under a blanket on our couch with a pint of ice cream and watch Netflix?"

"Why are you coming out with me then?"

I laughed as she held out her glass to clink with mine and we sat back to enjoy the delicious wine.

3

DAMIEN

"Is this a family intervention?"

I spared my younger brother Gage a glare as he strolled into the room, fifteen minutes late.

"Glad you could make it," his fraternal twin, Broderick, tossed out from next to me.

We were sitting around an enormous table in one of the many conference rooms in a building that had been dubbed "Cross Tower" due to a lot of our operations utilizing space at this location. Broderick and I had arrived on time to this mysterious meeting, while Gage stayed true to his colors and walked in after we were supposed to arrive.

"Happy to see you too, Ric."

I shook my head at his snark and mentally prepared myself for Broderick to snap back because Gage had shortened his name. This was something that always riled Broderick up when they were kids, and it came as no surprise when they sometimes reverted back to it. My eyes drifted toward the door to see if our father had arrived. What was surprising was our father was late and that was unlike him. Maybe he was operating under the assumption Gage was going to be late, as usual, and was wrapping up a few more things before joining us here.

We all shared brown hair, although the twins' hair was a couple of shades lighter than mine and my father's. Dad's hair was becoming more salt and peppery by the year. He and Gage shared the same hazel eyes while Broderick and I inherited our mother's blue eyes. I smoothed down my black tie, which was usually what I wore to work, and turned to look at the door when I heard it open.

"How about you two cut the bullshit before you revert to five-year-olds?" This was a waste of time.

"Good afternoon, boys. Thanks for coming over on such short notice." Dad walked into the conference room, not hearing any part of the conversation that had just happened.

While I watched him close the door, any other thoughts I had vanished. The one that remained had been nagging at me since he summoned us here just a few hours ago: *Why had Dad called us here with no warning?*

"Gage, have a seat," Dad said as he took a seat across from the three of us on the other side of the table. Gage and Dad arrived at their respective chairs at the same time and took a seat with no fanfare.

"Dad, what's up? What's with the urgency to get us here?" I was glad Broderick addressed the elephant in the room first.

Dad said nothing as he straightened his posture.

"The Meyers merger is moving forward."

Relief flooded the room. We had all been pulling our weight to make sure the deal occurred, and finally our efforts had paid off. Of course, all of this would need to be approved by the board of directors but getting Meyers and Company to this point had taken a couple years of hard work. The board had been ready to approve the deal a year ago. Dad had been the CEO of Cross Industries since our grandfather retired and now Broderick, Gage, and I served as senior vice presidents outside of the ventures we took on outside of the parent company.

"And that's another one added to the empire."

Gage wasn't wrong. Our family had done really well over the years after my great-grandfather had started his first company in the 1800s. It eventually became one of the biggest banks in the United States. That helped start what people called the "Cross Empire" in New York City and around the world.

Dad went into more detail about the next steps in the merger over the course of twenty minutes. We spent a couple of minutes talking about other business before Dad pushed his chair back, signaling that we could wrap things up.

Once we were done, Broderick stood up. "Thanks for calling us in for this, Dad."

"I wanted to keep you up to date. After all, this will shift the focus of the end-of-the-year board meeting a bit, but we should have a call with the rest of the team about it. Before you leave, I wanted to remind you three about the holiday bash your mother is putting together in a couple of weeks."

I smirked when I heard Gage groan. I was sure all of us were thinking it, but two of us had enough sense not to make those feelings known. Mom organized an annual holiday bash for New Year's that I didn't think any of us were particularly fond of, but we attended because she wanted us to.

"Okay, you three can leave now."

We got up and headed toward the exit. My brothers left the room first, and just as I was about to trail after, Dad called me back. "Damien?"

I turned around to face my father.

"A moment? And could you shut the door?"

I raised an eyebrow before complying. I placed both hands in my pockets as I walked back over to the conference room table. Dad slid a folder across the table to me, and it landed just out of my reach.

"What's this?" I asked before I leaned across the table and dragged the file toward me with the tips of my fingers. I flipped the cover open and skimmed part of the first page. In it was information about James Monroe, CEO of Monroe Media Agency. I looked at my father for a second and picked up the folder. He and my father shared similar salt-and-pepper hair, but James's hair was shorter. The photo must have been recent because he looked similar to when I last saw him. The next photo in the file was of a good-looking woman around James's age. It took me a second to confirm she was Ilaria Monroe, James's wife. I flipped through more of the pages until I came across a photo of a stunning brunette with bright green eyes, much like James's. Her skin was paler than his and my mind flirted with what her body would look like underneath me. Who was this? I could see the family resemblance, so she had to be their daughter. When I found her name, I looked up at Dad again. I knew he had caught me staring at the photo for too long based on the look on his face.

"This is the information Dave said you asked him for regarding Monroe. I offered to bring it to you."

I had almost forgotten I'd asked Dave, our in-house private investigator, to dig up some more details on Monroe. "I'm having another meeting with James in the next couple of days."

Dad did a double take. "You let him have another chance? Are you turning over a new leaf?"

"Let's just say I'm feeling jollier, given the season, but this will be taken care of as soon as possible." Her bright green eyes were imprinted on my mind. The second photo showed what the first had missed: her slim yet athletic frame. An idea of how I could make sure that I was paid for my generosity started to form because I knew there was no way Monroe could pay me back in time. Having her come to me willingly would be the ultimate payment.

"Are you sure? You seem...distracted." The gleam in his eye told me we both knew who he was talking about: Monroe's daughter.

My father's voice brought me out of the thoughts I was having. "He borrowed the money from me, and he's going to pay it back. If he doesn't, Monroe Media Agency will go under and be gutted and brought into the Cross Empire."

"And there is the Damien that I know."

I nodded at my father as my thoughts faded back to the woman whose photo was imprinted in my mind. This was new because women sailed in and out of my life on a regular basis and I got what I wanted before I got out.

The ringing of my phone broke my concentration on the woman in front of me. I pulled out my phone and recognized the number.

"Dad, I need to take this."

"Sure. I'll see you later."

I waited until he left and then I answered. "Yes?"

"Tate didn't have the money he owed you."

"Finish him."

"You mean—"

"You know what I mean."

"Do you want it to be quick or slow?"

"I trust your judgment. Just make sure it's handled."

I hung up and returned my phone to my pocket before my eyes drifted back to the file on the table. The women in my life had to submit and I could tell that she wouldn't, yet my attention was focused on her. I knew I needed to find out more information about Anais, the woman whose picture was staring back at me.

"Thanks for coming to my office today. I apologize for not being able to make the trek to your office."

I could feel the nervous energy flying off of James in droves. I couldn't blame him. After all, he didn't know what I might say or do that could upend the life he had built.

It was the day after my father had tossed the folder of information about the Monroe family into my lap. According to what Dave had provided in the file and my own deductions, I figured there was no way James Monroe was going to pay back the money he owed in six weeks.

"It wasn't a problem, and no hardship on my end," I said as I sat down in the chair in front of his desk as he did the same with his chair. Although his demeanor highlighted someone who had a lot of confidence, I could sense the nervousness dripping off of him like raindrops in a storm.

"Mr. Cross—"

A knock on a door interrupted us. James rubbed a hand over his face and said, "Come in."

The door opened and in walked the stunning brunette, from the folder. Anais Monroe. Her eyes darted between the two of us.

"Oh, I'm sorry. I didn't know you were busy. Your calendar said you were free."

"This is something that came up last minute," James said.

I nodded along with him because the meeting had just come together, maybe an hour and a half ago.

I took my time studying the beautiful woman in front of me. She wore her brown hair down, cascading in soft waves on her back, and her eyes had finally settled on her father, even though I knew she was well aware of my presence in the room. She wore a white blouse, navy blazer, and dark blue jeans with beige heels. Thoughts of her hourglass shape wearing only those heels slid into my brain before I could stop it. I discreetly adjusted myself and turned my attention back to her.

"Anais, is it anything that needs to be discussed right now?" James asked. "Oh, wait. Let me introduce you to Damien. This is Anais, the head of our social media team and the person who I have the privilege of calling my daughter. Damien is here to talk to me about a few business things."

I stood up from the chair and leaned over to shake her hand. Her palm was warm and soft, but the handshake she gave me was firm and sent a slight jolt to my cock. I could tell she felt the same, because her eyes lingered at our hands for a second too long before she pulled away and turned back toward her father.

"No, Dad. It can wait, and I'm sorry for interrupting. Nice meeting you, Damien."

"It was nice to meet you too," I replied automatically. *And it won't be the last time.*

4

ANAIS

I hadn't been to one of these events in a while. The urge to run in the other direction was real as Ellie and I walked through the doors of the Olympus Hotel. Our heels clacked along the floor before we both paused, trying to get our bearings, because it seemed as if we'd entered another dimension. The owners designed the hotel in a sophisticated, regal way with reds and golds displayed throughout. The intimidation I felt as a result of attending such a high-profile event with high-profile people crept in.

I thought I had quietly sucked in a deep breath, but the glance Ellie threw me proved otherwise.

"You okay?" she asked, leaning over to whisper in my ear.

"Yeah, I'm fine."

"Are you sure?"

All I did was nod my head. The urge to explain my worries and fears to her was there, but this was neither the time nor the place.

"You know, I was shocked you wore red, but I'm loving this gown."

The dark red gown had been sitting in my closet for well over a year, because I didn't have anywhere to wear it. The split down my right leg made it easier for me to walk in the black strappy heels I had also owned for a year or two and barely worn. I finished my look by throwing my hair into a French twist on the top of my head and applying a dark red lipstick to match the dress. Although my shopping excursion with Ellie hadn't been successful for me, she looked stunning in her new dark green V-neck gown with spaghetti straps and an open back. She wore her dark brown hair down over her shoulders.

"Thanks. Honestly, I should have worn black. That would have fit my mood better tonight."

"Hush," Ellie said. "This'll be over before you know it."

"Will it, though?"

"May I help you?" A woman dressed in a black suit and black shirt greeted us.

"We're here for the Project Adoption gala."

When Ellie finished her sentence, the woman in front of us lit up. "Oh, it's right down this hall and to your left. May I check your coats?"

"That would be great." We both took off our coats and handed them to the attendant, who then took them to coat check. She returned to give us our tickets.

"Thank you so much," I said as Ellie gave the woman a smile and nod before we trekked down the hall. "I hope we don't have to stay here too long. These heels are going to rob me of circulation in my feet."

"But they're beautiful."

"That's true," I said, glancing down to admire the shoes as we continued down the hall. It didn't take long for us to figure out which room we were in based on the sign sitting on a stand outside the door. Moments later, Ellie and I were standing off to the side, opposite the entrance, sipping on glasses of wine and taking in the scenery in front of us.

"You know, I think people watching is my favorite sport."

"I think it's mine too," I replied as I let my eyes float around the room. It was then that I looked back toward the entrance and a gasp fell from my lips.

"Hey, what's wrong with—"

I didn't hear the rest of Ellie's question. That was because my eyes settled on a man who struck both excitement and fear into me at the same time. I couldn't stop the shiver that flowed through my body once his blue eyes landed on mine. The way they perused my body made me think he was undressing me in his mind, similar to the vibe I had gotten when we'd met in Dad's office. I offered Damien the same treatment back as I stared at him from the top of his flawlessly styled brown hair to his shoes that looked barely worn. The standard black tuxedo reminded me of the suit he had worn to my office, but instead of wearing a black tie, he switched it out for a bow tie. It fit his body to perfection, and I would bet my paycheck it was custom made. Well, that bet wouldn't be worth too much, seeing as I didn't know how long I would have one.

"Hey, Anais—"

Out of the corner of my eye, I could see Ellie go from staring at me to the tall, dark, and handsome man standing across the room.

"Earth to Anais. Come back down from the clouds."

The words she whispered caught my attention. "Wait, what?"

"You've seemed to have caught Damien Cross's eye. Word on the street says that is both a blessing and a curse."

"Can you give me an overview here?"

"Mr. Tall, Dark, and Handsome over there is as dangerous as he is good-looking. Not to mention he and his family are richer than Bill Gates. I've heard stories about some of his exploits and not just the ones that were mentioned in the tabloids. Are you even listening to me?"

"Nope," I said. At least I was being honest. "We've met before. Briefly."

"And you didn't tell me?" Ellie's question came out as a harsh whisper, but I could hear the shock and knew she would tell me off later.

"I didn't think it was a big deal."

"I didn't think it was a big deal," she mumbled under her breath, lightly mocking me.

I snorted in return, used to this behavior from her. I saw movement out of the corner of my eye and a glance at Ellie forced me to break eye contact with Damien.

She took a deep breath and said, "We need to talk later." Ellie's eyes shifted between us rapidly. "Oh, yeah, we definitely need to talk later."

I looked back in Damien's direction and saw he was still looking at me. Before anyone could do anything, a voice broke through the chatter in the crowd and asked if everyone could take their seats because the program was about to begin. Ellie and I sat down, and I was disappointed we weren't sitting at the same table as Damien, but there was nothing that could be done about that. It wasn't surprising he was seated at a table near the front and we were seated a couple of rows back. The table and the room were decorated to resemble an A-list event, playing off the reds and golds that were a part of the décor of the hotel. Project Adoption made sure to include pets in their theme. Each name card included a picture of an animal on it. I smiled at the dog on mine.

The MC of the night caught my attention when he walked up to the microphone and announced what we would be seeing this evening to support Project Adoption. He kept the gala interesting and lively, removing some of the hesitation I had about attending the event in the first place. About an hour into the gala and during a pause in the musical numbers, speeches, and auctions on stage, I leaned over to Ellie and whispered, "I'm going to go to the ladies' room."

She nodded, and I grabbed my purse and walked out of the large hall. It took me a moment to figure out where the bathrooms were, but once I spotted them, I walked as fast as my heels would let me. Thankfully, I made sure my gown wouldn't take too much time or effort for me to use the bathroom. Within a few minutes, I was drying off my hands, ready to head back into the gala. I opened the door and stepped outside.

"Nice to see you here."

I whipped around to find out where the rich timbre had come from. I was startled to find Mr. Tall, Dark, and Handsome standing just a couple of feet away. His blue eyes shone even brighter now than they had when we'd met in my father's office a few days ago. I looked to see if anyone was around before my gaze landed back on him. I forgot to breathe for a second as I examined him without trying to make it too obvious. I couldn't deny that he looked good.

"What are you doing here?" I asked.

He said nothing but motioned for me to take a step closer.

When I did, he put his hand on my lower back and led me toward a row of windows overlooking the entire city. His scent, a woodsy and spicy fragrance with a hint of something floral, crept into my nose, embraced, and consumed me. Yet there was still a sense of danger that I couldn't pinpoint. I knew I wouldn't be able to smell this aroma again without thinking of him. When he stopped walking, I took a step back, even though I craved the warmth his touch brought on my bare skin. It felt very intimate for someone I barely knew.

"I can't attend an event to support animals? I do like them, and I assume you do too."

"Sure you can, but that doesn't require you to stop me from getting where I want to go. Excuse me."

I tried to remain as polite as possible as I took a step to the left to get around Damien, but he blocked my path. I moved to the right and he blocked me again.

"Move." My voice was low and menacing. I didn't want to cause a scene and embarrass Ellie and her parents, but I also had no problem doing so to get away from him. "Get the hell out of my way."

"No, and the quicker you realize that no one can tell me what to do, the better."

I rolled my eyes. "What do you want?" I asked.

"I have a proposition for you."

His eyes were stuck on mine. They didn't waver once. The blue orbs turned cold when I talked back to him. Confidence oozed off of him, making me feel intimidated by his presence, but I refused to back down.

"Well?" I asked, waiting for him to proceed.

"I wanted to talk to you about a deal I have with your father."

My eyes narrowed as I tried to figure out what he was getting at. "What type of deal?"

He put both of his hands in his pockets and said, "I'm sure it comes as no surprise to you that Monroe Media Agency is having money troubles."

I could have growled at him because he dared to utter my family business's name and spread information I hated to say was true. I glanced around once more, making sure no one was within hearing distance before I took a step closer. "This deal was the reason why you were at our office?"

"Yes, your father owes me money after I offered to help Monroe Media Agency survive about two months ago. I gave him an opportunity to pay it back, but he couldn't so I extended the deadline. Even with the boost Monroe Media Agency has received recently, it would take a miracle for him to pay me back everything I loaned him." He paused. "But there's a catch."

"And what is that?"

"Your father has six more weeks to pay back the loan, and based on the meeting I had with him and my research, that will not happen." He licked his lips and continued, "But I have one extra provision I want to include in this deal that, if it happens, would pay off his debt."

"Oh, really? And what is that?"

"You."

I took a step back as my glare became more prominent. "Excuse me? What do you mean me?"

It was clear who was running the show here. One side of his lips curved upward. "I want you."

My blood turned as cold as his eyes. "Can you repeat that?"

He took a step forward, entering my personal bubble once more. "I rarely repeat myself, but I'll make the exception just this one time. I want you."

I couldn't stop the feeling that he had become my worst enemy.

5

ANAIS

"I heard you, but I must be stuck in another dimension because I'm not comprehending it. What do you want with me?"

He took a step closer and said, "You will be mine for thirty days. Whatever I say goes." He leaned even closer and I got another whiff of his cologne.

I didn't want to admit it, but the scent spoke to me like how the smell of a decadent cake would make your mouth water. Yet his words and the intimidation he swung around like a sword made anything that could have been wet dry up like the Sahara.

"I'll even be generous and give you a couple days to think it over."

"Are you saying you want to have sex with me in exchange for paying off my father's debt?" The question flew out of my mouth and I didn't care. It didn't matter that it drew attention to us and could cause a scene.

"Those were your words, Anais. Not mine."

No.

No way.

No way in hell.

He didn't deny my interpretation of his proposal. It had always been hard for me to keep my feelings from showing on my face, but I succeeded and my face remained neutral. Inside, I was mortified at the words that had flown out of my mouth, but I was also too enraged to let that feeling take over. My body tensed up as I subconsciously tried to control the heat that was threatening to take over my face. Who did he think I was?

What further pissed me off was the fact that I could see a smile tugging at his lips. I was itching to slap him but thought better of it. "How do I know you're telling the truth?"

"I don't appreciate my honesty being called into question. You and I both know I'm not lying, but I'm happy to show you proof." He pulled out his cell phone and showed me a screenshot of what looked like a contract that my father had signed. "Now, as I said, this will be for thirty days. You will do anything I ask. If I were to tell you to run up and down Seventh Avenue naked, the only question you may ask me is for how long. If I said to stop in my office for a quick fuck, then you'll do it, without hesitation."

His comment left me speechless, unable to comprehend how this man could be this much of an asshole. My lips trembled, not with tears, but frustration and anger. Not once throughout our whole interaction had his demeanor changed. Even as he reached into his suit jacket pocket, the same calm and arrogant man who approached me was still present. It was like the demands he gave were just an everyday transaction. Hell, maybe to him they were.

On the other hand, my stomach felt as if it were racing to my chest, demanding to be let out of the prison it was in. Funny enough, based on what he said, I felt as if I was about to be thrown into one. He pulled out what looked to be a cream-colored business card and handed it to me.

"And if I don't agree to this...arrangement?" I glanced down at the card and realized that it was indeed his business card with a number scrawled onto the back.

"Your father needs to pay me in full in six weeks. And if he doesn't...well. I don't think you want to find out what happens if he doesn't. I look forward to hearing your answer."

I was sure he heard me gulp after his statement as I tried my best to not avert my gaze from his. I could handle clients like Edward all day, defusing tension as I went, but this was different. He was different and he was demanding so much more of me. He wanted my body, my soul, and my dignity.

The smirk that appeared on his face before he turned to walk away sent a small shudder through me. *Is this even legal? But even if I protest it, will I get anywhere with it?* He knew he had me between a rock and a hard place, which, if I was being frank, was exactly where he wanted me...in more ways than one. Thoughts raced through my head as I tried to process the conversation we had shared. Was it even worth me returning to the gala? My mind was going to be elsewhere anyway.

No, I would head back in, sit down next to Ellie, and make it through this evening. I would not let him see that he had gotten to me. When we got back to our apartment, I needed to do my research on Damien Cross. I didn't want to bring Ellie into this, but I knew her vast knowledge of people in this city would be helpful. Right now, I needed all the help I could get.

I locked my knees for a second to avoid sinking to the ground. There was no way I was going to faint if I had any control over it. I took a deep breath and marched back toward the gala with my back straight and my head held high. I didn't know who might be watching and I wanted to show that what had happened hadn't affected me. Ellie threw a glance in my direction when I sat back down in my seat but said nothing. Not that she needed to anyway, because I knew what the question would be: *Where were you?*

"Well, that wasn't so bad after all," I said as Ellie and I walked outside of the Olympus Hotel. I shivered briefly when the cold air hit my face and pulled my coat's collar tighter around my neck. After sitting inside of a warm room for a couple of hours, my body was not ready for the cold, blistering wind.

"Yeah, it was fantastic. Even the fifteen minutes that you missed when you went to the bathroom."

Most things didn't get past Ellie and I shouldn't have expected anything different here. I debated summarizing my encounter with Damien but paused, because of course he was standing a few feet away.

"He would arrive in a limo," Ellie whispered as we watched the driver walk around the back of the car and open the door closest to Damien. Damien paused and looked over his shoulder. Our eyes met once more and I swallowed hard, wondering what he might do next. All of that was for naught because he gave me a small nod and got into the limousine. His driver shut the door and walked around the car again before getting into the driver's seat.

"What's going on? What's up with him staring you down? This is at least the second time that has happened tonight," Ellie whispered.

I heard her, but didn't respond right away. Instead, I was spellbound by the menacing aura of the man who had thrown this challenge at my feet. It was then that I realized I hadn't said anything in a while.

"I'm not even sure." I knew that there was some hesitation in my voice based on the side-eye Ellie gave me. I could only admit to myself that I was lying. I knew exactly what was up with Damien Cross.

"Well, good thing we live together so we have plenty of time to chat about this."

"Yeah. Let's do that."

"Ma'am?"

We both turned toward the unfamiliar voice. An attendant from the hotel was standing a few feet away, trying to help with traffic and to make sure that the guests left the hotel safely.

"Can I get you two a taxi?"

"Yes, please. That would be great," Ellie answered for the both of us. Before you could snap your fingers, a taxi pulled up and both Ellie and I were sitting inside on our way back to our apartment.

I was waiting for Ellie to bring up tonight's events on the ride home, but she didn't. It, for some reason, made me nervous. Usually, she had no problem talking my ear off about things that were happening in either of our lives, so her silence was odd. When we arrived, Ellie stopped to grab the mail out of our mailbox in the lobby while I summoned the elevator so that it would be there when she made her way over to me. The elevator reached the lobby before Ellie reached me, so I stepped inside and held the doors open.

"Ellie!"

"Coming! I'm coming!"

Once she was on, I moved my arm away and watched the doors close. "Would it be weird if I took these shoes off right now?"

"A little. We are thirty seconds from our front door."

She was right and once my feet hit the door, I snatched the heels off and sighed. My feet on the rug near our front door felt heavenly.

Our apartment wasn't much, but it was home. It was on the smaller end for two people, but we made it work. It had a living room, kitchen, one bathroom that Ellie and I shared, and two small bedrooms. We could afford to upgrade to a place that was a smidge bigger, but we enjoyed the convenience of having the subway and buses nearby.

"I'm going to change and then we can chat."

"Sounds good. I'll do the same and make popcorn so we have something to snack on. There's never enough food at those things."

With that, I went to my room and changed out of the beautiful gown that I wore this evening. Then, I grabbed some makeup wipes and headed over to my mirror to remove my makeup. As I was wiping my face, I found myself staring in the mirror, still shaken by the demand Damien had made.

Although he had presented the deal as if I had a choice, something deep down in my heart told me I didn't have one. It was either be his for thirty days or have Monroe Media Agency go under and deal with those ramifications. The cold, wet cloth did little to soothe the irritation that was growing within me as I tried to find a way out of the predicament that I was in. The audacity he had to even suggest a thing showed how much of an asshole he was.

"Anais?" Ellie called through the door.

"Ah, yeah?" I looked down at my hand and found that I had stopped rubbing the wipe across my skin and had crumpled it in my fist without even noticing.

"Popcorn is ready."

"I'll be out in a minute." That was the second lie that I told tonight.

I walked into our joint bathroom across the hall with another wipe and did my best to remove as much of the makeup as I could without causing my skin to flare up. I then washed my face, mostly in an attempt to cleanse it, but I hoped that it would cool down the rage that was coursing through my body.

When I finished drying off, I walked over to my dresser and took out the pins holding my hair in place. The tension that was released from my scalp brought some relief as I threw my hair up into a messy ponytail. My hoodie and sweatpants marked the start of what should have been a quiet night, but the thoughts flying through my mind would make that anything but. One quick glance in the mirror proved that this was as good as it was going to get, and I walked out of my bedroom and moved toward the living room. Just before I entered, I stopped in the doorway. I was hit with how much Monroe Media Agency meant to the people who worked there and the services that we provided to our clients all around the world. Now, all of that might go up in smoke unless I did this.

"Anais?"

Ellie's voice caused the thoughts in my mind to stop turning. I looked at her and said, "Ah, I'm sorry. What's up?"

"I asked if you wanted water or wine. Is everything all right? You looked like you were elsewhere."

"Yeah, I'm fine. I have a lot on my mind," I said, turning toward the kitchen.

"Does that include Damien Cross?"

I hesitated for a moment before continuing on my way. Just mentioning his name was enough to increase the edginess that I was already feeling. I grabbed the popcorn that Ellie made and put a couple of pieces into my mouth.

"Aha!" she exclaimed. "I knew it."

"Yeah, but not for the reason you're thinking," I mumbled.

"What was that?"

"Nothing."

"So, what was up with tonight? Seemed that anytime you were in his sight, his eyes were glued to you."

I didn't know how much about my brief history with Damien I should tell Ellie. Would she somehow get dragged into this? I was willing to bet he was petty enough to do it. It took me a moment for me to think of what I deemed safe enough to tell her. "So, I met Damien when he came into our office this week. He had a meeting with my dad."

"Oh, is Monroe Media Agency gonna be working for the ever-growing 'Cross Empire'?"

"Something like that. I'm not sure because I wasn't in the

meeting. My dad forgot to block out his calendar for that time, so I ended up interrupting them."

"Hmm, and now he can't seem to take his eyes off of you whenever you're near."

I scoffed. "Well, I wouldn't say that. I highly doubt he's interested in me." *Interested in humiliating me? Yes. Interested in dating me? Ha. No.*

"Of course you wouldn't, but you never do. That's part of the reason you've been single for so long." She leaned over and snatched some popcorn from the bowl while I rolled my eyes.

"I'm single by choice, thank you very much."

"Oh, I think you just bury yourself in work to avoid having to deal with dating. It gives you an excuse not to."

She was right, in part. I had been working longer hours, but it wasn't so I didn't have to date. I buried myself in work so that I could do my part to make sure that the company succeeded. I thrived on helping our clients market their businesses. Monroe Media Agency had a lot of blood, sweat, and tears from my father built into its foundation and once I graduated from college and joined the company, I put in my fair share of them as well.

"That's ridiculous. I've been on dates recently." This was a silly disagreement to be having, but I let it continue because it stopped us from having to talk about Damien.

"Oh, really? When's the last time you went on a date?" She folded her arms and leaned back on the kitchen counter.

"Maybe six months ago?"

"Exactly."

I stopped myself from rolling my eyes again because I had proved her point.

"Now you've caught Damien's attention and you need to make a decision about what you're gonna do about it."

She wasn't wrong. "I'm not sure what I'm going to do, but since you know everything there is to know about everyone, why don't you tell me more about Damien?" I couldn't avoid it anymore. It was time to learn more about the man who had gone from a very attractive businessman to my adversary in less than a week.

Ellie paused. "Before I begin, you might want to grab a drink and follow me to the living room because what I'm about to tell you will be plenty of entertainment for us. Who needs a movie?"

I shook my head and followed Ellie after I grabbed a glass of Merlot and the bowl of popcorn. She settled down on the couch and looked at me.

"I will fully admit, some of what I know about Damien and his family is hearsay, but I'll start with the facts. Damien is the oldest of three boys who were born to Martin and Selena Cross. His brothers are named Broderick and Gage and they are twins. I believe they got their start generations ago and have built their business and power ever since. The Cross family have amassed a fortune through their different business ventures as far as I know."

"Oh, yeah?" I said and stuffed my mouth full of popcorn. I cradled the glass of wine and said, "I might need something a little stronger to deal with this conversation."

"I don't blame you." She paused and threw a couple of pieces of popcorn into her mouth.

"Thanks for understanding," I said, bringing the glass to my lips. I was shocked I could take a sip given how much my mind was racing and my hand was trembling. Ellie didn't act like she noticed, though.

"Damien is a pretty well-known playboy. Most women he's with don't last for more than a month or two tops based on what the gossip blogs say. There have been rumors that he either goes to their place to have sex or he has his driver pick them up and drop them off back home the same night. Sleeping over at his place is a big no-no. I learned that from a source that leaked it to the tabloids. There are also rumors that he might be a co-owner of Elevate."

I choked on my wine. It took everything in me to hold it in and not splatter the contents of my mouth all over everything in front of me. Elevate was one of the hottest nightclubs in New York City. It had a dance club and bar on the main floor and was rumored to be a sex club in the basement.

"Are you all right?" Ellie hit my back as she tried to clear my throat.

I got the remaining wine down and nodded. "Yep. I'm fine." A small tear formed in the corner of one eye. I wondered if it was from the choking or the rabbit hole my thoughts were determined to jump down. I wasn't a virgin by any means, but I was worried about what Damien might do to me.

Ellie looked over at me once more before she continued, "I preface this by saying, once again, this is all rumors as I have personally never interacted with him, but it wouldn't be a bad idea for you to let loose a little bit, you know? You haven't gotten laid in months so what would be so wrong with having some fun with him? Chances are it won't last long anyway."

"Uh-huh." That made sense. And the thirty-day time limit

he put on our arrangement fit the playboy description Ellie gave him.

"That's what I heard. I wouldn't even call it dating him if I had to be honest. When the women he's fucking become addicted to him, he cuts them loose. And when he's done, he's done. He doesn't do relationships. If he gets tired of you, that's it."

I nodded as an idea started forming in my head. I could annoy him to the point that he would get over me and let me go. Based on my brief interactions with him, I bet that wouldn't be too difficult. He thrived on being in control of everything and everyone, and although there was no way that was happening here, maybe I wouldn't even have to make it the full thirty days.

I shook my head. Had I already decided that this was what I was going to do? Well, technically I guess Damien made it up for me because I didn't have much of a choice to begin with outside of going to maybe the police, who would probably laugh me out of the precinct. But with those barriers removed, would I go to the authorities? Conflicting feelings ran through me, so I used my conversation with Ellie to force myself to think about something else.

"So, tell me more about Elevate."

Ellie stretched and said, "Well, there's not much to tell."

"What do you mean there isn't much to tell?"

"It's extremely exclusive. Not much has gotten out about it. They force everyone to sign forms stating that they won't reveal what happens downstairs. It's hard to get on the guest list to just party on the main floor. Trust me, I've tried."

"That makes sense," I said. "I mean, they're probably trying to protect the identities of whoever is attending."

"Right. If I had to make a guess, I would say the club probably caters to New York City's elite based on the lack of information about the place and who the Crosses associate with. Now, I mean this with all the love and care in the world, and I don't mean to offend, but I'm not sure why Damien would be so laser-focused on you. Yes, you're stunning with a kick-ass personality and have a million and a half great things going for you. But the fact that you're in his crosshairs is a huge deal. I don't know if I would call it a good thing or a bad thing."

I licked my lips as my hand made its way to my temple to gently rub it. "I wouldn't say that he is laser-focused on me. We met recently and saw each other at the gala tonight. That's it."

"Oh, really?" Ellie asked. "Then why do you have his business card?"

"Wait, how did you know I have his card? And it isn't uncommon for me to have business cards."

Ellie held out a small cream-colored piece of paper. "I don't think you closed your clutch tightly because this fell out." She flipped the card around. "It has a number scribbled on the back of it that I would bet money is his personal phone number."

"Give that to me." I snatched the card out of her hand.

"Anais, you can try to explain this away, but I know what I saw and what this looks like."

"We just met once and he's doing some business with my father and—"

"Anais, I'm not judging you. I'm all for you getting some, but if you play with the devil, you will get burned." She ran a hand through her long brown hair before she continued,

"Don't forget that you two don't run in the same circles. He has the ability to do more than we could ever dream of. He has enough money to protect you from everything yet destroy you with a flick of his finger."

I knew she was one hundred percent telling the truth about that.

6

ANAIS

Later that night, I was lying in bed and the things that Ellie said made the hairs on the back of my neck stand up. The kicker about the whole thing was that she was right about what Damien wanted with me. Sure, there were easier ways for him to find someone who would be at his every beck and call, so why me? I tried not to jump to conclusions because I knew I would spend my time overthinking instead of figuring out how to get out of this mess.

I knew that beyond any doubt I needed to talk to my father. Why had he decided to go to Damien, of all people, instead of going to a bank and asking for a loan? Hell, couldn't he do that now and use it to pay off Damien? If he could have, why didn't he do it already?

That made me sit straight up in bed. What had kept my father from trying to get a loan from a bank versus going to this man who had just threatened to take his daughter for his own pleasure? These questions caused a surge of energy to run through my body and motivated me to pull myself together in order to get ready for work. It didn't take me long to get it together because I had my weekday morning routine down to a science and I knew exactly how much time I could waste before I had to jump in the shower.

When I was done, I walked into the hallway and found Ellie's door closed. She probably had an early day today and had already left for work. Once I had my coat on, I grabbed my purse and keys and headed out the door. As I waited for the elevator, I dug around in my purse and found my headphones. They would allow me to ignore the world for a bit as I rode the train to work.

It didn't take long for me to reach my office and I dashed through the lobby and went up to my floor on the elevator. A quick check of the time told me that I wasn't late, yet I was still anxious. By the time I reached my desk, I let out a huge sigh. My anxiety was because of Damien's proposal and the questions I wanted to ask my father, since that seemed to be the only thing I could think about. I looked through my doorway, which gave me the perfect angle to see my dad's office. Based on the lack of lights on in his office, Dad still hadn't made it in.

"That's odd," I mumbled as I walked around to sit at my desk. I flipped open my laptop to wake it up. I pulled out my phone and sent a quick text to my father.

Me: *Dad, are you coming into the office today?*

I set my phone down and began reading the emails that had accumulated after I left the office yesterday. I had been so engrossed in what I was reading, I hadn't realized that thirty minutes had flown by until one of my subordinates, Jake, was standing outside my door.

"Sorry, I got caught up reading emails. What's up?"

"FYI, Edward is probably going to call you in a few minutes. Every time I give him an explanation of why a post wasn't performing well, he listens to me and then says that he has to speak to you."

I sighed and closed my eyes. "That's fine. Thanks for giving me a heads-up."

"Don't mention it." Jake lingered for a second longer before he left. I knew that at any moment Edward would call me, and it was pointless trying to work on something new when I was just going to get interrupted. So, I picked up my phone to check to see if Dad had texted me back. I confirmed he had, and I turned my phone on vibrate before I read his message.

Dad: *Yes, I'll be in the office shortly. Had a meeting this morning, probably forgot to mark it down on my calendar.*

A quick search proved that he had indeed forgotten to mark it down. To be honest, this wasn't shocking given the number of things he was balancing on a regular basis.

Me: *Dad, you really need a secretary or an assistant.*

I added a smiley face at the end of the text message and pressed send when a knock on the door startled me. When I looked up, I saw the woman I had passed at the front desk this morning holding a bouquet of pink orchids.

"Anais?"

I nodded.

"These are for you."

I hesitated before I stood up and walked over to take the flowers. "Thanks so much for bringing these up," I said.

"Not a problem. Looks like someone wanted you to know that they were thinking about you."

"Yeah, I guess so," I said as I stared at the flowers. "Thanks again."

With a smile, she left, and I closed my office door.

My phone buzzed before I could inspect the flowers further.

Dad: *I should be in the office in a couple of minutes. I'm about a block away.*

Me: *Sounds good. I want to chat with you about the money thing.*

I knew the flowers had to have been from him, unless it was some secret admirer that was coming out of the woodwork. With that, I placed my phone down on the desk and found the note card that came with the arrangement.

Anais,

Looking forward to hearing your decision.

Damien

The growl that left my lips shocked me. His arrogance jumped off the small piece of paper, as if he knew the answer that I was going to give. My thoughts were interrupted again by the buzzing of my phone. Apparently, I was popular today. I picked it up. I found a message from a number I didn't recognize, and the words caused a small amount of bile to rise in my throat.

Unknown Number: *Did you get the flowers?*

Me: *Damien?*

Damien: *Would someone else be sending you flowers?*

My head jerked back involuntarily when I read his response. The possessiveness rolled off his words in droves. Who the hell did he think he was? I didn't owe him an explanation, period.

Me: *How did you get this number? And I don't owe you any explanation about anything going on in my life.*

He didn't reply right away, and I figured either he was doing it on purpose, or he might have gotten pulled into a meeting. I stared my phone down for a few more seconds before looking at my office phone. *Wasn't Edward supposed to call me?* A knock on the door removed that thought from my mind.

"Come in!"

Dad opened the door and stepped inside, closing it behind him. "Hey sweetheart, do you want to talk? I have a few minutes before my next meeting."

"Dad, I'll cut right to the chase. How much money do you owe Damien Cross?"

"How did you know I borrowed the money from him?"

Shit. I hadn't realized he hadn't told me that he was borrowing money from anyone. "Uh. I put two and two together when you didn't tell me that he was a new client of ours." Thank goodness for my ability to think quickly on my feet.

He didn't respond at first, but he seemed to buy my explanation. He walked over to one of the chairs that I kept in a corner of my office and pulled it closer to my desk before he replied.

"About $270,000."

"Dad!" I exclaimed.

His gaze darted toward the door, probably checking to make sure that no one had heard me through the closed door. "I know, I know."

"$270,000?" I said. I knew I sounded like a parrot, repeating what he had said, but I couldn't help it.

"Sweetheart, I know."

"Are you anywhere near being able to pay that money back? Like, would you be able to get it in six weeks?" I knew the pleading in my words and the uncomfortable nature of this conversation were getting to him because he still hadn't looked at me.

"Potentially."

"What do you mean potentially!" I sounded frantic to my own ears. I paused and said, "I mean I know what *potentially* means, but why aren't you sure? And what happens if you don't?"

"Monroe Media Agency is no more." He stopped and ran a hand across the back of his neck. "We'll have to shut our doors. I'm not sure what your mom and I will do but we'll figure out how to make it work."

"Why didn't you go to the bank and get a loan?"

"Interest rates, and I wasn't sure that they would loan us this amount."

"I've heard some things about Damien Cross, and I don't think he's someone to mess with."

"I know, but I had no choice. No bank was going to loan me that type of money that quick." His eyes made their way around the room before they met mine. "He made me an offer I couldn't refuse. I did it to save this business. To save what you, me, and everyone here worked so hard to achieve, and to give me some more time to fix everything. New companies were springing up and taking our clientele and we needed some more money in order to compete."

I could see tears welling up in his eyes as he ran a hand through his salt-and-pepper hair. I looked down on my desk in order to not start tearing up again myself. Not only had

Damien made my father an offer he couldn't refuse, he had done the same to me.

At the end of the workday, I found myself staring at my phone. Damien had responded hours ago at this point, but I didn't have an urge to read it until now.

Damien: *I have my sources. One more day.*

Reading the words again and again made my lip quiver. Although I was scared there was something else there—a tiny bit of excitement about the unknown? I didn't know if I would call it that either. The fact that I was even considering doing this and not just telling everyone involved to go screw themselves told me a lot about myself. As I was staring into space in the direction of my phone, it lit up alerting me that I had just received a message. It was from Ellie.

Ellie: *You'll never guess what happened.*

Me: *This sounds dangerous and I'm not going to even try to guess what happened.*

Ellie: *Fine. Sometimes I wonder why we're friends. Anyway. You'll never believe this.*

She didn't type for a moment, drawing this out even more.

Ellie: *I just got you and me into Elevate.*

I felt my eyes almost bulge out of my skull.

Me: *You got us into a sex club?*

Ellie: *I got us into the dance club portion. I hope you're ready to party because we are definitely going tonight.*

I sighed and mumbled, "Damnit." I was not prepared for this. Not at all.

7

DAMIEN

"You don't look like you're having much fun. Not that you have much fun to begin with."

I glanced at Broderick and I fought the urge to roll my eyes. "I know how to have fun."

I hadn't intended on coming to Elevate tonight. The twins had insisted, and I didn't give them much of a fight. We had opted to stay in the VIP section of the bar, and I was glad. The sleek black, gray, and gold was a theme across both the bar and the adult club in the basement. The atmosphere of the bar and dance floor could be changed on a dime by switching the music and the lighting, which was one of the reasons we had gone along with this option when the interior designer had suggested it. We knew it made the place look more expensive and that had been the aim when it came to making our money back on the investment. And we did, and then some.

Instead of wandering down to the basement, I stayed up here and nursed the whiskey that had been thrust into my hand when I arrived. Based on where Gage's attention lay, he might have found a woman to take home tonight. He leaned over Broderick and said to me, "Well, pull the stick out of your ass and have some fun."

Broderick shook his head, and I took another sip of my whiskey. Broderick was sitting between us, making it harder to talk one-on-one, not that I was complaining. The music blaring through the speakers didn't help either. Although it was quieter in VIP, it was still difficult to hear.

Both Broderick and I ignored him, and Broderick placed both of his elbows on the back of the couch we were lounging on. My brothers and I had always wanted to go in on a project together but could never agree on anything until we saw that this space was available. Elevate was born and it had been a tremendous success. The grand opening was a couple of years ago, and nothing had stopped the steady stream of people coming through its doors. We made it a point to make both the bar and club somewhat exclusive because we thought that would attract more attention and consumers and it had. Besides, there were well-placed rumors flying around that the three of us co-owned it although no one had proved it.

Gage was right. I did have a stick up my ass because I didn't want to be here and because of a certain brunette that I couldn't shake no matter how much I tried. I spent most of my adult life focusing on work and finding the next company to conquer, but now things felt strange because I couldn't escape my thoughts about her. My quality of work hadn't suffered, however, and I made sure to keep it that way.

There were plenty of women who came in and out of my life. We had our fun, and when it was time to let go, we let go.

I can't remember the last time a woman, especially one who I barely knew, stayed on my mind for this long.

I took another sip of my drink and stood up. Broderick looked over at me and before he could ask, I said, "I'm going to check out the crowd tonight. I'm tired of sitting."

"I'll go with you. I don't want to be stuck next to him."

I looked at Gage and shook my head. He was flirting with a server.

"Come on," Broderick said and together we walked over toward a balcony that overlooked the entire ground floor. It was clear as day that drinks were flowing, and people were dancing and having a good time.

"Excellent investment." Broderick held up his glass and I joined him in a silent cheer before we took another sip. "So what else do you want to take over?"

"What do you mean?" I asked, answering his question with a question.

"Well, you are a mega tycoon, according to the supermarket tabloids." We'd definitely turned the nightlife scene on its head with Elevate in more ways than one. It was then that I spotted her, and my gaze narrowed. "You're one of the most powerful men in New York City. What's next?"

"Same could be said about you and Gage."

"That's not an answer."

"Maybe a media firm."

Broderick took a glimpse at me, his eyes widening before he caught himself and turned back toward the balcony. He was trying to find what had made me say it. "Do you know her?"

"Know who?"

"Good job on being evasive, Damien." Broderick looked

down again over the balcony. "It's the woman in the gold dress, isn't it?" They were making their way across the dance floor and I almost strained my neck in order to get a better look at what she was wearing.

I didn't answer, instead taking another sip of my drink.

"Is there something going on here? Are you fucking her?"

"No." *At least not yet.*

"But you want to."

"That's none of your business."

Broderick snorted. "And that explains why there is a bigger stick up your ass than normal. Maybe you *do* need to fuck her."

"Can you shut up? Or go back to watching what Gage is up to?" His brother didn't need to know that fucking her wasn't out of the realm of possibility given the deal I came up with. I never had to worry about whether I would be able to find someone to share my bed with. There was a mutual understanding between me and the women I slept with. Sometimes things got dicey, but it wasn't anything I couldn't handle. Relationships were something I didn't want to deal with. Period.

Broderick looked behind him prior to turning back to me, a smirk firmly planted on his face. "Looks like Gage struck out."

His words made me turn around to confirm. Gage was now by himself, looking at his phone. "Bet he thought he was going to end up taking her downstairs." Broderick shrugged as I shook my head and downed the rest of my drink.

Another server walked by and said, "Can I get that for you, sir?"

"Yes," I said, and the man took the glass and placed it on his tray. I buttoned my suit jacket.

"Where are you going?"

"I have something I need to take care of. I'll probably be back." With that, I headed off to find out exactly what Anais was doing here.

It didn't take long for me to get down the stairs, but I had lost sight of them. Anais had somehow gotten into Elevate with what looked to be her roommate, based on the pictures and captions Dave had found on Anais's social media profiles. And I wanted to know how and why.

"Damien?" I glanced over and saw Kingston. He was my cousin and was doing us a favor by subbing in for one of Elevate's security guards who'd called out sick. He was stationed near the stairs to stop people who didn't belong in VIP from getting through. "Do you need anything?"

"No, I'm good," I said, just as I spotted the two women. They were making their way toward the bar. I walked around the periphery for a bit because I didn't want to draw attention to myself, nor did I want Anais to spot me before I was ready.

I watched as her roommate leaned over and whispered something in her ear and then she started making her way through the crowd leaving Anais alone at the bar. I knew it was my turn to strike. It took little effort for me to get to Anais and once I was close enough to touch her, I paused. She'd left her long brown hair down and it was a blessing and a curse because I thought about running my fingers through her hair while she gave me a blow job. The gold dress left very little to the imagination, and I could tell I wasn't the only one near her who thought the same. I noticed a guy to our right making his way over to her with his eyes stuck to her body as I assumed mine had been.

His eyes shyly shifted off of her and toward me and all it took was a look before he backed away. The person next to her grabbed their drink and shifted out of the way, leaving an opening for me.

I slid into the space and leaned down to ask, "What are you doing here?"

I could tell she was about to snap, but once her eyes landed on me, the words were gone. It took her a few seconds to recuperate from her shock but when she did, the feistiness returned.

"What do you mean what am I doing here? What are *you* doing here?"

"That's none of your business."

"And the reason I'm here is yours?" I saw a ghost of a smirk appear on her face, probably because she thought she'd won this battle. All I could think about was ripping that slinky dress off of her and fucking her on the bar. *In front of patrons? Why not?*

"Careful. You don't want to piss me off. And being that I'm the co-owner of this establishment and I don't like you being here because you're going to be mine, I could have you escorted out right now. Hell, I have no problem doing it myself."

I could tell when my words registered because her eyes widened. She knew I wasn't joking about doing it either.

"I haven't said yes to your arrangement. You're assuming that I will."

"I'm not assuming anything." I folded my arms across my chest. I was enjoying this sparring match a bit too much. The fire in her eyes was a stark contrast to the coolness that her green eyes had given off before. I knew she wasn't willing to go down without a fight and because of that there would be many good days and nights ahead. "You know what I'm looking forward to?"

"What's that?" I barely heard the words because she whispered them.

"Tomorrow, Spitfire." I turned around and took a step forward, back toward the VIP section.

But her words stopped me. "Don't call me that."

I turned back around and shifted my body closer to her. "I can call you whatever I want. Do you want to know why you'll come to me willingly?"

She was forced to look up at me even with the three-inch heels she was wearing.

"Because your father doesn't have the money and he won't have it by my deadline. You don't want to see Monroe Media Agency close. The stakes are too high." *In more ways than one.*

This type of deal wasn't something I usually did because I didn't have to. This time, I didn't want to take a chance that she would slip through my fingers. I wouldn't lie and say that I wasn't drawn to her when I first saw her photo. I let my gaze wander down her body before it made its way back up to her eyes. I could see that her eyes were staring at my lips when they drifted up to mine.

"But there's something else, Anais."

Before she could say anything, I bent my head down to kiss her, giving her a small preview of what it would be like to be mine. At first, she didn't react, but when she started to get into the kiss, I pulled away.

"You want to know what it's like to be fucked by me." I took a small step back and didn't fight my urge to smirk. "Wear something like this tomorrow." I turned and walked away, leaving her beautiful swollen lips ajar.

"Hey, Kingston," I said. "Have your men watch that woman in the gold while she's here tonight. She should be here with another woman. If she tries to make her way downstairs stop her." I had no problem monitoring her from my position in VIP.

"Got it. I'll switch positions and head toward that door just in case." Kingston leaned away from me and started talking into his earpiece, conveying the message I had just sent.

A smile crept onto my face as I walked back up the stairs to VIP. I knew that in a short period of time, Anais Monroe would be mine.

8

ANAIS

Coming here had been a bad idea. After Ellie told me about how she suspected Damien might own Elevate, I knew there was a chance that he would be here tonight. Now lo and behold, he was. My phone vibrated in my hand. I looked down and saw a text notification.

Damien: *Be ready at 7:30 p.m. tomorrow. My driver will pick you up.*

"You still haven't ordered a drink." Ellie appeared next to me.

"You almost gave me a heart attack. I forgot to order one."

"Is everything okay? We talked about it and then I went to the bathroom."

I leaned over to whisper in her ear, "I was preoccupied. Damien appeared."

"Wait, what?" Ellie's voice cracked, causing her to sound almost like a parrot.

If this were an everyday situation, I would have laughed. It wasn't and I couldn't bother to try to fake one.

"Yeah, and there's more that I need to tell you." It was time to come clean. I would do it once we got home.

"Okay. Do you want to stay here or head home now?"

I admired her for offering to go home with me even though we were in one of the most exclusive bars in New York City. Who knew when or if we would have the opportunity to do this again?

"No, let's stay. We should also at least get a drink while we're here."

"Good plan. This time I'll do the ordering."

I rolled my eyes at her little jab and turned to face the bar again. When we had our drinks in hand, I let the coolness of the mojito coat my throat in an attempt to calm down the raging fire that Damien's presence and words had caused to erupt. Ellie and I continued chatting among ourselves while drinking, but the entire time, I felt as if there was someone watching me.

"Did you want to go downstairs?"

"Downstairs? For what?" I played dumb even though I knew what she was referring to.

"To see what it's like? Supposedly, there is a lounge of some sort, or maybe it's another bar where people can meet other people and decide if they want to head farther into the club. I wouldn't want to go that far but figured the lounge might be a good place to get a feel for the atmosphere."

My mind drifted back to my interaction with Damien a few minutes ago before I came to a decision. I knew that if he found out what we were doing, it was going to further piss him off and I didn't care. I didn't answer to anyone and I could do whatever and whoever I wanted. Well that was what

I liked to tell myself, although I never had done anything like this before. "Sure, why not?"

I polished off my drink and followed Ellie as she made her way through the crowd. How she knew where the entrance to the sex club was, I would never know. We made it over to the bouncer, who I didn't remember seeing when I walked in, and Ellie turned on her charm.

"Hi, we would like to go downstairs."

"Are you both on the list?"

"Uh, maybe?"

I couldn't help but roll my eyes. She knew damn well we weren't on any list unless Ellie had done it without telling me.

"Where's your coin?"

She looked at me and then looked back at him. "What do you mean where's your coin?"

He looked at her and shook his head. "If you don't even know what I'm talking about, I know for sure that you're not on the list to get in. Please move aside."

"This is ridiculous. No one needs a coin to get in here."

"I said what I said. Now move aside." His stern voice told me he meant business and I noticed when his eyes stayed on her for a moment too long. Still, he didn't budge.

"Look—"

"Are you trying to start a fight with me?"

I grabbed Ellie's arm and she looked at me. "This isn't worth it, E. Especially if it's an invite-only type of thing."

"I think you should listen to your friend."

I could feel the anger in Ellie about to boil over. "You're being completely asinine about this because there is no coin needed for entry!"

"Big words there and you're annoying me."

"I don't care if I'm annoying you. Listen—"

"No, and now I'm going to escort both of you off the premises."

I could see Ellie fuming and if we were in a cartoon, smoke would have been coming out of her ears. The bouncer walked us halfway to the door when I paused for a second and looked up and saw Damien standing at the balcony. I didn't know how long he had been standing there, but the look he was giving me and the small wave he sent my way told me he had something to do with us getting kicked out of Elevate tonight.

"THAT GUY WAS SUCH AN ASSHOLE."

"Ellie."

"You don't need a coin to get into the club. I would have known."

I watched Ellie pace back and forth in front of me. Hopefully her stomps weren't loud enough to piss off the tenants underneath us.

"Ellie."

"He kept us out of there on purpose."

She definitely had that right, but she was giving me a headache on top of the thoughts that were already doing laps in my brain. "Ellie."

"I can't stand—"

"Ellie!" My hollering did the trick.

"What?" She stopped walking to look at me. "What's wrong?"

"There are some things I need to tell you."

She walked over and sat next to me on the couch and curled her feet up under her. That was when the dam of words broke. I walked her through everything that had fallen in my lap over the last few days. Monroe Media Agency's impending collapse, my father going to Damien Cross for money to help save the agency from failing, and then Damien approaching me about the deal.

"Oh, honey," Ellie said for what seemed like the fiftieth time. "I take back everything I said about you becoming involved with Damien. Fuck him, excuse the pun. We'll figure out a way to get you out of this."

If I wasn't worried about the situation, I would have laughed. "I feel like I have no choice but to say yes." I ran a hand across my forehead and into my hair. I barely stopped myself from yanking the strands.

"No, there has to be another way. We can go to the police."

"Ellie, we can't call the police. They probably wouldn't believe me anyway, and I don't want my father to know any of this."

"There has to be some way to get you out of this. Maybe if we both take out loans. I could try going to my parents..."

Ellie's words made my head snap in her direction. I stared her down for a moment before the words I wanted to use came to me. "There is no way I would drag you into this."

"Shit," she mumbled. She kept whatever else she was thinking to herself.

"I know."

Ellie closed her eyes for a moment and when she opened them, they zeroed in on me and it didn't take much for me to read the sadness in them. "At the very least, if you go through with it, it's only thirty days, right? If you could stay strong for thirty days, maybe it won't be so bad? None of this sits right with me."

Me either. I thought about Ellie telling me that he had enough money to make me disappear with the flick of his finger, but if he could do that to me, he could do it to my father as well.

Visions of that happening to my father crowded my brain and involuntarily made me shiver. I muttered a cuss word and threw my head back on the couch. I assumed it meant that anyone that was in my family or close friend circle would have a target on their backs if Damien didn't get either his money or me.

It was a few moments before I sat back up and gasped. "There's one thing I forgot to tell you!"

"Well?"

"The night I went to have dinner at my parents' house, some random man shoulder-checked me on the way back to our apartment. He told me to watch myself. I also thought I might have been being watched at Elevate but wrote it off as me being paranoid. After all, it was hard to not have at least someone's eyes on you when you're in a crowded place."

"Based on what we now know Damien is capable of, I wouldn't put it past him to have you being watched."

"Me neither. Plus, it would feed into his desire to intimidate me."

"When is the deadline for having to tell him?"

"Tomorrow. He told me to be ready by 7:30." I opened his message on my phone and showed it to Ellie. "It's not even worth me running away."

"Nope, because he'll find you. The only way I could see this working out is if you could get all of the money your father owes him by tomorrow, but we both know that's damn well impossible."

"Yeah, I know." I ran a hand through my hair and watched as my tresses fell onto my shoulder.

Ellie grabbed my other hand and squeezed. "Just remember, you need to make it out unscathed. You can't get addicted to him."

"That won't be hard. I hate the man."

THE NEXT EVENING, I watched as the time grew closer and closer to when I was supposed to be picked up. I could finally admit to myself that I would go to him, but I'd be damned if I was going to wear anything that resembled the dress that I had worn last night at Elevate. I threw my hair up into a high ponytail and changed into a green sweater, fresh denim jeans, and white Chucks that had seen better days. I looked more like a student than a working professional nine years removed from her college days, but I didn't care. I wasn't going there to please him; I was doing this to save Monroe Media Agency and all of its employees. And if he didn't want me this way, that wasn't my problem.

That pep talk helped energize me for whatever would happen tonight. That was the thing: I didn't know what was coming next, nor did I know what to expect and I was sure he'd use that to his advantage. When the clock struck 7:28 p.m., I stood up and zipped my winter coat. I double-checked that I had my mace with me and closed my purse. It was better to be safe than sorry.

I shuffled toward the front door, my heart pounding harder with every step.

I watched as a set of headlights appeared at the corner of my street. The car moved past my building and, as I stepped out, the driver made a U-turn before pulling in front of my building and parking the car. A man in dark-colored clothes stepped out of the vehicle and, based on what I could see, he was the man who had picked up Damien from the Project Adoption gala.

"Miss Monroe?" he asked, which was him being polite because I was pretty certain he already knew who I was if my assumptions about Damien were correct. He was wearing what looked to be a black suit, which matched the sedan's exterior. He looked more muscular than he had the night that Ellie and I saw him, but that could be my fault for not paying much attention to him because Damien had dropped his demands on me.

I rolled my shoulders back and looked him in the eye. I refused to be intimidated. "Yes, that's me."

"Right this way. My name is Rob and I'll be taking you to Mr. Cross's home this evening," he said as he opened the door.

I stepped inside, without saying another word and he closed the door behind me.

Something in me was expecting to see Damien sitting inside the car just to throw me off, but he wasn't there, so I had more time to myself before I had to deal with Satan in the expensive suit. Once Rob stepped into the driver's seat and closed the door behind him, I heard the locks engage and I wondered if he had done it on purpose to keep me prisoner or if that was an automatic feature of the car.

"Could you tell me where we're going?" I asked, just as Rob pulled out of the parking spot.

"We are going to Mr. Cross's home. Let me know if you need anything." He gave me a small smile and raised the divider between us.

I knew that was done as a way to get me to stop asking questions because he hadn't given me the answer I wanted. Soft jazz tunes played in the background as we glided through New York City's streets. Since I was alone, all I could do was think of all the different scenarios that might come about tonight. An idea popped into my head and I pulled out my cell phone to send my location to Ellie just in case something terrible happened. Once I had done that, I put my phone away. At the very least, someone would know where to start looking for my body. The thought of that made me tremble as I tried to ease concerns that something might happen to me.

The ride to Damien's gave me even more time to think about his deal. Taking this deal didn't mean that he got to set all the rules. There were some hard limits to what I was willing to do and he was going to hear about them tonight whether he liked it or not. Some of the items I wanted to discuss I had been mulling over, but several of them I thought of on the drive to Damien's. I typed them up on my phone to pass more time on my journey to what I called hell.

About twenty-five minutes later we were pulling up to a townhouse and I was somewhat shocked we were still in Manhattan. Rob carefully parallel parked the car as I held on to my phone like a crutch, hoping that it would calm my nerves because at least I had that lifeline still available to me.

"I'll walk you up to the front door." With that, he opened the door, letting himself out.

"Well, at least I won't be going on my death march by myself," I mumbled, making sure he didn't hear me.

Rob stepped out of the vehicle and I watched him walk around the car before he reached my door. Every step he took made the blood rushing through my ears louder. I looked around and found myself on a relatively quiet Manhattan street that was filled with other townhomes that looked just like the one I was standing in front of. I waited for Rob and together we walked up the stairs to the front door.

"How long have you been working for Damien?" I asked.

"I've worked for Mr. Cross for seven years now."

"Hmm. So I'm sure you've seen a lot."

He didn't respond, which told me all I needed to know. That did little to help my anxiety as we stood in front of the door.

"If you need anything, just press the number one on any phone in his place. I'm sure he'll tell you to do the same."

I nodded and he walked down the stairs as I was left staring at the red door. I knocked on the door and took a step back. I held my breath, awaiting what would be my fate.

9

DAMIEN

"And you need to be here at 10 a.m. in order to catch the meeting with Ben Nichols. Information for that meeting will be on your desk and in the calendar invite."

"That should work. Thanks, Melissa."

Melissa had been my assistant for about three years, and I admit I would be much more disorganized without her even if it meant her staying at work until after seven to make sure I had everything I needed.

"Is there anything else you needed?"

"That will be all."

"Have a good evening."

I hung up my phone and walked into the dining area. I watched as Lucy, my personal chef, finished lighting the candles on the dining room table and I checked my Rolex. Anais and Rob should be arriving in about five minutes. I knew Rob was always punctual so if they were late, it was more than likely a result of Anais being stubborn. It was something I was looking forward to yet was the exact opposite of what I usually went for when it came to finding someone to fuck.

"The apple pie should be done pretty soon, but you'll need to set it out to cool on the wire rack. I put that right there." Lucy pointed diagonally behind her. "I have everything else either covered up so that it stays warm or in the other oven."

I nodded and she walked around me before she headed toward the hallway that led to the front door.

"Good night, Mr. Cross."

"Night."

She closed the front door, and I was alone once more. Some might say a house with five bedrooms and six bathrooms was excessive for one man, but I didn't care about what other people thought I should do with my money. Plus, the only reason the public really cared was because the tabloids wrote about it and it sold copies. It was a never-ending cycle.

A glance around my home told me that everything was perfect. The cleaning service had finished up several hours ago, so my home was immaculate. Although I was barely here, it didn't hurt to have someone freshen up the house frequently. I'd bought this townhouse several years ago when I decided I wanted to have somewhere to lay my head down in NoHo. It didn't hurt that the house had a gym already in the basement. One less thing I needed to wait to have built. It also wasn't unheard of for me to stop by for a quick workout after a conference call and grab lunch here before the next event or meeting I needed to attend.

The wine room was heavily pushed by the seller's real estate agent as a bonus. I walked over to my bedroom door and locked it without looking inside. That was the last place I wanted her to go in case she had decided to snoop. Something told me if she got the chance, she would take it. No one stepped foot in there without my permission.

I couldn't deny that I enjoyed Anais's grit and determination to fight to get what she wanted even if it meant fighting me to get it. I was used to having people fall over me to make sure that I was well taken care of, and it was a nice change of pace to have someone who wouldn't just take my shit. It also made the fight and eventual takedown even better. I knew this experience would be enjoyable for both of us once she learned what being mine was all about. And she would learn quickly.

I walked back into the kitchen and looked at the notecard Lucy had laid out on the counter for me. She had done everything that I had requested to prepare for tonight's meal. Part of me wondered if I was doing too much as I saw the candles flickering out of the corner of my eye. Was I trying to get a good reaction from Anais by doing all of this? I would say so, but only so that I could catch her off guard and get my way in the end. To make her think that this little arrangement would be no big deal as I laid my requirements on the table. She didn't know what she was getting herself into and I looked forward to her reaction. I checked the clock again and straightened my suit jacket. I went for my standard all-black suit without a tie. I ran a hand through my hair and then there was a knock on the door.

"Right on time," I said to myself as I took one more sweep of the room before heading to the front door. So, she hadn't put up a fight to come here. *Interesting.*

I looked at myself in the hallway mirror that my interior designer had insisted on installing and made sure that I had gotten nothing on my suit. I opened the door and startled Anais based on her wide-eyed look.

"This isn't what I had in mind when I said you should wear something similar to the dress you had on at Elevate." An image of her in the shimmery gold dress that ran on repeat in my mind made my dick shift. I could have said hello first, but where was the fun in that? Plus, it was the truth. I expected her to be rebellious given the conversations we'd had, but I hadn't been expecting this.

"I must have forgotten," she said with a shrug as she entered my home. "I'm surprised you opened your own door."

"I'm very capable of opening a door. But you don't seem to be capable of following directions. That will be rectified." My words had their intended effect when she averted her gaze before facing me once more. I gestured for her to walk into the foyer and I closed the door. She looked back for a second before she walked farther down the hallway.

"I'm shocked your place is nice. Then again, you have enough money to buy anything, including women."

I knew she was doing her best to change the subject, but this wasn't the last she was going to hear about her ability to not listen to my instructions.

Is her plan today to cause as much irritation as possible? Nice try. "Thank you. Dinner should be ready in a few. I'll take your coat. We'll go downstairs and pick out a bottle of wine." She handed me her coat and I placed it in the coat closet.

"I didn't say I wanted a glass of wine."

I raised an eyebrow at her since I had done my homework. "Follow me."

I nodded my head and walked toward the stairs leading to

the basement. I flicked on the lights and walked down with Anais trailing behind me.

"Pick any bottle." I held open the glass door that led into the wine room.

It seemed as if Anais's mouth was permanently open as her gaze moved from bottle to bottle. "Some of these bottles of wine have to be hundreds of dollars."

"Some are even a few thousand."

It took a few seconds, but she closed her mouth and continued studying the bottles of wine. Finally, she picked one. "Here, I'd like to try this one."

"Excellent choice, this bottle is from Tuscany."

A ghost of a smile appeared on her lips briefly before it vanished. "Is this a thousand dollars?"

"It's not." I didn't tell her that it was damn close to it. "All right, come on and I'll open this up." I let her go upstairs first before I turned the lights off and followed.

Once we were upstairs, I walked past her giving her the opportunity to roam around the open area that was my living room, kitchen, and dining room. I poured myself a finger of whiskey into a glass I'd set out a few moments ago. While I was opening the wine bottle, I glanced up to find her examining my home.

"If it wasn't cold outside, I'd take you up to the roof so that you could see all of Manhattan."

"I wouldn't be interested."

"Don't lie to me."

I grabbed both glasses and walked over to her. She settled on looking out the window closest to my couch. When I approached, she took a seat on my couch and I handed her the wine glass. Small talk during regular business meetings annoyed me to no end and this wasn't much different. "So, you decided to come, which means you are agreeing to our deal."

"Yes, but I'm going to negotiate the terms." She leaned forward and placed her wine glass on the coffee table.

"You think you have negotiating power in this situation?" It was amusing to think that she did, and I could see that she was getting upset.

Her eyes darted around the room and she clenched and unclenched her hands. She was probably imagining slapping me across the face and the thought forced me to hide any excitement. I dared her to do it in my mind just so she could experience what type of punishments I would unleash if she defied me.

"So what you want me to do is strip and lie on my back, so that I'm in prime position for you to take me whenever you want? Is that what you want? Well here, then." She pulled off her sweater and I saw hints of the plain black bra she was wearing underneath.

I scoffed as I leaned forward to place my glass on the coffee table next to hers. "Stop. Is this your way of exerting power? You have no leverage here, Anais. It's cute that you are trying to act as if you do though." I could see when the realization hit her because her entire mood changed. Her face switched from being upset to downright angry. What she did next surprised even me.

She whipped out her cell phone and lay back on my couch. She ignored me for several seconds and I leaned over and snatched the phone.

"Hey—"

"Are you trying to order a vibrator?" I asked. There wasn't

much in this world that surprised me, but I would admit that this did it. My lips twitched as a chuckle threatened to come out my lips. "Is this supposed to get under my skin?"

"I figured since I wasn't going to get any pleasure from this, a vibrator would be an excellent investment. Or maybe I can grab mine from home."

"You won't be needing any kind of toy unless I'm the one using it on you. Here's the thing, Anais. You control nothing for the next thirty days. I do. I control your pleasure and everything else. When and how, it's all up to me. Once you understand that, this arrangement will be beneficial for both of us. Now we are going to sit down and enjoy a meal together."

I knew the edge in my voice got to her because her eyes refused to meet mine. My little speech had rendered her temporarily tongue-tied because all she could do was look down at her hands. The dinging of my oven timer cut through the tension.

"Dinner?" she asked, her head shooting up from its prior position.

"Yes, you know the meal that comes after lunch?" I asked her with an eyebrow raised. I stood up from the couch and made my way to the kitchen. My open-concept townhouse allowed me to easily see her in the living room from the kitchen. "That would be the pie that Lucy left."

Her eyes turned to me. "Who is Lucy?"

"My personal chef."

She visibly relaxed at my answer. *Fascinating.*

"Hiring a chef was the best option for me because of work and traveling." I put on an oven mitt and turned to grab the pie out of the oven.

"Or you could just meal prep like the rest of us."

I silently chuckled to myself before I said, "What was that?" I stood up and turned to face her, placing the hot dessert on the counter.

"Nothing. I said nothing."

This might be more fun than I thought after all.

10

ANAIS

Dinner was awkward to say the least. I stayed quiet, only opening my mouth to eat the meal that Damien's chef had left for us. The melt-in-your-mouth lobster tail was delicious, along with the truffle mac and cheese and sautéed spinach.

"There's pie for dessert."

I thought it was a bit much to make all of this food for someone who was coming over to settle a debt. Then again, it wasn't like Damien had spent the time making it himself. I didn't know how I was going to fit any more food in my stomach after what we'd just eaten. That, however, didn't stop me from nearly polishing off my second glass of wine. I hoped it would help calm the anxiety I was feeling about what would happen after dinner was over.

"More?" he asked, gesturing to my almost empty wine glass.

I shook my head because my goal was to keep a straight head and two glasses would keep me there.

As I took another sip of the wine, I looked around the

townhouse that Damien called home. I would describe it as a bachelor pad, although the outside of the house looked like a pretty standard New York City townhome. The modern-sleek dark décor that was in Elevate was present in his home, which made me wonder if Damien or his interior designer played a part in the club's design. The wood floors were stunning and something I hoped to have one day when I owned a home.

"What time can you move in tomorrow?"

I glared at Damien. "Say what?"

"You heard what I said."

"And I can't believe that you still have the ability to leave me flabbergasted. I'm not moving in with you. I refuse to pay rent for my apartment if I'm not living in it."

"You won't have to worry about that because it will be taken care of. The entire thing."

I raised an eyebrow. "You mean Ellie's portion too?"

"The entire thing. I don't like to repeat myself, Anais."

My mouth had no filter when it came to Damien. I also couldn't help myself, but something inside of me worried that I might dig a deeper hole and I still had so much to lose. He shouldn't be allowed to treat me or anyone else like this. I thought that my words might anger him. Instead, he gave me a small smile.

"You and I are going to have a lot of fun."

His voice deepened when the word *fun* fell from his lips, sending a small current of electricity through my body that I refused to acknowledge. There was still fear, however. Fear about not knowing what he had in mind or what he had planned. That seemed to be one tactic he used to keep his enemies guessing.

"You're moving in here and there's no room for discussion. If you don't, the deal is off and I don't think you can afford that, can you?" His words sent a tremble down my spine. Once again, he was right. I couldn't afford for the deal to be off. Too many people were counting on me to cancel this debt, even if they didn't know it.

"Can I make one request?" I asked, attempting to take a fresh approach.

He shrugged his shoulders. "You're allowed to ask. Doesn't mean I'm going to grant it."

I placed my fork down on the table and folded my hands. I peeked out the window before turning my attention back to Damien. "I don't want anyone to know that this is happening."

He tilted his head to the side, seemingly digesting my request. "Are you trying to keep me as your dirty little secret?"

I rolled my eyes. "Call it what you want. I don't want people to know that the reason why you and I are together is because I am trying to settle a debt on behalf of my father. That includes my parents. Now, I assume that there will be questions if we're ever seen out in public, but I want to keep this as tight-lipped as possible. I also want it down in writing that you will cancel this debt once the conditions are... met."

"I can work with that."

I was shocked I was able to get that minor victory, but I didn't make a big deal about it. "I also still need to go to work because Monroe Media Agency clients count on me to do my job." I had the ability to work from home and flexible leave, but that wasn't something I wanted him to know. "Oh, and I don't want to sleep in the same bed as you."

"Anais, you will get used to the idea of what I say goes. I

had no intention of you not going to work or doing your job so you're in the clear there. And you won't be sleeping in my bed because I don't sleep with anyone. I sleep alone."

I mentally thanked Ellie because his revelation didn't startle me. I watched as he placed his utensils on the table and a dark look took over his face. The smile that appeared didn't do him any favors either.

"I can't wait to break you." His voice was low and deep, causing the words to come out sinisterly.

"So that means I'll have my own room?"

He nodded. "You'll have your own room and bathroom. No one enters my bedroom but me unless I give you permission."

That was the first time I had felt relieved all night. At the very least, I would have my own space away from him. But it did draw up questions about why he was so protective of his bedroom.

"I assume since you have a chef that you have a cleaning service. Are they not allowed in there either?" I asked the question as innocently as possible, hoping to not make him suspicious about the fact that I was digging for information. I hadn't planned on entering his bedroom, but the secrecy made the red flags in my mind fly high and proud.

"They are, but they mind their business."

I had to force myself not to roll my eyes as I picked up the double meaning behind his words. "You make it sound as if you have a red room or something."

He snickered. "Funny you should mention that because we are going to go to Elevate at some point soon. That way you don't have to beg and plead for Kingston to let you into the basement."

"I did nothing of the sort." I could feel my body betraying me due to his comment, but I would never admit to it.

He sat back in his chair and folded his arms with a smug look on his face. "Yes, you and Ellie did, and I'm sure it was just to see what was going on down there. I'm happy to take you on a tour of the aspects of Elevate that you haven't seen yet. Trust me, there are plenty."

"Oh, no."

He can't do this.

"Oh, yes."

Yes, he can do this.

"I already told you, I'm in control of your pleasure and it will be a *pleasure* for me to take you there."

I could feel my pulse racing. I raised my hand and placed it on the side of my neck. *He can't be serious, can he?*

One glance at his face told me he was.

I cleared my throat and said, "Last, I want us to be monogamous during this arrangement."

"Is this in reference to my reputation?"

I did my best to keep my voice even. "No. This is something that I wanted and thought you might agree."

He didn't answer right away, and I couldn't tell if he was thinking about my suggestion or doing this on purpose to make me sweat. If I had to be honest with myself, it was a bit of both.

"That works for me since I don't share what's mine."

"I'm not yours."

"You are for a month."

He had me there.

Damien pushed back from the dining room table, stood,

and walked over to the living room area. "Why don't we get started now?" He tossed the question over his shoulder.

I thought the way I dressed to come to dinner would have turned him off. I jumped up and stomped behind him, my heart rate picking up speed. "But I'm not dressed—"

"Whose fault was that? You seem to have a very hard time following directions." He sat down on the couch and lazily let his eyes roam over my body. "Did you think that just because you dressed down that would stop me from collecting what's owed to me?"

The smug smile appeared once more on his face and I wanted to knock it off.

This was all a game to him. "Since you were in such a hurry to take off your sweater earlier, why don't you do it now?"

I didn't move right away. I disliked this man more than anyone I had ever met, yet his words started a small ember in my body that I couldn't control. Ellie's words about not getting addicted to him rang in my ears as I moved to take off my sweater.

"Wait a second," he said, pulling out his phone. A few swipes led to the blinds closing, and the lights in the room dimmed to a warm hue. "Stand up."

This time instead of giving him any attitude I did as I was told.

This is only for a limited time. You can make it through this, Anais.

"I said, take off your sweater."

I turned, took off my sweater, and let it fall to the ground with a soft thump. I stalled. It wasn't that I was ashamed of my body. I worked out pretty regularly and ate healthy most of the time and I knew it showed. But feeling his gaze burning a hole into my back stopped me from turning around because I would have to face his gaze head-on.

"Anais." His voice was stern with a hint of annoyance. That was what finally got me to turn around. "Was that so hard?"

Don't answer him. It will only encourage him to act more like an asshole. The ember that he lit under my skin continued to grow, although I did my best to tamp it down. His inspection of my body made the tension in the room thick as a cloud of billowing smoke and I could feel my nipples harden as they brushed up against the soft yet firm fabric of my bra. I couldn't even blame it on being cold because it was warm in his home.

"Take off the bra and touch yourself."

"What do you—"

I watched as Damien's eyes darkened. "I'm not repeating myself again."

My eyes migrated down from his eyes to his chest and cock. Although it was more difficult to see beneath his pants, I could tell that he was affected by the display he wanted me to put on. A slip of his tongue peeked out from his lips. I could feel my cheeks heating although I wished they wouldn't. This wasn't my first rodeo, although I had never been with someone who was this demanding.

My hands made their way toward my back and unhooked the bra. I let it fall off my shoulders and watched it hit the floor with a light tap. They then journeyed to my breasts, gently massaging them as I imagined he would do. But who was I kidding? I knew he would be rougher than that.

I got up enough nerve to look him in the eye and noticed

that his eyes veered from looking at my movements to looking back at my face, as if he were studying me. I wasn't expecting him to stand up so when he did, I took a step back and immediately scolded myself for doing so. He took another step toward me and I stood my ground and didn't move an inch. I didn't even try to breathe because I didn't want him to mistake that for me being intimidated.

"I'm looking forward to our time together." His tone took on a rough, raspy timbre that sent a jolt through my body. His eyes said something more, but I was having a hard time reading them. However, his words soon tossed clarity on the table, making it easy for me to understand. "Stop touching yourself and put your clothes on. Pack your things tonight and I'll see you tomorrow."

His words were like ice-cold water being dumped on my head and they snapped me out of my thoughts, making me realize that once again, this was all a part of the game he was trying to play with my mind and body. What sucked was that my body betrayed me and no matter how much I tried to deny it, I wished that it was his hands on me instead of my own.

Damien backed away from me and left the room without tossing another glance my way. I threw on the clothes as if my ass were on fire. I had been dismissed without a care in the world and I didn't know how to process it. When I made myself presentable, I rushed to the closet where Damien hung up my coat and didn't even have time to throw it on before I dashed out his front door. As I left the townhouse, I saw Rob sitting in the car. The slam of the front door behind me caused him to look over and a moment later he got out of the sedan. I walked away from the door, putting my winter coat on one arm at a time, and by the time I reached the car, Rob already had one of the back doors opened for me. Rob slightly nodded his head in acknowledgment but said nothing.

I wondered how often this happened. Ellie had mentioned that Damien had his fair share of women come and go, but had he made similar arrangements like this in the past? *Wait. Why did I care?* I shifted those thoughts in my head as the car started moving. Once I was settled in the car, I laid my head back on the chair and let the events of this evening replay in my brain. As I thought about it, anger rose in my veins replacing feelings of humiliation, embarrassment, and shock that I'd felt previously.

How dare he just kick me out like that? I wished I had gathered up enough courage to say something when he was in front of me, but I had been overwhelmed, given how quickly everything was happening. I needed to school myself on how to react to him and his mind games because I was sure this wouldn't be the last time this would happen.

What shook me to my core was realizing that I was fooling myself. I wasn't pissed because he had humiliated me before kicking me out. I was pissed because I liked it.

11

ANAIS

"Hello?" I called as I walked through the front door because I didn't know if Ellie was home.

She peeped her head from around the corner and that was when I noticed that water was running in the sink. "Hey! I was just washing dishes while I waited for you to come home. How did it go with Damien?" Her eyes widened and before I could say anything, she jetted back into the kitchen. The water shut off and she came flying out of the kitchen, wiping her hands on a dish towel.

"It went," I said, and I closed the door and walked into our apartment. I didn't even bother taking off my coat and then I flopped down to the couch. I put my hands over my face, and I tried to figure out what I was going to say. "So, he had his personal driver pick me up and he had dinner set out and ready to go when I got there."

Ellie sat down next to me on the couch. "That sounds sweet."

I looked at her in disbelief. "Sweet? That is the last thing I would use to describe Damien." My voice was muffled because of how hard I was pressing my hands against my face.

"Well, keep going," she said, clearly impatient and wanting to know the entire story.

"He told me to move in with him."

"Shut up." She paused to look at my reaction. "You're not kidding. What?"

"Yeah. For the next thirty days."

"Are you gonna do it?"

"I haven't decided yet but according to him, I'm moving in tomorrow."

"That's quick." Ellie folded her legs under her.

"Tell me about it. I would think that at most I would have to bring clothes because his apartment is fully furnished."

"Well, if you decide to move in with him, I at least know where you are."

I had forgotten I sent Ellie my location on the way to Damien's place. That had been some good thinking on my part.

"Maybe it won't be so bad?"

I slowly turned my head to Ellie, not believing what she just said. "Maybe not, but it's not something that I want to do. He's only moving me in because he wants me at his beck and call."

"That's true, but maybe there are some amenities you could take advantage of?"

"He has a personal chef."

Ellie's mouth opened wide before she closed it. "I don't even know why I'm shocked by this. He probably shits hundred-dollar bills."

I couldn't help but snicker. "Or maybe he wipes his ass with them. You truly have a way with words."

"It's a gift. Anyway, stop getting sidetracked. What else happened after he mentioned you moving in with him?"

"I told him I was worried about having to pay rent so that we could keep the place after I leave. Didn't know if that would be added to my debt as well."

"Oh yeah, that's right." I couldn't believe Ellie forgot that part, but I gave her a little leeway given what I had just spilled to her.

"And he said he would pay the rent, no problem. Including your portion."

Ellie grabbed my thigh. "Say what?"

I confirmed with a nod of my head.

"I'm not sure how I feel about that."

"You and me both."

Ellie started playing with the ends of her brown hair. "Heck yeah, I want my rent paid, but also feels like we might end up owing him something outside of what you're doing."

"I know," I agreed once more, trying to wrap my head around the whole situation. I debated whether or not I should tell her about how he had me on display. I didn't know what good that would do besides potentially embarrassing me even more.

"I'm going to head to bed soon. I have a lot to think about and I'm exhausted."

"Sounds good. I'll see you later."

I turned off the lights in the living room and turned off the television for the night while Ellie wrapped up cleaning things in the kitchen.

I walked over to our window to close the blinds and just

as I was about to pull one of the blinds down, something caught my attention from out of the corner of my eye. From the apartment building across the street, there seemed to be someone pointing something at our window. I could see slight movements and when I saw a flash, it all but confirmed it was a camera. I stopped moving for a split second before I acted as if nothing had happened.

I backed away from the window, without closing the blinds, and said, "Ellie?"

"What? I was just getting ready to—"

I put my finger up to my mouth, signaling for her to be quiet. "Can you hit the lights?" She did as I asked and walked over to me.

"What's going on?"

"I think someone is spying on us from across the street. If we back up enough and walk around the couch, we should be able to look from both sides of the window to see if I'm right."

"Okay," she said, and we both walked out of the range of what we thought could be seen into our apartment before reaching the window and slowly moving our heads to peek out of it.

Ellie gasped and then said, "I think you're right."

"Yeah, but by who?"

Ellie slowly closed the blinds, returning the apartment back to our private sanctuary. "It could be Damien. Making sure that you're doing what he told you to do."

"But he wants me to move in with him, so wouldn't having someone watch me right now defeat the purpose?"

"You haven't moved in with him yet," Ellie pointed out. "Could be his way of keeping you under his thumb until you do."

"That's a good point."

Ellie clapped her hands together and said, "Or what if this is his way of pushing you into his arms?"

I raised an eyebrow at her. "Do you think Damien has ever had to work to get a woman to fall into his arms?"

"Touché."

"Can we go to the police with this?"

Ellie returned the eyebrow and scoffed. "Are you kidding? With what evidence? Although we suspect this person is spying on us, he or she could just be taking a photo of New York City architecture instead."

I sighed and pulled my ponytail tighter. "If I'm going to move in with Damien for a month, I want you to remain safe."

"Don't worry about me. I'll be fine. You're about to enter the lion's den."

I'D BE LYING if I said I didn't toss and turn most of the night. My emotions were all over the place as I thought about what the next thirty days would hold. I didn't want to move into his home. I enjoyed having my own space, and more than that, I hated the thought of sharing a space with someone who wanted me to move in so I could be his sex toy for a month. So, I did what any reasonable person would have done and sent a text to Damien.

Me: *This moving-in arrangement doesn't work for me. I have no problem meeting up with you somewhere, but I'm not moving into your home.*

There was a moment of relief that came when I hit send.

Panic soon replaced it as I realized I sent that message at three in the morning. I wasn't too keen on him knowing that I was up this late thinking about him. Part of me didn't care that I might have woken him up. but I valued sleep and felt a tinge guilty about disturbing someone else's. Or so I thought until my phone buzzed in my hand. I flipped my phone back over, thanking whoever created the ability to dim the light on your screen, and read the notification.

Damien: *You'll be moving in tomorrow. Rob will be at your place at 9 a.m. sharp.*

I almost screamed in frustration. The fact that Ellie's bedroom wasn't too far away was the only thing that stopped me.

Me: *I'm not ready and I don't want to go.*

Damien: *I'll come over there and carry you out myself.*

"Good luck with that," I said. Since it was 3 a.m. and there was no way I could pull myself together for anything tomorrow, I emailed my father and Vicki, his vice president, letting them know I was taking the day off. I tossed my phone to the side and looked at my room. I was in no shape to move anytime soon. Clothes were everywhere because of me being too busy between work and life. Shoes weren't in their proper place in my closet. I made a note to myself to spend part of tomorrow cleaning for my own well-being because I had no plans to go to Damien's. I got up and closed the curtains. I flopped back onto my bed and turned over.

I fluffed up my pillow and placed it back under my head, wishing that sleep would overtake me. It wasn't too long before it did, but there were no dreams to be had tonight. Only darkness as I pondered what tomorrow would bring.

ALTHOUGH I HAD GONE to bed super late, I still woke up early because my body was used to getting up early for work. I was super sluggish seeing as how I was operating on about four-and-a-half hours of sleep. Nothing could be done about that besides drinking a ton of coffee. A quick glance at my phone told me it was eight in the morning and I had heard nothing from Damien after the conversation we had the night before. Shrugging my shoulders, I stood up and got my day started by grabbing that cup of coffee. Once that achievement was unlocked, I checked and saw that Ellie had gone to work. I started sorting through my clothes that were laid out around my room. I was done with that in about thirty minutes so next up was a shower. I stood under the hot spray feeling it beat down over my body as it helped to relieve some of the stress I had been feeling. Once I was dried off, I put my wet hair into a French braid and threw on a tank top and running shorts. I glanced at my phone again.

8:55 a.m.

Five minutes before I was supposed to go downstairs with whatever I wanted to bring to Damien's place. I placed my phone in my back pocket and walked into the kitchen as I thought of another chore I could do. Who knew avoiding moving in with someone could motivate you to clean up your apartment? As I was about to lean down to unload the dishwasher, there was a knock on my door.

After a quick debate with myself, I decided not to answer it. But when the person knocked louder, I hurried over to the door, not wanting them to bother the other tenants.

"What the hell? Clearly someone is either not home or

pretending not to be. Go away," I muttered. What if it was the person that we suspected of taking photos of us last night? I peeked through the peephole. The man that haunted my dreams and had become my worst nightmare was standing on the other side.

How could I forget that he had threatened to come over again himself and pick me up and carry me out of here? Denial swung and hit me like a brick. My fight-or-flight instinct kicked in and my immediate thought was to head toward the fire escape. As I moved to grab my running sneakers, his fist pounded on the door again, even louder this time.

"Anais, I know you're in there," his voice boomed, sounding as loud as someone who had a megaphone up to their mouth.

Even if I tried to make a run for the fire escape, there'd be a very good chance that Rob was waiting at the bottom. Without thinking twice about it, I walked back over to my front door and opened it.

He immediately stormed in causing me to back up unintentionally. The door slammed shut behind him and I was convinced that one of my neighbors would soon call the cops.

"Do you get off on defying me?"

I didn't respond, instead choosing to focus on the look in his eyes and the tone of his voice. His eyes darkened and he was definitely on edge.

"Anais, I asked you a question."

"No. I'm just not the type of person who jumps when you say to." I knew my mouth was going to get me in trouble.

"Looks like your lessons need to begin now."

Puzzled, I watched as he looked to his left, checking to see if we were alone. He grabbed my arm and pulled me over to my sofa and sat down.

"What are you—"

He lazily dragged a finger up and down my leg, causing goosebumps along the way. He took my phone out of my pocket and tossed it on the coffee table. "Lie down on my lap."

"Excuse me I'm—"

He stopped my words with a stare. His chest was rapidly moving up and down and I couldn't tell if it was due to all of the yelling and knocking that he had just done or if it was because he was aroused. There was only so far that I could push my luck and with that thought in mind, I laid down over his lap.

"What are you going to do? Spank me?"

The taunt had the opposite effect I wanted it to have.

"Funny you should mention it," he said, now running a finger softly up and down my spine. "And these little shorts you have on give me ample opportunity to do whatever I want."

His touch brought another shiver to my body. I hated myself for enjoying what he was doing to me as his finger made its way back down to my ass. He brushed a hand against my bottom before he smacked it.

A rush of air left my lungs, and I could hear the slap vibrating through my body. *He freaking did it.*

And then he did it again. The hits weren't hard enough to make me cry, but firm enough to make my pussy tingle.

And again.

I didn't trust myself to speak. I knew my words would betray me.

"No words, Anais?"

I still didn't respond.

"Such a shame. After all, I'm enjoying you in this position."

Another slap met my flesh. There was no way that my ass wasn't turning pink by now.

"I think we've reached an understanding now, don't you?" His words flew across me like a weighted blanket as his hands started a war on my body. They massaged the places he'd hit as they made their way to my center. Damien shifted my shorts and my underwear to the side letting a small breeze tickle my pussy. He slid two fingers inside of me and chuckled at what he found.

"You're soaking wet. I think you enjoyed that quite a bit. And I'd bet you enjoyed the show you put on for me yesterday too."

Before I could even think to speak, his hand started moving faster. A moan fell from my lips, the first sound I'd made in minutes. My breathing came out in pants as I tried to control my body's reaction to his motions, but it was useless. My body hadn't orgasmed in months and it was primed and ready for one right now.

"Are you close?" he asked.

All I could do was nod my head as I buried my face into his thigh. The sensations were so intense that it took all of my control to not roll off of his lap.

"I could stop right here and end it all."

When he stopped moving his fingers, I screamed, "No! Please don't stop."

He let out a noncommittal grunt and slapped my ass again before sticking his fingers back inside me. It was almost as if he hadn't stopped and I was ready and revving to go once more.

And it was then that he laid one last strike on my ass that sent me soaring and it was only because of my face being stuck in his lap that my scream was muffled this time. I hadn't expected to feel the rush of emotions that came about as a result of him playing with me on my living room couch.

"I'm in control of all of this. Next time you go against my orders, there'll be plenty more slaps and you'll count each one out loud. Now let's go."

There was no way both of us were going to make it out of these next twenty-nine days intact.

12

ANAIS

It took a few moments for me to pull myself together after Damien let me up. I headed into my bedroom to put on a pair of jeans and a T-shirt. Then I threw some clothing in my bag. I figured an overnight duffle would be enough for now. I could return to my apartment in a few days to get more things. I also grabbed my work bag, thankful that I hadn't bothered to take anything out of that and threw it over my shoulder. Just as I was walking out of my bedroom, Damien hung up the phone.

"Glad to see you're finally listening to directions. Better late than never. Let's go."

I bit my tongue as he walked to my front door and opened it. I snatched my phone off the coffee table and followed in his footsteps. Once I had locked up, I followed Damien down to the car where Rob was patiently waiting.

Rob helped load my things and opened the door to let me in. I quickly scrambled into the car, making enough room for Damien to fall in behind me, and raised an eyebrow at him when he didn't.

"I have another meeting that I need to attend not too far from here. Rob is going to take you to my place so you can get settled. I'll check on you after the meeting is over." Part of me wondered what kind of meeting he could have on this side of town. I didn't ask, scared to think that it might be something I didn't want to know. I saw his face as he left me in this car. Between the furrowed brow and the darkening of his blue gaze, I worried for the safety of anyone who was on the other end of the conversation with him. I nodded my head, and Damien took a step back, allowing Rob to close the door. When Rob pulled off, I strained my neck a little to look behind me, to see where Damien was. He had already started walking down the street, like a man on mission.

IT DIDN'T TAKE LONG to get us back to Damien's. Rob opened the door for me and offered to grab my bags, which I accepted. Once we were inside, Rob turned to me and said, "Here's the key to the front door and my business card. I'll take your things up to your room."

Rob brought my bags through the foyer and down a hall where I was able to get glimpses of Damien's home. From what I could piece together, his home was impersonal. There were no family pictures or books that I could see. It almost seemed as if he just came here to eat and sleep before hopping back up to conquer the next company.

The enormous TV I saw hanging on the wall when I glanced into the living room looked to have all the bells and whistles and screamed bachelor pad. I followed Rob until he stopped at an elevator and I gasped. Of course, Damien would have an elevator in his home.

When we entered, Rob pressed the number four, and the elevator took us to that floor. Neither one of us said a word. When we stepped off the elevator, Rob showed me to my room and placed my bags inside and then went back to stand in the hallway.

"You are not to go to the top floor at any point. Let me know if you need anything." And with that, he was off.

His warning followed him out of my room and when the door clicked shut, silence crept in, creating an unsettling feeling. The bedroom I was staying in looked like a dream come true with its wooden floors, floor-to-ceiling windows, and a king-size bed that required me to climb into it. It resembled a hotel room and that I was okay with. If my ten-year-old self could see this bedroom, I knew she would describe it as a bright neutral-colored room that reminded her of a princess room without the frills. The room was decorated in whites, grays, blush, and other neutrals. The room had a few abstract paintings in those colors hanging on the wall and the bed was piled high with pillows. I loved the ivory roses that were sitting on one of the end tables. Who wouldn't want to stay here if the circumstances were different?

I turned to the dresser and found several pieces of paper and a pen. I took my time reading through the document and saw that it was two copies of a contract dictating that Damien would wipe my father's debt clean if the conditions of our arrangement were met. His signature was on the last page. *He had kept his word.* Feeling wary about signing a contract that a lawyer hadn't looked over, I did it anyway and placed it back on the dresser.

I began unpacking and neatly placed my things in one of the dresser drawers. After that, I took a step back before pivoting to head to what I thought would be a closet. When I opened the door, I gasped in both surprise and horror.

The closet was filled to the brim with women's clothes. Clothes in all different colors and styles, including dresses, slacks, jeans, and T-shirts. It was much more than I could have ever dreamed. I could only imagine how much these things were worth. I pulled out a red dress and checked the tag. I was shocked that he got my size right, and then I was shocked it was Valentino, which I knew could retail for several thousand dollars. Had he bought these specifically for me or were these hand-me-downs from another mistress?

I picked up a white cashmere sweater and felt the material between my fingertips. This was without a doubt the real thing given how soft the fabric felt and I knew this sweater alone had to cost a couple hundred dollars. What was the point in buying me these clothes? To make sure that I fit neatly into his world? Although I enjoyed having new clothes like the next person, irritation rose in my body, because I didn't know what the purpose of all of this was. Thoughts of whether or not I should switch rooms crossed my mind because it would irritate him, but I decided it wasn't worth the hassle. Plus, I loved the room that I was staying in so that solidified my decision to stay.

I grabbed my phone from my back pocket, snapped a picture, and sent it to Ellie. After debating the idea in my head for a moment, I waited to talk to Damien about all this in person the next time I saw him. I tossed my phone onto the bed and continued unpacking, but it didn't take me long to get settled, since I didn't bring much. As evidenced by the wall-to-wall clothes in the closet, I didn't need the little I had brought.

Once I left the bedroom, I debated going downstairs to the living room or going upstairs to his bedroom and looking around. Curiosity got the best of me and I listened for any sounds. I softly strolled over to the stairs. Hearing no one, I walked up the stairs when I reached the top level, my eyes ventured off to look at the only door that was closed. Something told me that that was the master bedroom. I approached the door and tried the doorknob, but it didn't budge.

I rolled my eyes. I should have known he would have locked the door, given that he was forcing me to move in here and he knew I would be alone in the house at some point. Part of me wanted to pick the lock, but I didn't want a charge of breaking and entering on top of whatever punishment he would dole out. His punishment was meant to "correct" my behavior, but the opposite happened. The spanking made me feel more alive and aroused, something that I wouldn't have guessed in a million years. It was the quickest I had ever found my release, wonderful in theory, but I hated the idea that I wanted to do it again.

I turned around and headed back down the stairs. As I reached the landing, I heard the front door open. I nearly jumped out of my skin at how close I'd been to having to explain myself to Damien.

I put a hand on my heart as I tried to slow my breathing down and walked over to the stairs to meet Damien. Once I reached the next floor, the man of the hour looked at me with a raised brow.

"What are you doing?" His voice was thick with suspicion.

"I was walking back from my room. Last I knew, I could do that without having to run it by you." Technically, what I said wasn't accurate, but he didn't need to know that.

He shrugged, accepting my answer. "You should have everything you need. I'll take you on a tour of the rest of the house and if you need anything, Rob is the person who you should call."

"Okay."

He nodded and checked his watch and looked back at me. There was something brewing behind those crystal blue eyes, but I knew he wouldn't tell me. "Lunch should be delivered in about an hour."

"Sounds good."

Damien started to leave but stopped as he reached the door. He turned to look at me over his shoulder. "Anais, if you ever try to open my bedroom door without permission again, you won't like the consequences."

With that, he left me standing there speechless, wondering how he knew I had ventured to the top floor.

DAMIEN HAD to take a call from work, so I ate lunch alone. I was glad. It gave me some breathing room, something I so desperately needed after having to shift my entire life to fit his. It was quite lonely, and I had only been here for less than a day. I usually took lunch meetings or would get lunch with a coworker so not having anyone around was strange. I looked around some more, purposefully avoiding his bedroom because there was no way I was getting in there anyway with him being home.

The sights I saw earlier barely scratched the surface of everything there was to do in Damien's home. I found out that he had a chef's kitchen, a gym, and what I'm sure might become my favorite room in the house, the wine room. Although the house looked compact on the outside, due to it being a townhouse, it had more amenities than anyone could ever want on its five floors, and that didn't include the terrace on the roof. Plus, it was in a prime location in NoHo. I could see why he wanted this place.

I daydreamed about what it would be like living here full time before shaking my head. There was no way that I could live with Damien. Now, if he moved and decided to leave me the house that would be a different story. How I wasn't about to crash from pure exhaustion right now was beyond me, but I knew I was running on pure adrenaline. I decided to go work out in his home gym.

When I got back to my room, I realized that although I'd worn my running sneakers over, I hadn't brought any workout clothes. I walked over to the giant closet that was filled to the brim with clothes. I searched around and found something appropriate to work out in and threw on a black sports bra and black workout leggings. The clothes fit well, almost like a second skin, and the fabric was breathable.

"How did he know my size?" I asked the empty room, not expecting an answer. The thought troubled me, but there wasn't much I could do about it at the moment.

I checked that my French braid still looked decent and grabbed my phone before walking toward the stairs.

I walked downstairs to the gym. There were quite a few machines including an elliptical, an exercise bike, and a treadmill, which was what I was hoping for. I also found some water bottles, some towels, and an extremely fancy water dispenser. I did a mental high five because I didn't need to go back upstairs to the kitchen to retrieve the water I had forgotten.

It didn't take me long to grab some water and to get set up on the treadmill. Once I had a podcast queued up and I finished my workout warm-up, I was ready to go. I was in the zone as I ran and listened to the words of social media leaders talk about the latest trends. It provided a great way to ignore that I was jogging in place versus actually being out and about on hilly terrains and smooth walkways.

Exercise was great for my brain and allowed me to feel as if the fog that was around me was clearing up. Once I finished my cardio, I hopped off the treadmill and wiped it down. I grabbed my towel and wiped the sweat from my body. Then I started doing my abdominal exercises on the floor in one corner of the room. I closed my eyes as I let the movements take over and tried to breathe deeply while I was performing each move.

"This isn't how I expected to see you, on your back."

Damien's voice was louder than the podcast episode and I jumped, interrupting the groove that I had going.

"Don't stop on my account."

"I was just wrapping up anyway. You can leave now."

By my tone, anyone else would have backed away, but Damien took several steps closer. He was in my personal space and acted as if it were his own.

"Don't you have something to do outside of bothering me?"

"I'm not bothering you because I own you. I tell you what to do, remember? Or do I need to remind you?"

I huffed. "What do you want?"

"I was looking for you because I wanted to. Your sessions start now."

"Nope. You don't get to order me around whenever you please."

He reached out with his hand and gently grazed my cheek. "That's exactly what I get to do." He dropped his hand as if my cheek burned him. "You have exactly twenty minutes to shower and when you are done, you are to be naked, face-down, ass up on your bed."

"And if I'm not?"

"Don't test me. You won't like the consequences, Spitfire."

13

ANAIS

I stood in front of the mirror looking at myself. If I had any sense of self-preservation, I should be walking into my bedroom and presenting myself to Damien. In part, the thought of that made me sick. What made me want to shake myself was that being with Damien made me...excited, and I hated him and my body for it. The thought of him putting his fingers inside of me again made me wet, but I'd never admit that to him. I tightened the robe that I threw on after my shower and heard my bedroom door open.

I knew I was in trouble.

"You refuse to do as I say at all costs, don't you?" He was leaning on the door frame of the bathroom and I stared at him through the mirror. "Let's see if you understand this. Go stand near the bed."

I turned around and he moved out of the way, barely giving me enough room to get by him. When my body brushed up against his, my desire for him grew, even though I couldn't stand him. This time I did what he asked, and I stood near the foot of the bed.

"Spitfire, now was that so hard?"

"Oh, go fuck yourself."

"No. I'm going to fuck you. Do you know how long I've waited for this moment? I've been very patient with your smart mouth, but maybe now it's time I,fuck it."

He looked at me, studying me like he was a predator, and I was his prey. I knew I was about to meet my end. He was still dressed in his suit and put his hand on his bulge, feeling himself through his pants. I wasn't sure if I'd ever seen anything more mesmerizing.

My heart rate quickened, and my breathing became more and more heavy to the point where I wondered if I was going to hyperventilate from watching him touch himself. He hadn't whipped his cock out yet but based on the bulge that had formed in his pants I knew he was hard. He took measured steps toward me and when he was finally standing just inches away, he placed his index finger under my chin and lifted my head up so that I looked at him. My eyes were drawn to his lips and lingered a bit before they made their way up to his eyes. I gasped when I realized that this man had given me an orgasm, yet our lips had only touched once.

Until now.

I had never been one to get hot and bothered over kissing.

Until now.

When his lips landed on mine, my mind lost all thoughts of anything except Damien. My primary goal was now making sure that Damien Cross, one of the most powerful men in New York City, lost control.

The kiss became harder and he captured my lips between his teeth, tugging on my lower lip before consuming me once more. It caused my temperature to spike and sent my pulse racing as we both tried to get as close as we physically could to one another. With his body on mine, his hard body against my softer one, I was eager to rip his clothes off. That thought jolted me since I couldn't stand Damien, but I chalked it up to not having sex in months. A few seconds later, he slipped his tongue between my lips and groaned in response as our tongues declared war with one another, neither one of us wanting to be the winner for fear that it might stop. The sweltering heat that this kiss brought to my body was enough to send me off and we hadn't done anything else. Yet.

He broke the kiss first as he moved down toward my neck, where it was only a matter of time before he—

I moaned when he found the sensitive spot on my neck and continued to assault it, causing me to squirm and groan. All he did was chuckle and continue his actions. I was disappointed when he stopped and pulled back.

"Lie down on your back."

"I thought you wanted me with my ass up in the air?"

"The time for that has passed."

I did as he said, and he yanked open the top of my robe exposing my breasts. He wasted no time in going after what he wanted. He immediately placed one nipple in his mouth while his fingers massaged and played with my other nipple until it became a taut peak. He then switched breasts and I clenched the bed sheets. One of his hands made its way down my body and it wasn't until I felt his finger in my pussy that I almost jackknifed off the bed.

He let my nipple fall out of his mouth with a decisive pop and asked, "What do we have here?"

"Damien." His name came out as more of a moan.

"I thought you said you hate me. That doesn't sound like you hate me."

"I do."

"Your body doesn't," he said as he removed his fingers from me and took his time licking each and every one.

His actions made me almost want to scream at him and beg him to put his fingers back where they belonged.

It was as if we were communicating telepathically because he placed his fingers back between my thighs and I made a noise that I couldn't even describe. His fingers moved like a maestro, in very distinct motions, as if he were playing my body like an instrument. This time, he moved faster and when I felt a familiar tingle, he slowed down and gave me a dark smile.

"Tease."

He didn't deny it.

But what I thought was teasing turned into a whole new realm of pleasure when he added another finger to my heat, and it was quite literally all downhill from there. My legs involuntarily opened wider and when I realized it gave him the ability to increase his speed, I threw my head back in ecstasy.

"I'm getting close."

"Don't."

I balked at his words. He had to be joking.

"I can't hold—"

"I said don't." The deepness of his voice sent another wave of pleasure through me, making it even harder to control.

"Dam—"

"I'll tell you when."

The urge to let myself go as a result of his finger fucking

was becoming way too much to bear. If he didn't let me—

"Let go."

There were no words I could use to describe the feeling that was coursing through my body or the cry that fell from my lips when he finally let me over the edge. I felt him leave my body, but I was too exhausted to even look up to see where he went. That was until I heard his belt buckle. I looked back at him and he'd already removed his shirt. It took everything in me to keep my eyes on his face. His lean yet muscular body wasn't a shock to me. I felt the power under his hand and his slacks did little to hide his muscular thighs. I was shocked to find he had just taken the belt off and had thrown it next to me on the bed. Was he thinking about spanking me? Or tying me up?

He took off his pants and boxer briefs next, and I was mesmerized once more by his cock. His dick stunned me, and my eyes widened before I could control my expression. It was long, thick, and hard and I couldn't deny that I became wetter at the sight of it. He slowly walked forward again but instead of approaching me, he went to one of the nightstands in the room and opened the drawer. He took out condoms and tossed them on the bed next to the belt. He joined me on the bed and climbed over my body. He completely unwrapped my robe and leaned forward to kiss me on the lips again hard before he pulled away.

"Now I want that ass up."

I did as he asked without questioning and by the time that I was ass up, he was already lining up his cock at my entrance and diving in. His decision to fill me up completely in one go took me by surprise as the yelp that left my lips turned into a moan.

"I knew this pussy would be tight around my cock."

His words turned me on even more and when he slid out a little, I braced myself for him to launch himself back into me and when he did, I saw stars. His movements picked up velocity and at first, I could barely keep up, but once I started meeting his every pump he groaned.

I could feel myself getting close to the brink again, but there wasn't any way I was going to have a second orgasm. It was too much, and I couldn't do it again. "I can't."

"Yes, you can."

"No. I can't."

"I know you can." He slowed down a bit and began playing with my other lips and I groaned from the sensations.

When he stopped and started pounding into me again, that was all it took for me to go over the edge. "Damien, I'm—"

My words were cut off after I let out another unhuman-like sound and it wasn't long before Damien was following behind me. He slowed down to almost a dead stop as he leaned over me, putting his head on top of my sweaty back. When he pulled himself back up and slipped out of me, I collapsed onto the bed. I heard some rustling behind me, but I was too weak to move. I closed my eyes for what I thought was a minute.

Damien's voice made me open my eyes. His expression was emotionless as he zipped his pants and said, "Dinner will be at six thirty. Meet me in the dining room and don't be late. I suggest you clean yourself up first."

He turned and walked out, pulling the door closed behind him. As the door clicked shut, I felt used and lonelier than ever.

14

DAMIEN

"Shit!" My voice came out as a harsh whisper as my eyes sprung open. I glanced around the room, confirming that I was at home and in my bed. I wiped the sweat from my forehead and felt a headache forming. I had another nightmare tonight.

I got out of bed and threw on some pajama pants that I had haphazardly thrown on a chair in my bedroom. I left my room, closing the door softly behind me, and walked downstairs, thinking that that was the quietest way to head down to the main level. I went to the liquor cabinet and poured a finger of whiskey before sitting in a chair near my fireplace.

I watched as the embers in the fireplace flickered to the point of extinction. It seemed like a good idea to light a fire on a cool December evening, but what it ended up doing was making my mind drift to places it went only when I was asleep. Images of flames clouded my mind, and I couldn't shake them. I took another sip of the whiskey I poured for myself. I knew it wasn't wise because of the headache I was dealing with, but right now it didn't matter. I knew it was the wee hours of the morning, yet all I could do was stare at the light as it slowly dimmed. Nights like this weren't uncommon and lack of sleep was what my brothers would say was the reason I don't do relationships, but it was more than that.

I'd seen life given and taken away in a single instance, which would haunt me until the day I left this Earth, and there was nothing I could do about it. I finished what was left in my glass and stood up, ready to face the demons that came only when I closed my eyes. When the last ember went out, it was showtime for another party that occurred only in my subconscious.

Every time Mom asked me when I was going to settle down and get married, I shifted gears, refusing to answer. But I didn't want to bring anyone permanently into my personal hell. It's why having very casual relationships worked best. No harm, no foul. That was what made everything with Anais so much better.

Dinner with her tonight was less eventful because she was more quiet than usual, but I chalked it up to her being tired from her move here. The deal we struck, though, was one of pure magic. She'd stay here for thirty days, which should be plenty of time for the urge to fuck her to burn out, and by day thirty, it would be done. Yet now I was jumping through hoops to make sure that everything was perfect for her when she came over for dinner and inviting her to live with me. The demons that haunted my nightmares must have done a real number on me to even consider something like this.

But I had never made this type of deal with another woman. Nor had I had another woman move into my house for any length of time. Doing things spontaneously was not wired into my psyche and I admitted that this whole arrangement with her was an impulsive decision. When I hopped into anything in life, whether it was for work or in my personal life, I researched as much as possible before forming an opinion or making a decision. Here, I had done the complete opposite because I was drawn to her in a way I couldn't explain. I had to do whatever I could to make her mine, even if that meant spinning up this foolish deal.

Having a taste of her drew more attention to how this deal shouldn't be occurring and how clouded my judgment was. I knew it wouldn't happen again, for both her sake and mine. I shook my head at the idea. That was the whole point of her being here, or at least that was what I told myself.

I could let her go, that way I could guarantee that she would remain unscathed, but the selfish part of me refused. I knew I would always be the tattered man who seemed to have it all on the outside, but inside, I was miserable, and I knew she would get hurt from this deal.

They say that money can't buy you happiness, but in my case, it's money that can't buy you peace.

15

ANAIS

Several days later, I exited the elevator and looked around the corner to see if anyone was standing near my office door. Seeing no one, I walked as quickly as my legs would allow me to my office and took off my coat. I hung it on the back of my door and winced when I stretched a bit too far to place it on the hook. My eyes drifted toward my desk chair and I sighed. I gave myself a small pep talk and headed over to my chair.

Things had been weird since Damien had blown any expectations that I had in the bedroom out of the water. He hadn't come to fuck me since the first time. In fact, I barely saw him and only in passing. Conflicting feelings floated around my mind about it. I felt relieved to not have to feel his intimidation around every corner, but I secretly hoped we would go for another round...or two. As much as I wanted to tell myself I hated the situation I was in, he was right. I would come to him willing and wanting.

"Anais?" I looked up from my laptop and found my father standing at the door. "Do you have a minute?"

"Sure. What's up?"

Although he had asked a question, it felt as if he were making a demand. He didn't look angry, but I could tell he was taking a more measured approach with his words instead of speaking freely. Dad closed the door and sat down in one of the extra chairs in my office. He didn't speak right away and seemed almost hesitant to tell me why he wanted to talk. I sucked in a deep breath, waiting for what I was worried would be more bad news.

"You know I don't try to get into your personal business, but is there something going on between you and Damien Cross?"

It took every ounce of control that I had in my body to not react to his words. "What?"

"Are you two dating?"

"No." *Technically that wasn't wrong.* I had done my best to keep our arrangement under wraps and the only person I had talked to about this was Ellie, who I knew wouldn't tell a soul. She was my best friend and I trusted her, but she also knew how high the stakes were. "What gave you that idea?"

"This." Dad pulled out his phone, swiped a few times, and then handed it to me.

There was Damien and me all right. The picture was blurry and grainy, but I knew it was from the night that Ellie asked me to go to Elevate with her. The gold dress that I was wearing was unmistakable and we were standing in front of the bar on the main floor of the club. I was relieved that the photographer hadn't caught the explosive kiss we'd shared. Looking at the photo, it would be hard to tell who either person was, especially Damien, whose back was to the camera. I moved my thumb along my father's phone screen, hoping to discreetly check who might have sent the photo. The email in the field was a nonsensical address filled with random letters and numbers, but the subject contained my name. Who was the person who snapped the photo and then leaked it? Wasn't Elevate supposed to have tight security against this type of thing?

My focus turned to the man who shoulder-checked me and the guy Ellie and I believed was spying on us near our apartment. Someone was tracking me. I turned away from my father to hide my trembling lip. I closed my eyes and took a deep breath, trying to calm the fear that was running through my veins. There was no way these incidents were all a big coincidence.

Damien. He always seemed to be several steps ahead of me and nothing seemed to happen without his approval, so he had to know about this. The anger built up inside of me, but I did my best to keep it under control in front of my father. Although I was an adult and could do what I wanted when I wanted, the last thing I wanted him to do was to get a whiff of this and tie it back to the debt.

"Ellie and I ended up at a nightclub the other night and Damien was walking around asking people if they were having a good time. Maybe he owns the place? Anyway, I told him I was and that was it." I knew I didn't have to explain myself to anyone, but if it stopped any suspicion, it needed to be done.

Dad's eyes shot down to the photo before looking back up at me. My anger turned to guilt. I hated having to tell even the smallest of lies but felt it was necessary in this case.

"Let me know if he tries to contact you again, okay?"

"Why? Is there something I should know about him?" I waited with bated breath after I said those words.

He stood up from the chair and looked down at me. His facial expression changed from one of relief to one I couldn't quite pinpoint, and that was frightening.

"The Cross family owns this town. Nothing gets past them in this city and if you want to do certain things, they need to approve it first. They are known to dabble into dangerous things, although there has been no legitimate proof that has been brought to the authorities. Hell, it might have been, but they probably have all of them in their back pockets anyway."

A quiver ran down my back as his words. My gut told me I should be afraid, but having it confirmed was another matter entirely. I needed to find out more, but I wasn't sure how most of the things I wanted to know might be completely scrubbed from the Internet. Another thought popped into my head. "Is that why you went to them to bail the company out instead of going to a bank?"

"In part, yes. I looked into several loans and none of them would have expedited the amount we needed as quickly as we needed it."

Part of me wondered if that had anything to do with Damien, but I didn't want to raise my father's suspicions about what Damien and I were doing. But this was something I needed to know. "Dad, what dangerous things has the Cross family done?"

He shifted his weight and ran a hand through his short-cropped hair and then he replied, "There have been talks of potential ties to the Mafia. Not that they're in it, but they might have some dealings with them."

I kept my face unreadable. "And I'm willing to bet it was swept under the rug, right?"

My father nodded. "Be careful, Anais. If Damien contacts you, let me know, okay?"

Not sure what you could do even if we weren't sleeping together. "I will, Dad."

"I love you and we should try to go out to dinner with your mother sometime soon, okay?"

"Okay, and I love you, too."

Once he left and closed the door behind him, I threw my head into my hands, wondering what I had gotten myself into.

16

DAMIEN

"Melissa, I'm going to need those files from Samson after this meeting."

"I'm on it, Mr. Cross." I said nothing else as we walked toward the conference room door, so Melissa continued, "Don't forget you have 2 p.m. and a 3:15."

I checked my watch. Ten minutes until the meeting. I nodded and she started to walk away before she turned back to me. "Thanks for the fruit basket."

I was taken aback by her comment, but I didn't show it. It took a second then it clicked about what she was talking about. "Happy birthday." I'd made a standing order with a local company to send Melissa a fruit basket for her birthday every year.

She smiled at me and walked away again, I assumed back to her desk, which was stationed right outside of my office. I walked into the conference room and grabbed a seat near the door.

"How are things going with the woman of the hour?"

"What are you talking about?"

I didn't even bother to look at Gage as I patiently waited for the meeting to begin. My father, brothers, myself, and other staff were coordinating to have a plan ready to go for one of the biggest board meetings that Cross Industries had ever seen. Hence the need to make sure we were aptly prepared for just about anything that might happen or any question that might come up.

"We already know that the woman we saw draped in gold at Elevate the last time you were there is now living in your townhouse," Broderick chimed in from across the table.

I saw Gage sit up in his chair out of the corner of my eye. "You moved her into your townhouse too?"

"Are you all done?"

"They better be because we have work to do."

All eyes were on Dad as he walked into the conference room shutting down the conversation. It was rare that I heard Dad use a tone that reminded me of how he used to talk to us when we were children doing something that we had no business doing. Clearly, that tone was still effective because we all fixed our postures to get ready for the meeting. It didn't take long for the senior staff to file in. The meeting started and my mind was focused on all things related to our business ventures.

When it was getting closer to the end, my thoughts turned to Anais staying at my home and keeping my dick wet. Due to our busy schedules, we didn't get to spend much time together.

"Mr. Cross?"

The meeting had just wrapped up. Everyone swung around to face the voice since they didn't know which Cross Melissa was talking to.

"I, uh, meant Damien." She looked somewhat surprised that she had said my first name. "There is someone here to see you."

I stood up and walked over to her. "Who is here to see me?"

"She said her name was Anais Monroe. Said you would know who she is."

I checked my phone to see if she had left a message, but I didn't see one. *She pulled this off as a surprise. Interesting.*

"Did I do the wrong thing? She's sitting in the lobby."

I glanced at Melissa after I put away my phone. "No, what you did was fine. I'll take care of it."

I excused myself from the conference room without causing a fuss and headed toward the lobby. It didn't take me long to spot Anais sitting in the first row of chairs closest to the door. By the look on her face, she was pissed. I took my time to appreciate her coming to my office in a red pencil skirt. She was also wearing those "fuck me" beige pumps that she had worn the first time we met.

"Ms. Monroe." She looked up at me and the look in her eye told me this was going to be a fun meeting. "Please follow me to my office."

I placed a hand on the small of her back and guided her through the cubicles on my floor. I could see everyone's eyes avoiding mine, but I knew they were watching as we marched to my office. I was glad that my brothers were either still in the conference room or had gone to their own floors to manage their operations because I would never hear the end of this, and it was the last thing I needed. I could feel my subordinates' ache to gossip about the scene that was occurring in front of them and I knew they would once we were

out of sight. Not that I never had business associates come to
my office to hold meetings, but she was different. The energy
around us was different and I understood why it would send
tongues around us wagging.

The walk to my office ended with me closing my office
door. "To what do I owe this pleasure?"

She seemed stunned as she took in the room. I will admit
that my office was pretty remarkable. It was located in one of
the corners of the floor and had large windows that allowed
me to look at the tall skyscrapers featured in New York City's
skyline whenever I wanted. I had a big-screen TV on one wall
in case I wanted to watch the news or the stock exchange.
The other walls featured charitable and business accolades.
While she was caught trying to take in as much of my office
as she could, my mind drifted to visions of her bent over my
desk. That was when she snapped out of it and turned her
attention back to me with fire burning in her eyes.

"What the hell do you think you're doing?"

"What are you talking about?"

"Did you tell my father that we were doing whatever
this is?"

What the hell was this about? "No. I had a phone call with
your father about the loan and we may have a meeting later
this week. You were not brought up at all."

"Did you have someone send him a photo of us from
Elevate?"

"I wouldn't lower myself to leak a photo. Elevate has strict
security protocols and you're saying someone disobeyed my
rules?" Someone had the audacity to not only leak a photo
from Elevate, they leaked a photo of Anais and me? The
anger that her accusation and a leak in my club caused in me

went unchecked. How dare she think that I would do such a thing? Before she responded, I continued. "An investigation into who took the picture will occur. Never accuse me of going back on my word. We had an agreement and I've kept my word."

I checked my wrist again. I had less than ten minutes until my next meeting. There wasn't enough time to bend her over my desk now but there was always next time.

She snorted. "I can't trust you. You lie to people all the time."

I got close to her and tilted her chin up to force her to look me in the eye. "I have never lied to you and I never will."

She said nothing, and I wasn't sure that she accepted what I said or not.

"Here I thought you were just here to get fucked across my desk."

Her eyes darted from the desk and back to me. "This isn't about sex. This is about my father suspecting that there is something up between us and it's something I didn't want him to know."

"It had to have been someone you know that told him."

"How dare you attempt to accuse Ellie!"

I locked the door behind me, a decisive click letting both of us know what had been done. "I didn't accuse anyone. I know that my people keep their mouths shut and have sworn their loyalty. It sounds like there might be a problem on your end that needs to be solved. We'll get to the bottom of who is attempting to leak this." I took a step toward her forcing her to back up. I did it again and again and again until she was up against my desk. "This isn't really an issue, that you're linked to me. You're already mine."

And that was when my lips slammed down on hers. The kiss turned serious fast and it was intoxicating. I broke it to whisper to her, "Place your hands on the edge of my desk and don't move."

She did as I said without argument and I growled in satisfaction. *Thank fuck because I don't have time to waste anyway.*

My mouth usually went to her neck first, to the spot that I found that drove her wild, but I mixed it up. My eyes zeroed in on her tits that were currently hiding from me behind a bra and white shirt. How had I still not gotten enough of them? "Unbutton the shirt now or I'll rip it off you myself."

Once again, she followed directions and soon she was standing in front of me in her lacy beige bra, her shirt falling off her shoulders, and her mouth slightly open, her breath coming out in light pants. Her green eyes told me that she was waiting to see what I was going to do next.

My mouth made its way to her breast licking a small trail along the top of it, while my hand massaged the other because it deserved some attention as well. When I heard a moan escape her lips, my dick stiffened in my pants and I was already regretting not being able to put it in her tight pussy due to this meeting that could have taken place over an email.

After my tongue made its way to the start of her cleavage, I used my other hand to yank that bra cup down and put her light brown nipple into my mouth. I glanced up and watched as she threw her head back and let out a groan, not caring who could walk by and hear her. A minute later, I moved onto her other breast, paying as much attention to it as I did the previous one. I loved to hear the sounds that were coming out of her mouth as she lost her mind because of what I was doing to her. When I was done, I let her nipple out of my mouth with a loud pop and knelt to get ready to go toward the main course of this meal.

"Remember what I said. Don't move your hands away from the desk or I'll stop."

She nodded her head, but words were past her at this point as she didn't say anything, but her breathing became more erratic the lower I went.

"I can't wait to get my mouth on this pretty pussy." I glanced up at her and found her eyeing me as I pushed her skirt up and shifted her panties to the side and touched her folds with my fingers as she shuddered. "You're already wet for me and I've only just begun."

I pulled two of the chairs that that were sitting in front of my desk a little bit closer and she intuitively knew to put her heels up on the chairs and that's when I submerged myself into her and she told me that I had done the right thing when she bucked forward, but I held steady and reached around to grab her ass, making sure there was no way she was getting away from my mouth.

Part of me wanted her to thread her fingers through my hair just so I could punish her when we got home, but so far, she was doing her damnedest to keep her fingers clutched tight on the desk, honoring what I'd told her earlier. My tongue made its way to her clit and even if I didn't know I'd made the right decision, her body would have told me I did based on the cuss words she was spewing. Her taste was sweet, something that I could see myself wanting to have for the rest of my days although I knew that couldn't be.

I switched between sucking and licking, not sticking to a particular rhythm so she didn't know what was coming next and I could feel her losing control of her body. The harder her breaths became, the harder my motions, and when I felt her fingers in my hair, I hid my grin. *I got another thing I wanted.*

"Damien." My name came out as a groan and I almost moaned too. I knew I would never tire of that sound and I continued consuming her as if I needed her to live.

A few more seconds and she fell apart and I licked every drop of her, enjoying the taste of her in my mouth. When I pulled back, she looked as if she had been properly fucked with her tits on display and her pussy still glistening from the havoc I had just wreaked on it.

I sat back on my heels and then I stood up, pulling my suit jacket down to cover my dick, which was now at full mast. I checked my watch and bit back a cuss. This had taken eight minutes instead of seven.

"I have a two o'clock and need to head out. Stay in here as long as you need. I'll see you at home later." I paused for a moment. "Take your time too because you look as if you've been properly fucked."

I gave her a small smirk before I exited my office, closing the door behind me.

17

ANAIS

"We can talk about this later."

"Sounds good, Jake," I said as I walked into my office and closed the door. I eased down into my chair, finally able to show that I sore show all over my face after Damien had taken me this morning. I was just about to make a phone call when my phone buzzed alerting me that I had a text message.

Damien: *Be ready to go by 7. Rob will pick you up from home.*

I closed my eyes, first trying to calm myself to tame the urge to send a snarky text message. It would have been nice if he'd asked me if I had any plans. I also would have appreciated more than a few hours' heads-up that I had to go somewhere. There was also the fact that he called his townhouse home to me, when previously he'd always referred to it as "my home." Could be a slip of the fingers, but when has Damien ever slipped up? Before I could analyze it any further, a second text message from Damien popped up on my phone.

Damien: *Don't worry about picking out something. I had my stylist send a few options.*

I furiously typed a message back to him.

Me: *No. I'm not going.*

Damien: *Yes, you are.*

Me: *I don't get a say in this? Shocking. Could you have given me more than a few hours' heads-up? I don't want it to leak that we were seen together and have it get back to my father.*

I pressed send and placed my phone face down on my desk. A frustrated growl escaped my mouth after I checked the time. It was almost four, which meant I should start wrapping up things here soon in order to get back to the townhouse to be ready in just a few short hours. My phone buzzed again.

Damien: *My father was supposed to go to this event but can't and asked me to take his place instead. We could entertain each other.*

Well, at least he too had found out last minute. That lessened some of the anger that I felt. I noticed he hadn't said anything about news about us being revealed to the press. I was worried about more photos leaking and my father finding out that I lied by omission, but I didn't push it further.

Me: *Could you at least tell me what this event is about? That might help me decide on an outfit that's appropriate.*

Damien: *It's a cocktail and dinner event. I have to make an appearance and act friendly.*

Me: *Act is right. You mean until you take over their companies and portfolios?*

Damien: *You got it. Rob will get you from work at 4:45. You will be ready to go by 7.*

THE RIDE to Damien's took longer than usual with traffic factored in, but I made it there with plenty of time to spare. I jumped into the shower but avoided wetting my hair in order to save time. When I got out, I noticed a black off-the-shoulder cocktail dress, a dark red sheath dress that dipped a bit in the front, and a long-sleeved forest-green boatneck sheath dress hanging on a small rack in the bedroom. On the floor near the foot of the bed were black pumps and I was thankful that at least they were basic, and I didn't have to make a choice between shoes as well. They hadn't been there before I entered the shower, making me wonder who had left them. If it had been Damien, I was shocked he didn't stop by the bathroom to see me, assuming he didn't let the stylist come into my bedroom. Knowing that it was December, I walked into the closet that was filled to brim with expensive clothes, wondering what the reason was for asking his stylist to bring clothes when I could have found something suitable. I found a beautiful long white peacoat and placed it on the bed next to the forest-green dress I decided to wear tonight.

It didn't take me long to put my dress on and apply my makeup. I thought about spending some time putting my hair up but kept it down for the sake of convenience. As I finished putting on my heels, there was a knock on the door.

"Come in," I said and was shocked to find Damien on the other side of the door. He had knocked instead of barging into the room? Was I living in an alternate universe? He was focused on how tight the dress was in the bodice area before his eyes made their way down the rest of my body to stare at my legs.

He liked what he saw although he said nothing about my appearance.

"Wear these," he said as he handed me a small box.

My heart temporarily jumped into my mouth because of its shape, but my brain finally caught up to my eyes and noticed that it was too big to hold a ring. When I opened the box, I found a pair of rectangular-cut diamond and emerald earrings. On top was a diamond and dangling from it was an emerald.

I almost slammed the box shut and dropped it.

"You want to ask a question."

"Whatever could have given you that idea?"

"Because you never shut up."

I couldn't tell if he meant that as a compliment or an insult, but I took it as the former.

"How much did this cost?"

"That's not important. It's a gift."

"Will this be added to my debt?"

His eyes flared. "What part of 'it's a gift' don't you understand?"

Was giving earrings that were probably worth more than what I had in my savings account just an everyday occurrence for him?

"Why did you buy them?"

"Because they reminded me of your eyes. If you hadn't picked the green dress to wear, I hoped these might have convinced you otherwise."

I had nothing else to say and although I felt uncomfortable wearing something so expensive, in the back of my mind, I knew part of my job tonight was to be a representation of him and all of the companies that were a part of the

"Cross Empire," so I put the earrings on. I could talk to him about not being able to accept these later.

I put on the white coat and grabbed the black purse that I was going to be using for the night. When I looked at him, he nodded, turned around to walk out of my room, and waited in the hallway. I checked my makeup one more time and I followed behind him, closing the door on my way out. We waited for the elevator to take us down to the main level and when we reached the front door, he held out his arm for me to grab as we descended the front porch stairs where Rob was waiting with our ride. Damien waited for me to enter the sedan before walking around the car to enter on the other side.

"Is everything okay?" His actions raised my bullshit meter and I wanted to know what this was all about.

He didn't say anything, but he looked at me.

"You're acting like a gentleman and I want to know what's up."

"Are you questioning me?"

"No." I thought about arguing further but figured if I wanted to have a nice evening tonight, it wouldn't be worth what this was about to turn into.

As he said, the ride to the event was short and I clutched Damien's arm as we made our way through the crowd of people that were in attendance. We were gathering in the enormous living room of someone who had more money than I could ever imagine. I could see what looked to be part of a large, stunning staircase down into the hall.

Almost as soon as we arrived, everyone wanted to talk to Damien and therefore me since I was on his arm. While people were talking to him, I watched as Damien's eyes scanned the room. What he was looking for, I didn't know. I prayed that this wouldn't get back to my father, but if it did, what good was it worrying about it now? What was done was done.

I felt my body tense up, and Damien must have sensed it too because he rubbed his hand up and down the small of my back, providing a small sense of comfort in the very crowded room in an unfamiliar place.

"Damien, hello!"

Although we were in the middle of a conversation, this man, whose name I didn't catch, had to let his presence be known. Damien's eyes narrowed. He was supposedly talking to Damien, but his eyes were zeroed in on me. "Take your eyes off of her if you ever want to breathe, let alone work in this city again."

Damien's words sent a tremble down my spine. The people in our immediate vicinity heard Damien's words and either took a small step back or looked at him with wide eyes. I did neither of those things because I suspected something like that might come out of his mouth based on the irritation he had with this guy and his hand, which had been on my lower back, had now moved to my waist, holding me to him like a vise. All this man did was look at me and that was enough to make Damien go off. I refused to admit to Damien or anyone else how much it aroused me.

The man in question got the message quickly and his attention was on Damien before finding an excuse to leave us alone. I was relieved because I truly thought Damien might kill him.

I leaned over to whisper in Damien's ear. "Was that really necessary?"

"What did I say about questioning me? I didn't like how he was looking at what was mine and I let it be known. End of discussion."

The conversations continued until at one point, Damien excused both of us and pulled me away to where we could be alone.

"Do you want to get a drink or anything?"

I thought about it for a moment and said, "I think I'm going to go with water."

"Not Merlot?"

I snorted. "Trying to keep a clear mind instead of drinking and turning into a lush."

"Damien, long time no see."

Damien and I turned to find a tall, tan-skinned man standing behind us. His aura was off-putting. I looked at the stranger in front of me and then back up at Damien. It was clear as day that this individual was no stranger to Damien.

"Will. It's good to see you." Damien's tone said that it was anything but.

I knew my instincts were correct.

"Likewise."

"I just wanted to come over and say hello after I saw you across the room." His eyes turned to me and he said, "And you are?"

I hesitated for a moment before I said, "Anais."

"Well. What a beautiful name for a beautiful woman."

I thought about rolling my eyes at his very cliché comment, but something told me that wouldn't go over well. Who was he?

"I'll let you get back to it. It was nice seeing you again."

"Likewise," Damien replied.

When Will left, I turned to Damien and asked, "Who was that?"

"Just someone I knew a long time ago. You don't have to worry about him."

Although I didn't think that was the end of it, his voice, thick with assertiveness, was reassuring and it scared me.

18

ANAIS

"Damien, I don't think I'm properly dressed for an evening at Elevate."

"It doesn't matter what you look like since you're with me."

I rolled my eyes and threw my head back onto the headrest. I knew Elevate would be fun, I just also knew I was overdressed no matter how much Damien said I wasn't, but I was ready for a more relaxed vibe after spending most of my evening at a function I didn't care to be at. But had the security issue been taken care of? It irritated me because I kept thinking about it, but I didn't want to deal with the fallout from it.

"But—" I leaned forward to argue with him because this was a terrible idea.

"The security issue is being handled and the majority of people that will be there tonight won't see you."

I sat back because he ripped the wind from my sails when he answered my question.

It didn't take long for us to arrive, but we drove past the

entrance. The SUV turned down an alleyway and we were escorted into the building through a door behind the building. Damien led the way as we went up to the VIP lounge where we were seated and given drinks.

"Not too bad, huh?" Damien asked as he dipped his head to whisper in my ear.

I shook my head. "No, this is great. I don't know if I've ever been in the VIP portion of a bar or club."

"Well, there is always a first time for everything."

The way he said those words both aroused and frustrated me. Ellie's words about becoming addicted to Damien replayed in my mind. I closed my eyes briefly, tossing her words aside because there was nothing wrong with enjoying how he made my body feel. No emotions required.

"We're going downstairs tonight."

"I uh — wasn't expecting that." I wasn't opposed to it and the thought of trying something new with him down there was more than enough to get me excited. I had just thought we might get a quick drink and head home. Visions of what he might have planned flashed through my mind. If he brought up anything outside of what I was comfortable with I was walking out.

"You should always expect the unexpected, especially when it comes to me. We'll head down after you finish your drink." His eyes dared me to fight him on it, but I didn't want to.

What I wanted to do was continue to press his buttons and I did that by drinking my drink even slower than normal.

I could see him growing impatient while I cradled my drink, determined to draw this out as long as possible. I stood up and walked over to the balcony. I sipped from my drink and looked out at the crowd. The atmosphere in the club was electric and part of me wished I was partaking in the festivities below. The VIP area was secluded from the rest of the night life, making me feel both envied and envious.

"Let's head downstairs," he said as I took another sip of my drink.

I hadn't heard him walk over nor had I felt his presence, so his voice caused a small tremble. "I haven't finished my drink yet."

"I'll get you another."

His annoyance with my stalling was obvious. I swallowed a mouthful of the liquid left in my glass, polishing it off. My attempts to stop the inevitable were over.

It was now or never. Damien grabbed my hand and together we walked down the stairs and came face-to-face with a security guard. This time I had no problem getting in with Damien leading the way.

Damien led me down a dark hallway and the first stop on the tour was a lounge that looked like the bar upstairs, but the vibe was different. The energy was more sensual and pure sex. Although there were couches in the large room, most people were on the dance floor grinding on one another and having a great time. The lack of clothing helped set the mood as I watched a woman in what I would call a dominatrix outfit lead a man, who was just in his boxers, around on a chain.

I leaned forward and asked Damien, "Would you ever let me take charge like that?"

The look he gave me told me what I needed to know, and I bit my lip as we walked past a gigantic room that seemed to go on forever.

Bang. I jumped several inches in the air at the loud noise that came from my right. The noise came from a woman who was now leaning up against a glass door that looked out into the hallway we were walking down. Her hands and breasts were plastered against the door as her partner appeared from the shadows and started fucking her from behind.

It was Damien's turn to whisper in my ear. "I can tell by your reaction you wish that was you."

"It was also a sudden loud noise."

"Uh-huh." He didn't believe me, and I didn't believe myself. The look of pure ecstasy on the woman's face said it all. "Maybe you'll be interested in some of the other themed rooms."

"It's up to you since you control my pleasure."

"Now you're starting to get it." The look he gave me when he said those words had me ready to confess every secret I had as long as it led to him giving me that look and so much more. We continued down the hall, passing a few play areas including one that was safari themed and another that had a nautical theme. When we passed a room that was dressed in different variations of red lights, almost painting the picture of flames being on the walls, I noticed Damien visibly stiffen, but before I could ask, he was pulling me toward a door.

"Here we are," Damien said. We walked inside and he closed the door behind us. The room he picked was much more like what I deemed to be his personality. He chose a dimly lit room, whose light was coming from a fake fireplace. The king-size bed in the middle of the room was the only other thing that I could see. "Strip. Down to your bra and panties."

Normally I had no problem arguing with him, but the

darkness of his tone sent a shiver down my spine that I tried to hide. I didn't want him to know the effect that he was having on me out of fear that he might use it against me. "You're going to have to unzip me."

I turned around and pulled up my hair giving him plenty of room to maneuver. He placed his hands on my thighs and they drifted up my sides, where he briefly touched my breasts before moving his hands toward my back. He slowly unzipped my dress and when it was about halfway down, I let my hair down, allowing it to swing loosely down my back. His quick intake of breath told me he enjoyed that image. I dragged the green sleeves off my shoulders, allowing the dress to gather at my waist.

I wore a black lacy bra and panties under my dress. It had been a splurge purchase about four months ago and I finally wore it tonight, to give me some more confidence. It somewhat worked, or maybe it was the drink I had. He was enjoying what I was wearing although it wasn't for him.

I rolled my eyes before I stopped moving an idea formed in my mind. Damien loved being several steps ahead, but I wondered if I could get the upper hand here. I slowly unzipped the dress and made a bit of a show of getting the tight dress off of my body by bending down, letting him see all of my cleavage as I dragged the dress over my waist and down my legs.

"You think this act is cute?" His voice came out a little hoarse, so I knew my "act" had done what I intended it to do. "You're not in control here. I am."

"There is one thing I am in control of. We haven't talked about any boundaries and I want to clarify that I'm not doing anything that I'm not comfortable with. If it pisses you off, so be it."

His eyes narrowed and then a smirk appeared on his lips. "I was waiting to see if you would say something. You always have a choice." With those words, he backed me up against the wall and I loved the sensation of the cool wall against my warm back.

"What do you want?"

His question startled me for a split second. I answered honestly. "You. I want you."

"Undress me."

Feeling bold, I didn't hesitate to reach for his pants, wanting to take his cock out. I took my time unbuttoning his shirt and once all of the buttons were done, I peeled the shirt off, removing it from the hard muscles on his shoulders and down his arms before I threw it on the floor. I bit my lip as I undid his pants' button, unzipped his fly, and unbuckled his belt and watched his pants fall down, leaving a pool of cloth at his feet. He quickly removed them along with his shoes and socks. I couldn't help but stare at his perfect form before our eyes met. The desire that flashed in his eyes made me even more wet as I looked at his hard abs and the black boxer briefs that he had on. I felt as if his bulge was teasing me, and I couldn't wait for him to fuck me. No emotions, just pleasure.

"I shouldn't want this," Damien murmured as he lifted my head with both hands and kissed me. My senses went on overload as his desperation seeped through. The kiss became more wicked and his hands left my face and made their way down my neck and to my breasts. He was the first to break the kiss and launched an attack of kissing and sucking on my neck. I expected him to work his magic there, but he switched it up on me when he pulled back and bent down, wrapping his hands around my legs, and pulling them around his waist. I wasn't expecting the motion and I squealed in response. When I looked at Damien, I saw a hint of a smile on his lips.

He carried me across the room and gently tossed me on the bed. "You know, it's been a while since I heard you say anything, Spitfire. Let's turn this up a notch."

He peeled my bra straps down my shoulders and my tits sprang free from their enclosure. I heard him groan under his breath, trying to keep a lid on his yearning for me. Looked like all of this was turning things up a notch for him instead of me. That was until his lips landed on my breasts. When his mouth met my nipples I moaned, mentally acknowledging that he had turned the tables. He worshipped my breasts as if they were everything he needed to survive and slowly his hand made its way down my body. When he touched my pussy, I was ready to drag his cock inside me. He pulled back and looked down at me, his eyes moving between where his fingers lay and my eyes.

"Who made you this wet?"

Forming words wasn't on my agenda so I didn't make a peep, even fighting back the moan that was dancing in my throat.

"Anais." His voice was low and full of warning. "I'll move my hand."

"No! Fuck! I'm wet because of you."

"Good answer." With that, his finger slipped between my folds and I let out the moan that I had been fighting for what seemed like forever. How was I already revving up to come this quickly?

His fingers moved in and out of me with a finesse that

none of the men I had been with previously had. When he added another finger, it didn't take long for me to soar above the imaginary clouds that had formed in my mind. I rode out my orgasm on his fingers and when he removed his fingers my orgasm was cruising back down in altitude. I thought he would give me a breather, but he wasn't done yet.

"Get on your knees. Put your fingers on that cunt while I get ready."

My body moved on reflex and I found myself on all fours on the soft king-size bed. I felt empowered as my fingers rubbed my clit and I could feel his eyes zeroed in on the motions that my hand was doing as I pleasured myself. I heard the ripping of the condom wrapper.

"You don't know how much I love this ass," Damien murmured as I heard him get closer to me.

Not being able to see him heightened my other senses and I almost buckled when I felt his dick teasing my entrance. I loved when he ran his cock up and down my seam, because I never knew when he would enter me. He did it repeatedly and I wondered if he was waiting on me to beg. He wasn't.

He entered me and I whimpered, feeling relieved that he finally satiated my need to have him inside of me. Him entering me from behind was a novel experience and the sensations that Damien set off in my body as he fucked me took me to another planet. His pace quickened and it didn't take long for the first smack to land on my ass. The sting from the hit sent another load of pleasure through my body and got me closer to my second orgasm. When he did it two more times, I could feel myself about to take the deep dive once again.

With a few longer strokes, I cried out, reaching the tipping point. Damien didn't let up the pace until he succumbed to his own orgasm after I had. He collapsed on my back, removing himself from me. Damien got up to head to the bathroom, leaving me alone in the room. Although I knew I could feel safe in this place, my gut told me that danger wasn't too far away.

19

ANAIS

I looked down an aisle and didn't see what I wanted, so I moved on to the next. I made an impulsive trip to a drug store near my office after work to grab a couple of things before heading back to Damien's. I saw the aisle that was full of nail care items and hurried to pick out a new nail polish color. Smiling when I found the one, I plucked the container off the rack and placed it in the basket I was holding. The deep brown that I found was a perfect color for winter.

I headed toward the front and got in a small line that had gathered near the cash registers. I zoned out for a moment, wondering what I was going to do for the rest of the night.

"Thank you. Have a good evening."

My head shot up not just because I was next in line but because of the voice I just heard. Why was it familiar? I looked to my left and noticed a man with a black hoodie and baseball cap walking away.

That was when it dawned on me. The scratchy voice was

similar to the man who shoulder-checked me outside of my apartment before this deal with Damien began. I hurried to the register and tossed my things on the counter with a tight smile. I hoped that the sales associate in front of me would have no issues ringing up my purchases because I needed to find this guy.

Thankfully, the clerk had me out within a couple of minutes.

I knew better than to confront him by myself because I didn't know what type of danger that posed, but I wanted to get a good look at him. There was no way I was going to believe that it was just a coincidence that he walked into the same drug store as me. I rushed toward the front door and the cold air hit me like a slap in the face. After looking up and down the street several times, I couldn't find him. The person that was following me was still out there and I couldn't do anything about it. I snatched my phone from out of my bag and called the first person who came to mind.

"Anais."

Just him saying my name helped warm me against the cold that was caused by the chill of the wind and the fear in my soul. "Are you at your place?"

"I'm a few minutes away. Why?"

"I think I'm being followed. Can you stay on the phone with me until I get to your place?" The confident mask I usually wore around Damien was cracked.

"Where are you?" His no-nonsense tone soothed me a bit and I hated to admit it.

"Two blocks away from your house."

"You'll get there first because of traffic. When you arrive, lock the doors until I get there. I'll stay on the line until you do."

I sighed. What could we talk about? "Tell me a funny story." I looked over my shoulder but found nothing out of the ordinary.

He didn't miss a beat. "One memory that I have from childhood is that I was in the living room finishing my homework with my mom helping me. I couldn't have been more than six at the time. With three boys under the age of seven in her house, she knew that something was up when things were a bit too quiet. She found my twin brothers playing in her makeup when they were around two or three. I remember the horrified scream she let out."

I snorted. "I'm sure she wasn't too thrilled to have to clean them up." I felt some relief wash over me when I spotted Damien's house in the distance.

"Nope, but I couldn't lie and say that I wasn't happy that they were getting in trouble."

The small amount of glee in his voice made me smile as I walked up the stairs to Damien's place, almost forgetting the reason that I called him.

I COULD FEEL myself waking up even though my body was telling me it wasn't time to do so yet because I was still exhausted. After talking with Damien and discussing my potentially using Rob to go to and from work I came up to my room and went to bed early.

A low beeping noise was playing, but I couldn't tell if it was something in my dream or in real life. It took another second for me to become fully awake and to sit up in bed. I heard the door creak and I turned and found that Damien was in my room. I scrambled to get out of the covers and when I looked at him, he put a finger to his lips, letting me know that I should be quiet. I reached over and pulled a hoodie on over my tank top and sweatpants.

"What's going on?" I whispered, fumbling to fix the clothes on my body.

He didn't answer right away, and my eyes widened until he held up one finger. That was when I realized he was attempting to listen for any strange noises. Did this have anything to do with the low beeping noise I'd heard earlier?

"Someone is attempting to enter the house and tripped the alarm."

I listened once more, and I heard the beeps sound a couple more times and then they stopped. He pulled out his phone and opened up what looked to be an app, but I didn't recognize the icon.

"Come with me," he said, and I dashed over to him. He wrapped his arm around my waist, and his bare arm on the small of my back provided some of the warmth that I didn't know I wanted.

He guided me out of my bedroom and quietly up the stairs. He stopped in front of a closed door and I held my breath when I realized he had led me to his bedroom. With one swipe of his phone, he opened the door.

Given the situation and the lack of lighting, I didn't take the time to look around the room like I had wanted to. I watched as he walked over to a corner, guided by the light from his phone, and placed his fingers just under the tabletop of his desk. I took a step toward him, not totally understanding what he was doing, and a beat later I heard a door open on the other side of the room.

He rushed back over to me and said, "Anais. Listen to me. This is not the time to argue with me. I want you to head over to that corner of the room and go through the door. The door will close behind you and I need you to stay put until I can get you."

I nodded and followed Damien back toward the open door.

"Rob has called in reinforcements and this is just a precaution."

I nodded again and walked through the door, not sure what might meet me on the other side. When I walked in, an overhead light turned on. I glanced around before turning to Damien.

"I'll be back as soon as I can. If I'm not back in fifteen minutes, use either that phone or that panic button under the desk to call the police." He pointed to a black phone that looked to be connected to a landline in the corner.

I moved my head so I could see the circular red button on the underside of the desk. "Okay."

Damien gave me one last look before he left, closing the door behind him, and encapsulating me inside. I took a deep breath and turned around to continue examining my surroundings. I found a storage container full of dried food and water. Another contained at least two first aid kits, blankets, clothes, flashlights, hand crank radio, portable toilet, and toilet paper. The final container had what looked to be cards, a portable chess set, and a couple of other things to serve as a way to pass the time. Essentially, there was anything and everything that you would need to survive for several weeks in this room.

Damien had taken a lot of thought in putting these materials in this room and had made sure that whoever was in here would be prepared for just about any instance, that was for sure. And that feeling helped calm my nerves temporarily. I patted my body, trying to find my phone, and realized I had left it in my bedroom.

"Fuck," I muttered as I debated what I could do. I reached into the bin and took out the cards and started dealing them out to play a round of solitaire. It wasn't how I thought I'd be spending my Wednesday night when I should have been sleeping.

As the game went on, I noticed that my hands were becoming clammy, although I was in a cool room. I checked the clock on the wall and if it was correct, only seven minutes had passed, so I continued playing.

A couple of minutes later, I heard a slam that nearly caused me to jump out of my skin. "What the hell was that?"

Of course, silence answered my question as I stood up and walked over to the door. I hoped that Damien, Rob, and whoever their backup was would be okay. I placed my ear against it for a few seconds and I realized that wasn't a good idea because if someone started shooting, I would more than likely get hit by a bullet. With that thought in my mind, I backed away quickly until my back reached the other wall. It didn't take long for any lasting confidence that I had to fall by the wayside and the sense of dread to creep into my veins. Sweat broke out over my skin, causing me to tremble for a moment. When the tightness in my chest started, it finally clicked what was happening: panic attack. I slid down on the wall in a fetal position on the hard, wooden floor.

I hadn't had a panic attack like this since I was a teenager, right before I had to present a group project in biology. Now was definitely not a good time to be having one.

I tried to take deep breaths to at least ease the tightness in my chest, but it wasn't doing much to help. The nausea that rolled in soon after was interfering with my breathing, causing me to struggle even more. The tears increased and were free flowing down my face and although I tried to keep somewhat quiet, I knew I was failing.

I didn't know how long I was in that position, but seconds turned into minutes that then turned into what felt like hours as I waited for someone to free me from this room.

"Get it together," I tried to tell myself and that lessened my tears some. I slowed my heart rate down to a point that I could force myself to crawl over to the desk and looked up at the clock on the wall.

"Three minutes to go," I muttered to myself and pulled open some of the drawers, thinking that maybe looking through them would take my mind off of what was going on in the house. I found some papers in the top drawer, but I didn't have time to read them. I opened the bottom drawer, and my eyes widened. A gun was staring back at me. I pulled it out of the drawer and wondered why Damien hadn't mentioned that it was in here. I studied it for a minute before placing it on top of the desk. This might come in handy in case someone tried to break into the panic room. The only problem was that I'd never fired a gun, so I hoped the safety wasn't on so that if I needed to, I could just pull the trigger and ask questions later. I'd deal with whether or not I could pull the trigger if the time came.

I had so many questions that needed answering, but there were several that stood out to me. Who the hell would break into Damien's house? And why did he find it necessary to install a panic room in his home?

20

ANAIS

Just as I got up to make the phone call, I heard the creaking of a floorboard outside. My feelings jumped from being terrified to attempting to calm myself in order to think rationally. I heard another creaky board bow under the pressure of someone's weight and that caused me to get into position. I snatched the gun and flicked the lights off and bent down, crouching down in front of a counter.

"Anais?"

My name came off his lips in a hushed whisper. But that was all I needed to restore a sense of calm. In my mind, we were safe.

I backed away as the door opened, dropping the gun at my feet. Damien sprinted inside.

"You're all right."

"Yes," he responded and then he acted as if he was checking me for bruises, as if I was the one who had just gone out to face whoever had tried to break into his home. "Are you okay?"

"A little shaken up, but I'm fine."

"You're not fine. You look as if you've been crying." He wiped the remaining tears from my face. "Whoever sent that asshole to my house is going to pay for putting those tears in your eyes."

"With everything going on—" I was staring at his face until I noticed a small red smear on his cheek. "Is that blood?"

I moved to take a closer look and that was when I finally got a look at his hands.

"Damien, your hands are bleeding."

"It's not mine. You need to pack a bag." He didn't hide the fact that he was changing the subject.

"Wait, what?"

"We're getting out of here," he said, getting ready to pull me along behind him, but I pulled my hand back.

"What do you mean we're leaving? We should probably call the cops and wait for them to get here."

He shook his head. "Don't worry about the police. Pack your duffle bag with a few essentials and the rest can wait until we get there."

"Get where?"

"Anais, right now is not the time to be asking a million questions. Just do as I say. Rob should be standing outside your door just in case."

"What are you going to do?"

"I'm packing as well."

I nodded and Damien walked me to the stairs. Sure enough, Rob was standing at the bottom close enough to guard my bedroom door, so I sprinted down the stairs. Rob gave me a slight nod as I entered, and I packed up as much as I could before Damien appeared back at my door.

"Are you set?"

"Give me one second." I threw on a sweatshirt that I had brought from my apartment and grabbed a thick winter coat from the closet. "Yes, now I am."

"Okay. Let's move."

When we made our way downstairs, another man that I swore I had seen previously was standing near the sink washing his hands.

"Kingston, we are going to head out now."

Kingston turned around as he was drying his hands and looked at both of us. That's when it hit me. "You're the security guard from Elevate."

"I am. I'm also Damien's cousin."

"Oh lovely, there are more of you Crosses in the world." Watching Kingston dry his hands triggered another memory as I looked at Damien's face and hands. The only thing that told me that he might have gotten into a scuffle was the bruising that stained his knuckles.

The men chuckled. "We need to get a move on," Damien said and faced Kingston. "If you hear anything, let me know."

Kingston nodded and said, "You know I will. It was nice seeing you again, Anais."

I was shocked that he knew my name. "Likewise."

Damien and Rob grabbed the bags and I followed them out to an awaiting SUV. I found a couple more men that I had never seen before standing with their guns drawn. "What the hell?" But no one said anything as we got into the SUV and it took off into the dark of night.

I turned to Damien, who was busy on his phone next to me and hadn't said a word since we left his home.

"Is now a good time to ask questions?" I couldn't believe how meek my voice sounded and Damien must have thought the same because when he looked up, I saw a hint of concern in his eyes and his expression.

"Hold on." He dug into his pocket and handed something to me. It was my phone. "Email your father and whoever else and tell them that you're working remotely for the time being."

"Okay but—" The look he gave could melt steel. As I pulled up my email, I said, "You need to explain what's going on. I'm tired of being left in the dark."

"Don't worry. I will once you send the email."

I did as he asked and then turned to him. "Did you find whoever tried to break in?"

"Yes."

I was shocked by his response. "Well? Did you turn them over to the police?"

"No, but they've been taken care of."

When he said that, I thought back to how bruised and bloody his fist had been and the smear of blood that had been on his face before we left the house.

He must have noticed that I put two and two together because he leaned over and said, "You don't have to worry about that guy anymore."

Unimaginable thoughts ran through my head and it was enough to get me to stop asking questions for the time being. Although it was warm in the car, a shiver crept through my body as realization hit me. Damien had no problem killing someone who crossed him. Would he have no issue doing the same to me? The thought caused a headache to form so I curled up as much as my seatbelt would allow and stared out the window. Some of the exhaustion, both mental and physical, had taken over my body and I fell into a restless sleep.

"WHERE ARE WE GOING?" I asked a while later. I was still groggy but feeling a bit more human as the SUV continued on its journey to who knew where.

"Upstate to a remote location that is more secure," Damien said. He had pulled out his laptop at some point and was now working on that as well. "Thought it would be nice to get out of the city for a bit and give my people enough time to clean up and add more security to my properties in the city."

I stopped my eyes from bulging out of my head. He had multiple properties in New York City? The townhouse we were staying in had to be worth about $13 million by itself. I glanced at my phone and saw that my father had replied. He wanted to talk to me, probably questioning my reason for working remotely.

"Will we be back by Christmas?" I tossed that question out there because Christmas was a week away and I wanted to be back with my family to celebrate it by then.

"Yes."

I sat back and got comfortable again and watched as we cruised down the highway to a place unknown by me. Thankfully, it wasn't long before we pulled up to a vast estate that seemed to go on for miles.

The enormous white home was something that dreams

were made of and the snow that lined the property made it look like something out of a movie. When Rob steered the car up the round driveway, I noticed a couple of black cars parked there too. *I was certain those were more security guards.*

"Do you own this house?" I asked Damien as the car came to a stop.

"No. My parents do."

"What? Why didn't you tell me we were going to your parents'?"

"Look, this is probably one of the most protected locations in the state outside of a government facility. This was the best option unless we flew out of the country. At least until we figure out who sent that asshole to the house."

"Did you tell your parents about all of this?"

Damien closed his laptop and placed it into his bag. "Yes, they know what happened and I told them about you. They split their time between the city and here, but they are here right now."

I played with my clothes. If he had mentioned it before, it would have given me an opportunity to at least look more presentable since I would be meeting his parents for the first time. Then again, why did this even matter? This wasn't real and would be over soon. He grabbed my hand, stopping my movements.

"Don't worry about what you're wearing. We are just going to go in there, we'll talk to my parents for a minute, and then we'll shower and change. Everyone understands what happened."

I quickly attempted to pull my hair into a ponytail, hoping that would make me look more put together. The doors on both sides of the car opened and I grabbed my purse and laptop bag. After I stepped out of the car, Damien followed suit and offered to hold my laptop bag as the two of us walked up the stairs to the home.

Someone had been expecting us because the door swung open and a man in a suit greeted us.

"Hello, sir."

Damien smiled back at him and this might have been the first time I had seen him smile. It was strange to see his lips turned up into a smile. He turned to me and said, "This is Bernard. Bernard, this is Anais."

"Nice to meet you." I held my hand out to shake his.

"It's nice to meet you too, Ms. Monroe." Before we could say anything further, a handsome couple entered the room. I could immediately tell that they were Damien's parents. It was easy to see that Damien got most of his looks and height from his father, and his eyes came from his mother.

"Oh, dear. You're okay, right?" The woman reached over and held Damien's face in her hands. "I swear I've been holding my breath until Rob pulled into the driveway."

"Everything is fine. We're safe and we're here now."

When she turned to me, she said, "You must be Anais. We've heard so much about you."

I gave a polite smile because that was news to me. I had barely heard anything about them and what I knew had come from Ellie's or my research. "Thanks for welcoming me into your home, Mrs. Cross."

"Of course! Any friend of Damien's is welcomed to our home, and please call me Selena. And this is my husband, Martin." She gave me a warm smile as Martin stuck his hand out to shake mine. "Do you need anything? I could have Maddie whip something up."

"Could she throw together something for breakfast? We haven't eaten."

"And when he hasn't eaten, he becomes harder to manage. Trust me I know this well." Selena smiled at me and faced her son.

"Sure, I can go do that and you'll show Anais to the Hampton guest room? That one should be ready. Damien, your room is still how you left it so that's where you'll be."

"Sounds great." He looked over at me before letting his eyes float back to his mother's and said, "I think Anais and I will probably change our clothes. We're wearing the clothes we've had on since last night."

"Right." Selena moved back and allowed us to move farther into the home. "I'll be in the kitchen or living room if you two need me."

"Damien, we should chat when you're done settling in," Martin said.

Although there was nothing that shouted out to me that something was up, I could tell that Martin's words had a different meaning to Damien than they did to me. The look he and his son shared told me that.

"Sounds good. I'll show Anais to her room."

Damien, Rob, and Bernard grabbed our things and we headed up the stairs and down a long hallway. It was lined with photos and paintings, most of which seemed to relate to the family in some sort of fashion, including photos and paintings of her children when they were small. When Damien stopped in front of one door, Rob and Bernard placed the bags they had been carrying down. Damien thanked them and the two went back the way we had come.

"So, you're right here," he said and opened the door he

was standing next to. The bedroom had all the standard amenities you'd expected in a guest room but was brighter and the complete opposite of the dark colors Damien seemed to stick to. The king-size bed had a beige comforter and a ton of pillows, and there was a dresser and windows that overlooked the huge backyard. The Crosses definitely took pride in having everything you could ever want. I was sure it would be a steep transition to go back to completely fending for myself.

"You have your own bathroom that is connected to your room."

"Wow. This home is beautiful. I can see why your parents wanted to live here."

"We have had some wonderful memories here." His tone was softer than his usual you-must-obey-my-orders tone. It made me want to dig deeper into his fond memories, but I knew he wouldn't respond.

"Well, I have to go get ready for a few conference calls, so I'll see you later."

I nodded as Damien turned away from me and I did the same. I walked farther into the guest bedroom after shutting the door behind me. Although I was tired of uprooting my life on a whim, I'd be staying here for a period of time and I needed to make the best of it.

I unpacked my things for what felt like the millionth time before walking into the bathroom and gasping. This bathroom belonged in a luxury suite of a hotel. The vast bathroom was big enough to fit my entire bedroom in it. Ridding my body of the clothes that had long since worn out their welcome, I turned the showerhead on to what I suspected was closer to hot than cold. I was right and when the water's temperature was where I wanted it, I stepped into the shower and almost swooned. Inside, the water beat down on my body and I felt as if I were under a warm, powerful waterfall. The force from the water felt so good, I could almost compare it to the massages that I had gotten when I stopped by Ellie's job for a session. I didn't know how long I had been in the shower when I swore that I saw something out of the corner of my eye and I was surprised to see Damien leaning on a door jamb. I cracked open the shower door and asked, "What are you doing here?"

"Just because we've switched locations doesn't mean the circumstances have changed. You belong to me and I get to do whatever I want."

"Even if that means interrupting a shower."

"Even that."

"Don't you have a conference call to get ready for? I wasn't expecting to see you for another few hours." I was looking forward to having some time alone, but I wasn't about to admit that out loud.

"When you're the boss, you can do whatever you want. Right now, my cock wants to get inside that smart mouth of yours and I'm happy to oblige."

21

DAMIEN

I closed the nightstand after stashing a box of condoms and walked to the bathroom. It would have taken no time for me to ditch my clothes at the door and enter the shower, but I didn't. I took my time removing them, letting the anticipation build because Anais didn't know what I was going to do. I kept my eyes on her naked form, thankful that Mom hadn't bothered to install frosted doors for this shower. Instead, the glass of the door was clear, allowing me to get as much of an eyeful as I wanted. Once I finished that task, I stepped into the shower.

"Get out of here. Can't even take a shower in peace." I didn't think she was trying that hard to fight me on this. It might have to do with her not being able to keep her eyes off my cock for longer than a second.

"I'll do you one better. You're going to suck my cock and you can sit on that marble bench right there and do it. No hurt knees, right?"

I could see an argument was at the tip of her tongue, but I preferred that something else was. She flipped her hair back and wiped the water from her eyes, and they landed on mine. I dipped my head, letting her know it was time. She drifted toward the bench before sitting on it and I could see her lick her lips as she came face-to-face with my dick. Her first move was to lick the head of my dick and I closed my eyes as I enjoyed the light sensation. Another lick almost made me buck my hips, hoping that she would take me deeper in her mouth.

As if she could read my mind, she took me in her mouth and gagged for a moment before she relaxed. She took me deeper than the previous time, realizing that she needed to relax her mouth in order to calm her gag reflex so that she could take more of me in. It worked. She took more of me and I could feel when my cock hit the back of her throat. I sucked in a deep breath and groaned in satisfaction.

She looked up at me as she was taking my cock and I nearly lost it. The feel of her mouth on me made my knees buckle slightly. Her tongue glided over the tip and alternated between that and taking my throbbing member into her mouth. Each time she started this cycle over again, she sucked my cock harder and I threw my head back with my eyes closed. She chuckled and that led to more vibrations heading straight to my dick. She moved her mouth back and sucked the head of my cock harder. I looked down at her again and the image was a lot for me to handle.

"I can't wait until you swallow every drop, Spitfire."

That and the fact that my hands had found their way into her hair seemed to give her a kick because she started enthusiastically alternating between sucking me deep, licking the head of my dick, and massaging my balls; all things that had me creeping closer and closer to the edge.

My hips moved involuntarily trying to get closer to her so she could take me even deeper than before. I groaned again before I took control over my body and plunged it in and out of her mouth. If I thought the image of her sucking me off was too much, seeing me pump my dick into her mouth was unbearable.

A roar preceded my orgasm and I watched as she made sure not to miss a drop. She looked up at me, a hint of a smile playing on her lips as she stood up and smirked.

"Now, I would appreciate it if you let me take a shower in peace." Her smirk betrayed the tone of her voice. I ignored her words and watched her for a moment before leaning down to pick up the shampoo and poured some of it into my hands. The light coconut fragrance hit my nostrils and I knew she must have smelt it too because she looked at me, water dripping down her face.

"Turn around."

She did as I asked without an argument and I placed my hands in her hair and began washing it, covering every inch. A low groan left Anais's lips as I massaged her scalp.

"Feels good?"

"You have no idea. Okay, I'm going to rinse this out and then you can do whatever you need to do under the showerhead."

"I'm getting out," I said, not offering an explanation. I knew it was time for a phone call that I needed to take, and this distraction took longer than I planned. I glanced at Anais and exited the shower. Her mouth was slightly open as she narrowed her gaze and turned away from me. I got a quick look at her ass, which was much appreciated, and grabbed a huge fluffy towel. I dried myself off and wrapped the towel around my waist before I grabbed my clothes and walked out of the bathroom.

It didn't take me long to get from Anais' room to my childhood room that had been revamped a couple of times since I had moved out. My parents kept the dark navy-blue color that I had liked as a teenager in the room but had changed some of the furniture out to flip it into a guest room if need be. Gone were the posters I'd hung on the wall, replaced by some of the paintings my mom had taken a liking to and wanted to be displayed in her home.

I tossed the clothes that I had been wearing previously into the hamper and checked the time on my phone. I had about twenty minutes until I had to be on a phone call that I didn't want to take. I threw on my trademark black suit and tie and styled my hair. I checked myself in the mirror and headed out the room and down to my father's office.

Of course, he was already there when I entered and briefly glanced at me before holding a finger up. He was on a call with a member of the board that I assumed would wrap up pretty soon.

"Thanks, Don. I'll talk to you later this week." Dad hung up the phone with a decisive click and stood up, grabbing his suit jacket, and putting it on.

"I thought we had a call with the twins and some potential organizations that wanted to expand their horizons in good old New York?"

Dad walked around his desk. "Change of plans. We're headed out and I'll explain it in the car."

22

ANAIS

After my shower, I looked for Damien, but didn't see him, so I went down to eat on my own. His mom joined me for only a moment then had a phone call she needed to take, and I didn't see her for the rest of the day. The evening was low-key, and I had to admit, I preferred it that way. I spent the evening alone, mostly resting and reading books on my phone. I thought Damien might come in and check on me, but he didn't. I was partially relieved and disappointed, but I didn't want to go seek him out. I went to bed early and felt rejuvenated the next morning. That was until I forced myself to text my father.

Me: *Hey Dad. I'm doing well. Just wanted to get away for a bit, but I should be back in time for Christmas.*

Dad: *Sounds good. Mom and I were worried about you.*

Me: *No need. Everything is fine and I'll see you soon.*

Dad: *Okay and don't forget to call your mother.*

I rolled my eyes but still sent a message back.

Me: *Will do.*

Once I rolled out of bed and was presentable, I headed

down to breakfast and found Selena in the dining room. It was bright with its white, beige, and gold décor and the similarly colored table sat fourteen. Selena matched the sophistication of the room with her black slacks, cream sweater, and her pinned-up hair. I wasn't shocked to see that Damien wasn't there. When we were back in his place in the city, he rarely was home for breakfast anyway. What was interesting was that Martin wasn't there either. I glanced at the chair next to me and sat down at the only other seat that had a placemat and utensils in front of it.

"Like father, like son. Am I right?" Selena smiled, which told me that she had read my mind and was used to the absences too. "I hope you don't mind that I had Maddie fix a few different dishes. I wasn't sure what you liked, and I forgot to ask you before we retired for the night."

"Oh, no, that's completely fine. I'm not a picky eater anyway, so I'm sure whatever you have will be fantastic."

She smiled at me again and made me wonder how Damien turned out to be the exact opposite of his mother in that regard. She was friendly whereas he was intimidating. Though, like his mother, Damien was caring. The way that he took care of me when someone broke into the townhouse, when he found me in the panic room, and how quickly he took charge to get us out of there. The way he made sure that I orgasmed during sex before him. These were just a few of the things that made me see him in a different light, and I wasn't sure how to feel about it.

"Did you sleep okay?"

"Ah, yes, I did. I slept like a baby." That was only partially true. I always had a hard time falling asleep when I was in an unfamiliar place and staying here was no different. When I did eventually get to sleep, it had been fine, but it was pointless to divulge all of that.

"That's good. I was hoping you would get some rest. I can only imagine how you must feel having had to deal with a break-in."

"Yeah, I wasn't expecting it and in addition to that, we aren't sure who did it." At least I wasn't sure. As soon as the words left my mouth, Maddie walked in with breakfast.

My stomach growled as I smelled the freshly cooked bacon that was sitting on the plate. Maddie also made Eggs Benedict and had cut up an assortment of fruit that she quickly retrieved from the kitchen once she left the hot foods for us to eat. She also brought out coffee. It seemed as if the coffee was an alarm because Martin and Damien walked into the room when she placed the hot pot in between Selena and me.

"Is there anything I can get you two?" Maddie asked, looking between Martin and Damien.

"We came in to get another cup of coffee and it seems like we were right on time," Martin said. That's when I realized that both of them had mugs in their hands.

"You could have rung me up and I would have brought it in there. That wouldn't have been a problem," Maddie replied.

"Coming in here wasn't a hardship. Trust me," Martin said as he strolled over to his wife and planted a kiss on her lips. Although he whispered his next words, I heard parts of it.

"How are you doing? I missed you this morning..." They continued to have a private conversation and to anyone looking on, you could see how much love and compassion was between them. Just watching as he gently massaged her shoulders as he spoke to her and the way her eyes lit up when she looked up at him. It almost made me wish that I could find the person to share that kind of connection with. I looked back down at my plate, feeling a little weird for having intruded on such a private moment between the two, before shoveling a forkful of eggs into my mouth.

"Ahem."

I almost forgot that Damien was there between watching the elder Crosses and deciding that food was the most important thing in this world right now.

"Yes?" I asked as I looked up at him.

"Did you have a good night's sleep?"

"I did. Thanks for asking."

"If you need anything, you know you can call—"

"Bernard," I said, finishing his sentence. "I know." Having a chef at Damien's house who came and cooked was weird. Getting used to having a butler that people repeatedly told me I could ask for help was weirder.

Damien gave me a peculiar look and walked around my chair and grabbed the hot pot of coffee. Martin leaned over and placed his mug near Damien's and Damien poured the coffee for both of them. They didn't linger around the dining room for much longer and once they both left I went back to eating the food.

"Mm-hmm," I said just as I grabbed my napkin from my lap and wiped my lips. "I need to go thank Maddie when we're done. This is so good."

"She always does such a good job. It's why I ask Martin to pay her whatever she wants because if she ever leaves, I don't know what we'll do. And he knows he didn't marry me for my cooking skills, and he could burn a pot just by boiling water. That literally happened when we were dating."

Thankfully, I hadn't eaten anything when she said that because the snort that I let out was so loud that it almost hurt. "That is hilarious."

She waited a moment before she asked, "What are you doing for the holidays?"

"I'll spend Christmas with my parents and then maybe go out with some friends for New Year's."

"That's what we usually do for Christmas too. Early in our marriage, I made Martin promise me that no matter what, he wouldn't work on Christmas. I wanted us to spend it together as a family and that was it. He's kept that promise every year. So that's what we do, and it has been ingrained into my boys' heads that unless something happens, everyone comes home for Christmas. I can't wait for them to bring their own families here too. We have so much room in this big house and I can't wait to fill it up with more of our extended family."

I said nothing about that as I took a sip of my coffee. I looked up from my plate and found Selena looking at me, before going back to eating her food. Was I reading too much into it or was she alluding to me? I had a feeling that me coming here might give Damien's parents the wrong idea, so it made me wonder why he had done so.

"You should make Damien bring you up here for our New Year's party. I know it's short notice, but I promise it will be a lot of fun. Plus, maybe it will make it more bearable for him. He, Broderick, and Gage have been trying to get out of the party for years because it's just a gathering of a bunch of stuffy suits, as Gage affectionately told me one year."

I chuckled. "Maybe I'll be able to make it." I couldn't

make Damien do a damn thing, but I'd let her live under the illusion that I could.

"I'M SO happy that you're spending some time with us."

"Thanks for having me," I said as I sat down in their great room, with the fireplace adding even more warmth to the room. Selena and I had been spending a great deal of time together over the last few days when I wasn't working because of Damien's and Martin's busy schedules. It included watching movies and television shows and doing a few work-outs together in their home gym. We even got Maddie to teach us a few things in the kitchen, which both Selena and I appreciated. It was nice to socialize with someone in person. Just talking to Ellie and my parents on the phone or by text message and my coworkers by email had sucked.

Selena crossed her legs and said, "Sometimes it gets a little lonely because Martin works a lot. I have my projects that I do for charities here and there, but with it being winter and having poor weather more frequently, it makes it harder to get around. Sometimes some of our staff jokingly get offended when I try to help out. It's because I want to keep busy and I want that social interaction, you know?"

I couldn't believe that Selena was telling me this because we hadn't known each other for very long.

"I've also noticed some changes in Damien since you've been here, and it's been wonderful to see. There is a light back in his eyes that I haven't seen in a very long time."

I wondered where this conversation might head as I thought of what to say next. This might be the perfect opportunity to connect the pieces of the puzzle that had existed in my mind.

"What happened, if you don't mind me asking?"

"Hm?"

"What made him lose the light in his eyes?"

Selena stood up, adjusting the pretty pink cardigan she had worn today, and walked over to one of the many windows that lined the walls of the room. She looked outside for a moment before turning to look at me over her shoulder. "Some of us have heinous demons that continue to haunt us in everything we do. Some of us can move on and continue living life as we always have, but others have struggled to breathe because of the turmoil we have faced. I can't be the one to tell you what happened to Damien. It has to come from him."

I understood that. How could I have expected a mother to talk about her son behind his back?

"Tread lightly, my dear. I love my husband and sons very much, but I also know they've seen some things that no one should ever see. That has made them into the men they are today."

"Lunch is ready, Selena."

Selena looked toward the door and smiled.

"Thanks so much, Maddie." She looked back at me. "You don't want to know how many years it took her to drop 'Mrs. Cross.' That's my mother-in-law, rest her soul." Selena walked over to Maddie and turned to face me.

I got up and walked over to the other two women and together we went into the dining room to eat, but the questions in my mind remained.

23

DAMIEN

I let the water drip down my face, not caring if it painted an abstract pattern on my white T-shirt. I had just gotten back from the in-home gym my parents installed once they saw mine and was about to shower after a grueling workout. A text message notification on my phone from Kate, my publicist, was still running through my mind.

Kate: *The press is asking questions about Charlotte.*

As I turned the shower faucet on, my mind drifted to thoughts of what it was like growing up here. Being in this house brought back so many memories about my family, my childhood, and what used to be my life. The times that I would chase after Gage and Broderick after they entered my room when they weren't allowed when we were kids. Or the meals we would all share when Dad was home. Those times had been mostly great, but there were also the bad times that had colored in the lines of what made me into the man I am today.

The fire haunted my nightmares.

There was nothing I could do to stop the feeling that

came over me. I thought about the fact that I was the one who survived. She didn't. I was forced to leave Charlotte behind. Because who knew what kind of shit would have been written had my name been directly connected to the incident. At least that's what my father told me. When he practically threw me into the back seat of his car, and we sped down the empty road. I could remember hearing the sirens blaring in the background. But they weren't coming for us. They were coming to find Charlotte, the woman I had tried my damnedest to get out of the house, but it had been too late.

I remembered Dad pulling over on the side of a dark road miles and miles away from the fire. Tears welled in my eyes as my body hacked up the remnants of what was left in my stomach. He came over to me and gave me one pounding on the back.

Once I had stopped heaving, my father walked away and when I looked up, I saw him leaning on the hood of his car. I walked over and found him smoking one of his trademark cigars.

"Why didn't you let me go back and get Charlotte?" I had asked.

He tossed a glance my way before he shook his head. "Because then you both would have died. You're lucky that you happened to be downstairs and I could get you out in time."

"I don't feel lucky. I don't think I'll ever be able to get the fire—"

"I know, son. It will more than likely be etched in your mind forever."

I was upset. I wanted to mourn the life that had just been

lost, but nothing came out. No emotion. No tears. No wanting to break something. I felt almost...numb.

"Can I ask a question?"

"It's better if you don't."

I knew given some of the things I had overheard in the past that it was better to not ask questions, but this was something that was going to bother me for the rest of my life.

"I need to know the answer to this."

He took another puff of the cigar and said, "Go on."

"Did you have anything to do with that fire?"

I could see when Dad looked over at me and not even the darkness could hide the glare that was radiating from his eyes. I was fully expecting him to yell, which was rare, but he didn't.

"I had nothing to do with it. I was, however, tipped off that something was going to happen, and I clearly got there just in time." He put out his cigar and started walking toward the driver's-side door. "We need to get you home."

And that was the last time we ever spoke about what happened to Charlotte DePalma.

24

ANAIS

I adored the fact that the Cross estate also had a gym on its property. It gave me the opportunity to continue my workouts and not have to venture outside, which might cause a big distraction with security that needed to be involved. Plus, it was cold outside and if I could stay in the house that was what I was going to do.

About twenty minutes into my workout, I got a notification that Ellie had texted me. I waited until my workout was completed in ten minutes. During the last two minutes of my exercise routine, I had a flurry of text messages come through, making me wonder if something was wrong. During my five-minute cooldown, I picked up my phone and scanned the messages.

Ellie: *Hey?!*

Ellie: *Where are you?*

Ellie: *How are you?*

Ellie: *Is everything okay?*

Ellie: *Call me as soon as you can!*

Shit, I had forgotten to tell her that I was at Damien's

parents' house. I called her and the phone rang once before she picked up. She didn't say hello when she answered the phone.

"Is Damien there?"

Her question made me look around the room to verify what I already knew. No one was in the room with me. "No, he's not here. What's wrong?"

"Where are you?"

I noted that she still hadn't answered my question, further raising alarms in my mind. What was the meaning of all of this?

"At his parents' place, upstate."

"Why are you there?" The panic was clear in her voice, making me even more concerned.

I thought about telling Ellie what happened, but I was worried about dragging her into anything and causing her to worry. "A minor incident happened at Damien's place and he decided to spend a few days with his parents. Everything's fine." *Was it though? Was everything okay?*

The words that I said aloud made me remember just how much of this show Damien was running. I hadn't gotten a choice in whether or not we went to his parents'. I hadn't gotten the opportunity to talk about what had been going on, yet I was thrown into harm's way and had to hide in a panic room. Then while things were being investigated, I moved my life once again to be under lock and key in upstate New York. Hell, even the decision for me to enter this arrangement seemed predetermined because if I didn't, hundreds would have suffered. "What's going on?"

It felt as if I had asked that question for the billionth time, yet I was still no closer to finding out the answer. Almost everyone in my life seemed to operate several steps ahead of me while I was playing catch up. I was over it.

"There's more about Damien than you're aware of."

"Ellie, so help me if you don't start actually telling me what is going on, I'll—"

"I'm not sure how much there is to say because a lot of this is hearsay, but you need to find out who Charlotte DePalma is, what happened to her, and what Damien's involvement is in all of it."

"Who is Charlotte? What does she have to do with anything? Did something happen recently?"

"No, no, no. It was something that happened years ago, but I don't know exactly what. The press seems to be hinting around at it, but no one wants to be the first to say it. Probably fear of retribution."

"Okay, but what does this have to do with anything?"

Ellie waited a beat before she responded. "Stories have been circulating in the press that Damien is connected to Charlotte and that she died unexpectedly. I'm going to send you a few links to some stories. Is there any way we can find the rest of the money that is owed to Damien and give it to him? I don't know if he was involved or not, but I don't feel comfortable with you being up there with him and not closer to home."

Neither did I after all of this information was coming to light, and I couldn't stop myself from over-analyzing the situation as it all clicked into place almost simultaneously. Was Charlotte the actual reason he wanted to hide away at his parents' home for a few days? To give this time to blow over and to coordinate with his family on what the response would be? And why hadn't Damien told me anything about this? The startling realization that I was in way over my head shook me to my core. I did not know what I was facing and that terrified me.

ANOTHER NIGHT, another fitful time of tossing and turning as I tried to get comfortable and fall asleep. But this time it was different. I was worried about whether I would survive to the end of this deal or not.

Now it was a fear. Fear of not knowing what Damien was capable of. Fear of losing what I had worked so hard for. Fear of not understanding Damien before I became addicted to him. I told myself I would not let myself become a victim of whatever game Damien was playing. The danger that seemed to grow as a result of me being connected to Damien was pretty damning as well. Although things felt somewhat more peaceful as time had gone on there was still the fact that I knew he was keeping things from me and it had nothing to do with being in a relationship. This was why I needed to turn any rational thoughts off and just get through the next few days because thirty days were almost done.

But there was more than that.

I knew that once day thirty came, I would never be the same. That was something that I would grapple with into the New Year.

A loud groan that turned into a scream made me sit up in bed and freeze. I looked at the door to the hallway. A thump followed and made me jump out of my skin and my first thought was that someone was trying to break into this house too. I got up and walked over to my door, knowing that that was the direction the noise had come from. I slowly opened the door and peeked into the hallway.

Nothing.

A few lamps provided some light in the dark abyss. I waited to see if I could hear anything else. It only took a few seconds, and I heard another groan that sounded like it came from Damien's room. I walked a few feet and then stood in front of the door before knocking softly. Although I didn't get an answer, I twisted the knob, and found the door unlocked. Telling myself that he needed help, I walked inside and found a dim room and a sight I never thought I would ever see.

Damien was sitting on the edge of his bed with his head in his hands, a single lamp illuminating both him and part of the room. I also saw what could have possibly made that loud thump—a huge book, just a few inches away from the end table that the lamp was on.

"Damien," I said, my voice just above a whisper. "Are you okay?"

"I thought I told you not to step foot in my bedroom at all? The rules from the city still apply here."

"But I thought you might—"

"Just leave."

Instead of doing as he asked, I walked farther into the room and stood in front of him, placing my hand on his shoulder. "Is there anything I can do to help?" I fully expected him to snap at me because I had once again disobeyed his orders, but what I saw was something more heartbreaking. He moved his hands from face. Although he wasn't crying, there was a lot of hurt in his eyes. Something felt special about this moment and I wondered if he shared this side of him with anyone else.

Something had replaced the hurt and anger that I felt toward him, something more intense that I couldn't quite place.

"Anais, go back to bed." His tone left no room for questioning, but it still sounded weaker than his normal terse commands.

"Okay, but feel free to come over if you need anything." I could tell that we were both shocked by the words that left my mouth because at the beginning of this arrangement, I wouldn't have said that. There was no way to take them back if I wanted to, and I didn't want to, which left me even more baffled.

I stumbled back to his door and closed it behind me and walked back across the hall to my bedroom. I knew the chances of me getting back to sleep were slim, but one of the burning questions that had been on my mind had been answered. If he was having trouble sleeping, it made sense why he didn't want to sleep in the same room as me. I wondered if the secrets to the demons he fought at night lay in the room where he went to sleep.

I drifted in and out of sleep when I heard a creaky sound from across the room. "Who's there?"

"It's me." My body recognized his voice immediately. I listened carefully as his feet shuffled along the floor as he made his way to my bed.

"What are you doing here?" I whispered once he was standing over me.

"Getting into bed."

I was thankful for the darkness that surrounded us

because he would have seen my jaw hit the floor. He climbed into the bed and did as he usually did when he was in a space: took over. But I had no problem with it because he wrapped me up in his embrace. Together we fell asleep, and I hoped that whatever had woken him up would remain in the depths of the shadows so that he could get some rest.

25

DAMIEN

The next morning, I awoke and was taken aback when I didn't find myself in my childhood bedroom. It took my eyes a moment to adjust and the first thing that hit my nostrils was a subtle smell of coconut.

Anais.

Her hair smelled like the shampoo that she used while staying here. Visions of what had occurred last night and her finding me in a vulnerable state didn't sit well with me. She caught the end of what sometimes happens when Charlotte's memory haunted me in my sleep. This was never supposed to happen, and I had always been careful not to let anyone know what transpired when I closed my eyes to sleep.

After she checked on me, I'd felt compelled to go to her. Once I stepped into her room, I couldn't stop myself from crawling into her bed. When I was next to her, it didn't take long for me to pass out between the soft cream sheets. Although I had been woken up in the middle of the night, it was the most rested I had felt in a long time. Rejuvenated in a way that I hadn't expected.

Anais was lying on her side with her back toward me. I shifted my arm that was around her waist and dragged my finger along the smooth skin that had become exposed during the night. She stirred, and I didn't feel an ounce of guilt about it.

In the early morning light, I watched as she turned to face me, a smile playing on her lips that made me stop and stare. She mumbled something that I didn't catch, stirring as she fought between being awake and staying asleep. My cock hardened against the pajamas pants I was wearing.

"I want you. Right now." My voice came out more gruff than normal, something I barely recognized.

"I'm not saying no."

"But are you saying yes?"

"Yes."

That one word set all things in motion. I turned her head toward me and claimed her lips. She turned her body so that she was now lying on her back, making it easier for me to deepen the kiss. My hands slid down her sides to the waistband of the short shorts she had worn to bed. She held her breath as my hand made its way to her mound. I smirked at what I found.

"Either you were having a pleasurable dream or that kiss was as hot for you as it was for me."

"I plead the fifth."

I swallowed a retort when I felt how wet she was. She helped me remove her pajama shorts and underwear and I started playing with her nub before I pushed a finger into her cunt.

"You know what I can't wait for? To take this ass."

I said it to get a reaction out of her and I got one. She threw her head back and moaned and my cock was rock hard against her hip. I didn't know if that was because of the sex-induced haze she was currently in, but we could address that later.

"Flip back onto your side with your back to me again."

While she got back into position, I stood up and took the condom out of the nightstand, thanking myself for having the foresight to think of it. It took no time for me to rid myself of my pants and placed the condom on my erection prior to running my cock up and down her slit.

"I like when you do that."

"I know," I responded as I entered her. I closed my eyes briefly, enjoying the feeling of her tight walls around my cock. One day I wanted to know what it felt like to have no barriers between us.

Entering her from this angle was a fresh experience for the both of us together as my hands alternated between fondling her breasts and her clit.

"Yes," she hissed out, voicing the same sensations that were going through my body. Every time my cock drove into her, I wondered when this would be it. When this would get old. When I would want to cut this off. Those thoughts vanished the closer we got to our peaks. It didn't take long for both of us to reach our climaxes, her going before me. We took a moment to catch our breath and then I pulled out of her, almost immediately regretting the motion.

"That was a way to wake up," Anais said as I felt her turn to face me.

My eyes were closed as I stopped to enjoy the euphoria I

felt after the high came down. "That it was," I said, but she didn't respond. Instead, I felt her snuggle deeper into my chest and play with some of the hair on my happy trail. Something had been swirling in my head, just before I woke her up by pleasuring her. I debated whether or not I wanted to say anything. The silence around us was so peaceful. I didn't want to do anything to jeopardize it.

"Damien?" she asked.

I opened my eyes and looked down at her. "Yes?"

She looked stunning in the pale light that the sun was casting on the room, with her hair sprayed out across the pillow behind my arm. This was a sight I could get used to seeing on a regular basis. I expected myself to flinch at the thought because of the events that transpired with Charlotte. I thrived on remaining single and dating when I wanted, but this felt different. And I didn't know if thirty days were going to be enough. She was going to be mine, period.

"Do you want to talk about what happened last night?"

And just like that, ice-cold water surged through my veins as I shifted my body to get from underneath her. "No. I don't want to discuss it."

"But I thought—"

"You thought wrong," I said as I got up and out of bed. I put on the pajama pants that I had worn when I entered and walked toward the door. No one needed to know the pain that that night had caused, and I wasn't ready to talk about.

I didn't look back even when I heard her sniffle and the barrier between us closed with a soft click.

26

ANAIS

"I'm an idiot," I mumbled to myself as I paced my bedroom. After Damien stormed out of my room, we had done our best to avoid one another over the last couple of days, which hadn't been hard due to us both claiming the work we needed to do for our jobs was more of a priority than anything else.

It was two days before Christmas. I felt like a mouse in a glass prison that needed to get the hell out. I knew going into this there was a chance that I might become addicted to him. His touch. The way he made me feel. Him allowing me into parts of his world. I thought I'd done my best to prevent it. When Damien didn't want me, I avoided being near him, but even that hadn't protected me and my thoughts from migrating to him.

I had done what I said I wasn't going to do. I was addicted to Damien Cross and it was only a matter of time before he realized it and kicked me to the curb. The thought of him doing that made my stomach turn. I knew who he was before I became addicted and yet I still fell. No, I needed to get out of whatever this was first. He didn't even trust me enough to tell me what caused him to scream out at night. I could try to make it through the last week, but I knew I would be lying to myself and driving myself to the point of hysteria if I stayed. I also wasn't any closer to finding out who Charlotte DePalma was or her connection to Damien. This all troubled me and was why I needed to leave now.

There was another way that I could find out more information about Charlotte. I stared at my computer, lying on the made-up bed in this room. Ellie had done some research when she alerted me but hadn't found much at the time. Over the last couple of days, I hadn't been able to find anything and it didn't hurt to look things up one more time, did it?

I opened my laptop, typed in my password, and waited for my browser to load. Once it had, I typed in Charlotte's name and New York City to see if anything popped up. I got lucky because an article that was published four hours ago came up. My hand shook as my cursor hovered over the link. I took a deep breath and clicked. My eyes scoured the article, taking in every word about an event that took place years ago. An arsonist burned down a cabin, killing one person: Charlotte DePalma. The murder was tragic, but one of the pictures that was included with the article was an image of a younger Damien. It had been easy to spot, outside of him looking much like the man he was today, because of the pictures Selena had hanging around her home. He was listed as Charlotte's boyfriend and the last person she was seen with although he was never charged with a crime. My emotions jumped from sadness, to fear, to anger more rapidly than I could deal with. This needed to end.

I figured Damien was either in his childhood bedroom or in his father's office, and since I hoped to catch him alone, I walked across the hall to his bedroom first.

A quick knock on the door confirmed that he wasn't in there, so I went downstairs to the office, hoping that both Damien and his father weren't in there. I knocked on the study door.

"Come in." It was Damien's voice.

I took a deep breath to steel myself because I hadn't been expecting him to be there, and I was about to face the devil himself.

I opened the door and he looked over at me from his place at one of the windows behind the huge wooden desk. He was alone. "Is this urgent? I have a phone call in five minutes with some important investors who are overseas."

"Who is Charlotte DePalma?" I wanted to give him an opportunity to explain himself, although I knew way more than he thought I did. I walked further into the room and stood several steps in front of him.

"Why do you care?"

"What happened to her?" I believed this was the first time since Damien and I had met that I had shocked him. His eyes widened briefly yet an indifferent expression moved into place.

"You need to mind your business," Damien said, still as calm as ever. That only further enraged me.

"I'll tell you who Charlotte DePalma is. Charlotte DePalma is your ex-girlfriend who died in a horrible house fire when you were eighteen."

His silence was palpable.

"Wow." Damien's silence spoke volumes. When he still

hadn't said anything, I continued, "Why didn't you tell me about any of this?"

"It wasn't your concern nor your business."

Tears welled up in my eyes and it finally became clear to me where I stood in all of this and how much I had truly fallen.

"This whole time you were hiding this from me."

"Anais, this wasn't any—"

"Stop with the bullshit!"

His blue eyes darkened, and I could feel their stare trying to freeze me into place. "Watch your words. Unless you want me to punish you by—"

"You can go fuck yourself." Any threat that he had behind his words didn't mean a thing to me at this point as I unleashed the pent-up anger and frustration that had been inside of me for far too long. "Did you have her killed?"

Damien's demeanor turned hard. "I don't have to explain myself to you."

"What? She didn't want to play any of your little games, was that it? Is that why you did it?"

"You have no idea what you're talking about."

"I know I wasn't there fifteen years ago, but what I do know is that you still won't tell me the truth and you locked me in a deal that I had no choice to be in."

"Bullshit, Anais. You always had a choice. You could have walked away at any point, and I would have let you go." Damien took two steps toward me.

I scoffed. "No, the whole point was to use me until you got tired of me. If I left, my family's company would have gone to shit, and you wouldn't have given a damn about it. That's because you care about no one but Damien Cross."

My words had their intended effect on Damien because he stopped walking toward me. "Well, the opportunity to leave is still open."

"Does that mean you'll still wipe my father's debt? That's the only reason I'm here." The taste of freedom was almost too much to bear.

"Given the number of days that you've been here and seeing that there is only a week left, if your father pays the rest of the money that your services didn't provide, the debt will be wiped."

I knew he used that phrasing to get under my skin. It did sting, but I didn't care. I prayed my father had that money and it wasn't my problem anymore.

"This whole arrangement is over, and I don't care if the thirty days aren't up. As someone who said that they would always keep their word, I trust that you will wipe my father's debt clean once he pays off the rest of what I couldn't as it states in the contract."

Damien took a step back and looked out the window in his chair. "Pack your things and I'll make sure that Rob drops you back off at your apartment."

"Thank you," I said, and turned and walked away. I could feel his eyes burning a hole through my body. And it wasn't until I closed his office door behind me that I wiped the tears that were flying down my face.

I bolted up the stairs and reached the room that had become my second home. It didn't take long for me to pack the items that I'd brought with me and once I was ready, I carried my bags down the stairs. I felt bad for leaving under such short notice and after Selena and I had gotten friendly with one another, but I didn't think I could face her at the moment. Bernard greeted me at the door and wished me well on my trip back to the city.

I thanked him and he opened the door just as Rob was exiting the car. The two men helped load the few bags I had, and I gave a sad smile to Bernard. I stepped across the threshold to enter the waiting car that would soon take me back to the life I once knew.

ALTHOUGH ALIVE AND BUSTLING, New York City's streets seemed lonely even as we passed hundreds of people. It wasn't long before Rob dropped my bags off at the door of my apartment and gave me a small wave. He walked back down the stairs and into his car. It took me a minute to find my keys, since I hadn't used them in about a month.

Once I walked inside, I felt that loneliness creep up again. Ellie was at work so there was no one to greet me at the door like there had been at the Cross residence. Although I had been renting this apartment for three years, it was like entering a new home for the first time. This didn't feel like me anymore. It wasn't the place I used to know, although everything looked the same. It wasn't the apartment that had changed. It was me.

27

ANAIS

"Thanks for coming over for dinner."

I smiled at my mom as she grabbed my hand and squeezed. There was a lighter expression on her face, one that I hadn't seen in quite some time.

"Of course, it's Christmas. Where else would I be?" We both chuckled as Dad joined us at the dining room table.

My father cleared his throat. "There's something I wanted to tell both of you."

My hand immediately went to grab my wine glass, bracing for the worst.

"The debt is fully paid."

I was glad that I hadn't taken the opportunity to take a sip because I knew it would have ended up everywhere.

"What?" My mother was the first to speak.

My father nodded. "Looks like there was a Christmas miracle. I wasn't expecting the call at all since I still had a couple of weeks to pay it, but the entire thing has been wiped clean. I didn't have to pay a cent."

Wow, Damien hadn't even charged my father what he and

I had agreed would be paid before I stormed out of his parents' home. I was stunned, yet ecstatic about the news, but I wondered what the catch was because it seemed as if Damien never gave up on anything without a fight.

"To make matters better, this officially puts Monroe Media Agency back in the black and clients are coming back in droves. I think—no, I know—things are going to be much better." He hugged my mom first and then reached over to hug me.

"That's wonderful news, Dad. I'm so happy. Sounds like drinks are on you tonight."

My parents chuckled and we enjoyed the rest of our Christmas evening.

THE CHRISTMAS HOLIDAY came and went, and the next few days flew by in a blur. It didn't take long for me to get back into a similar routine that I had before Damien came into my life. I went to work, and I came home, and the same thing happened the next day. Ellie and I hung out a few times, but life got in the way once more and it wasn't as frequent as both of us wanted it to be. Damien hadn't said a word to me since I left, and word never got out about our arrangement or fake relationship rumors. The talk about Charlotte also died down around the same time and I wondered if he had something to do with that. To top it all off, I had found nothing else about the man who was watching me, nor the break-in at the townhouse. At the very least, he seemed as if he wasn't watching me anymore and for that I was grateful.

New Year's Eve and Day came and went, and I thought

about the Cross family more often than I wanted to admit. Although it wasn't my style, I would have liked to have been there to support Selena, especially given how nice she had been to allow me to stay in her home.

On the job front, work was going well. Monroe Media Agency was still gaining new clients and I could see the stress leaving my father's face as the days went on. I couldn't be more thrilled. I was busy with the new clients too.

A couple of days after New Year's, I was reading an email from a coworker when my father stepped into the office after knocking on the door.

"Hey, what's up?"

"Your mother can't make it to a meet-and-greet event tonight. Could you join me?"

I looked down at the several-years-old-but-still-in-good-shape black A-line dress I was wearing and looked back at my father.

"What you're wearing is fine because it's not a huge formal affair. Plus, it's been a while since you and I have had some father-daughter time anyway."

I put my head on my fist as I leaned on my desk. "Dad, if you wanted to hang out, we could hang out."

"I know and I think we should do more of that. Things are looking up and we're both going to have more free time to do more with one another, your mother included. She and I have a date set for Friday night."

I smiled. I was glad they were still going out and keeping the romance alive. "And did she give you that fancy Rolex that you have on your arm?"

Dad actually blushed and nodded but didn't offer an explanation.

"Yeah, I'm not doing anything tonight so I can go with you."

"Perfect. I'll see you at five and we can walk over together."

"Sounds good. See you then." We shared a small smile, and he left my office, closing the door behind him.

"THAT WASN'T SO BAD, was it?"

He was right. The event had been fine, and we spent most of the time talking up Monroe Media Agency to some of his friends and potential clients. Plus, I got to spend time with my father and have a glass of wine. What more could I ask for?

I glanced at my father and said, "No, it was fine. You know I'm not a huge fan of schmoozing."

"But you're wonderful at it. And you've definitely gotten better with it over the last couple of months."

"Thanks, Dad."

We walked over to get our coats that had been checked and I smiled when Dad helped me put mine on. We walked over to the exit of the building where the fundraiser was being held and looked around. "Do you want to go home with me so you can see your mother? Then I can drop you off at your place or you can stay in your old room."

"Sure. We can split a cab."

"Okay, I'll see if there's one nearby. You stay near the building and keep warm." His suggestion made sense. It was still cold in the city and standing near the building would probably be warmer. Plus, this street wasn't well lit, and I appreciated being closer to a source of light, versus trying to find a cab in the dark.

Only seconds later shots rang out and I dropped to the ground so fast I lost every ounce of breath that had been in my lungs. Chaos surrounded me as people ran in different directions, trying to outrun whoever was firing the gun.

Although my ears were still ringing, my first thought was finding out where Dad was. "Dad?"

I didn't get a response.

"Dad!" My scream was more of a shriek as I panicked and tried to pick myself off of the ground.

It took me a moment, but I saw a motionless body lying a small distance away and I took a few steps toward the body, shoving people who were running toward me out of the way. It was then that my eyes landed on the watch, the one I had complimented my father on just hours before.

"No, Dad!" I screamed as I tried to run toward him. I could see something dark seeping out from underneath him and the urge to get to him increased tenfold. My forward mobility stopped when someone grabbed me from behind and covered my mouth. My muffled screams did not attract any attention as people ducked for cover.

"Get off of me! Let me go!" came out as a mumbled mess, and the person continued to pull me in the opposite direction of where I wanted to go. It was then that I was thrown into the back of an SUV that then sped off. When I tried to sit up and open the door, the childproof locks were engaged in one swift motion and the next thing I knew, something was thrown over my head and my hands were tied behind my back. My screams did nothing to deter my kidnappers and the SUV sped off to its destination unbeknownst to me.

SCARRED EMPIRE

BLURB

She is scarred.

When I stormed into her life, it was supposed to be temporary.

Anais was supposed to be like the rest,

Then I became addicted.

My past caught up with me and she walked out before I could make her mine.

Tragedy strikes and I have no choice but to bring her back into my world.

In order to protect her, I convince her to wear my ring.

But I fear even I can't protect her from the turmoil we're about to face.

PLAYLIST

911 - Lady Gaga
Save Your Tears - The Weeknd
Use Somebody - Kings of Leon
Kings & Queens - Ava Max
Dirty Little Secret - The All-American Rejects
Everybody Talks - Neon Trees
How to Be a Heartbreaker - MARINA
Alice - Lady Gaga
Be Kind - Marshmello and Halsey
Never Really Over - Katy Perry
Still Into You - Paramore
I Miss You - Adele

The playlist can be found on Spotify.

1

ANAIS

P anic.
Silence.
Fear.

That was all I could hear and feel as I was carried somewhere. I struggled against my captor. My hands were restrained but that didn't mean I couldn't make his life difficult. I kicked my legs and moved my body as much as I could. Tears streamed down my cheeks, but they were absorbed by the cloth that covered my face.

I heard something click to my right and I held my breath, wondering if someone had cocked a gun. I briefly wondered how long it would take for me to feel the piercing pain that my father endured just before he ended up in a pool of his own blood. But nothing followed the sound. I shook my head and felt the cloth that was covering a portion of my face loosen. A few more shakes and I was able to get the fabric below my eyes and I squinted. The blinding light directly over me was disorienting, but for as bright as it was, it did little to light the entire room. It took a moment for my eyes to adjust, but I didn't know where the hell I was.

Where is my father? Dread filled my heart as I thought back to the scene that unfolded in front of me. The memory of seeing his lifeless form just before I was kidnapped made my body turn cold. My lips trembled and my teeth chattered as fresh tears burst from my eyes. I shivered, but when I tried to bring my hand forward, I couldn't. My hands were tied with what felt like some type of plastic. I looked behind me and found that a zip tie held my hands together.

Fuck. My mind raced because I knew I had to get out of this. Nobody was coming to rescue me and I would have to do this myself. I took a few breaths, calming myself enough to stop the shivers. *Now, Anais, what are you going to do?* I knew there was no way to break out of this without hurting myself. *How can I free myself? Is there a tool I can use to rip these cable ties open?* I took another steadying breath and steeled myself before I examined my surroundings.

This room was foreign to me and had barely anything in it. There was a brown sofa, an outdated television sitting on a tiny stand, and I was sitting in a brown chair that had seen better days. I spotted a single closed door, but no windows or any signs that anyone actually lived or worked here.

Panic once again rose in my throat as the events of the last couple of hours flooded my brain. My heart thumped harder in my chest, and I knew that if I didn't get myself back under control, fear would take over again.

I couldn't allow that to happen because I had to get out of here. I took a deep breath and wondered if I could yell for help. Maybe my kidnappers were gone, and someone would hear me. It wasn't the best plan, but it was all I had. I took a deep breath and started screaming. I prayed that it wasn't for naught and that my screams wouldn't do anything but steal my voice.

"Help! Help! Help! Is someone there? Help me!"

"Would you shut up!" a deep voice from the corner of the room yelled.

I flinched and my mouth snapped shut. Fear returned tenfold. My heart sped up, beating a rapid drumbeat in my chest. I wasn't alone.

The door opened, and I hadn't heard it. Two burly men walked into my line of sight and just beyond them, I could see someone else was stationed at the door. I thought about rushing at them, but that wouldn't be smart.

There was no way I would make it very far. As if he understood what I was thinking, one of the men walked closer to me. A sliver of terror rushed down my spine. I pushed back into the chair, trying to shrink away from him.

I pulled my legs up to my chest and shook my head, whispering, "Please, no... don't do this... please!" but it was barely audible as my throat was so tight with fear.

The bald stranger gestured for me to get up and turn my body.

I didn't know what to do, but I knew I had better do as he asked before he killed me right here. Maybe on my feet I could figure out a plan of escape. I struggled to get to my feet, but before I could get myself standing, he grabbed one of my arms gently, helping me up.

Confusion flooded my mind. *What is he going to do?* My breathing turned erratic, as he turned me around. *Is this it? Is this dirty brown chair going to be the last thing I see?*

He surprised me further by snapping the zip tie that had

been holding my hands together, freeing me from my bonds. Questions continued to surge through my head as I examined my arms under the light. *Why is he freeing me? Who are these men? What do they want with me?* I rubbed my wrists which were red and hoped the marks would soon fade. I brushed the tears from my cheeks and spun around, ready to confront my kidnappers.

"What's going on? Why am I here? Where is my father? Did you leave him to die on the street!" I stepped up to one of the men, who had to be double my size, and said, "So help me if you don't get me to my father, I'll..." The words tumbled out without a filter as my mind raced a thousand miles per hour.

The men looked at each other before turning their attention back to me.

"It's not our job to tell you anything," said the man who broke the ties that bound me.

"Who are you? Could you at least tell me if my father is okay?" I pleaded.

"It's not our job to tell you anything."

I could feel the urge to snap at him growing in my gut. "How dare you?" My anger overflowed. "Where am I?"

I knew we had driven for a while, but I wasn't sure how long exactly. It felt like an hour or so, but it was hard to keep track with my face covered and with no phone. I patted my pockets and found that I indeed didn't have a phone, nor did I have my purse. Had it gotten lost in the scuffle of throwing me in the SUV, or had the assholes who kidnapped me snatched it? I sank down into the chair, my body sagging onto the cushions as I could feel the adrenaline from the night's events wearing off. "Where's my purse?"

The stranger said, "You'll get it back when you leave here."

I took a step back and looked at him. This was the weirdest kidnapping I'd ever heard of...not that I got kidnapped often. I looked at each man as closely as I could, given the lighting in the room. If I had seen either man before, I didn't remember them.

"Who are you?"

Before anyone could tell me it wasn't their job to answer my questions, there was a knock on the door. One of the burly men opened the door a crack before opening it wider.

I recognized the woodsy scent first, and my jaw hit the ground when he came into view.

"Damien?!"

"Anais."

He walked further into the room until he was standing mere feet from me. I could see his eyes scanning me, checking to see if I was hurt. Damien didn't look surprised to see me, but he looked angry. My body shook, but no longer with fear. It was as if someone had injected a surge of energy into my veins.

It was as if a switch went off and I became enraged. Every ounce of anger I had in me was directed at him. I glanced at each man in the room, judging whether they would be able to stop me, before I launched myself at him.

"You did this!" I roared.

My hands curled up into fists and they went flying. At first Damien did nothing, letting me release my anger against his broad chest. The calmer he was, the angrier I got. Tears of fury streamed from my eyes once again and I screamed unintelligible words as my fists beat a steady rhythm against him.

After a couple of minutes, Damien caught my arms, stopping me from hitting him. One of the men grabbed me around the waist, trying to pry me off him.

"Get your hands off of her." The words that came out of Damien's mouth sounded deadly.

The other man let me go without a word. Damien looked down at my arms and lightly touched the red marks.

"You shot my father and then kidnapped me!" My breath came out in heavy spurts as I stared at him. I hoped he could sense the hatred I felt for him.

"I did nothing of the sort. In fact, I did the exact opposite. I saved your life." He paused and turned to the bald man who freed me, "Carter, we will have the room and if you ever lay your hands or leave a mark on her again, I'll kill you myself. Understood?"

Carter nodded and he and the other men exited.

"How could you?"

"You're upset right now, so I will say nothing about the tone of your voice."

"Oh, go to hell," I said without giving it a second thought.

"Watch it."

He was still trying to dominate me, bend me to his will and my desire to fall back into his arms made me question my sanity. *Is this his fucked-up way of getting back at me for leaving our deal early? But he did say he isn't responsible. If that is true, what is he doing here?* I swallowed the retort on the tip of my tongue because if I wanted answers pissing him off wouldn't get me any.

"Where is my father? Is my mother okay? What do you know about all of this?" I wiped at the tears that continued to fall. *Why did I survive without getting hurt, while my father was lying in a hospital bed?* Any attempts at keeping my emotions in check were pointless. I wanted him to give me the answers I desperately needed.

"Your father is in one of the best hospitals in the city under the care of some of, if not the, best doctors and nurses in the country and your mother is there. She is safe."

He didn't say he was dead, and Mom is okay. Thank goodness. Weariness seeped into my body as I took a seat on the couch with a *thump*. The news brought some solace to my tired heart, but it wasn't enough. "I want to see him. I want to go to her...I need to." I hated that my voice broke, and I sniffled to top it off.

Damien sat next to me. "That is being arranged, but first we needed to make sure that you're safe."

He pulled the pocket square from his suit jacket and wiped my tears. His touch was tender. When my gaze met his, I didn't see the coldness or indifference I was expecting. There was something warmer there. His thumb grazed my cheek, sending a tendril of warmth through me. I thought for a brief second that he might lean down and kiss me. Why was he being this way? The man had just kidnapped me. That thought revived my anger, and I pulled away from his touch.

"Why the hell did you kidnap me? I could be with my family right now!"

Damien remained calm, and that did little to help my racing heart. He stood and walked over to the chair that was across from me. When he didn't answer me right away, I jumped up, ready to yell in his face.

"Sit down," Damien said.

"I need to be there for my mother. Take me to my parents."

"I will."

But he didn't move.

"Why aren't we going right now? Time is of the essence! Give me your phone. I'll call my mother while we're on the way."

Damien didn't move, instead keeping his eyes on me.

"Well?"

"Anais, we have to do this as securely as possible. I'm waiting until my men get in place before we go to the hospital."

I drew my eyes into slits. None of it made sense. I needed to be with my parents as soon as possible, and I could tell he was avoiding my questions. "What aren't you telling me? And don't tell me it's none of my concern. Because all of this is my concern. This is my business."

Damien glared at me before his expression shifted to one I recognized. His face was hard as stone and nothing could be done to break it. He stayed silent.

"Damien, please." I deserved to know what was going on and how it would affect my life and my family. My plea finally broke through the wall he had built.

"Based on the information we currently have, this was a targeted hit on your father. The reason I brought you here was to prevent them from attempting to kill you too."

"Why would anyone try to attack my dad? Why did you have them blindfold and tie me up?"

"Your guess is as good as mine. He might have asked the wrong person for money. The blindfold was to prevent you from seeing where the safe house was. I assume the zip tie was to stop you from attacking one of Kingston's men. I didn't intend on them hurting your wrists and I will talk to Kingston about that."

The glare I tossed Damien's way would set anyone ablaze and turn them into a pile of rubble. He didn't even flinch, which made me angrier.

"So, is your plan to keep me locked in here like you did when I was staying at your house?"

Based on the ticking of his jaw, I could tell that Damien didn't like my cheap shot. I was far from caring about his feelings. "Anais, you had a choice. You could have left at any opportunity and I told you that."

"Yeah, and risk the livelihood of hundreds of people. I totally had a choice." I knew I was playing with a time bomb. Based on what I'd heard since being with him, Damien had ordered people's necks snapped for less. And yet here I was pushing his buttons.

But I didn't care. Nothing else mattered except getting to my parents.

A knock interrupted our stare down and our eyes moved to the door. Carter peered into the room. "Damien, everything is set up at the hospital. Mrs. Monroe is there."

Damien dipped his head, and the man left and closed the door behind him.

At the mention of my mother, I stood up and walked toward Damien and grabbed his forearm, digging my nails into his flesh. He looked down at my hand and back up at me, daring me to keep it there, but I prevailed and didn't move. I wanted to quake in my shoes, but knew better than to show weakness, especially in front of him. "If you so much as touch my mother, I'll become the scariest bitch you've ever had to face."

I was serious. Dead serious. I didn't care about any consequences. If a hair was missing on Mom's head, he and I would have words that would lead to more drastic actions.

He snatched his arm from out of my grasp. "Anais, it's clear that you have little faith in me."

"That is a massive understatement."

Damien adjusted his position and his imposing stature forced me to back up until I hit a wall. "Spitfire." His words were dark and calculated. "I've been more lenient with you than probably any person in my life, but you're pushing it. I know you've been through something traumatic, but I've had enough of all of this and I'm the only person you can trust right now."

"Why should I? In what way have you shown that I can trust you?"

"I didn't leave you out there to die." His eyes darkened as his voice rolled like thunder in a storm. "Now let's go."

2

DAMIEN

I knew I'd shattered her world, but she wanted the truth, and that was some of it. I couldn't have foreseen anything like this happening, but I'd known I had to be prepared to save her in case something happened.

Anais had taken over my mind. Completely and utterly consumed my thoughts. Before her, I spent most of my days thinking about work and most of my evenings thinking about who I was going to fuck. Now all of that had changed. The day she walked out of my parents' estate was one that I would remember forever. No one had ever left Damien Cross. I was the one who always cut things off, but I let her go.

It was a punishment I was inflicting on myself. She didn't need to be caught up in the battles I was fighting. But that all changed when someone dared to shoot her father.

I might have let her leave, but I'd kept a close eye on her as soon as she stepped out of the safety net of my parents' home. We were trying to track whoever sent that fucker to break into my home and with this person still on the loose, things could be dangerous for Anais. It was my job to protect her, whether she liked it or not.

Since the break-in, I'd hired more guards from Cross Sentinel, the security company that Kingston cofounded, to watch over her in case someone tried something. Their job was to keep her safe from a distance so she wouldn't suspect anything. If something happened, their goal was to get her out of there immediately. That was how the guards on her detail extracted her from the situation safely when someone shot James. When Kingston briefed me on the situation on the way to the safe house, I was told one guard pretended to be a stranger on the street and made sure that the paramedics got to him as soon as possible, while another followed Ilaria to the hospital.

And now, here we were, sitting in the back of one of my many SUVs as Rob drove us to the hospital. I glanced over at her for a moment before turning my head back to my computer. Getting her out of harm's way could have gone smoother, but I knew my men did what needed to be done in order to keep Anais safe. The ride to the hospital with Anais was quieter than the one my men had reported to me when they were bringing her to the safe house.

Although she hadn't said a word since we had gotten in the SUV, Anais kept clenching and unclenching the hand that was resting on the seat between the two of us. Being in her presence again gave me a sense of peace that I wasn't willing to admit out loud. I could only imagine the thoughts that flew through her mind as we raced to the hospital. If we went any faster, we would get pulled over. Even though I could get us out of a ticket, it would delay us further. I reached under my seat, grabbed something, and placed it in her lap. She looked down at it and back at me.

"Thank you," she said, opening her purse to check the contents.

The trip didn't take long and almost before the vehicle could come to a stop, Anais jumped out wordlessly, her dark strands billowing in the wind behind her. Understanding her urgency, I opened the door on my side and stepped out, buttoning my suit jacket as I went. Carter and Stone, another guard on her detail, had already caught up with her by the time I rounded the vehicle and I quickly fell into step with them as the hospital doors slid open. We stopped to get our visitor passes before heading for a bank of elevators that would take us to her parents.

In the elevator, I took a moment to observe Anais. The first thing that struck me was the way her head was down, her hair almost creating a shield around her. I watched as her shoulders moved slightly before she lifted her head, her lip trembling. I nudged Carter aside and stepped closer to her. When my arms engulfed her, I didn't dwell on how great it felt to have her head on my chest again. Tears flowed down her cheeks, and I hid her face from the view of everyone else in the elevator while I stroked her hair. This woman who took the world by storm was coming apart right before my eyes. I knew I'd made mistakes with how I was handling her, but I didn't know what else I could do besides keep her safe. Seeing her this way made me want to scorch this city until every person that caused her pain was dead.

When the elevator stopped at the floor we wanted, I wondered if she would try to break out of my embrace. But she didn't. We were in our own little world, taking a moment together before finding out her father's fate. She looked at me before we stepped out of the elevator, and her eyes were swollen and red. The tears painted on her face only made me want to rage further. Whoever tried to mess with what was mine would pay.

"There's so much we need to talk about." Her words came out barely above a whisper. They paused the thoughts that were flying through my mind about revenge, and I turned my focus on the only thing that mattered: her.

"Not now. Let's get you in to see your father and then we can figure out the next steps."

She took a small step back and nodded. Anais wiped her eyes and together we walked to the nurses' station to find out where her father was located.

"He's currently in surgery, but your mother is down the hall."

Anais sprinted down the hallway, only pausing so her eyes could frantically search for her mother. I spotted Kingston sitting with Ilaria right away. His muscular form was blocking her from Anais's view. Ilaria let out an ear-piercing wail that sent Anais dashing in her direction, her purse swinging wildly in her wake. Ilaria met her halfway, the women falling into each other's arms, sobbing. They stayed like that for a few seconds before Kingston led them to a couple of chairs in a smaller waiting room, where they could sit down and not be in the middle of the hallway. When I reached the group, I nodded at Kingston and sat down next to Anais and Ilaria as they quietly wept until Anais pulled herself together and spoke.

"Mom, what's the latest? Please tell me what you know. There was so much blood," Anais sobbed.

"Oh, honey," her mother said, just before she took a big gulp of air.

Ilaria's hand was trembling, and Anais moved her own hand to hold her mother's. I could see that Anais was trying to be strong, but I didn't know how much she had in her after what had occurred in the elevator just a few short minutes ago. It brought back memories of how my own mother had tried to comfort me after the fire that took Charlotte's life. I pushed those thoughts back to where they belonged as Anais leaned over to wipe the tears that were flowing freely from her mother's eyes.

"Your father was shot in the thigh and hit his head on the cement when he went down. The bullet missed his femoral artery, thankfully. It could have been so much worse." Ilaria sniffled. "Paramedics stabilized him on the way to the hospital and when he got here, doctors checked for brain damage before taking him to surgery for the gunshot. That's all I know. Where were you? Are you okay? I mean you saw it all happen for crying out loud. They could have killed you!" She flung her arms around her daughter again before Anais could speak. They stayed like that for a moment before Ilaria unwrapped her arms, allowing Anais to sit upright once more before she grabbed her hand.

"I'm fine. Damien took care of me and I came here as soon as I could." Her words sent a sensation through me that I didn't want to dissect. "Dad is going to beat this."

"He's a fighter, that's for sure and…I don't know what I'd do if I lost him." She took several deep breaths before she continued. "I should have been there, but because you took my place, I put you in harm's way. I don't know how I'll ever forgive myself."

"Mom, there is no way you could have known."

Her mother's eyes shifted from looking at Anais to looking at me. "Are you Damien Cross?"

I nodded.

She let go of her daughter's hand and reached over to hug me. "Thank you for all the help getting James here so quickly and for helping me get here." She turned to her daughter. "Damien called me right after the shooting and said he was sending someone to pick me up. I'd heard his name from your father, but you know me, honey. I wasn't getting into a car with strangers, so I met them at the hospital. Kingston followed me and hasn't left my side."

I'd heard everything she'd said from Kingston when I was en route to Anais. Her eyes moved between Anais and me.

"I didn't expect you two to come in together. Did you know he also offered to help pay for all of James's medical bills including any rehabilitation expenses?"

Anais studied me for a moment before she said, "No. I didn't know that."

"It's so wonderful and one less thing we need to worry about."

Too bad she doesn't know what else Anais needs to worry about.

I fought to keep a smirk off my face. I had plans for my little Spitfire, and I wasn't going to be deterred.

Not now that she was back in my debt.

ANAIS

"Where are we going now?"

I'd followed Damien into the back of an SUV before it occurred to me to ask. Kingston, who had been following me around while I made sure my parents were being well taken care of at the hospital, was in the front seat with Rob driving. Damien had always been nearby, but he let Kingston shadow me while he made phone calls to keep his empire running smoothly, I assumed. Under normal circumstances, I might have fought Damien on this, but nothing about this was normal. I knew I needed protection. That didn't mean that I believed that Damien had nothing to do with my father's shooting.

I thought I'd escaped his control when I walked out on him just before Christmas. When Dad told me he was debt free, I let out a breath I hadn't realized I was holding. Thoughts of trying to find another way to pay Damien off crowded my brain, suffocating me. Not only had I danced with the devil, but I'd left him in a pretty dramatic fashion, when he was the one holding all the cards. Yet he hadn't demanded retribution when he had every right to. That was why I wondered if Damien had anything to do with the events that occurred tonight, even if he claimed he'd saved me.

Dad's surgery had gone well, and he was now resting. That sense of relief was short lived because I knew I needed protection because whoever had done this was still out there. That didn't mean I wasn't still pissed about the protection Damien provided. I rubbed my wrists, remembering the way the zip tie felt as I waited for him to answer my question.

"We are on our way to my penthouse."

I jerked my head around. "Why are we going to your penthouse? Wait, you own another home in the city?" He nodded but didn't elaborate, so I kept talking. "I assumed you would drop me off at my apartment."

"You thought wrong."

I snorted. "Of course I did."

I tried my best to stop the yawn that was begging to come out and failed. After the evening and night I'd had, there wasn't much keeping me from passing out. Sleep would be hard to find because of my father's condition, but I knew I had to try.

The silence in the vehicle gave me plenty of space and time to think about everything that had occurred over the last several hours. We had left the hospital once we were sure that my father was stable, and the police had taken my statement. I was thankful for the darkness that helped hide my feelings. Only flashes of light from the streetlights revealed hints of my despair. I would do almost anything to take away the pain my father was in. *It should have been me.* Tears stung my eyes before cascading down my face like a waterfall.

I tried not to draw attention to myself, but I should have known that Damien was attuned to my moods, to my needs, to my desires. He grabbed my hand, my smaller one inside his, creating a warmth barrier and a sense of comfort. I longed to be in his arms again, much like we were in the elevator, but our seatbelts prevented it.

The SUV glided through the streets because it was early morning and most of the city still slept. It felt as if seconds later we were pulling up to a gate and Rob flashed a badge at a scanner before the gate whirred to life. Here I was, entering Damien's world again, a world that was all-consuming and something I still didn't understand.

As the car maneuvered around the underground garage, my heart continued to sink. I glanced down at my phone and watched as the bars showed my cell phone's signal decreasing from four to three to two to one and finally zero. The countdown until I was under Damien's lock and key once more was done.

When the car was parked, Damien opened his door on the other side, clearly not patient enough for Rob to open it for him, while Rob opened the door for me. I walked over to his side of the car and Damien placed a hand on the small of my back as he led me to a door and into a smaller room with an elevator. Damien pulled out a badge and placed it on a scanner near the elevator. The doors opened immediately. Damien led me into the elevator and the doubts that entered my brain while we were driving back to his penthouse encouraged me to stand as far away from him as physically possible, which wasn't far. That amused him based on the smirk that played on his lips. Damien leaned over and pressed a button labeled "64", the highest number on the panel, and he brushed against my arm.

He took a step back and crossed his hands, but he didn't say a word as the elevator started moving. The silence made the elevator ride seem to last forever. My eyes stayed glued to the numbers as they lit up across the elevator panel.

Sixty-one.

Sixty-two.

Sixty-three.

Sixty-four.

The elevator lurched to a stop. When the doors opened, I took a deep breath and stepped out of it, following behind Damien. The elevator opened into a long hallway that only had one door at the end. Damien still hadn't said a word as we walked toward the door and he opened it.

He turned on the lights as I walked across the threshold and finally said, "Welcome home."

My mind wanted me to tell him to fuck off, but I was too tired to fight him. Frankly, staying in my apartment right now kind of scared me, even if Ellie was there. That jolted me out of my thoughts as I closed the front door. "What about Ellie? Is she okay? She can't stay at the apartment by herself if someone is after me."

"She's fine."

And there he was, not elaborating on things that were important again. "I would feel better if I talked to her." I dug into my purse and pulled out my phone. But it was dead. "What did you mean by she's fine?"

"I arranged for her to stay with her parents in New Jersey. We didn't want to take any chances given the situation. She also has a security guard."

I placed my hands over my face, leaned back on his counter. How had this gotten to the point where Ellie was dragged in? "I'm such a fucking idiot," I mumbled, not talking to anyone in particular.

"No, you're not. Most, if not all, of this was out of your control. Hence why from now until I settle all of this, you'll have at least one security guard with you at all times when you leave the penthouse. While you are here, we'll have someone check up on you every so often just to make sure that everything is okay. Between Kingston's men and the security in the building, you'll be safe. And you'll be working from home. Got it?"

"Damien, I have to go into the office at some point. I have to live my life. Got it?" I threw the phrase he used back at him because it pissed me off, even though the hardness in his face and his voice told me it was nonnegotiable.

"I will not get into this with you." He took a step toward me. "The more you argue and fight me, the greater the urge is to have a repeat performance of when I threw you over my knee in your apartment." His steps continued until he had me backed up against the door.

I took in a quick breath because I wasn't expecting him to say that. I didn't want to admit how much had changed since he came into my life, even at this very moment. My eyes were focused on his chest, given how quickly he had trapped me against the door. They slowly made their way from his chest up to his face and to his eyes.

"You didn't do this, did you?"

Damien's body stiffened and his face hardened. My question wasn't going over well.

"No. And whoever did this is going to pay for it. With their life."

The gravity of his words gave me the urge to take a step back, but I had no space to. The door leading to the outside world was now locked and I was fully enclosed in Damien's private oasis. He placed a hand under my chin, even though I was already looking at him. His movements and his eyes told me that he was in control and that it would be smart to watch my words and actions around him. That thought frightened me because I was supposed to hate him. He was supposed to be an enemy even though he saved me from suffering the same fate that my father had, or worse, and I didn't know anything about the person who shot my father. *The devil you know is better than the devil you don't.*

The intensity in his eyes increased just before his lips crashed into mine. It was the first time our lips had touched in a couple of weeks and I had missed it, though I refused to admit it. But I didn't know how much I'd missed his raw energy until now. The kiss turned feverish, his mouth on mine as we battled it out for who would take control. It became clear soon after that Damien would wrestle control from me when I gasped into his mouth. He took advantage of that opportunity and slipped his tongue into my mouth, forging another survival of the fittest. That was until he pulled back suddenly, leaving me in a daze for a moment before I could recollect my senses.

By the look on his face, I knew he needed this as much as I did, but even though I wanted to keep doing what we were doing, there were still some things that needed to be squared away.

I touched my lips, still reeling from what had just

occurred. My brain floated back to the conversation we were having before he used his lips to turn my brain into a pile of mush. Damien's argument about why I should stay at his place probably made sense temporarily. I wouldn't need to be in the office for a while anyway.

"That is correct. Everything will be fixed so that you will work from home."

Did I say those words out loud? Of course, he had already thought of everything that needed to be done, and I tried my best to hide my annoyance. Once again, it felt as if he had removed my ability to choose. "Did you also grab my things from my apartment while you were at it?"

Damien nodded. "And from your office. If you need anything else, we can arrange for someone to either pick it up or you can stop by with security."

"Would it kill you to ask me before you just uproot my life?"

His expression remained unchanged, and my annoyance grew the more tired I became. How I hadn't fallen asleep while standing on my feet, I would never know.

"Just because I'm letting you get away with all this, doesn't mean that it's just going to be smooth sailing."

That got his attention. He looked over at me, and I could see the smirk forming on his face. "I wouldn't have it any other way."

"There's something else we haven't talked about that happened back there."

"What are you referring to?"

"That you're paying my father's medical bills, including his physical therapy."

"And making sure that your father has the best doctors

the world has to offer. You can tack it onto our next arrangement. After all, you left before the terms of our last deal were
met. Due to that, the stakes in our next contract will be
higher."

Anger simmered below the surface after he mentioned
the last deal we had and the potential for a new contract.
"Damien, you cancelled the debt, effectively ending the deal
we had. There is no need for a new one." I kept my voice
neutral, trying to not escalate the situation.

"You walked out on me and I still cleared your father's
debt. Now you're looking at another massive debt even with
his health insurance. That's not including the security I'm
providing. All you have to do is sign a new contract and I will
take care of it for you. Same rules apply with one small
addition."

"My God, you are such a petty asshole!" Well, that flew
out the window.

"I've been called worse. Do you want to hear what the
new term is?"

As I stared at him, something clicked in place. "No. All of
this is because you're hurt that I left you."

"Of course not. I'm showing you what happens when
someone goes back on their word. Yet, I'm still being generous. Now whether you admit it or not, you need me to fix this.
Medical and security bills are expensive, and you don't have
the wherewithal to cover it. I do. All you have to do is agree to
the new deal."

I thought about throttling him but couldn't find something I could use as a weapon in the general vicinity. He must
have sensed my anger was reaching a boiling point because

he turned to look at me, not displaying any feelings on his face.

He moved toward me, taking my chin between his thumb and forefinger, staring into my eyes. "When I allowed you to leave, it was not a permanent thing. When I said that you were mine, I meant it. When I'm done with you is when we are done. Not the other way around."

His words made my heart shatter into a million pieces. I knew I had been brave when I told the man who refused to take no for an answer that I was leaving, but now I knew why he let me leave with little fight. It was almost as if he knew I would always end up right back where he wanted me.

4

ANAIS

I slowly opened my eyes and found myself face-to-face with the sunlight streaming in from the window. The warmness from the light served as a warning that it was time to get up. I groaned, putting an arm over my face to block the light and give my eyes enough time to adjust to the new day's brightness. The lack of sleep the night before made itself known as I forced my brain to think. Images of what occurred yesterday flooded back into my mind. Thoughts about the state that I left my parents in caused me to jolt out of bed. I needed to check in with them.

I tripped over my own feet as I dashed to the door, adjusting the clothes I threw on as I went. I remembered being so pissed after he had kissed me senseless, and then what he said about creating a new arrangement had sent me over the edge.

I'd given him the one-finger salute because that was the only thing I could muster as exhaustion had taken over. He'd watched as I opened the first door I walked to and almost sang with glee because it was a bedroom. I hadn't bothered to find something more comfortable to change into. Instead, I'd stripped down to my tank top and panties, leaving my clothes in a pile beside the bed. A quick check this morning had told me they had been moved. I'd looked around and found them neatly folded on a chair in the corner. That had all but confirmed that Damien had been in here at some point.

That was when I realized I hadn't taken an opportunity to look around Damien's penthouse last night. The room I stood in was spotless and had dark furniture that looked as if it could fit in with the décor in Elevate. From what I could see, there were three doors in the room. One led to the living room, and I assumed the other two led to the bathroom and a closet, respectively.

The television hanging on one wall was huge, and when I looked over at the end table on the other side of the bed, I did a double take. There was a bottle of cologne sitting on it. I walked over and smelled it. A faint woodsy aroma that I associated with Damien reached my nose. Was this Damien's room?

I listened to see if I could hear anything that would indicate that someone else was home. Hearing nothing at first, I walked over to a door that I knew wasn't the one that led into the living area. When I twisted and pushed on the knob, I found an enormous closet, much like the one that I had seen back in Damien's other home just a few weeks ago. It was filled with different dark-colored suits, white shirts, and ties. There was also an assortment of shoes, including sneakers, which I had never seen Damien wear. This discovery confirmed that the room I had found was Damien's and that I had slept in his bed last night. Had he slept next to me? Figuring that I would delve more into that later, I went to the next door and before I could open it, I heard what sounded like Damien, but it was muffled. I rushed to the door that led to the living area and listened.

"Do we know anything more?"

I put my ear up to the door to see if I could hear what was being said a little clearer.

"He's still stable and things are looking good," Damien replied. I assumed they were talking about my father.

"How is Anais?" The phone was on speaker.

"She slept through the night, which I wasn't expecting, but I'm glad she did."

"That's good. I'm sorry that all of this is happening. It brings back memories of what happened with—"

I recognized the voice. It was Selena Cross...Damien was talking to his mother about me?

"Mom, now is not a great time."

"I know, I know, but I'm glad that the result of this was better. Is there anything I can do? I'll have some food delivered if that's helpful, and if you need me to come, just let me know."

That made me smile. Although Damien could probably buy anything he wanted several hundred times over, Selena's offer was motherly.

"Okay."

I heard them wrap up the call and counted to ten before I stepped out from behind the door. Damien looked up at me as I entered.

"How much of that did you hear?"

"The ending. Your mom is really sweet."

"That she is."

I looked down at the counter and found my phone charging. "Ah, there it is." I picked it up and noticed dozens of notifications. Coworkers wanting to check in, social media comments, and more emails than I cared to think about. I cleared most of the items without reading them. The thought of dealing with any of it was stifling during a time like this. I only cared about the ones from my mom and Ellie. I knew I could at least text them without feeling overwhelmed. Ellie was up first since I hadn't heard from her since everything happened.

Me: *Hey, just wanted to tell you I'm okay and am with Damien. Feeling a bit overwhelmed, but I'll call you soon.*

Ellie: *Yes, please call me when you can!*

I then wrote a text message to my mother.

Me: *Wanted to let you know I was fine and that I should be at the hospital soon.*

Mom: *Okay. Your father's condition hasn't changed but we can talk about it when you get here. I'll see you soon.*

Before I put my phone down, it buzzed in my hand, telling me I had an unread email. The message was an alert I set up to send me a notification if Monroe Media Agency was mentioned online. It turned out that the notice was from an obscure website that I had never heard of and the headline was: **James Monroe, Founder of Monroe Media Agency, The Intended Target?**

The post included vague details about my father's shooting, but once I got to the end, I sucked in a quick breath. It included speculation about why my father might have been shot. One of the assumptions was about him owing someone money.

I placed my phone on the counter and looked up at Damien. "When can we go see my father?" I told myself if I didn't like his answer, I would take a cab down there by myself, not giving a damn if Damien had any objections to it.

"Soon. But there are some things we need to discuss first."

"Okay," I replied, waiting on him to elaborate so we could get this show on the road.

"A lot has happened in the hours since your father was shot."

"I know, and I'll figure out the best way to go about doing everything that needs to be done. I need to check in with work."

I assumed my coworkers knew about Dad and that none of us would be doing much of anything for the rest of this week. I made a mental note to send Vicki Thomason, Vice President of Monroe Media Agency, a text because I didn't have the brain capacity to check my emails at the moment.

Vicki and I had a good relationship, and I knew that she would have no problem standing in my father's place. I also didn't think she was involved in his shooting. I leaned back and closed my eyes. My hands grew warmer rapidly, so I clutched the edge of the counter, which provided a much-needed cooling sensation.

"That's not everything." That made my eyes pop back open. "The media have picked up on this case and it's running wild. You don't want them to start picking up on a potential motive. I could step in and control the narrative and dull the flames. But I want something in return."

He's right. If they connected the motive to say, my father's money troubles, Monroe Media Agency would be ruined. "What?"

"You. I want you to be mine permanently in exchange for

me quieting the noise around the shooting. You're going to sign a contract and we're going to get married."

My eyes almost bulged out of my skull as his words ran through my mind. It took a moment before I drew my eyes to him, his expression not showing whether he was joking. That lit a fire under the rage I felt for Damien that lay dormant because of everything else that was going on in my life. "You must have lost your mind."

"I have not." The hardness in his voice told me the same. His glare should have made me quiver in fear, but I refused.

"You are a member of one of the most powerful families that this city has ever seen. You could squash any media attention toward my father with a flick of your hand."

"I know I can, but I don't have to. And I think you care too much about your family business to let this—shall we call it an opportunity?—pass you by."

I pushed off the counter and started pacing. "Fuck you. How is this an opportunity? You're blackmailing me into an engagement."

He shrugged. "You can call it what you like. Take it or leave it."

"You can't be serious."

"When am I ever not serious?"

I agreed with him there. "But you don't do relationships. What benefit do you get out of this? I don't even know what you're protecting me from!" The last statement ended in a screech that at any other time would have embarrassed me. Not today. I knew Damien would sink low to get his way. I didn't think he would go past hell to do it.

"The benefit I get from this is that I get to bend you over my desk and spank that ass of yours. Anytime I want. You get to come under the Cross Empire, so stories about the shooting and your father being desperate for money, so desperate that he came to me, will be squashed."

"How would that get out?" I asked. "I assumed no one but you, me, and my parents knew about it."

"People talk. There were rumblings about it, but nothing concrete. Who knows who might have been tracking him. After all, Monroe Media Agency was working with some big names before the decline. There are plenty of ways the information could have gotten out there. Now, news of this has not been proven true, but if we were engaged to be married, I know I can stop it. Here is the contract."

There was that confidence oozing out of him as he handed me several pieces of paper while I tried to prevent the bile from rising in my throat. Although I craved Damien's touch and couldn't stop thinking about it in the days after I skipped out on our deal, it didn't mean we were compatible for marriage. This was all too much. "I need time to think about this. There's a lot going on at once, and I need time to process it all."

"You can have as much time as you want. Just know that the clock is ticking because who knows how long the media will keep a lid on these stories. Who knows who might know that Monroe Media Agency was struggling to survive? Hell, one reason I brought you here is because the photographers and reporters had swarmed your apartment to find out more about what happened to your father. Thankfully, your parents' home has a doorman and a rear entrance like this one, so it's been easier for Ilaria to slip in and out when she goes home or leaves to go back to the hospital."

He wasn't wrong about that.

"That's another reason why I talked to Ellie before I reached you. It was best that she went somewhere else. They will not leave you alone until they get what they want, or someone brings down the hammer."

I knew he was right. Because of the high-profile nature of some of Monroe Media Agency's clients and the reputation that my father built, I shouldn't be stunned that this caught the attention of the press. Once the media got word of a story, they weren't going to let it go until they found out the truth, which made sense, but it didn't benefit me. I flopped my body onto the couch, the black leather making a swooshing noise under my weight. "Do we have any more information on who might have shot my father?"

Damien shook his head. "What I know, you know."

I highly doubted that was the case. "What is the media reporting? Or do I have to go on social media myself and find out?" My sarcastic question was dripping with venom. None of that mattered to Damien. He didn't look impressed or amused. His face remained impassive.

"They're just saying the usual and when they reached out to the police, they didn't receive a comment other than that they were investigating the situation. I'm launching my own investigation and I'm using multiple avenues to find out what happened. The only thing I know for sure is that he was the intended target. In the time it took to grab you, the shooter still had an opportunity to shoot you or anyone else in the area too, and yet they didn't. Now, I want an answer about our impending engagement as soon as possible." He walked away from the living area and headed toward the kitchen.

"So, once again, I don't have a choice in this matter," I said, standing up with rage flowing through me because he tossed another "choice" at me that I had to decide on within his timeframe. I knew this was all a game that he liked to play in order to get his way. "I don't want to get married to you, and I know you don't want to marry me."

Damien stopped in his tracks. The words flew out of my mouth without me giving much thought to them. I'd spoken out of anger, but there was truth to my words.

His face was still unreadable, but his eyes weren't. I thought my response might have pissed him off, but instead of his eyes becoming ablaze, they froze over, causing me to shiver for a millisecond as I waited for his response. "You don't know what you're talking about. The longer you wait to give me an answer, the worse it is going to get. And like with our other arrangement, you've had every opportunity to walk out that door and never see me again, but you know the consequences of that."

With that, he stalked toward another room in the apartment and slammed the door shut, putting a barrier between me and him. That was the first time I'd ever seen Damien show pure rage.

5

DAMIEN

A painting fell to the floor as the door slammed. Thankfully, the abstract design that my interior designer had insisted on hanging in here had just been a canvas, as opposed to framed in glass, so there was nothing to clean up. I picked up the picture and put it back on the hook. Then, I gripped the edge of my desk and tried to calm my fury as I watched my knuckles turn white.

I don't know what I hoped her answer would be when I told her we would get engaged, but I hadn't expected her to say that she didn't want to marry me. The rejection hurt me more than I was willing to admit, but I could see why she might have felt that way, considering she'd blamed me for her father being shot and the way Kingston's men had treated her. The shock on her face that followed her defiant words gave me pause because I wasn't sure what it meant. Did she merely want to piss me off? I knew that when I came up with her nickname, Spitfire, that it fit her perfectly, but I didn't expect it to backfire on me.

Nothing I was doing was helping to quell my anger. I

prided myself in being able to rise above the fray no matter what happened. It allowed me to keep people off balance in my personal life and in my professional life, yet I hadn't controlled my temper in front of Anais. I couldn't remember the last time that I had snapped like that with anyone. What made her different from any other person I dealt with I didn't know, and that frustrated me. I needed to control my emotions when it came to her.

It didn't do me any good to have anyone who was pressing my buttons know they were doing it. I thrived on making people squirm, but I seemed to give her more leeway than I gave members of my family. When she fought me, my cock twitched at the thought of her lips taking me, giving us both something else to do. The thought of her kneeling at my feet and taking me in her mouth made me harder. I adjusted my dick, although it was pointless since my thoughts revolving around her got me here in the first place.

I thought she would jump at the chance to marry me. I lost count of the number of proposals that I had received, even as I ended the relationships I'd had with some women. To hear that she didn't want me made me want to punch my fist through a wall, but I stopped myself there. Had I really expected her to say yes? We hadn't seen each other in weeks, and we didn't exactly part on good terms.

When I came up with the idea that we should be engaged, it was a complex plan, but even I knew my emotions were overruling my brain about this. Being engaged to her provided another liability for me. Outside of the contracts that needed to be worked out and signed, being named in a high-profile affair with me would turn her world upside down for a third time.

I never expected it would be me initiating any arguments relating to getting married or taking a relationship more seriously than just a quick fuck. Whenever talks of marriage came up in conversation, I shuddered at the thought of not only being tied down to one person, but how much of a microscope anyone in my life would be under. Yet here I was planning to break all my own rules and put a ring on her finger in order to guarantee that she and her family stayed safe. *Who the hell am I becoming?*

My phone's ringing stopped my thoughts and made me growl. I didn't appreciate being interrupted at any point in time, but especially when I was trying to calm myself down. I pulled my phone out of my pocket and glanced at the caller ID. Well, at least this was someone I wanted to talk to. The device rang again, and I put it up to my ear.

"What do you have for me?"

6

ANAIS

"There is no way in hell you can marry him, Anais."

It was two days after Damien's declaration, and I found myself staring at my laptop in disbelief. I almost wished I had decided to call her on the phone versus hosting a video call so she couldn't see my expression. "Ellie, do you think I don't know that? Could you imagine me being the next Mrs. Cross?"

The thought made my stomach turn and that was beside the glaring red flags flashing in my mind. Everything inside of me was telling me how horrible marrying him would be. His possessiveness would launch him into a rage at the sight of someone looking at me wrong, but there was a sliver of comfort in the fact that if it came down to it, he would do whatever he could do to keep me and my family safe. Hell, he had even convinced Ellie to go back to New Jersey to live with her parents for a bit with the security guard. As headstrong and street-smart as Ellie was, even she got the hint that it was probably wise for her to do as he said.

"Based on the hints you've given, at least the sex would be amazing?"

She wasn't wrong there. We hadn't been intimate since I left him just before Christmas, but there was no question that he knew what to do to set my body ablaze. Only that wasn't important right now. Or maybe it was. It was definitely doing its job to scramble my brain even more. "I might have an idea."

"Spill."

A knock on the door stopped me from saying anything more.

"Hold on, someone's at the door." A quick check at the clock on the wall told me that it was almost noon. "Ah, it might be my security detail doing their rounds to check on me. Give me a second."

"No worries."

I muted the phone, walked over to look through the peephole, and found Kingston on the other side. I opened the door. Kingston gave me a small smile and a nod before he did a quick scan of the home. "Are we still on for visiting your parents in a couple of hours?"

I nodded. "That was still my plan."

"Okay. We'll be ready to move then."

"And after we come back, you'll take a break?" I saw Kingston multiple times per day when he came in to check on things inside the apartment. Although it had only been two days, since I'd been cooped up in here, it seemed as if he was always doing something. A small goal of mine was to break the frosty exterior that he exhibited toward me since it was clear that I would be seeing a lot of him for the time being.

He dipped his head and then exited the apartment just as quickly as he'd entered. I walked back to my seat on the couch and unmuted my laptop.

"I don't think we need to go as far as to get married. Shouldn't a fake engagement be enough? It will get people talking, spread all over social media, and will cause enough of a distraction that Damien could squash any rumblings behind the scenes."

"I'm not positive, but wouldn't that drum up more interest in your father?"

"Not if Damien organized a few backroom deals that guarantee special access to us regarding our wedding plans in exchange for not publishing stories related to my father. Don't celebrities do this type of thing?"

"Rumors say that some have. Do you think Damien will go for it since he said that he wanted to marry you?"

"I mean, he doesn't do relationships, and this is probably the best way that will lead to the least amount of baggage. No need to go through lawyers when the arrangement is done. Hopefully."

"Aren't you assuming that he's viewing you in the same light as his other relationships? 'Cause based on what I know, and I've told you this before, this is not how he usually does things."

"No, it came from his mouth. He told me this himself, so I don't know why he brought up this talk of getting married."

Ellie scoffed, "Damien Cross can do whatever he wants. He could protect you and anyone else you wanted to protect, along with killing any of these stories, without getting married. I highly doubt anyone would try to go up against him."

I knew she was right, which made his behavior even more puzzling. We barely had anything in common, and I couldn't tell if he wanted to snap at me or fuck me until I screamed. He probably wanted to do both at the same time, and I couldn't deny that the feeling was mutual, especially when we went to Elevate. I just wouldn't say this out loud.

Something else filtered into my mind. His words about how I was his and his desire to have control...and that's when it all clicked. Our last deal had an expiration date on it, this one didn't. I thought he was being threatening when he mentioned that he wanted me to be his permanently, but maybe it went beyond that?

"Shit."

"What's wrong?"

"I don't know what I'm going to do." I covered up what I was thinking because I wasn't ready to share it now, if ever.

"This is a pretty big ultimatum that just got sprung on you last minute and with only a few days to think about it. Has he even taken you out on a date?"

I couldn't remember a single time that he had taken me out on a date. That needed to be rectified if we wanted to go along with this engagement charade and make it believable. Maybe if it was photographed, it might be another opportunity to take some heat off my father.

As I rubbed my hands over my eyes, I sighed. "I'm still thinking it over, but I need to come up with an answer."

~

"DAD, you look good. I'm glad they'll be letting you out of here soon."

I sat down in a chair at my father's bedside, looking at the man who had always been so strong, now looking almost frail after the trauma he was trying to recover from. Seeing him attached to these machines terrified me, and not even knowing that he was receiving the best care would change that.

"Don't lie to your old man."

I was lying. Dad looked frail but I was still optimistic. The hope was that he would be out of the hospital within a week, but we needed to see how his body responded to treatment.

"Seeing you like this is a helluva lot better than the last time I saw you. The blood... I—" My voice broke as I tried to maintain my composure but failed.

Dad and I looked at each other, the soft sound of the machines monitoring him bouncing off the walls of the silent room. Mom had gone to the cafeteria with a member of her security detail, while Kingston stood outside the room guarding it.

"You know, even with all the pain you're in right now, I know how much worse this could have been. I'm glad that you're okay."

"Me too, kiddo."

WHEN I CAME BACK from the hospital, I realized I hadn't heard from Damien all day and for that I was glad. Over the last couple of days, he tended to either work from his home office or go into the office to handle whatever business he had to take care of. Part of me was relieved that I didn't have him breathing down my neck, but I also felt lonely. Without having work to distract me, I watched a lot more television and read more books. I threw my purse down on the couch and removed my outerwear before I pulled out my phone. I checked my work email, vowing not to spend more than three minutes on it. An email from Vicki was the first thing that caught my attention. She reiterated that she had everything under control at Monroe Media Agency and that if I needed anything to let her know.

I sent a quick thank-you note before there was a knock on the front door. I walked over to the door with my phone in hand. When there was another knock, I checked the peephole and saw Rob on the other side. *What is he doing here?* I thought he might have gone to pick up Damien, who I assumed would get off work soon. I opened the door and he handed me a white rectangular box.

"This is for you." It was a flat box that looked as if it might have clothes in it. "This is also for you," he said as he handed over a white envelope.

"Thank you," I said, and he gave me a small wave before he turned away to walk back down the hall.

I closed the door and brought the things he gave me over to the counter to open them. When I lifted the top of the white box, I gasped. Inside was a stunning navy dress. It resembled a long slip that I knew would cling to my body.

"I think I might have some beige shoes that will go with it...." I stopped myself from going any further when I realized I should have probably opened the envelope first. I flipped it over, pushed the flap up, and took out the card. To the surprise of no one, it was from Damien.

Wear this tonight because we're going out. Be ready to go by 6:30 p.m.

He didn't sign the note.

"Could you, just for once, *ask* me to do something?"

After I put the card back in the envelope, I threw it on the counter. I debated whether or not I should go before deciding that it probably made the most sense to do so. I remembered the first time I'd denied him, when I'd refused to move in with him, and he'd left me in a puddle of mush. I smirked as I wondered what he would do if I didn't put the dress on.

Since I needed to be ready by 6:30 p.m., I had just a couple of hours to do everything I needed. I hurried into the guest room, which I was now sleeping in after asking Damien to give me time to think about his "proposal," and started getting ready.

What does he have up his sleeve tonight? Maybe he put this together because he was trying to help me relieve some stress due to everything I was dealing with. Although Damien sometimes drove me mad enough to scream, I couldn't say that I wasn't looking forward to spending this evening out with him, even if it meant he might try to weasel an answer out of me about marrying him tonight.

7

ANAIS

I was ready with a few minutes to spare. I wore a long beige coat over the navy dress and wore my hair in loose curls down my back. My fingers fluffed my hair once more when I heard Kingston's knock on the door at 6:30 on the dot. Nerves bubbled under the surface of my calm exterior. I grabbed my dark brown purse, peeked through the peephole, and opened the door.

"Ready?" he asked.

"Yes. Thank you," I replied before I locked the door behind us. It didn't take us long to get to the elevator, travel down to the car, which Rob had parked in the garage in order to avoid me potentially having to be spotted by anyone. With the media sniffing around, who knew who might be watching especially because I hadn't agreed to anything yet. The coast was clear and when I was safely in the car, I breathed a sigh of relief before Rob backed out of the parking spot.

"You okay?" Rob peeped at me before focusing on the backup camera on the console.

"Yeah. I just feel as if I'm stuck in an ivory tower and I

only leave the house to go to the hospital, outside of right now. I've already binged a season of *Friends*." Rob just shook his head, while Kingston stayed silent. "Come on, don't act like you haven't seen even one episode."

Kingston said nothing, but Rob did. "My wife loves it."

"See!" I turned my attention to Kingston. "Maybe you should watch it too in your free time."

"I don't have any free time." Kingston's response made me smile.

"You've told me that before. Everyone has some free time."

He shrugged, so I turned back to Rob. "I hope Damien lets you take some time off to spend it with your family."

"He does. In fact, my wife and I are going on vacation soon."

"Great. Where to?"

"Colorado. She wants to spend some time on the slopes and I'm happy to oblige."

I smiled and sat back in my seat as we made our way to a destination unknown. At least to me.

"Where are we headed?" I asked.

"Mr. Cross wanted it to be a surprise. He knew you would ask." Rob looked at me in the rearview mirror with a smile. "Let me know if you need anything."

I was glad that our relationship had at least warmed since we'd first met, and it stayed consistent, unlike what I went through with Damien.

"Of course he did," I responded.

The surprise was fine by me. Furthermore, I was able to get out of the house instead of being by myself with just those four walls to keep me company besides when Lucy came by. I wondered where we could be going as Rob drove the SUV to our destination. It wasn't long before Rob slowed down and pulled up in front of a gigantic building. When I saw the small yet prominent sign, I gasped.

"I'm going in there?" I asked. My eyes jumped between Kingston and Rob, as I waited for one of them to confirm.

"Yes, Miss," Rob replied. He parked outside of Thirteen Park Avenue, one of the most expensive restaurants in New York City. My heart jumped into my throat. This was going to be an amazing evening.

Rob opened my door and I waved at both men before I was quickly swept into the beautiful restaurant by the door-man. The high ceilings and tall windows reminded me of Damien's penthouse, but that's where the similarities ended. The décor was more classic, fitting the smart and sophisti-cated ambience the restaurant was known for. It was defi-nitely fancier than I had imagined, and the gigantic chandeliers were a wonderful touch. I was fully immersed in the atmosphere and couldn't be happier. When I greeted the host at the front podium, she took my coat and led me to a private room on the second level of the restaurant. She placed my coat on the coat hanger a few feet from where we would eat and directed me into the room.

Of course, Damien was there already, and as he stood he gave me a heated look. He wore his usual uniform—the black suit that fit him impeccably and his simple, yet expensive black tie. He didn't say anything as he pulled out my chair and when I sat, he pushed my seat toward the table. His fingers brushed against my shoulders gently, causing me to tremble slightly. I longed for him to touch me again, but he took his seat once more. We both listened intently to the things that our server told us before gesturing to the menus in front of us. I smiled and waited until the server left the room before turning to Damien.

"What's this all about?" I asked. I tried to keep my voice light, even though I was trembling inside about the decision I needed to make.

He took a sip of his water, and that's when I noticed there were two other seats at the table. My heart sank when I realized that this dinner wasn't exactly what I thought it was going to be. "A couple of people will join us in a few moments."

"Good job on elaborating. Is this work related?"

"Yes. I thought you might enjoy being here and having a fancy dinner."

That wasn't completely wrong. I swallowed the words I wanted to say and focused on attempting to get through this dinner. Why did I even remotely think he had asked me out on a date? This was just another work function, and I was supposed to sit here and look pretty.

"So, have you made your decision?"

This question startled me, although I should have been expecting it. "I assume you're talking about the marriage proposal." I made air quotes with my fingers when I said, 'marriage proposal.'

He raised an eyebrow after my comment and titled his head slightly. "What do you—"

"Mr. Cross." I heard another voice come from the doorway, and it took everything in me to not throw my head back in relief. I was almost willing to bet money that he wouldn't try to get me to answer this question while in front of others. He wanted me to agree to this on my own and even Damien had the decency to know this conversation would be out of line in front of others. Even if his marriage demands were fake.

I turned my head and watched as two men entered the room. Damien stood up as they walked over and shook their hands before introducing the men to me. "Anais, this is Jon and Will. You've met Will before."

The men shook my hand and I immediately got a bad vibe from Jon. The way his hand squeezed mine longer than necessary while he looked me up and down as if I were on the menu tonight made me want to shudder. But I stayed steady and spared a glance at Damien. Based on the narrowing of his eyes, he wasn't pleased. Thankfully, when we all sat down, I was sitting next to Damien, not Jon. It didn't take long before the conversation devolved into business. I listened to the conversation somewhat, but I wasn't exactly sure what they were talking about. I sighed from boredom but sucked in a quick breath when I felt Damien's hand land on my knee. Those thick fingers drifted north, bringing my silky dress with him, before he stopped a couple of inches above my knee. It took every ounce of control to make sure I didn't show how he was affecting me.

Our server came back and asked for our orders, and once he was done, the men went back to talking about whatever business they were discussing. The longer the meeting went on, the more frustrated I became. I grew tired of Jon's boisterous laugh and the looks he was giving me, but my body was waging a war within me as I waited to see what Damien's hand was going to do next. When his hand moved once more, I held my breath as part of me wanted to reach down and stop him from going any further, but I was also excited about his hand inching toward my pussy in public. The further his palm moved, the wetter I became, and I could feel my nipples hardening into peaks underneath the navy slip dress. The cool fabric rubbed against them, causing my arousal to increase.

I was in my own world as I waited for Damien to make his next move, ignoring the other men in the room. That was until Jon brought me into the conversation.

"So, Anais, what do you do?"

It shocked me that he was looking me in the eye, because I thought my nipples were blaring off signals I was aroused. "I am the social media director of a media firm."

"Oh, that's cute."

His reply made me see red. Damien clenched my thigh for a moment, causing my gaze to land on him. Before I could say anything, Damien leveled a glare at Jon that was so glacial I almost felt bad for him.

"What Anais does is very important, and you have some fucking nerve to downplay her work. She creates a social media strategy that could help these companies' reputations and help them thrive on social media. She has to turn her knowledge of marketing on its head, in some cases, to navigate and adapt on social media."

Damien's words caused me to look at him again, because I didn't think I'd ever heard him say such positive things about me. I tried to keep the shock off my face.

"I don't worry about social media because I don't have to. It's a child's playground and is not based on the reality of what happens in the real world."

Will eyed Jon, but said nothing so Damien responded,

"Tread lightly, Jon. Especially about something you know little about. Now apologize."

"Sorry." Jon looked down at the table before glancing at Will.

I knew the apology was bullshit. It was written all over Jon's face, including the smirk he was trying hard not to show. Damien's defense had filled me with warmth, but now it turned cold. I was pissed at Jon for his comments, but I was also pissed that Damien felt the need to jump in when I could defend myself. It didn't take long for something to snap in me. I'd had enough.

"Jon, you and I both know that you're not sorry. Damien, I don't need you to defend me, thank you very much."

"You're feisty, huh? Reminds me of someone I used to know."

That was the first time Will had addressed me outside of shaking my hand. I watched Damien sit up straighter out of the corner of my eye. Before I could inquire further, our server came back with our meals. I made it halfway through my smoked duck before I picked up a napkin and patted my lips.

"Excuse me," I said as I stood up. "I'm going to use the ladies' room."

Anger bubbled below the surface of my polite mask, but I wasn't about to let them know that. I walked out into the hallway and glanced at the coat rack across from the bathroom. I made a split-second decision and grabbed my coat and dashed down the hallway.

"Miss?" I turned around and found our server standing behind me.

"Yes?"

"Is there anything I can get you?" He was eyeing my coat, probably wondering why I'd left just after he'd served our meal.

"Can you let Mr. Cross know that I was feeling unwell and that I will see him later?" I saw a small bit of fear light his eyes, so I quickly added, "It had nothing to do with the food, I promise."

"Sure, that won't be a problem. Feel better soon."

"Thank you," I said before I turned away to walk to the exit. I debated whether to call Rob on my walk to the door, but I didn't have to because he was standing at the entrance. I assumed the reason Kingston wasn't there was because I was supposed to be with Damien. "Please take me home now."

"All right," he responded as I got closer to him.

"I'm just not feeling too great."

"Do you need anything? I can take you back to the penthouse and come back and get Mr. Cross." It didn't take long for the valet to grab the car and soon I was sitting in the back seat of the SUV with my head against the car window. I was glad to be leaving behind the misogynistic attitudes that had joined what I thought would be a peaceful dinner, yet I missed Damien's hand on my leg and wondered where that would have gone if I hadn't left.

I had never given him an answer.

8

DAMIEN

I checked my watch for the third time, wondering where the hell Anais was. She had only been gone for a few minutes, but it was enough to make me wonder if something had happened. I knew Jon had irritated her.

Jon and Will were there to talk over a deal they hoped to bring to the Cross Empire as a whole. We had intel proving they were trying to continue operating a drug-trafficking ring on behalf of the Vitale family and they wanted us to turn a blind eye. Little in the way of business, legal or otherwise, happened in this city without our knowledge or approval. They thought they were being slick by inviting me to dinner first to warm me up before bringing in my father or siblings. I had a history with Will. One might even describe us as friends at one point. He should have warned Jon to be on his best behavior and that I was someone they should be scared of. Especially after the way Jon spoke to and about Anais. Their deal was dead on arrival, but Jon's behavior confirmed my decision was the right one. Now I had to decide if he was going to stay alive.

Thoughts of Anais floated through my brain as I glanced toward the bathrooms, almost demanding for her to return this instant. She had looked exquisite when she entered the room. The designer I'd hired had outdone themselves. That dress reminded me of silk sheets and had made me want to cancel the meeting, pull the straps down, yank the skirt up, and fuck her right there on the table. The only thing that mattered to me when she first walked in was getting a taste of her—five-star meal be damned. I had reined in my desire to lose control in order to be professional at this dinner. I had always compartmentalized work and play, but it seemed the more time I spent with Anais, the more the lines blurred.

Our server approached the table again and I asked, "Have you seen Anais?" I thought about calling her but didn't want to pull that trigger just yet.

"Oh, I'm sorry." The server stared at me like a child whose hand got caught in the cookie jar. "W—We got a little backed up in the kitchen and I didn't have an opportunity to come back here. Yes, she said she wasn't feeling well, and that she was leaving."

I kept a straight face as I stood up and said, "Excuse me."

I pulled my phone out of my pocket and saw a text message from Rob.

Rob: *I got her. We're on our way back to the apartment. She's okay. I'll pick you up once I make sure she's safe.*

I didn't respond because there wasn't anything left to say. She had left and now she would pay the consequences unless she was actually sick. My instincts told me she was faking it, and I believed my gut. I sat back down and gave the men a tight smile.

"Gentlemen, I think we need to wrap this up, but I

enjoyed having you as my guests tonight." That was a lie. I couldn't have cared less. "Since I'm leaving early, why don't you guys have another couple of rounds of drinks on me and we'll have a follow-up meeting later this week." That got their attention.

I wrapped up things with the bill and within minutes, I was heading to the exit. Rob pulled up as I was exiting, and I opened my own door before he could get out and sat down in the back seat. "Tell me everything."

"Well, sir, I was standing at the front door and Anais came out looking flustered and asked if I could take her back to the apartment because she wasn't feeling well. I made sure she got upstairs, and I contacted the security team before I drove back to you."

"Thank you," I said, and I pulled out my phone to send a text message.

My fingers were suspended over my screen as I tried to figure out what to type. When was the last time I checked in on someone when they were unwell? Years?

Me: *Is there anything I can get you?*

I watched for the signs that she was typing back, but there were none. Should I tell one of the guards to go in and stay with her until I get there?

No. I'd be there soon, and I could take care of this then. Yet I continued to stare at my phone, speculating what had happened to her to cause her to leave.

I replayed the events of the night while I waited for Rob to navigate us through traffic. Her mood shifted when Jon and Will appeared, as if she hadn't been expecting others to join us. Had she thought this was a date? It didn't help when Jon talked about her job as if it were a speck of lint on his suit that he had just flicked off. His dismissal of her profession had angered me, but I knew I had to keep a level head. Going off the deep end and shoving him up against the wall would have felt good in the moment, but there were other options at my disposal.

I tapped my fingertips on my knee and tucked my phone back in my pocket. Now my focus was on getting back to Anais and taking both of our minds off of the transgressions that had taken place tonight.

9

ANAIS

I saw Damien had sent me a text message and nearly dropped my phone in the water. I couldn't recall Damien ever asking me how I was. My world revolved around him, filling his needs and desires, not the other way around.

Was that really true? It seemed as if he knew what I wanted before I knew, at least, when it came to my sexual desires. The struggle we both had for dominance outside of the bedroom was another matter entirely.

When I entered the apartment, I decided that a soaking was in order to ease the tension in my muscles. I clipped my hair up and stepped into the warm oasis as I thought about the high hopes I had for the evening. Those hopes were ruined by Jon and by me for setting expectations for tonight that I shouldn't have. Now I was filled with anxiety and turmoil as I debated how to respond to Damien's text message. A few seconds later, I typed out an answer.

Me: *I don't need anything. Thanks.*

I washed myself before I sank lower into the massive tub

and almost felt guilty about enjoying this luxury. It should be illegal to have a bathtub this nice. I watched as the water swirled around with every movement I made, and my mind floated away, wondering what would happen if I was as free as these ripples. It was only a matter of time before Damien stormed into his home and demanded to know what made me leave dinner, but my answer wouldn't be simple, and I didn't know if I was ready to have that conversation.

I heard the front door slam. Warning lights blared in my head as I had mere seconds to prepare for the onslaught about to be thrown my way. I felt my body tense up, and no amount of warm water in a relaxing bath was going to stop it.

"Why couldn't the traffic be heavier right now?" I mumbled.

My eyes drifted toward the closed bathroom door. I wished I had locked it before stepping foot into the tub, but I also realized that chances were a locked door wouldn't have stopped Damien from finding a way inside. Plus, I could already imagine him saying something along the lines of this bathroom was his, as was I, and how dare I lock the door. Seconds turned into minutes, which felt like hours, as I waited for the doorknob to turn and for Damien to charge in here, like a bull on the run, but he didn't. I was taken aback. Was he attempting to keep me on my toes?

My question was left hanging in the air because I finally saw what I had been expecting: the doorknob slowly turned. I held my breath as I wondered what his entrance would bring.

Damien let himself in but didn't cause a scene like I had been expecting. He seemed subdued.

"You could have at least knocked."

"And there's the smart-ass mouth I love sticking my cock into."

I rolled my eyes at his cheap shot. If he thought that was going to get a rise out of me, he was wrong. "Don't you have something more important to do? Like go buy another company or something?"

"I probably could have done that if you hadn't left." I refused to feel guilty for leaving a situation where I didn't feel comfortable, although he might not have realized that. "Buying another company can wait, but this can't. Why did you leave?"

"I didn't want to be in the same room as those assholes anymore. I don't appreciate being talked to that way." When he said nothing right away, I thought I had crossed the line, but at that point, there was no reason to hold back, and he was keeping me from relaxing in this tub. "You can leave now."

Instead of moving, he took off his suit jacket and threw it across the top of the toilet bowl and began unbuttoning his sleeves, all without taking his eyes off me. I could clearly see a vein in his arm as he moved, and as strange as it might have sounded, it was one of his most erotic features. The devilish look in his eyes told me he was thinking of something, and I knew it was wicked. Damien constantly kept me on edge because I couldn't read his facial expressions or him. This was his way of keeping his opponent off balance.

"You were there when I handled it. Neither one of them will ever talk to you that way again."

"Yes, but I didn't need you to do that."

"Jon also won't ever work with anything related to any of the Cross subsidiaries again."

I sat up fast, causing the water to splash out of the tub. My once-covered chest was no longer hidden behind the bubbles, putting my breasts on full display for Damien's eyes to peruse.

"But I've found a way to put you to work for me."

"There's always a catch with you, isn't there?" I could see my comment stung based on the way his eyes shifted away from me, but it didn't take long for him to zero back in on me.

"Get up."

"Damien, I—"

My words fell on deaf ears and his crystal blue eyes stared back into my own wordlessly telling me he didn't want to hear my objections. The hunger in his eyes increased as our stare down continued, and I blinked as I stood from the tub as gracefully as I could, feeling the heat from his eyes as he watched the water cascade down my body. When my eyes made their way back over to him, I found him holding out a thick, white, fluffy towel. It had been on the towel warmer when I walked into the bathroom. The warmth of the towel provided a soothing sensation that left my body once I stood up.

"You have six minutes to finish up here, and I want you naked on the bed when I return. Wear your hair down."

His cocky reassurance kept me on edge now, just as much as it had when we interacted at the Project Adoption gala, which felt like a lifetime ago. I'd be lying to myself if I said that his words hadn't turned me on, but it was more than that. It was his presence, his aura when he entered the room. The heated gaze that traveled up and down my body both when he knew I was watching and when he didn't.

Figuring I had nothing to lose but everything to gain, I

dried myself off, tossed the towel in the hamper, and rubbed lotion on my body. I removed the clip from my hair, allowing it to flow down my back and shoulders like a river running wild. With one last glance at the mirror, I turned off the light and walked out of the bathroom.

I strolled into the bedroom and was greeted by the same sight that I had left before I entered the bath. It was as if Damien's presence had been a mirage, and the only thing that told me it had been real was the lingering scent of what could only be described as Damien. I'd always thought most men smelled the same, but Damien had a unique scent that did things to me I couldn't always explain.

I climbed on the bed just as the bedroom door opened, signaling that Damien had reentered the room. I looked over my shoulder at him and found him staring back at me, a finger of whiskey in hand. He leaned on the doorjamb with his feet crossed.

"This is a welcomed sight." His words made my cheeks warm due to how uncovered I felt. The position I was in left nothing to the imagination. "I'm shocked you listened to directions, Spitfire, but I'm very pleased. The last time you played with yourself in front of me was done to prove a point. This is strictly for pleasure."

I looked up at him through my lashes and swallowed. The last time I had played with myself in front of him was when I'd first come to his mansion in NoHo and had threatened to order a vibrator in order to please myself. I hadn't been this exposed then, and I only had to fondle my breasts, whereas here I knew he wanted to take it many steps further.

"And that's what I want you to do this time. Lie down on

your back, your legs bent at the knee and spread shoulder width apart."

I did as he said. I made my way up to the pillows and rested my head before getting into position, taking my time to prolong the inevitable.

He followed up with, "Play with yourself."

I had a feeling this would be his request and to my amazement, I wasn't opposed. I had never had someone watch me bring pleasure to my own body, but there was always a first time for everything. My hand, which had been resting beside me, moved to touch my breasts, and I watched him as he looked at me, his eyes concentrating on the motions I was making. With one final squeeze, my hand left my breast and slid down my stomach, past my belly button and reaching my thighs. His eyes followed me every step of the way and I knew I was driving him as wild as I felt.

I let my fingertips dance along my thighs, and it took a couple of seconds before they made their way to my mound. I played with my trimmed dark curls before my fingers touched my clit.

If I wasn't in tune with my body and didn't know that I was aroused, the wetness that I felt when my hand reached my center would have told the tale. I heard a moan leave my lips as I played with my clitoris, a sound I hadn't realized was sitting on them. My eyelids grew heavier as I tried to keep my eyes on Damien. I wanted to watch his reaction, to see if he was getting closer and closer to the edge.

I found him clutching the glass of whiskey. I wanted to tell him he should probably put the glass down before he cut himself, but I couldn't say the words. Almost as if he could read my mind, he walked away from the door, placed the glass down on the dresser, and walked back over to the door to close it. That was when I made my move. I took my finger that had been rubbing my clit and stuck it between my folds.

Damien let out a small groan that sounded as if he was trying his damndest to restrain himself. His sound and his apparent desire to watch this show encouraged me to continue. Plus, I wanted this now more than anything.

I added another finger and increased my tempo and my eyes drifted closed, fully immersing myself in the pleasure my fingers were giving me. I heard something in the background, but I didn't care.

"Stop."

His voice was throaty, but I couldn't. I was too far gone. My finger rapidly moved in and out of me. My hands stopped when I felt a dip in the bed, and I knew I wasn't alone. I pulled my fingers out of myself and opened my eyes to find Damien kneeling on the bed, completely naked, stroking his cock.

"Do you enjoy making me lose control?" His question was a rhetorical one as he leaned forward and grabbed the hand that had been pleasing me. He stuck my index finger in his mouth and groaned. "I need to taste you again, but right now, I need to be inside of you. Open wider."

I did as he requested and shivered with anticipation when I felt his condom-covered dick at my entrance. *Had I tuned out him ripping the condom package?* The seconds felt like minutes as he rubbed himself against my folds, teasing me as anticipation continued to build.

"I swear if you don't—"

Apparently at that moment, he'd had enough of waiting too, because he entered me slowly with a groan. A breathless sigh left my lips when he started picking up pace, and I was grateful that I didn't have to tell him to do so or how much more I wanted him. After all, I wasn't sure I could form the words. I met each one of his thrusts with ones of my own as we both feverishly tried to go over the edge.

A fog took over my brain as our movements fell into a primal rhythm. His growl lifted the daze I found myself in. It took a moment before my gaze found his, but when it did, I found devilishly hungry eyes staring back at me. It was as if his eyes had put me under a spell because I couldn't look away. Not now. Not ever.

He took that opportunity to switch up the pace once more, going even faster, as if it was a matter of life or death.

"Um—ah, I'm so close," I screamed, not recognizing my own voice as he plowed into me.

His motions became more erratic, and I screamed again, the sensations from everything proving to be too much for me to control anything. My climax hit me like a ton of bricks, and it didn't take him long to follow behind me, roaring as he rode the waves of pleasure.

The only thing that could be heard were our labored breaths as we tried to calm our racing hearts. Damien rested his head in the crook of my neck as we slowly but surely found our center of gravity once more. After a few more seconds, he dragged himself out of me and I immediately missed the feeling of our union.

We looked into each other's eyes, but didn't say a word, sharing a moment without making a sound.

10

ANAIS

"I need to get out of here," I said to Ellie. "Being cooped up in here is bad for my mental health." Having a scheduled video call with her was nice, but I needed more.

"I'm sure being stuck in the house is just the tip of the iceberg when it comes to the list of things affecting your mental health. I mean, you saw your father get shot, for goodness' sake."

"That's true, but I feel like I'm going insane because I'm stuck in here. Heck, I'd even take going into the office as long as it meant I got to leave here for a few hours. I think I'm going to see if I can go down the street to pick up some groceries."

"Doesn't he have people on staff that do that?"

"Yes, but I'm more than capable of doing it myself and it would get me out of the house for a bit. Hell, I'll even take shopping online and picking it up at this point; I want fresh air."

"Do it. Speaking of getting out of the house, I want to

come back to New York City. I miss my life. I miss being able to go to work, hanging out with you, furthering my career. A lot of what I hear now is my parents complaining about said career."

"I know and I miss you, but we both know you need to stay in Jersey for now. We don't know when this shooter might strike again." Guilt crowded my brain again because Ellie had to uproot her life because of her connection to me. "I'm so sorry that this has happened."

"Stop apologizing. Outside of me having to be careful and have a security guard, my parents are pretty happy that I'm home now. They've been trying to convince me to stop being a massage therapist, but other than that it hasn't been bad."

Her words did little to extinguish my guilt. I should have taken more care of Ellie's feelings considering all the changes she was having to make instead of focusing on me.

"How are you holding up?"

"I didn't expect to be back at home with my parents, but seriously, I didn't realize how long it had been since I visited them. At least I had somewhere to go until this blows over, so I can't complain too much."

"Yeah. Thank you for willingly doing so. I know this isn't what you wanted, but right now we don't know what is going on. Hopefully, Damien finds out some more information about what's going on and then you can come back here, even if it means having someone watching the apartment while you're there."

"I hope so too because I miss being in the city. I felt like we were finally hitting our goals and that there was nowhere for us to go but up. Now, it's like we've hit a stumbling block.

Side note, has Damien asked you anymore about his new 'engagement' deal?"

Damien's proposal felt like a boulder sitting on my shoulders. I felt as if I was going to have to give him another part of myself in order to fake this relationship with him.

"Not really. It's been four days since he told me about this fucked up deal, and he hasn't mentioned it yet, so I haven't said anything either. He's given me some space and that's been helpful, but honestly, I've been more focused on my dad than anything else. I'm still visiting my parents every day."

"How's he doing?"

"Good. He should be released within the next couple of days as long as everything continues going well. I'm happy about it, but it also makes me nervous because someone tried to hunt him down. What if they try again?"

"True. Any word from the police on any evidence they've found?"

"Not much yet, but it's still in the early stages. They've been keeping my parents up to date on their progress and my mom summarizes it for me. Damien has little faith in the police being able to solve this case, so he told me that he is putting feelers out there for more information. My key priority is figuring out how to keep both of my parents safe once my dad's out of the hospital."

"Is that something you could talk with Damien about?" Ellie asked before I heard shuffling on the other end.

"Eh. I probably should and—"

"Hold on a second."

I could hear Ellie talking to someone in the background as I waited for her to return to our conversation. I tapped my fingers on the table as I waited for her to return.

"Oh shit."

"What's wrong?"

Ellie glanced to the side before looking at me. "My mom was on her computer and found a post on social media related to your father."

My heart dropped. "Can you send me a link to it? Does the post have any interaction?"

Ellie reached off screen and when she moved her hand back into frame, she was holding a phone. "Not much interaction but, I'll send you the link."

"Thanks so much."

"I'm going to sign off because I have a couple of things I need to do around the house, but I'll be in touch. Sending you the link now."

"Ah, okay. Well, I'll talk to you later."

"Yep, I'll text you. Let me know if anything changes."

"Sounds good. Bye."

I ended the video chat and thought about what I should do next. I could start trying to catch up on work, but to be honest, I didn't want to. After all, I had taken time off so I should be off. My phone buzzed and I clicked the link that Ellie sent me. It had the same headline as the post that I found several days ago, with a link redirecting to the blog. *Who was trying to make sure that news of this spread?*

"Screw this," I mumbled before I grabbed my phone and sent a quick message to Kingston. I needed to get out or all of this was going to drive me up a wall.

Me: *I would like to go grocery shopping. Is that possible? There's a store only a couple of blocks away. We could walk there.*

Kingston: *Ask Damien about that.*

I growled. There was no way I was asking Damien for

permission to leave the house. I had no problem informing him about what I was going to do, but asking him? Hell no. Maybe there was a compromise that could be reached. I would let him know I wanted to go grocery shopping, and that the security team was organizing it, and that would be it. Instead of sending him a text message, I risked him not being in a meeting and called him. A phone call would be easier and quicker.

"Anais," he said after the phone rang once. The way he said my name gave me goosebumps.

"Hey, I can't remember if I shared this with you or not, but someone has been trying to connect the dots about my father's shooting to his money troubles. I'll send you what I've found. Probably should be told to the police too."

Damien was silent for a moment before he said, "Yes, send it to me."

"Should we be concerned about it?"

"No. I'll look into it. Anything else?"

I told myself to take Damien at his word, but I still had a nagging feeling about it. Getting out into the fresh air would help with that. "Also, I'm going to go grocery shopping to get out of the house. I'll take security with me."

"You know you can just order delivery or have Lucy grab it?"

I rolled my eyes. No shit. "I know that. I've done that. But that's not what I want to do right now. I want to breathe in some fresh air and stretch my legs a bit. Just being out in society instead of trapped in this bubble that has become my life would be beneficial to me."

He was silent for a moment and I wondered if he was going to say no. Technically, I hadn't asked him, so even if he said no, I would just say screw it and find a way out of this building.

"Fine. Kingston will be waiting for you. There's a credit card with your name on it in the guest room."

"Damien, I can pay for my own groceries." I hadn't paid for food since my father was shot because Lucy did most of the cooking for us, and if I needed a snack, the kitchen was usually fully stocked. My goal was just to grab a couple of things and to get out of the house. I released a sigh of relief. Although I had to go out with security, at least I'd be outside mingling with society. I wasn't going to use that credit card, however. "Well, I guess I'll talk to you later."

"Okay." He paused again. "Anais?"

"Yes?"

"It's a good thing you asked instead of just going. I would hate to have to spank that ass, even though we both know you like it when I punish you."

Before I could snap back at him that I was telling and not asking him, I heard a click on his end, letting me know that he had ended the call.

"Asshole. Asshole!" I exclaimed.

I took a deep breath before I headed into the guest room to change to go outside for something other than traveling to the hospital. It didn't take me long to throw on a sweatshirt and walk back out to the living room to grab a pair of sneakers and a coat.

Once I was dressed, there was a knock on the door, and I grabbed my purse and smiled at Kingston before we headed to the lobby. I closed my eyes as I enjoyed the feel of the cool crisp breeze on my face that lightly whipped my hair. Carter joined us and together, the three of us walked down the street. The number of people in the store reminded me of how I used to view this as a chore just a month ago. Now, it seemed like a treat.

Carter offered to push the cart for me and once I was done gathering the items I wanted, I got in line with the two beefy men on either side of me. When we were the next people in line, Carter made his way up to the conveyor belt, and Kingston stayed behind me as I hung back a bit to check out the snacks and candies that were stationed right before the register. That was when I saw the magazine.

A blurry picture of me and him entering his apartment building was on the cover. The text in bright yellow letters said: **Settling Down? Damien's Journey to Love.** I stepped back in shock. Kingston saw my face and stepped over to look at the tabloids. I heard him mumble a cuss word under his breath, but he did his best not to draw attention to us. It would be hard to recognize me, but clearly Kingston wasn't taking any chances. He grabbed a couple of the magazines and tossed them onto the conveyor belt, and I walked over to Carter so that I could pay at the register. When the magazines moved toward the register, Carter raised an eyebrow and scanned the covers without reaction. Carter monitored me until I was finished paying for the groceries, which Kingston grabbed.

Once we were out of the store and back on the street, both Carter and Kingston scrutinized the general perimeter of where we were and the three of us hurried back to the apartment. As soon as we got inside, Kingston pulled out his phone and tapped the screen, before pressing it to his ear.

"Hey, Damien. We have a problem."

11

DAMIEN

I put the phone down and knew Anais was raging. I'd tossed that comment out there before I hung up because I knew that it would get her.

A knock on my door dragged my attention away from the conversation. "Come in."

Melissa, my assistant, opened the door and stepped inside. "Your next meeting is here. Also, Jon Moretti has called twice already today."

"Send Quincy in and if Jon calls one more time, direct the call to me." Jon had already sent me a couple of emails since the dinner, and I told him that I would get back to him when I had time for a follow-up. Clearly, he hadn't gotten that message.

Melissa spun on her heel and left the room and was soon replaced by Quincy. I wrote a note to myself and Quincy stood in the doorway for a few moments. I already knew this meeting would be a quick one. I slowly placed the pen down on my desk and looked up at the frumpy man in front of me.

His eyes darted around my office, refusing to land on me. *This would be too easy.*

"Have a seat." I gestured to the seat in front of my desk.

He scrambled over to the seat, further wrinkling the suit he had on. "I'm not stepping in to settle a score that you have with the Vitale family." Quincy came into my office last week on behalf of his boss asking if I would step in to help squash the increased tensions between the two factions.

First, I was already annoyed that Quincy's boss hadn't asked me himself, instead wasting my time with his underling. Second, this wasn't my business, and they could figure it out amongst themselves. If it crossed into my business interests, then we would have a problem.

"I can't go back to my boss with that answer."

"Excuse me?" I stood up from my desk and folded my hands over my chest. I saw a slight tremble run through his body as a smirk grew on my face.

"I—I didn't mean to offend. It's just that—"

"Then take my message back to your boss before it changes to one that ends with you in a body bag on his doorstep."

Quincy scurried out of my office just before my phone rang.

"Kingston."

"Hey, Damien. We have a problem."

12

ANAIS

Kingston and Carter worked on trying to figure out how the photo was taken while we waited for Damien. The desire to throw a meal together in order to add some normalcy back to my life went out the window. Would things ever be normal again?

I read the articles while we waited, and it relieved me to see that it was pure speculation and that they didn't know my name. However, they had officially forced me to take Damien's offer.

Someone was playing a game and was backing me into a corner. If the blog post and this tabloid leak were telling me anything, it was that it would only escalate from here. This person knew enough information to release as much information as they wanted when they wanted, and it was only a matter of time before my father's money woes would be announced. I didn't know if Monroe Media Agency could weather that storm.

The front door swung open, drawing all of our attention to Damien as he stormed in. He stopped in front of me and studied my face, searching for signs I was in distress. Once he was satisfied, he turned to the other men in the room.

"Where's the tabloid?"

Carter handed him the paper and Damien snatched it out of his hand. When he was done searching for whatever he was attempting to find, he tossed the paper on the counter and looked at Kingston.

"I want to know every rumor that is circulating and what every tabloid in this city is investigating within the next twelve hours. This wasn't supposed to leak until I said so. Anais and I have some unfinished business that needs to be taken care of in the meantime." His eyes were trained on me and I knew he was referring to the proposal.

"No problem."

A shrilling ring disrupted the room, causing Damien to snatch his phone out of his pocket.

"What?" Damien barked, adding to the tension in the room.

The heaviness in the room made me realize I was scared. Scared of the unknown, scared of what all of this meant.

"I think you can handle this and if I'm wrong, you'll pay the price." His simple words sounded deadly, and I felt bad for the other person. "Send an update to Dave and he'll get everything to me." He ended the phone call with a resounding click and turned his attention to me.

"Anais and I have to talk."

Carter and Kingston needed no further prompting to leave. Damien's gaze followed them out the door until it was closed and then all his attention was on me.

"Who's Dave?"

"A private investigator who works for Cross Industries."

I stored that tidbit away for later.

"It was only a matter of time before something like this leaked."

"I know." I looked everywhere but at him. His stare was burning a hole through me, one that might never be repaired.

"And it's only going to get worse."

"I know," I repeated because I knew how the tabloids worked. Once someone latched on to the story, there was no way they were letting go.

"I've let you go without answering my deal, but that ends now."

"Yes. I'll accept your proposal." The words came out low, and I almost wondered if he had heard them because he said nothing. "I'll sign the contract."

He was in front of me in two seconds flat, leaning down to take my lips. The kiss was powerful. I felt a slight shiver course through his body when my hands landed on his chest. When the kiss broke, I groaned, but before I could protest, he bent down and lifted me up in a fireman's carry.

"Where are we going?"

"Bedroom. Now."

The Neanderthal in him came out in full force, and I couldn't deny that his words made me wet. He didn't stop until he deposited me on the bed. I shifted my position and moved my hair out of my face to look at him.

"Pants off."

My heart shuttered as he tossed his cellphone on the bed and started rolling up the sleeves of his shirt. I never thought that would be sexy, but here I was growing more and more aroused as fingertips migrated to my own clothes. His eyes were staring me down as I unbuttoned my jeans and lifted my hips so that I could push them down. He took over, pulling them down as my hands moved to my thong.

"Did I say to remove that?"

I shook my head and stilled my hands.

"It seems you still have a problem with following directions. That will need to be addressed." He tugged at my pants until they were off and dropped them. "Spread your legs."

I hesitated for a moment before I did as he demanded.

He leaned down on the bed and planted slow, tantalizing kisses along my left ankle. Damien made his way up my leg, building anticipation about what he would do next. Once he reached the inner side of my knee, he took his time planting kisses along the sensitive skin of my leg before he reached the apex of my thighs. His piercing blue eyes studied my mound and the scrutiny caused me to grow wetter. Damien's hand moved to the thong and lightly played with the lacy fabric. "I'm glad you're wearing one of the pieces I bought you."

My eyes widened. Surely, he hadn't picked out the new clothes himself. I figured he had tossed the task at his stylist to do the work for him. Before I could ask him more, I felt his fingertips run up and down my seam before moving the thong aside. As he bared my pussy, I swallowed any words that I might have said as I waited for what he was going to do next.

Without warning, Damien dove into my pussy, letting his tongue dip into my warm slit before settling on my clit. Before I could blink, my hands were in his hair, attempting to anchor him to his current position.

"Fuck..." I said as my voice trailed off. My body was in an uproar over the sensations that his tongue was causing. My head thrashed from side to side as Damien continued his assault, leaving me dazzled. Thinking straight was out the window, and my only thoughts were of when an orgasm would overtake me. My body was getting closer and closer when a ping from Damien's phone briefly brought me out of the moment.

"Ignore it," Damien said, lifting his mouth from my sex before going back down on me.

The phone pinged again, and Damien growled, "Read it."

I grabbed the phone and said, "I don't know your passcode." My words came out in a breathy whisper. Damien's mouth was short-circuiting my brain.

"Four, eight, nine, zero."

I typed in the numbers as a moan left my lips. As I tapped the zero something clicked... "That's my birthday."

Damien lifted his head and looked at me. "Maybe I just like those numbers."

"That's not a coincidence."

He shrugged. "Read the text." And he went back to work.

Once he started back up again, my head flew back.

"I'm going to stop eating your cunt if you don't read that text message."

That was enough to make me look at the phone again.

"It's from Kingston. He said, 'We're outside.'" My voice was breathless as I relayed the message.

Damien gave me a wolfish grin and said, "Looks like we need to speed this up then. Tell him to give us five minutes."

I texted Kingston and said, "You think you can get me off in five minutes?"

"Three."

Damien sucked on my clit and started alternating his motions, driving me to the brink.

"Damien, I'm getting close."

He took that as a sign to back away and stuck his fingers inside me to bring it home. His eyes were glued to me and I felt my eyes roll toward the back of my head.

"Yes!" I cried as my eyes shut and I felt my orgasm take over. My heart was racing, and it took a couple of seconds before I could focus on opening my eyes. His fingers were still inside me, and only when I opened my eyes did he slide them out and stick them in his mouth one by one, licking them clean.

"If we had more time, I would lick you clean before we fucked, but I need to go talk to Kingston and Carter. If you want to join, feel free, but I'm sure you need time to recover."

He was correct.

DAMIEN PULLED BACK the covers and slipped into bed next to me. Kingston and Carter had just left for the second time that evening. I didn't join them this time because I didn't trust my legs to be steady enough to carry me into the living room due to Damien taking me to his bed and setting a world record in getting me to orgasm.

I couldn't deny that I loved the way he made my body feel, but that was where I drew the line. *How would my life change with Damien's ring on my left hand?* I shifted the thoughts of Damien growing tired of me that plagued me throughout the time we had spent together and decided to bask in the happiness that I felt right now.

I looked over at him, half expecting him to leave the bed once more, but he didn't. Instead, he was playing with my hair, twirling it around his finger. My head was resting on his chest and I felt completely at ease as I listened to his heart beating in my ear. I had something that I wanted to say, yet the soothing sound of his heart was lulling me into silence. But it needed to be said.

"I want to go into the office tomorrow."

His hand stopped moving, almost making me wish I hadn't said those words.

"Why? Don't you have everything you need here?"

I sat up, pulling the sheet and comforter with me, and looked at him. "Damien, I do, but it would also be helpful for me to at the very least stop by. Also, my getting back to work would show leadership. I've been off for a few days, but maybe going back into the office would help me take my mind off of things." I knew throwing out the word "leadership" might give me the upper hand since Damien owned a company and was all about leading by example to get results. "Plus, who knows how long my father will be out. I need to do my part to help Vicki make sure that Monroe Media Agency keeps a steady drumbeat."

I could see him tossing ideas back and forth in his head. "Sure, but I want you to bring security with you."

I knew a caveat was coming, but it didn't mean I had to like it. "Fine. Are we two for two on compromising?"

"I guess we are." He couldn't stop the smirk that appeared on his face, even though I wanted to throttle him because sometimes he made things more difficult than they needed to be, but this time he was more reasonable when I had thought it might be a tug-of-war. What he said made sense and this was a compromise I was willing to make. It made sense given everything that was going on.

"Speaking of security, did you hear anything else about the case?"

"It's been difficult to find all the people your father associated with even with the details he gave to you. Thanks for the information you gathered."

"It wasn't much of a hassle. I currently have all the time in the world, and I could find some information from calendar invites. That definitely isn't everyone he associated with, because sometimes he forgets to put meetings on his calendar. As you and I both know."

Damien's smirk proved he knew I was alluding to when we first met because my father hadn't noted his meeting with Damien on his calendar.

Dad was still in the dark about Damien's involvement in his care and now in investigating the incident. I knew hearing Damien's name would only upset him. It surprised me that my mother had kept everything a secret too, but I was happy about it because I wasn't ready to see the disappointment on Dad's face, along with the pain he was still in. But if having his help meant getting closer to whoever had shot him, I knew it was worth it.

The next thought that bubbled in my mind almost made me want to vomit. I knew that no matter what, I had to tell my parents about my engagement and Damien's involvement in all of this. Even if the engagement was fake, my parents needed to hear it from me before they heard it from a reporter. I took a deep breath before I said the words that had been stuck on my tongue, refusing to budge.

"I'm going to break the news that we're engaged to my mom and dad, and I'll tell him you're trying to help him find out who did this. Maybe that could help." I made air quotes with my fingers when I said "engaged." I never imagined that I would be indifferent about getting engaged, but given the circumstances, I knew I had to protect myself.

Damien said nothing, but I could feel his stare without looking at him.

"Is that a problem?" His voice was dangerously low, daring me to say something he wouldn't agree with.

"No. I just don't enjoy lying to my parents, and this is a pretty big lie."

"Would this make the lie seem more real?" He mimicked my earlier motions of putting invisible quotes when he said "lie."

He backed away from me and rolled over to get out of bed. My eyes stayed on him and I tried to hide the fact that I was checking him out. His body looked like a work of art when he moved with each aspect carefully sculpted to perfection. He didn't bother putting on his boxer briefs as he strolled across the room to where his slacks had ended up. He pulled something out of them and walked back over to the bed. It was a small, velvety black box.

"Is this what I think it is?" I asked, my heart pounding in my chest as I studied the small black box. There was no question what was inside it, unless he was trying to pull a prank.

"Open it." His voice made me jump, although he hadn't said the words very loud.

I did as he said. A sparkling diamond ring stared up at me. It was an emerald-cut diamond that I knew had to be quite a few carats on a white gold band. It screamed expensive, yet I was disappointed.

"It's beautiful?" My statement came out as more of a question. I glanced up at him and his eyes were focused on me, his expression once again unreadable.

He pulled the ring out of the box and I reflexively held my left hand out. When he placed the ring on my finger, it fit perfectly, but sadness flowed through my veins. It was a stunning ring, but it wasn't what I had in mind, nor was it my style.

My heart had always been set on something smaller no matter the type of stone with smaller diamonds on the band. This wasn't it.

I tried to find what words to say as I stared at the foreign object on my hand. I felt like an asshole for judging this ring so harshly, but it just wasn't me. Then again, this wasn't a real engagement, so why did it matter?

"Thank you." My fake smile was in place when my eyes drifted back to Damien. I found him studying my face, so I further pushed up my lips to convey a more sincere smile, hoping that I didn't appear as if I were grimacing in pain. "I hadn't thought about a ring being needed to seal the deal."

Damien stared at me for a second longer, before he said, "You will wear this to show everyone that you are mine. The ring on your finger will give people something else to talk about besides your father's shooting."

"Okay."

"You hate it."

His words took me by surprise, and I knew my face fell, showing the truth of the matter.

"No, it's fine." I gave him a small smile. *It's a fake engagement that I will have to endure before everything gets back to normal.* "I promise, it's fine."

Damien stared at the ring, moving it back and forth with

his finger before looking back at me. He stopped to tuck a strand of hair behind my ear, and I stopped myself from leaning into his touch.

I cleared my throat and said, "Please don't tell me how much this cost. If you do, I'll never wear it because I don't want something that could be a down payment on a mansion."

He chuckled. "Okay, I won't," he said before he went back to playing with the ring on my left hand.

I smiled at the light-hearted moment before I moved my hand and pulled the covers off of my body.

"Where are you going?"

Damien's question stopped me, and I turned to look at him. "Back to the guest room."

"Stay."

The gravity of that one word weighed on my shoulders as I placed the covers back where they were and laid down on the bed, just before Damien brought me into his arms.

13

ANAIS

I paced as my eyes darted back and forth between the clock on the wall and my laptop sitting on the coffee table. It was only a matter of time before I wore a hole in the soft carpet beneath my feet. I glanced at the door that led to Damien's office before my eyes drifted back to the computer. Hopes that Damien would be able to sit in on this call had been dashed because a last-minute meeting pulled him away.

Dad was doing better since he had been released from the hospital. Damien set them up in a secret location in the Hamptons to keep them safe while Dad recuperated. Damien told me he was tacking that on to the list of things I owed him.

My nerves flipped around in my belly and I debated rescheduling, but I'd rather rip the Band-Aid off now. Another glance at the clock told me it was time. I walked over to the couch and sat down on the cool black leather seat before starting a video call with my parents.

"Hi, Mom. Hi, Dad."

"Sweetie, how are you doing?"

I snapped my head back with my eyes open wide. Mom's voice came through my laptop's speakers loud and clear, with an emphasis on loud. My fingers rushed to turn the volume down and I bit my lip. I rubbed my hand down the side of my denim-clad leg. I could do this. "Good. How about you guys?"

"Not too bad, not too bad." My father's words temporarily put a grin on my face. He looked much better than he had when he was in the hospital after his surgery.

"How is physical therapy going?" I asked.

"Pretty good. Things are moving slowly, but there have been no setbacks so I can't complain too much."

"That's good. You'll be flying around like Superman in no time."

My father chuckled. "If only."

"What's going on with you, Anais?"

Mom's question didn't surprise me. She could always tell when something was wrong, which made it hard to get away with some things as a teenager. "Well, I was hoping to tell you both something."

My nervousness increased and I placed a hand on my knee to stop it from bouncing. I was scared to say the words, because there was no question what Dad's reaction would be.

"I'm engaged."

"You're what?" Dad's eyes widened as he tried to connect the dots. "We didn't even know you were dating someone."

My mom beat him to it. "Is it to Damien?"

Dad's eyes shot over to her before looking back at the screen.

I looked down at my left hand, eyeing the large diamond

on it, glistening under the light. I felt as if I was about to be scolded even though I was a grown woman. The emphasis on Damien's name must have summoned him from hell, I mean his office, because he sauntered into the room right then. He looked as if he had no cares in the world.

"You told me you weren't dating him when I showed you the photo someone sent me." Dad saw him come into the frame and once he sat down beside me, Dad's face turned even redder. "You."

Mom put a hand on Dad's shoulder, trying to calm him down, but he continued.

"Damn it, I knew you were dating him, even when you tried to deny it. But now you're getting married to him."

I didn't know how much redder his face could get. And my mom's eyes were darting from the computer screen back to my father and back to the screen.

"Dad, it's fine."

"No, it's not fine. I warned you about him. Do you know what type of man he is? This is not who I envisioned you would marry."

His words pissed me off and I snapped, "That's not your decision. I can marry whoever I want. This is not a discussion. I was informing you about what was taking place. The news might leak sooner rather than later, and I thought my parents might want me to tell them rather than find out by reading an article online."

I immediately regretted raising my voice, but I couldn't take it anymore. I knew my parents cared about my well-being and wanted the best for me, but they also needed to understand that I made my own decisions, even if I couldn't tell them the real reason this was all happening. A heavy hand landed on my knee, and a gentle squeeze told me that Damien was there supporting me even if he had said nothing. I appreciated him letting me fight this battle. Any intervention from him in this moment would cause an even bigger rift with my parents.

"Anais, I don't think—" Dad stopped speaking when Mom cleared her throat.

"Well, James. Who do you think is paying for all of your medical costs?"

I let out a small gasp at Mom's interruption of Dad's rant. That didn't stop her from continuing.

"Damien stepped up to help in a time of need, and we are grateful that he did. We wouldn't be where we are in your recovery without him. So, thank you, Damien," she said. Mom turned back to me. "Anais, I'm very proud of you, and I look forward to getting to know Damien when we are all back in the city. Now, I'm going to let you both go because we should let your father get some rest. On behalf of both of us, I want to say congratulations."

"Thanks, Mom. Before you both leave, I have a quick question for Dad." I glanced at my father briefly before I continued. "Dad, did you reach out to anyone else for money when Monroe Media Agency was doing poorly?"

Dad didn't answer right away, and I could tell he was debating whether he wanted to respond. "Other than the banks that wouldn't lend the money to me, no."

I shared a look with Damien before turning back to my parents. "I'll talk to you guys soon."

"Okay, bye, sweetheart."

That conversation was shorter than I had originally

planned, but I knew I had done the right thing by telling them now in case the story broke.

"That call seemed to go well." Damien stood up and walked over to his office door.

"You're hilarious."

"That is not something I have ever been accused of." He paused before he continued. "I have a surprise for you."

"Oh, really?" I closed my eyes briefly and moved my head back and forth, trying to release some of the tension that gathered there in anticipation of this phone call. When I opened them, I found him looking at me. His stare sent a tremble throughout my body and made my nerves go haywire again. "What is it?"

He walked back into his office and grabbed something wrapped in a red-and-white striped gift bag with red tissue paper flowing out of it. I don't know what I was expecting, but it wasn't this.

"I was...inspired by a performance you gave several days ago."

I opened the bag and dug into tissue paper and yelped. Any words that I had been considering left as my mouth fell open. It was a sleek black vibrator. I could feel the heat rising in my cheeks.

"You can only use it when we're together. Just when you think you're getting to the point of no return, I can shut it off and make you beg me to let you come."

His words should have pissed me off, but they made me want him even more. I was becoming a masochist. "Thank you? Do you want me to use it now?"

Damien slowly shook his head. "In fact,"—he reached over and took the device back—"I'm going to hang on to this for safekeeping. I want you to be thinking about this small, yet powerful toy constantly, because you'll never know when I'm going to pull it out and use it on you."

And once again, with Damien Cross, it always made sense to expect the unexpected.

14

ANAIS

The next morning, I found myself in the shower, repeating the same mantra I had started the night before: there was no way I was falling for Damien Cross. We had a deal and once whoever shot my father was caught, we would go our separate ways. It should be that simple, but it didn't feel like that was the case anymore. I kept reminding myself that I had agreed to his proposal so that he would protect me and my family. Nothing more, nothing less.

I stepped out of the shower and got ready for what I suspected would be a busy workday, and I couldn't contain my excitement. After I finished, I applied red lipstick and took one more look at the outfit I'd chosen to wear, mentally giving myself final approval. The black coat lying across my bed would offset the brightness of the red sleeveless blouse that I had on. The dark denim jeans and red heels that matched my shirt perfected the look. Since the pieces came from the clothes that Damien had bought me, I knew it looked expensive.

I grinned to myself as I put my coat on because I was

ready to get out of the house and be around my coworkers again. Something I didn't expect to miss was Edward's phone calls. Edward worked for CASTRA, one of Monroe Media Agency's bigger clients. I hadn't heard from him since I had been out on leave, and I would never give him my cell phone number because he would definitely abuse it. As I bent to grab my bag, something caught my eye that was sitting on Damien's, and I guess now my, dresser. I picked up the box and tugged out the expensive ring and studied it again. It still wasn't to my tastes, but I kept hoping it would grow on me. After a quick mental debate, I put it back in its black velvety box and put it in a safe place. The thought of wearing something worth a fortune was too nerve-wracking, even if I had Kingston with me.

I put the ring away and grabbed my bags and walked to the front door. When I opened the door, I found Kingston walking my way and gave him a small smile before I turned to lock up. When we arrived in the lobby, Kingston walked up to Carter and chatted with him briefly while I found Rob and followed him out to the car.

"Oh, you parked outside instead of the garage. This is an upgrade."

Rob chuckled. "I figured this might save time." Rob opened the car door and I got inside. Once Rob closed the door, I saw Kingston open the passenger door and fold his body inside while Rob headed around to the driver's side. When he pulled away, my eyes were drawn to my phone, trying to answer as many emails as I could on the way to the office.

Most of them were about my father and asking how he was doing and if there was anything more they could do for me. My team had taken on part of my workload while I was away, and I wrote a note to myself to do something for them as a thank-you. My phone buzzed in my hand, making me jump slightly as a text message notification popped up on the screen.

Damien: *Everything should be ready for you at your office.*

Was this his way of wishing me a good day at work? What did he mean by everything should be ready for me?

Me: *What are you talking about? We should be there shortly.*

My mind wandered, and I began thinking about Damien. I vaguely remembered him getting out of bed this morning to get ready for work, and I hadn't heard from him since. I assumed he would probably get caught up in the work he was doing and would reach out later. What annoyed me was that I felt myself longing for another text message because he'd been sending more lately. They went from telling me about something Dave found to him "just checking in". I knew he got regular updates from Kingston and Rob, so it had come as a surprise when he'd started checking in on me directly.

Damien: *Kingston's team swept your office. Everything looks good. Left a small gift for you too.*

His message came just as Rob pulled up to my office building. Rob came around and opened the door. I gathered my things, thanked him, and looked up to find Kingston waiting for me to follow him. He had a book bag on his shoulder that I hadn't noticed earlier.

"Are you going to sit in my office all day and watch me work? I hope you brought something in that bag to keep you entertained."

"I have a few things."

I felt bad that he had to babysit me for several hours, but

he wasn't complaining, and Damien was paying. It wasn't lost on me that Damien had his cousin guarding me, and although he hadn't said anything about it, I had a feeling it was because he trusted him the most. I'd also gotten him to talk a bit more, so at least I had someone else to talk to when he stopped by and checked the penthouse to make sure that everything was okay. Other than that, it had just been video chats with Ellie and my parents when Damien wasn't around for the last week.

I walked into the building and Kingston and I got into the elevator and patiently waited for it to reach my floor. Once we arrived, the employees who spotted me suddenly hushed as I walked to my office. I smiled when I saw what was sitting on my desk. An assortment of my favorite snacks were in a basket, except it was from a company that was known to provide high quality items at an expensive price. Someone had been paying attention to what I ordered when Lucy went grocery shopping. I made a note to myself to thank Damien, and as I set my things down, someone knocked on the door.

"Anais, hi. How's your father?" Vicki strolled in with a container full of mail. She placed the basket on a chair before turning to look at me.

"He's doing better. Thanks for taking over here while we made sure he was settled." Even though I knew they were safe, it didn't stop the worry I felt constantly. It also seemed that the New York Police Department had reached a dead end on finding out who exactly had committed the crime. I stopped myself from thinking about how my decision to become "engaged" to Damien might have led to more emotional pain for my dad.

"Of course." Vicki paused and gestured to the container.

"Here is everything that came for you since you've been gone." Kingston grabbed the container from her. She stared at him wide-eyed for a couple of beats before turning back to me. "We have a few meetings today. The most important is in about fifteen minutes if you're up to it."

"Yes, I had it on my calendar. Dad might try to call into it and listen. He's apparently going stir crazy, although the doctor recommended he rest."

That made Vicki smile. "I've known your father for over twenty years now and never have I known him to slow down, so I wouldn't expect anything less."

I gave her a smile back. "I'll see you in the small conference room soon."

With that, Vicki left me and Kingston alone once again. "I guess you don't need to come to this meeting with me."

"I'm going to sort through the mail while you're gone to make sure everything is safe."

He had an excellent point. I sat down at my desk and took my laptop out of my bag. It wouldn't hurt to read the meeting's agenda so that I was more prepared, and it felt good to get back to some of the normalcy I craved.

"WELL, THAT WENT WELL," Vicki said as we walked out of the conference room.

"It did, and Dad was happy to have been able to participate." I didn't want to mention that I thought he sounded weak, but that's to be expected.

I looked away from Vicki for a second when I saw Jake, a

member of my team, coming toward us. He gave me a tight smile and a wave just before he approached us.

"Is it okay if we chat for a second? Sorry to interrupt," he added quickly.

"That works. I was just wrapping things up with Vicki."

"I'll see you both later." Vicki nodded at both of us before walking past Jake and heading down the hall.

"What's up? Edward?" I guessed. When Jake nodded his head, I rolled my eyes before I could stop myself. "What happened now?"

"He's been a bit unhinged. More so than usual."

Jake's words alarmed me. "What do you mean?"

"Ever since you've been out on leave, he's been calling multiple people nonstop trying to get in touch with you. He's stepped things up a notch."

"Did he say why?"

"No, he claims that the only person who can help him is you."

I sighed, but it wasn't a surprise. I tried to keep my face neutral as thoughts ran through my mind about whether we should consider him a potential suspect in Dad's shooting. It was something I would raise with Kingston when I got back to my office. "Well, okay. Thanks for telling me. Anything else you need?"

"No. We debated calling the police, but we figured there wasn't much they'd be able to do anyway because he hasn't threatened anyone. He's just...very insistent on talking to you."

"Right. I'll see what I can do. I'm sorry you had to deal with that."

"It's no problem. I'll catch you later."

My feet started moving before my mind could process the information. My first thought was to reach out to Damien to tell him what I had found out even if Kingston was there. It surprised me that I wanted to tell him first, but I didn't have time to examine my feelings. I was pulling out my phone to call him just as I rounded the corner to reach my office when I stopped in my tracks.

"What the hell is all of this?" I asked, causing everyone in the room to stop moving except Damien, who stopped for no one. Why was Damien here? He looked at me but continued talking on the phone. He wrapped up his phone call as I closed my door. Although my office was a decent size, it felt cramped with Damien and Kingston in it.

"Someone sent you a welcome back package that wasn't very inviting."

"Wait, what?" My eyes shifted between Damien and Kingston, hoping that one of them would fill me in on what was going on. Neither one said anything, so I continued, "Someone sent me a package that was enough to drag you out of whatever meeting you were in to come down here? What was in it?"

I chided myself at how my voice wavered. I walked over to my desk to look inside, but just before I could, Damien answered, his words chilling me to my core.

"A gun."

"You've got to be shitting me." I leaned forward, peering into the box. Lo and behold, a gun was in the box. The black gun stared back at me, mocking me. The chill that was running through my bones got even chillier. I was even more determined to get to the bottom of this. "Is this the gun that was used to shoot my father?"

"Tests would need to be done on the pistol to verify whether or not it is. But if I had to take a guess, I would lean in that direction," Kingston said from where he was leaning on my desk, hands crossed over his chest. I closed my eyes and opened them before walking around Damien and sitting in my chair.

"Someone has to be taunting me."

"You mean taunting us," Damien chimed in from where he was standing. "Someone is fucking with what's mine and I will get to the bottom of it."

"Yeah, sure. Whatever," I mumbled, not wanting to deal with him referring to me as his in front of Kingston. It was the first time he had said it in front of another person. I gazed at the box on my desk once more and jerked forward when something caught my eye. I grabbed a pen from my desk to shift the paper that covered the gun in order to get a better look at it, while not contaminating any evidence further. The gun was surrounded by what looked to be magazine articles, many of them relating to Damien. Someone had confirmed that we were together.

"Damien?"

"Yes?"

"I think the news of our engagement is about to come out."

"Really? Because no one would know it because you aren't wearing your ring."

I rolled my eyes. "Check the box, Damien."

Out of the corner of my eye, I saw Kingston do a double take as Damien came closer to the box. Clearly someone else hadn't been told about our "upcoming nuptials", and I didn't think he had seen the ring since Damien gave it to me.

Damien stared at Kingston for a moment, almost daring him to say something, before he looked at the piece of paper that my pen was currently holding up. He muttered a curse before he pulled out his phone once more. I assumed he was going to call someone, but before he could, it rang.

Kingston and I waited while Damien listened to the caller. "Melissa, I'm going to put you on speaker, okay? It'd be best since all parties that will be affected are present."

He hit a button and placed the phone on my desk and said, "Continue talking."

"Mr. Cross, I've just gotten a couple of calls from reporters asking for a comment on your upcoming wedding. Is there anything I should say to them? I considered referring them to Kate but wanted to talk to you about it first."

I raised an eyebrow at Damien and wondered who Kate was. I looked back at the paper in the box and almost growled. Silly me had secretly hoped that maybe whoever had sent the box might have created the fake tabloid headlines about my father's money woes themselves to show us that someone else knew my father's secret. That could still be the case, but it was clear that someone had provided some information to the press. I looked over at Damien for a second before turning my attention back to his cellphone. I seemed to be the only one panicking about this.

"Refer them to Kate. I'm going to get her on the phone right now and we'll have this sorted quickly. Thanks, Melissa."

"You're welcome." With that, he hung up the phone.

"Who is Kate?"

"My publicist."

As Damien fiddled with his phone, I said, "Is there anything I can do to help? You know I—"

"Right now, we need to call Kate and get her recommendations. If she can't take my call, I'll have Melissa set something up. If I had to guess, she'll recommend we do a taped announcement and blast it everywhere."

"—am the head of social media for a company that specializes in communication. Not that that clearly means anything..." I said, but it seemed as if Damien hadn't heard me. I glanced over at Kingston and I thought he had, but he wasn't saying anything.

I sighed, frustrated with the fact that my opinion clearly meant nothing in this situation despite my expertise. Although I thought traditional forms of media were useful, the public often consumed their news online, and to me it made sense to create a social media plan of attack as well. "I'm going back to the penthouse." I made sure I said it loud enough so there wasn't any way that anyone in the room could ignore me.

I walked over to my desk, slammed my laptop shut, and left with Kingston trailing behind me. If Damien wanted a ride back to his home, he would have to meet us downstairs before Rob pulled away.

15

DAMIEN

The ride back to the penthouse was mostly quiet. Anais barely gave me the time of day and I would fix that with her later once I got everything sorted with my publicist.

I had questioned my sanity in offering to get engaged to Anais in exchange for my protection of her and her family, but it'd seemed like a good idea at the time. Now it seemed to do nothing but cause more headaches, and I wondered if it was worth it. None of that deterred the fire that burned deep inside of me that was determined to consume her. All of her.

I walked into this deal treating it like a business arrangement, but maybe that was the wrong approach. My thoughts were interrupted when my phone buzzed in my hand, alerting me to a message.

Kate: *We can tape the announcement tomorrow at noon at your apartment. The crew will arrive to set everything up at 11:00 a.m. and we'll do a quick run-through beforehand, so you don't have to worry.*

Me: *Okay.*

Kate: *And give me a warning about this next time, would you? You've already caused too many gray hairs.*

I shook my head but didn't respond. I turned to Anais and watched her staring out the window, looking like she had when we went to my parents' after the mansion break-in several weeks ago.

The gun being delivered to Anais's office caused a fury inside me that I couldn't explain. It also meant that we needed to confirm to the world that she was mine as soon as possible. The sooner people knew she was now under the protection of the Cross Empire, the better for her and her loved ones. I knew there wasn't much I could have done. Someone could have carried the box into the building, and it wouldn't have been caught because Kingston's team wasn't allowed to do a broad canvass of the building. If the owners had given us access, I could have done more to protect her. That would all change when I made plans to buy the entire building.

"We're taping the engagement announcement tomorrow."

I watched as Anais looked over at me and her expression changed from confusion to downtrodden. The fire that she usually had in her eyes was extinguished. I wished there was some way I could wipe the look off her face, but I knew there was none.

Anais didn't speak until we were upstairs in the apartment alone. "I could help you handle this. I work in marketing for crying out loud."

"There's no need because I'm taking care of this."

The growl that left her lips would have been almost comical if she didn't look as pissed as she did. "You know, you're a real asshole."

"That's accurate."

"Damien."

The tone of her voice forced me to look at her.

"You know what, never mind."

I didn't know how it could be possible, but she looked even more dejected than she had in the car. She went into the master bedroom and closed the door, putting another barrier between us.

THAT EVENING, I walked into a building nearly identical to my own and nodded at the person working the front desk. The elevator was already open, so I boarded and pressed the button for the floor I wanted to go to. I checked my phone to see if Kingston had texted anything but saw nothing. He and Carter were back on duty watching over Anais since I had left. I'd knocked on the bedroom door to let her know where I was going before I headed out, but she hadn't replied so I left. The ride to Broderick's didn't take long and soon I was standing outside of another door, knocking on it.

The door flew open, and Broderick looked me up and down before he said, "It's about time you got here. This whiskey won't drink itself."

"I'm sure that you'll have no problem on that front," I said as he let me in, and I closed the door behind both of us. We walked into his kitchen and as I waited for him to pour the whiskey, I looked at some of the changes he had made to the place.

The exposed brick throughout the loft apartment gave it an industrial look. It differed completely from the more modern style I preferred, but it fit with his personality. The dark furniture complemented the style well.

"So, what brings you here, big brother?"

"I want to talk through something with you."

Broderick and Gage and I usually talked about issues we were having, so it was natural for me to discuss this with them. Gage couldn't join us because he was busy tonight.

He dropped the glass down on his counter a little harder than necessary. "You want me to give you advice? Normally it's the other way around. About what?"

"Anais."

"Well, talk."

I gave him an abbreviated version of what had occurred with Anais over the last few weeks without diving into the contract specifically. "Wait, you asked her to marry you?"

"I did."

"And she said yes."

"She did." *Eventually.*

"Please tell me you told everyone that you're engaged and I'm the last to find out."

"Yes, although Kingston found out...unconventionally. I waited to tell you because I knew I could tell you in person. I told everyone else before I headed over here."

"Good, because I know Mom would have been hurt."

I nodded. "At least it went over well, Mom and Dad. You know, Mom is ecstatic to have me finally settling down."

"I'm happy for you, man. I knew you liked her a lot."

I crossed my arms over my chest. "Really?"

"Yeah. Why haven't you been to Elevate recently? You used to be there at least twice a month."

He had me there. I had stopped going to Elevate. The

club didn't have the same appeal it once did unless Anais was with me. "Maybe I'm becoming a prude in my old age."

Broderick's head fell back as he let out a belly laugh, and I did my best to hide the smile that was threatening to come out.

"Hardly. First, thirty-four isn't old. Second, the day that you become a prude will be the day that hell freezes over." He cleared his throat before he said, "What's with the change of heart? You once said that it was pointless to settle down with one woman."

"You agreed with me."

"Not the point. You texted me asking to come over to have a drink and to get some advice about...Anais. Well, continue."

"I don't know what it is about her. She has me doing these things I said I wouldn't do, and I can't get her out of my mind. Like I researched a company that could deliver some high-end treats for her so that it was at her desk when she arrived at work when I should have been paying attention to a conference call yesterday."

Broderick smirked. "You know, for all the money and knowledge you supposedly have, you can be an idiot sometimes."

I glared at Broderick before tasting the whiskey. Why was I here again? I could've gone to any random bar in the city. Oh, because my brother had a place nearby and all the alcohol money could buy and would take great joy in doling out advice to me. Plus, it was someplace Anais wasn't. My life had revolved around work for so long and somehow in the short time since Anais had entered my life, she'd taken over everything. Everywhere I looked, I found something that triggered a memory of her. The scent of her shampoo would linger in the bathroom after she showered, and the aroma lingered in my nostrils even when I left. Her presence seemed to be everywhere in my life, and I wasn't sure how to feel about it.

Given how much was changing in my life, I wondered if hell freezing over was in the cards sooner rather than later. Anais constantly kept me on my toes, even though I tried to make sure I was always one step in front of her. But I was used to being three to four steps in front of my opponents. Did I still consider her a conquest that needed to be conquered? When we had gotten together, my goal was to break her, but now things felt different.

I normally didn't give a damn about anyone outside of my family, but that position flipped when Anais entered my life. She was becoming a part of that circle as well. Speaking of women that we liked....

"How's Grace doing?"

That knocked the smile right off his face, and I knew I'd hit a nerve. Grace McCartney was Broderick's best friend's sister and one night after too many drinks, he admitted to having a crush on her.

"So, do you want to talk about how to deal with the feelings you have for her or is there something else? Spare me any of the screwing details, by the fucking way."

I rolled my eyes. I never shared details about my sex life. "She's pissed at me right now."

"That's a shock," he said.

I considered tackling him to the ground for his sarcasm but having to deal with hearing him whine and possibly spilling this smooth whiskey was enough to deter me.

"Do you know why?" he asked.

"There are several issues. I can't figure out what she wants."

"Did she tell you what she wanted? Usually, women have a way of telling us exactly what they want and need, but it can go completely over our heads."

Those words rang true. I could without a doubt say I knew what she wanted in the bedroom. Her interactions with me and the way I could make her body crave mine told me I did that well. Outside of the bedroom, I had no clue. I thought about my interactions with Anais. Her strength and desire to do things her way caused friction between us sometimes, but I didn't want it any other way. The women I had dated in the past let me get away with anything, and those relationships, if you could call them that, got stale quickly. Anais was a change I very much wanted and appreciated.

"I hate that I'm about to say this, but you're right. I haven't been doing enough listening. She wants to go out and interact with the world, but I keep her locked up in the penthouse, partly due to the murder attempt on her father."

"What can you do to fix that? Why don't you take her on a date?"

My eyes widened before I could stop it. "I don't do dates."

"Well, looks like you do now."

I cleared my throat. "Everything else is going well, but it's weird. After living on my own for so long, having someone to return home to is strange. It's taken some getting used to, yet I wouldn't have it any other way."

Broderick raised an eyebrow. "And you needed to get engaged to get her to live with you?"

The doubt hanging off of his question was justified. "I did it in order to pull her under our umbrella. I, and by extension we, can give her full protection from the media, and from whoever shot her father."

By the look on his face, I could see that Broderick wasn't buying it. "Couldn't you have done that without asking her to marry you?"

"What do you mean?" I asked, trying to stall for time and think of an excuse. I knew what he was going to say, and I had thought about it before.

"You didn't need to bring her into our circle to protect her. We have enough connections and people who would want to help. We also know enough people who owe us a favor or two to help stop just about anything, and it's only a matter of time before our guys find who shot her father."

"I wanted a way to lock her down so that I could fuck her whenever I wanted." The words sounded harsh coming from my mouth. As the lie fell from my lips, I knew I was opening myself up to be called out by him.

"Now that's the brother I'm used to." That was what I was hoping he would say. "So, how did you propose? Was it romantic? Did you pull out all the stops?"

"Trying to take notes so that you can do it sometime soon?"

"Nope. This is purely curiosity."

I rubbed a hand on the back of my neck because I could have done a better job. I had put little thought into it because I figured it wasn't worth the hassle. Determination to get her by any means necessary had forced me to pull the trigger without a plan. That wasn't usually my style. "I told her this is what we're going to do and bought the ring."

It was Broderick's turn to roll his eyes. "And you wonder why she's pissed at you."

I kept going as if he hadn't said anything. "I bought her a ring big enough to be seen from space that most women would squeal over, but I could tell by her expression that she was disappointed. She lied about liking it, and I wanted to call her out about it, but honestly, it was a conversation I didn't want to have."

"Do you think it was because of the ring or because of the person doing the proposing?"

"You realize that the only reason I'm not about to throw you through that brick wall is because Mom would kill me... but it might also be worth it."

"You came here. I didn't ask you to. I think you need to come to terms with the fact that she's different, and you can't treat her like everyone else. Show her that she means more to you. Show her that you value her opinion. Based on what you told me happened earlier today, with the rollout of this engagement, you steamrolled over her and her thoughts instead of taking them into consideration in a field where she has the expertise, not you. She probably feels like this is demeaning."

"I didn't—" But I had. I vaguely remember when I was trying to contact Kate, she wanted to talk to me about something, and I didn't give her the opportunity to. Then, before I came here, I brushed her off again.

"Let her shine because she will. She'll let you know what she wants and that will help you go about figuring out how to give it to her."

"Interesting advice from someone who hasn't been married or had a long-term relationship in a long time." There was no way I would admit that what he said made sense.

"I'm good at helping other people, but not heeding my own advice. I've seen this work in real time."

"What?"

"Dad does this with Mom all the time. He takes a step back and lets her tell him what she wants, and he gets it for her. Now I'm not saying that this is a one-size-fits-all approach and that there isn't more to it, but we have a prime example of how it has worked."

I glanced at him before finishing the last of the whiskey in my glass. I wouldn't admit it out loud, but he was right.

It was time to fix this.

16

ANAIS

Damien mentioned he was heading over to his brother's house tonight, allowing me to have the apartment to myself, but what could I do? I wasn't allowed to leave, so I did the only thing I could—chat with Ellie. I poured a glass of wine and started a video call.

"Hey!"

"Hi, sorry I'm a little late. What's going on?"

Ellie waved me off. "Don't worry about it and everything is okay. Can't complain other than what I've talked about before. How about you? How's your dad?"

"Okay... Dad is out of the hospital and they are staying in the Hamptons for the time being." I sighed and pulled my hair into a ponytail. "So, the whole engagement thing is a go."

"You accepted it?!"

I shrugged my shoulders. "Yep."

"How did he propose? Can I see the ring?" Ellie bounced up and down in the chat window.

"Hold on a second. Let me go grab it and I'll explain."

I grabbed the ring from its hiding spot and sat down in

front of the computer to show her. I took the ring out of the black box and held it up to the screen.

"Anais, that ring has to be worth a fortune."

"I know. I'm nervous to even wear the thing because I'm scared I might lose it. The proposal wasn't exactly romantic."

"Are you kidding me? This man has all the money in the world, and he couldn't at least try to make his proposal romantic?"

"I guess not." I shrugged to hide my feelings about how hurt I was. It would have been nice for him to have handled this a step above a business transaction.

"The ring is gorgeous, but it's not you."

"I know."

Ellie sat back in her chair in what I recognized to be her parent's living room. "I have a bad feeling about this. I didn't think you'd actually do it…"

I sighed. "I know… but I didn't have much of a choice. Damien told me if I wanted to protect myself and my loved ones, which includes you, we needed to be engaged to pull it off, so I did it. I'm happy I did too after what happened today." I filled her in on the package that was delivered to my office.

As I retold the events, I felt the anger that started as a low simmer turn into an untamable fury. Between someone having the audacity to mail what was more than likely the gun used to shoot my father to my office and me not having a say in the rollout of this fake engagement, especially given my expertise, I was fuming.

"Well, you've had a busy few days. I still can't wrap my head around this. Damien Cross concocted a scheme that involved appearing to be engaged. Mr. Forever Bachelor has no problem appearing as if he's coupled up. What gives?"

"That's the question of the hour." I could have filled in the blank about his obsession with me being his, but I refrained. "I assume he gets something out of having me on his arm."

"Of course he does! I could go into detail about how wonderful you are."

I chuckled, but it did little to change my mood. It was time for me to act. "Ellie, I just remembered something I have to do. I'll text you later?"

"Sounds good. I'll talk to you then."

I ended the video call and jumped up. I marched over to Damien's office and opened the door without thinking about it. There was a chance that I wouldn't find what I was looking for, but it was worth the shot. I was tired of waiting for the police, Damien, or Kingston's company to find a lead. I was going to find it myself.

I flicked on the light switch and walked over to his desk. I hoped to find something that might be a report or a file from Dave, but their correspondence might be all digital or he might keep the paperwork at his office.

No. He would want to keep the information close. But where would it be? I held my breath as I searched the file cabinet to the left of his black wooden desk but found nothing.

A sudden noise made me freeze in place. I listened for a moment. The only thing I could hear was my heart pounding in my chest at the prospect of getting caught searching through Damien's things. My heart rate slowly returned to normal when I realized I was still alone, and I quickened my pace. When I began the search through his desk drawers, the first thing I found was a solid black box. I lifted it up, briefly examining it and determined it was a safe of some sort. It didn't look big enough to contain any files and needed a fingerprint in order to open, so I placed it back where I found it and kept searching. When I reached the last drawer, I found a bunch of manila folders stacked neatly inside. *Is this it?*

I picked up one file and flipped it open. A quick scan of the documents in it confirmed I found what I was looking for. This must have been the intelligence that Dave found for Damien. The folder contained data on Jon Moretti, the man I met at dinner with Damien. The detailed report gave information from his physical stats, his mafia ties, to places he frequented, to the last person he slept with. Had Damien dug up information on him because of their business dealings or because of his disregard for my profession? Shifting the folder out of the way, I opened the next one and gasped.

It was a file that contained a report on my father. I read through the information that was all too familiar, but there were some surprises there too. "Dad got arrested in college? Didn't know that..." I mumbled as my brain processed the information in front of me.

The folder also contained a brief overview on my mother, but it was clear that he didn't consider her to be as high of a priority on his list.

My eyes widened slightly when they came across something I should have been expecting but couldn't have prepared myself for. Damien had gathered information on me as well. Most of it was the basics, which made me a little queasy. But what startled me were the photos that were included in the folder. I had vague memories of when they were taken based on what I was wearing and the background of the photos, including one that had been taken in the early fall. It looked like Dave had trailed me for a while. My thoughts flew back to the person who Ellie and I thought we saw taking our photo. *Did all roads lead back to Damien?*

I flipped through the pages again and found a document detailing my father's shooting. Reading the words forced me to relive the horrors of that night. Even though I tried to fight it, the thought that Damien could have done this seeped into my mind again. But why would he step in and provide care for my father and protect me and my family? To swoop in and be the hero?

No, that wasn't possible. Damien was anything but a hero and thrived on exuding power. But I wondered if the address that was highlighted in yellow on the sheet with a big question mark to the right of it might provide the answer that I was looking for. I was positive it was the bar near my apartment and that would put it close to the building where I saw the person trying to take photos of me through my window.

17

DAMIEN

I stepped into my black Audi R8 and felt the horsepower under my fingertips when I started the car. Before I could drive off, my phone rang.

"What do you have for me, Kingston?"

"You have time to head over to one of the safe houses?"

"Is it important?" My mind drifted back to Anais and how I wanted to get back to her quickly.

"It's about the Monroe case."

"You should have started the conversation with that. Send me the address and I'll be there as soon as possible."

"WHAT'S GOING ON?" I asked as Kingston and I entered the house and stood in the entryway. The inside was reminiscent of the home Anais was taken to after James was shot. The lack of material possessions made it clear that no one lived here full time. "Is Carter watching over the penthouse?"

"Yes. Said he would alert if anything happened."

I nodded. "On the way over here, I got an update from a contact affiliated with the NYPD. They still don't have much other than chasing down some leads that have gone cold. Interviews at the scene of the crime haven't helped much either. What did you find?"

"Anais told me about the erratic behavior of a client, and I looked into him. Edward loves talking to Anais directly, but nothing I found made me think that he's involved. Also, none of James's associates."

"Is there any good news?"

"Yes. I tracked down the person responsible for the blog post connecting James's shooting to his money troubles. He's sitting in a room down the hall. I wanted to wait for you before we began."

I knew exactly what he meant by "began". I gestured to the door down the hall and stalked toward it, not waiting to see if Kingston was following behind me. It was about time we got some answers.

Without thinking about it for a second, I opened the door with a resounding bang. The man that was sitting at the only table in the room jumped. One of Kingston's men who was watching over the suspect hadn't bothered to tie him up. I wouldn't have pegged him as someone who had any chance of escaping anyway.

"What's your name?"

"Gary."

"Gary, what do you know about James Monroe?"

"I—I uh don't know anyone by that name." He licked his lips nervously, before looking at every person in the room. *Was he weighing his options or worried about who would strike him first?*

I saw something flash out of the corner of my eye. Kingston was at my side and he handed me his phone. A quick glance at the screen told me he had pulled up the blog post on his phone. I placed the phone on the table in front of the man, making sure not to take out my anger on the device. "Do you own this blog?"

"Uh, yes. Yes, I do." His voice was more shaky than before.

"Then tell me why you made this post." I pointed at the phone.

"Look, I don't want any trouble."

I slammed my fist into the table, making him jump again. "The more you stall, the more trouble you'll be in. And I don't think you want my kind of trouble. Why did you make this post?"

The man in front of me didn't respond.

"Kingston, do you have a gun? Cause I'm about to put a bullet in this fucker's leg. Maybe that would encourage him to talk."

Control was long gone. I saw how devastated Anais was after her father was shot. That image would forever burn in my memory. James and I didn't have a great relationship, but I knew we both wanted to give Anais what she wanted. In this case, I knew it was getting justice for her father. *I was fixing this.*

"Okay! Okay! I said I didn't want any trouble." He took a deep breath and said, "I received a tip that it was a developing story, okay? Anonymous source, I couldn't find any information on the email address, but I thought it could be my big break if this person was right. So, I wrote a blog post and tried to make it go viral. It would be hard because James Monroe isn't a huge celebrity, but I knew that him and his company were well known in certain circles so that it might be picked up by someone bigger than me and I would get credit for it."

Although rage flowed through my veins, I knew inflicting pain on him would lead to a bloody mess that someone had to clean up. No, that energy would be better served for someone who deserved to meet their end.

"Tell us the email address, show us the email, and you can be on your way."

"That's it?" Kingston asked.

"That's it. He doesn't know anything else and won't be posting anything else about this. But if this person emails him another tip, I'm sure he'll be in touch. Right?" I raised an eyebrow at Gary.

"R—Right. Of course, I will! Anything for you guys."

Kingston and I left Gary and one of Kingston's men in the makeshift interrogation room. "You took it easy back there. The Damien I know would have shot first and asked questions later."

"I'm just ready to get home."

"I understand that. I did a quick search on the email address Gary gave us. He's right nothing popped, but I didn't expect it to."

"Makes sense due to the wide array of numbers and letters that were in the address."

"If I find out anything else, I'll let you know."

"Good."

I walked out of the house and sat down in my car, once again ready to head back to the penthouse. That was until I received a text that appeared on my dashboard.

Unknown Number: *You should do a better job of protecting what's yours. Would hate for you to lose it...again.*

18

ANAIS

I t didn't take much effort for me to throw on a pair of sneakers, a hoodie, a baseball cap, and a coat before I looked through the peephole. I knew that Kingston or Carter would sometimes stand guard outside my door, but I'm sure they relied on only authorized people being allowed to the penthouse. What they weren't counting on, was me leaving the building.

I opened the door a crack and found that the coast was clear. I hoped that if there were any hidden cameras in the hallway, no one was watching them. As I got on the elevator I immediately clicked the softly glowing "G" before the elevator started its descent. I felt as if I was holding my breath, waiting to get caught at any minute and dragged back up to the ivory tower that had become my home.

With a shaky hand, I slid my phone into my coat pocket and watched the numbers continue to go down. I hoped that no one else would call for the elevator, delaying my reaching the garage level. When the doors opened, I didn't stop to think as I quickly made my way through the garage and up

BRI BLACKWOOD

the ramp toward the street level. I had guessed that Kingston and his men weren't guarding the garage door because the only way you could get up to the penthouse from the garage level was if you had a special badge. I was right.

Once I hit the street, I waved down a taxi and rattled off my home address. I lowered my hat and sank lower in my seat as we zoomed away from the building that had become almost like a prison to me. I knew it was a privilege to say that, but it didn't change how I felt about the situation. When I knew for sure that I had made it away from Damien's home undetected, I double-checked that I had silenced my phone before putting it back in my coat.

The ride to my apartment was mostly silent, only the soft melodies from the taxi driver's radio guiding us along. When we hit the block where I was shoulder-checked, I let out a quivering breath. I might be onto something in the quest to find out more about who shot my father and why he was a target.

"Right here is good," I said, alerting the driver so that he knew to pull over. Once I drew out the money I had stuffed into another pocket in a hurry, paid the driver and exited the vehicle, I put my hands in my pockets and hurried down the street. I looked at my building, almost longing to go up there. It had been days since I'd been there, and the urge to hide away in my apartment was real. After all, it had been my safe haven for many years and once again, that had been taken from me.

I turned my head to look across the street and found the place where Ellie and I saw what looked to be a man with a camera aimed straight for our window. Thankfully, it was a quiet night, and no one was trying to stalk my place from what I could see. Did it make sense to go check that building out first? No, I wanted to follow Dave's lead; my eyes and thoughts were zeroed in on the bar that was just a few feet away. Why had Dave found this bar to be significant?

Hidden Tavern was a bar that I had been to a few times over the years to blow off some steam after a long day at the office. Its rustic aesthetic was nothing to write home about and would be considered a "hole in the wall" to most people, but the drinks were cheaper than a lot of places and the atmosphere was more relaxed. As I approached the front door, it swung open and a couple of young twenty-some-things left the establishment, one holding the door open for me as I entered.

I found a seat in the corner of the bar. I brought my hat down even lower, because I was worried someone might recognize me, but knew the chances of that were slim. What had Dave been watching here that made him highlight the address?

I scanned the scene and didn't note anyone who looked suspicious in the establishment, but that didn't mean the person or thing I was looking for wasn't there. I tried to look as natural as possible, while not drawing attention to myself as I people-watched. Ever so often, I would glance up at the television, as time shuffled by.

"Ma'am?"

I looked up and found a woman in jeans and a black T-shirt with Hidden Tavern written across the heart.

"Yes?"

"This glass of Merlot is for you along with this note."

"But I didn't order—" My words trailed off as I read the letter.

Nice to see you on the outside again. You didn't heed my warning to watch yourself.

It was unsigned.

"Who ordered this?"

"The only thing I noticed about him was that he was tall. Didn't get a good look at his face because he was wearing a cap, similar to yours. Oh, wait. His voice was peculiar. Almost like his vocal cords were damaged. He left right after he paid for your order."

That was all I needed for me to know that it was the man who shoulder-checked me weeks ago on my way home from work. I grabbed the note and jumped out of my seat, before running toward the front door. I swung it open and looked both ways down the street. How did I keep missing this man? Chances were, he hopped into a waiting car and sped off into the night. I mentally kicked myself for not staying completely focused on my surroundings, but who's to say how long he stayed before he ordered a drink for me.

Speaking of a car, I watched as a black vehicle with tinted windows drove up, stopping in front of me, only a few feet away. The passenger side window slowly lowered, and I gasped.

"Let's go."

My heart slammed into my throat and my eyes went wide when I saw Damien staring back at me from the driver's seat. His expression told me I better watch what I did and said, because the results might not be pretty. How had he known where I was?

"Get in, Anais."

The curtness of his words and the way he said my name had a chokehold on me, and for a moment I couldn't move.

When he started to open his door, I begrudgingly did as I was told. As soon as I was safely in the car, Damien sped off, barely giving me time to put my seatbelt on.

"How did you know where I was?" I tried to remain as calm as I could, knowing that my reaction could cause the situation to escalate.

"Your phone." He said it as if I had just asked him what the weather was.

The dam that contained my emotions broke. "You're tracking me? Do you get off on stalking a grown woman?"

The sneer Damien sent my way almost made me want to swallow my outburst. Almost. "Hardly. I had a feeling you might try to pull a stunt like this and asked Kingston to make sure I could track you via your phone. And I was right."

"How would you even know to look for me? Did you go back to the penthouse and see that I wasn't there?"

Damien's hands clenched and unclenched the steering wheel before he answered. "No, a text message warned me to watch what belongs to me or I might lose it. Currently tracking down who sent it."

"I don't belong to anyone."

He placed his hand on my denim-covered knee. The heaviness of his hand provided both comfort and control, reminding me of the contradictory feelings I felt for him. "That's where you're wrong, Spitfire. You do belong to me. I love the way that falls off the tongue."

"Fuck you." I threw the note at the center console between the two of us.

"What's that?"

"Looks like you're not the only one who got a message from a secret admirer. Someone ordered a glass of wine for me while I was at the bar and the server delivered it along with this note." I recited the terse letter to him and swore I heard a growl under his breath.

"What were you doing at Hidden Tavern?" He phrased the sentence as a question, but if anyone were to ask me, I would have said it was a demand.

I thought about lying but nixed that idea. "I read some files that Dave left for you in your office."

Damien took what I said in and slowly looked over at me. It didn't take the world's smartest person to tell me there was an inferno throughout his body and he was going to boil over in rage. "And what did you find?"

"That you were keeping a file on me and my parents. This address was listed there, highlighted in yellow. I assumed Dave had questions about it."

Damien didn't answer right away, and his expression remained stoic. "Anais, there are actors at play and events happening that you have no idea about."

"That you won't talk to me about. You are treating me like a child."

"And you're acting out like one." He glanced at me before turning his eyes back to the road. "You will lie low and do as I say. No more sneaking off, but since you failed to do that this time, I can't wait for your next punishment."

19

ANAIS

"Pull out the light blue dress in the corner. That might be a contender."

I looked around and grabbed the dress that Ellie mentioned and placed it on the bed. Damien's stylist had sent over quite a few options to choose from but none of the options felt like me. After all the compromises I'd had to make, I wanted this outfit to be something I felt good in.

As far as I knew, Damien didn't care what I wore because he hadn't mentioned it, nor had he laid out a dress in the guest room. His priority was making sure that we were ready when the crew got here and that there would be no problems while filming the video. He even asked Melissa to come over to the apartment at around 10:45 a.m. to help keep everything organized. He thought it was going to be that busy.

Yet here I was hiding in the guest room closet, trying not to freak out about what was going to happen in just a couple of hours. The three options that Ellie had helped me pick were in front of me, and it didn't take me long to decide.

"You're right. The light blue dress it is."

"Yes!" Ellie said. "I think it's going to look great against your skin tone. Maybe you can see if Damien could wear a light blue tie?"

I snorted. "Do you think Damien would listen to anything I asked him to do?"

Ellie shrugged. "I mean, you never know, but you need to shower and go get ready, so I'll talk to you later. Let me know how it all goes, okay?"

"You got it. Talk to you later."

Ellie waved and ended the video call. I took a deep breath and looked around. This had the potential to be a disaster, but damn, at least I was going to look good doing it.

I headed into the bathroom to start my shower and as I was brushing my teeth, I remembered I hadn't seen Damien much at all today. He had left the bed when I got up and I saw him briefly when I grabbed a bagel and cream cheese, but that had been it. I knew it was only a matter of time before he came in here.

My shower was quicker than normal because I didn't wash my hair, having washed it the day before. I picked out my makeup carefully, trying not to clash it with the light blue dress. Damien appeared in the doorway as I was finishing curling my hair and I knew it was almost time.

"You're wearing the blue dress that you have laid out on the bed?"

I looked at him through the mirror and took a quick second to admire the way he looked before he was completely done up. With his white shirt untucked and unbuttoned at his neck and his hair not yet styled, he looked like he might have just rolled out of bed and threw the nearest set of clothes on. I wasn't complaining, not one bit.

"Yes."

"Okay. Red tie or blue?"

He was asking my opinion on something? That was new.

"Blue. Thought you usually just stuck to black ties, you know, because they're dark like your soul."

I saw his lips twitch, but he said nothing before he left the room. I stared at the place where he'd just been standing before I went back to finishing my hair. Today was definitely going to be an interesting day.

WHEN I FINISHED PULLING myself together, I checked the time. I still had ten minutes to go before I needed to be out in the living room to meet the crew. I took a quick photo and sent it to Ellie to see what she thought.

Ellie: *You are going to knock them all dead. Good luck and let me know when the video is online so I can watch it.*

Me: *Thanks.*

I was going completely out of my way to make sure this farce of an engagement was believable in order to make sure that my family and I remained under Damien's protection. Or that was what I continued to tell myself. But had it become something more?

I took another deep breath, telling myself to pretend to be a blushing bride as I made my way to the living room. When I walked down the hall, my dark blue heels clacked along the wooden floor, alerting everyone to my arrival. When I appeared in the door frame, all eyes turned to me, including Damien's, who was talking with Melissa.

He told Melissa something before he used his long stride to eat up the distance between us. His eyes never left me.

"Perfect," was all he said as he looked at me, admiring my handiwork.

I didn't know if I'd made him speechless, but he didn't say anything else, and I knew I had to break the ice here.

"And I'm not late."

He leaned closer and whispered in my ear, "Yes, but that doesn't mean that I won't punish you later. You're lucky I didn't require you to wear the vibrator."

"I wouldn't have worn it anyway. It would have clashed with my outfit." I gave him a fake smile and he shook his head.

"Keep it up and you'll see what happens the moment these people leave. I didn't forget that I owe you for the stunt you pulled last night."

I didn't have a retort. I was thankful that a producer for the video came to give us a quick rundown of what we should expect from the video. The crew already had everything set up and ready to go. This wasn't going to be an interview, but more of a taped announcement and someone would guide us through a few takes until we got it right.

Before the recording started, I leaned over and asked Damien, "Why don't we just take a photo, post it on social media, and then send it to some of Kate's media contacts and call it a day? You leaking it would drive buzz alone. Then we could have a statement ready to go."

"Because that's not what people would expect me to do." He sat up and adjusted his tie.

I never would have guessed that he really cared what people thought. It wasn't unheard of for him to be completely extravagant and showcase how wealthy he was. My "engagement" ring was a perfect example. It felt like something that royalty would do. In fact, one article that Ellie had emailed me called the Cross brothers, "The Princes of New York."

"Let me do it," I said, watching him mess with his tie. I put my hand on his and pulled it away so I could fix his tie for him. Surprisingly, he didn't stop me. This might have been one of the few times he'd allowed me to touch him without it leading to sex. I figured everyone had their eyes on us anyway, and that this might be him trying to put on a good show in case any leaks happened from the behind the scenes. Actually, that was a pretty good idea.

All I felt was Damien's eyes burning a hole into me as I finished adjusting his tie until it looked perfect, like every other part of him. When I pulled back, Damien grabbed my hand, which had been placed on his heart, and he held it there for a moment. I looked up into his eyes and saw fire shining in them. I heard what sounded like a camera flash and the moment broke.

"Are you guys ready to get started?" the producer asked.

I tapped Damien, who had turned to glare at the producer. I pasted on a bright smile and said, "Yes. Let's get this started, please."

The countdown began and I felt nervous. Worried about perpetuating a lie, worried about whether not being with Damien would put an even bigger spotlight on my family. When it was showtime, I put on my best cheerful voice that didn't sound too fake and told the camera that we were engaged and how excited I was to become Mrs. Damien Cross.

When it was Damien's turn to speak, he said, "Anais is the

most beautiful woman I have ever laid eyes on. I'm not just talking about her appearance, but her soul. She'd do anything to take care of anyone and that was apparent the first day I met her. I can't wait to marry this woman."

He looked at me before he took my hand in his and stroked the ring. It was one of the sincerest moments we'd had in terms of public displays of affection. It almost made me think that this might have been all real.

"And cut." The producer smiled back at us. "Now we're going to do it a few more times just to make sure we've got the perfect shot, and then we can take some photos of the two of you and wrap things up. Do you guys need anything?"

"No," Damien said.

I shook my head. The next few takes were done and as we were getting ready to go up to the balcony to take some photos, I started feeling weird, as though I wanted to get out of there, but that wasn't an option.

"Are you both ready?"

"Yes." I glanced at Damien, who was looking out at the New York landscape before turning back to me. He didn't say a word.

"Hold her hand in yours again, much like you did during the taped segment, and place it here so that the ring is front and center." We adjusted our bodies to fit how the photographer wanted us and stayed that way until she told us it was okay to move. "How about you kiss the future Mrs. Cross?" the photographer asked.

I swallowed hard, then saw the big smile on her lips. She was clearly more excited than the couple to be capturing this moment. I looked back at Damien and I watched as his blue eyes darkened and his stare landed on my lips.

"That shouldn't be any problem," he said before he gently cupped my cheek.

My body felt electricity at his touch. My next breath left my lips just before he laid a sensual kiss on my lips.

"Perfect," the photographer whispered, but if she said anything else, it faded into the background. All that was left was Damien and me kissing on a balcony, in front of the New York City skyline.

We took a few more shots before the photographer said, "That should be good. That's a wrap."

We had been too caught up in another kissing session and it took us a second to pull our lips apart. When we did, I looked up at him and gave him a small smile that he didn't return. He turned to the photographer, leaving me standing by myself for a moment.

He shook the photographer's hand. "Thank you so much for coming on such short notice."

"It was my pleasure. These photos are stunning, and I'm sure you'll enjoy them when I finish and send them over."

The whole point of the photos was to "leak" them several days after the video to give the media something else to talk about. Then we would hopefully fade into the background a bit and be able to go on about our daily lives. Or maybe that was a pipe dream.

I shivered as Damien turned to me and without asking, took off his suit jacket and placed it around my shoulders. That left another good impression on the photographer, who smiled at us once more. If we had our photographer fooled, I could only hope that the public would be too.

ANAIS

I heard a sound play from my phone, alerting me to a text message. I sighed and put down my book.

Damien: *Grab the little black leather dress in your closet and meet me at Elevate. Your security team will be ready to go in an hour. It's time for you to receive your punishment.*

I blinked twice while staring at the message. There's no way he wanted to go to Elevate tonight. Why did he want to go to Elevate when we still didn't know who left us the anonymous messages? Damien hadn't let me go to work since the night I snuck out. I had also developed a false sense of security because he hadn't mentioned punishing me since the engagement photoshoot. I looked down at my clothes and back up at my phone. There was no way I was going to be ready in time. Another text message came through.

Damien: *You now have 59 minutes to get ready and if you aren't here on time, your punishment gets worse.*

Me: *Screw you and your punishments. I did what I felt was right to get the answers I needed.*

He didn't reply right away, so I figured that was the end. I should have known better.

Damien: *56 minutes.*

I cussed out loud as I got up and dashed into the guest room. I debated whether it was worth it to take a shower, but after taking one look at myself in the mirror, I realized a shower was needed. It was several days after the engagement announcement and I had thrown my hair up in a messy bun and lounged around in sweats most of the day. I hopped in the shower, thinking I didn't have any time to waste, and was out within fifteen minutes. I spent the rest of the time pulling myself together before I realized I hadn't picked out the dress yet. The pinging of my phone delayed me further. I shook my head when I saw what time it was and that the text was from Damien.

Damien: *You're late. I know you're familiar with the conse-quences.*

The words made me quake with excitement and a bit of fear. I was keeping one of the most powerful men in New York City and potentially the world waiting. I went into the closet and found a couple of black dresses, but they all seemed too formal or looked like work clothes. It took me another minute until I found a tight leather black dress built like a leather jacket. Although it was skimpy for the weather outside, as soon as I slipped it on I felt sexy. On the bright side, a coat would keep me warm, and I would be in the car for most of the time I was outside. Some black heels finished the outfit and I looked at myself in the mirror. I looked damn good, and I knew the perfect thing to add to my look. I walked back into the bathroom and found a dark red lipstick that I hadn't worn in a while and put it on. I tossed the tube in my purse and threw my coat over my shoulders.

The dress felt like a second skin on my body as my hands smoothed down the fabric. I had no idea what Damien had planned for tonight, and that excited me. I headed downstairs to the lobby where Kingston met me near the front desk.

The trip to Elevate took a little longer than I expected, causing the bubbles in my stomach to spill over. Rob opened my door and Kingston escorted me to the entrance to make sure that I made it inside and I gave him a small smile. A security guard greeted me at the front door and once I gave my name, another guard walked over and led me to Damien.

The music was thumping loudly in my ears. That plus my nerves being frayed made me jumpy as I was led up to the VIP area. I thanked the guard when he paused and directed me to another staircase. The added height the black heels gave me made it easier to find Damien once I was at the top of the stairs. He sat alone on a plush couch and looked like he was presiding over his kingdom from his throne. I wasn't entirely expecting to see any of his brothers here but based on the stories that Ellie had mentioned in passing, they regularly hung out in the VIP area and would split off if any of them went down to the basement. I didn't see them here tonight.

Damien didn't look at me right away as I approached, heightening any tension I felt from his last text message and my feelings from earlier today. Even as I walked up to the couch he was sitting on, he didn't look up, continuing to look straight ahead and sipping his drink.

I took my coat off, finally feeling his eyes watch me as the clothing slid off my shoulders. It was as if he just realized I was there. I sat down next to him and placed my coat over the arm of my chair. I stretched my legs out in front of me for a moment before crossing them, and when I looked up, Damien was staring at them, proving that his broody aloofness was an act. He appreciated the view. I glanced at my dress to straighten it and when I looked at him again, his gaze met mine.

"Drink?" he asked.

I nodded my head. A drink would help calm me down. Damien put in an order for a glass of Merlot when a server appeared at his side and I patiently waited for my drink.

"I'm surprised you wanted to come here after the incident at Hidden Tavern." I kept my voice level and smiled at the server who approached me, my drink of choice in hand.

"I controlled the variables the best I could. You were in safe hands from the moment you left until those fuck-me heels landed in front of me."

"Were?"

A sly smile appeared on Damien's face, but he said nothing as he took another sip from his drink. I followed suit and felt myself relax once the wine flowed down my throat. I wanted to believe that our experience at Elevate would be like the one we shared before, but something told me that Damien was about to switch it up. After all, this was his MO. For a few beats, we said nothing, and my mind darted between different ideas about what he might have up his sleeve for tonight. Before long, the silence was tiring, and I broke the ice.

"How was your day?"

Damien cut his eyes over to me briefly. "Have we become that couple?"

My eyes narrowed. "I was just trying to start a conversation, and I wouldn't call us a couple in a million years." I took a gulp of my wine.

"You still don't get it, do you?"

I waited for him to elaborate, but he didn't. Silence passed over us again as I took in his question. Was he referring to his constant need to reiterate how I was his?

The evening we met again at the gala shoved its way into my mind and I recalled how things had slowly changed when it came to what I thought of Damien. Yes, I still thought he was overbearing, but the time we spent together had shifted my perception of him. I felt that the words he spoke during the engagement announcement taping were about as close as I was going to get to a compliment from him, and I accepted that might be the only time I heard such nice things from him, and it was an act for an audience.

I took the last sip of my wine and Damien stood up. He grabbed his coat that I hadn't noticed he had thrown over his own chair. I grabbed my coat and purse as he held out his hand and I hesitantly put mine in his. I followed Damien's lead when he led me from the seats we occupied to the bar where we placed our empty glasses. We walked away, hand in hand, and descended the steps to VIP. We didn't stop until we passed the main level of Elevate and reached the basement.

Damien leaned over to tell me in my ear, "This vibrator is clean because I washed it personally, but I know you don't trust me. I'm going to give you three minutes to go to the bathroom and put it inside of you while I check your coat and purse."

"Excuse me? You must be—"

"Take the vibrator and place it inside you." He was losing patience.

"But—"

"But nothing. Although I can think of a few things to do with that ass. Put it inside you."

"You can go fuck yourself."

A sarcastic chuckle left his lips. "Why would I fuck myself when I can fuck you? If you don't do as you're told, and you aren't walking toward the bathroom in five seconds, I'll add that to the list of reasons I'm punishing you." He paused and took a step closer to me. "Even though we both know you enjoy my punishment too much."

Damien gestured to my coat and purse and held his hand out, all the while holding the small black box that I recognized. I snatched it from him and turned away before he could say anything else that made me want to combust.

It wasn't hard to find the bathroom and I appreciated the sleek design of the interior that matched the rest of the establishment. I double-checked that no one else was in the bathroom with me before I walked into a stall and took a deep breath before I moved the thong I wore tonight and placed the device inside of me. It slid in easier than I was expecting, a testament to how wet I was. I debated playing with myself but decided against it because Damien would know. When I was sure that the vibrator wasn't going anywhere, I left the stall and washed my hands. As I grabbed a paper towel to dry my hands, I jumped. Vibrations came from the toy and sent jolts of pleasure through me. I'd forgotten there was a remote that could control it from a distance. I could handle this. I looked at myself in the mirror and saw that my cheeks were already flush. Maybe I couldn't handle this.

I left the bathroom after a few more deep breaths and found Damien waiting for me, much like he had when he ran into me during the gala. A smirk lay on his lips; he clearly had no shame.

"Are you okay? You look...a little pink in the cheeks."

If I could have growled at him, I would have. Instead, my eyes were transfixed on his hand that was now moving to the pocket of his slacks as he increased the intensity of the vibrations a notch.

The tremors caused my eyes to widen as my body tried to become more accustomed to the change in settings. The smirk grew as he put a hand on the small of my back, guiding me along.

We passed the room that we played in the first time and I tried with every bit of my being to keep it together. But the anticipation of what was going to happen and the pulsing vibrator inside of me had me on edge.

It wasn't long before we stopped at another door and Damien turned to me. "It's time to take things up a notch."

He opened the door and took several steps inside. The theme of this room was jungle, and the different colored greens painted a beautiful picture, but my eyes were focused on the bed that was the main attraction in the room. The dark sheets were reminiscent of the sheets that I slept on in Damien's bed, and when I snapped out of the short daydream I'd entered, I turned around and found Damien leaning on the door. He trained his eyes on me as I once again watched his hand move toward his pants pocket, and I felt the vibrations increase not once, but twice. The sensations running through my body almost brought me to my knees. I couldn't stop the moans and whimpers that were flying out of my mouth as I felt myself coming closer and closer to my release.

I slowly made my way over to the bed as that was the closest surface I could lean on and sat down before I threw my head back. I pulled my head up and my eyes met his before they squeezed shut. Just a little more...

The vibrations stopped. I took a moment to catch my breath before I met his gaze.

"You thought I was going to let you come that easily? This is a punishment, Spitfire. It just so happens that it's pleasurable too. Stand up."

I stood up slowly, not trusting my legs. Damien walked over to me and if anyone else saw him, they would have assumed that he was unaffected. But I knew better based on the bulge in his pants. He got within a breath of me, and I felt his fingertips run up the front of my dress.

"You look stunning in this dress, but I know something that's even better: your naked body. His fingers made their way up to the zipper that was holding the dress closed, between my breasts. He slowly unzipped the garment and when he was done, he pushed the dress off my shoulders until it fell to the ground. The black strapless bra and thong were the only things that were keeping me from being completely exposed to Damien. I didn't move as I watched Damien take a small step back and undo his belt. He put his hand in his pocket and pulled something out before he went back to unbutton his pants and they followed my dress to the floor.

"I'm going to fuck your mouth." His eyes lowered to the spot in front of him, telling me that was where he wanted me without using the words. I did as I was told and took my time rolling his black boxer briefs down his body as he undid the buttons on the white shirt he wore. I didn't know what happened to it because my eyes were glued to the package that I had just unwrapped. Without a second thought, my mouth was on him, licking his head just the way I knew he liked. I teased him, much like he had teased me all night and almost as if he just remembered, the little machine came to life inside of me, sending sensational vibes to my core.

After several minutes of teasing his cock, I alternated between pulling him almost out of me and deep throating his pulsating dick. The groans that were coming out of his mouth were driving me wild and he turned the vibrator up again, causing me to moan around his dick. His fingers were in my hair, creating tangles I couldn't give a damn about. I was proud that it was me that was causing him to lose control.

Truly embracing the nature of this room, Damien pulled on my hair with one hand, not enough to hurt me, but enough to get my attention. His cock fell out of my mouth with a resounding pop, and as he looked into my eyes, he turned the vibrator up even more. Holy shit, this vibrator was powerful.

He leaned down and pulled me up, before bending down slightly to pick me up. For a moment he held me as if I were his bride and he was going to carry me over the threshold. Instead, he tossed me on the bed and spread my legs wide, before my eyes closed again, and my labored breath picked up. I could feel him drag the scrap of material that passed for underwear down my legs before he left the bed for a second. I tried to open my eyes to watch him, but I couldn't muster up enough energy to care. A moment later, I felt his fingers on my pussy and he slowly worked the vibrator in and out of me before he turned it off and removed it. I felt his condom-covered cock at my entrance just before he rammed it home.

The sensations slammed through me like severe thunderstorms coursing through me. I fought the urge to scream as Damien slammed into me, causing my arousal to soar. Why did this always have to be this phenomenal?

His movements didn't have the finesse that they usually did. It was almost as if his personality was taking on the theme of the room, and the beast in him was at the forefront. His hand clawed at my chest where he tried to massage my breasts, popping them out of the bra cups that were barely containing them anyway.

The way his body moved with mine was driving me closer and closer to the edge, and if he stopped me from coming this time, there would be hell to pay. Instead of slowing down, he continued to fuck me as if his life depended on it. The only noises that passed between us were moans and groans of satisfaction.

I cried out in pleasure as I felt myself crossing over the point of no return, and the grunt that he gave told me he had done the same. If this was a punishment, I couldn't wait to find out what was a reward.

DAMIEN and I walked out of the room and he led me to the bathroom that was a few rooms away. As I checked myself in the mirror to make sure I looked somewhat human, it hit me that I didn't recognize my own reflection. Just like every time Damien and I had sex, I could barely remember my own name afterward, but this was deeper than that.

I craved the intimacy that we shared. When we were together, nothing else mattered. The bags under my eyes proved that there was another side to all of this. Before Damien, I had lived a quiet life. Over the last few weeks, my life had taken a turn I could have never expected. The mixture of happiness, yet confusion swirled in my mind. I shouldn't feel this way about whatever Damien and I had going, but I wanted more. I deserved more, and I could finally admit that I hoped deep down inside Damien would be the one who'd give it to me.

I exited the bathroom and almost ran into Damien. Although it was dark in the hallway, I could still make out the look he was giving me, and my body involuntarily quivered with anticipation. He looked as if he wanted to take me down and have round two right here in the hallway, not giving a damn if anyone around us saw.

He glanced down at his phone and that was when everything changed. It was as if someone had poured a cold bucket of water down his back, the look was gone, replaced with passive indifference. There was the Damien I knew. I wondered what he had read that caused the shift. He held out my coat and helped me put it on before handing me my purse.

"We are leaving."

I nodded agreement. "Is everything okay?"

"Yes."

He guided me up the stairs, holding the small of my back as we walked back through the door to the outside world. Down here, we could ignore the drama that both Damien and I brought into whatever this was. Could I imagine my life being this way all the time? How would it affect my job and how hard I worked to excel? For the past couple of years, Monroe Media Agency has been everything to me. Everything I did was usually to the benefit of the company, to make sure that it continued to thrive and to prove to my father that I could do this. And now here I was with Damien, and I barely thought about work anymore.

We took a different route to exit the basement and ended up in a back-alley entrance.

"I didn't know this was here."

"Hardly anyone knows about this entrance. It makes it easier for me and a few others to slip in and out without being detected. I thought you might not want to go through the crowd in the bar."

I didn't react because Rob was pulling up in the SUV and in a matter of seconds, he whisked away us.

21

DAMIEN

S*moke.*

All I can smell is smoke.

It's the middle of the night and I'm in the kitchen getting some water, doing my best not to wake up Charlotte. That is until I smell smoke. My first instinct is to make sure that the stove is off. It is. I look around for another heat source when I hear a huge boom upstairs. Whatever fell makes the entire house shake.

"Charlotte," I yell. "Charlotte!"

"Damien, wake up." I hear a woman's voice call me, but I can't place it. "Damien, you're dreaming. Wake up."

My eyes shot open, and I sat up in bed. "Fuck," I mumbled, wiping my hands across my face. I was hoping things were getting better, because I hadn't had a nightmare about the fire in a while, but clearly, I was wrong.

"Are you okay? Can I get you some water?"

"No." I moved my hand over my eyes. The room was infused with light. Anais must have turned on the overhead light and the bedside lamp.

"Oh, let me turn that off," she said, scrambling out of bed

and dashing toward the light switch. When she came back, she sat next to me on the bed. "Is there something you want to talk about? It might help."

I looked at her in the soft light that was coming from the lamp. *Maybe talking to her about it would be helpful. After all, what do I have to lose?* I studied her face before I said, "Sure."

"Are these dreams why you're so protective of people going into your bedroom and sleeping next to you?"

I nodded. "Looks like I'm breaking all of my rules with you." I gestured to her, pointing out that she was currently sleeping in my bed. I saw a hint of a smile appear on her face before it went away.

"The first part of this you already know. I was dating a girl named Charlotte in high school during our senior year. We had only been dating a couple of months and one weekend we went away to one of her parents' homes in upstate New York. We were having a good time." I decided not to go into detail about what having a good time meant. "And then late on Saturday night, I headed downstairs to get a drink of water."

Anais leaned over and grabbed my hand. I looked down at our entwined fingers and wanted more in order to get through this. I pulled her closer to me as I lay down, thoroughly enjoying having her lie on my chest. Once we got settled, I resumed my story. "I smelled smoke. At first, I thought I was imagining it, but the smell didn't go away so I started looking for the source and couldn't find it. Then I went upstairs, and a beam fell from the ceiling. Deep down in my heart, I knew there was no way I was going to get to Charlotte without either severely injuring or killing myself, but I still tried. I bounded back down the stairs and before I could find something to cover myself up with, my father burst through the front door. He practically dragged me out of there, and we hopped into my car and sped down the street. That's most of what I remember happening, although I have several questions that still swirl around my head about that night, more often than I would like to admit."

I paused for a moment, giving Anais time to ask questions, but she didn't. Instead, she said, "Oh Damien, I'm so sorry."

"I don't need your pity," I said. It came out much harsher than I intended.

"I'm not giving you pity. I can feel bad without throwing pity around."

That was true.

"Have you talked to someone about it?" Anais asked.

"I have. It helped with the survivor's guilt but did little to help with the nightmares."

"There has to be something that could help. I wonder—"

"It's fine because it's not nearly as bad as it used to be. It mostly happens when I'm stressed. It was triggered by another text I received."

"The one you received a few hours ago at Elevate?"

Of course, she knew. I nodded once.

Instead of asking more about the message, she rubbed a hand up and down my back and I leaned into her, embracing the comfort she was providing. Despite her father still healing, and the investigation still ongoing for the person who had shot him, which I knew had her worried, she was trying to help me with a situation that had happened over a decade ago.

Having her by my side on and off for these last few weeks

was more than I'd imagined. I had grown used to coming home from work and her being there when I opened the door. It was a one-eighty from the person I thought I was, one who loved time alone and had no desire to share a space with anyone else. Now I craved having Anais in any way I could, and that was problematic. I knew I needed her more than she would ever know, but what if I was already too late?

22

ANAIS

"You looked stunning in the video, Anais. You both looked ecstatic to be engaged," Ellie said over the phone. We hadn't been able to catch up on the phone after the engagement news dropped until today.

"Well, I guess we did our jobs then." I placed the grocery bags on the counter with a huff. I mouthed *Thank you* to Kingston, who gave me a small wave before he exited the apartment.

"It was a hit. Everyone is praising the photos and fawning over the fact that Damien has finally found the one."

I was glad to hear that because I hadn't been keeping tabs on what people were saying. I knew that would drive me crazy with worry. It didn't help that I suspected they were picking me apart, wondering how I got him to propose.

"I'm glad most of the reactions were good." I took off my jacket and started unpacking the food to put it away. I had asked Lucy not to fix dinner for the next couple of days because I wanted to do it.

Ellie sighed. "You know there are always going to be

people who talk shit. There's nothing we can do about that."

"That's true. That's why I'm avoiding reading what people are saying. I know it would get to me."

"And that's why you have me."

I chuckled. "I appreciate you more than you know, and not just for your information-gathering skills."

"Thank you. How is everything going with you and Damien?"

I shrugged, even though she couldn't see it. "Things have been good. He still needs to be in control and that gets on my nerves, but we haven't had many disagreements. It's been... nice. Plus, the sex has been fantastic."

Ellie chuckled. "That's good! How's your dad doing? Any news on who shot him?"

"Dad is doing well! He's still recuperating in the Hamptons, and I've been talking to my parents at least every other day. And nope, we aren't any closer to finding out who shot him. NYPD are still investigating but have nothing concrete. Even though we found out about who created and was pushing the blog post about my father, that has been a dead end too. Damien hasn't mentioned it directly, but I think now the only way we're going to find the person is if they try something else. If I had to guess, it's a matter of when, not if."

"That sucks. I have something that might brighten your day."

I straightened my body. "What's that?"

"Nick, my bodyguard, mentioned that we might try to bring me back to the city next week."

Her words made my heart jump. I missed her terribly, especially with everything else around me moving so swiftly. "That's so exciting!"

"Yeah. I need to get back to work, so hopefully we can make this happen. Hey, I need to go help with dinner. Can I text you later?"

I glanced at the time and cussed under my breath. "That's fine. I just noticed the time myself and I have to do a couple of things before Damien comes home."

"Talk to ya later."

I hung up and busied myself on my computer, trying to finish the last few tasks I had left before I started dinner. Once our stew was going, I checked my phone and didn't see a message from him, which meant nothing was keeping him at the office and that he would be home for dinner.

I found cooking therapeutic and this was helping me get through all the other things going on. A couple of hours later, the front door opening distracted me from surfing the internet, and I looked at him wide-eyed as he came into the kitchen.

"Something smells good," he said.

"Hope it tastes as good as it smells," I replied. "I just have a couple more things to do, and dinner should be ready." I walked over to the pot and lifted the lid, stirring the ingredients in the one-pot stew that I had thrown together. It wasn't as glamorous as the meals Lucy cooked, but it was dinner.

He put his briefcase down near the kitchen counter. I didn't even try to hide my staring as he took off his suit jacket and rolled up his sleeves. His forearm flexed and my eyes went to Damien's hands. Images of how he'd fondled my breasts the night before flashed through my mind, and I wondered what he had prepared for tonight. I turned away after he whipped his tie off and stirred the dish once more. I wanted to continue staring at him, but I needed to tend to the meal.

"So, how was your day?"

"Why are you cooking for me?" His question came out accusatory, and I was taken aback by it. This hadn't been the first time that I had cooked a meal for us.

"If you must know, I was actually cooking for myself. Figured I would offer you some too." That was a lie, but my feelings were hurt.

"I have a chef who could cook for both of us."

I dropped the spoon I had been using to stir and it landed on the stove, sauce splattering on the counter and stovetop. "Listen, I'm trying to do something good, something nice. Something that you wouldn't know shit about. Then you come in here and start giving me the third degree."

He paused and stared at me. "You aren't here to cook food. You're here to be fucked and—"

"How dare you!" The rage from his comment came on quickly and I didn't let him finish the sentence.

I wanted to say the thoughts that were flying through my mind, but I couldn't because I was still in shock. His comment stung me more than I was prepared for.

"I had a rough day at the office. What I meant to say was that you could use my chef. Nothing more, nothing less. I apologize for saying that you're only here to be fucked."

I grabbed my chest and stared at Damien wide-eyed. Damien Cross had just apologized. But he was right. I wasn't here for anything other than to pleasure him. I turned around and the timer that I set earlier went off and I quieted it before I walked over to the sink with the spoon and rinsed it off. I dried the spoon and turned the stovetop off.

"Dinner is ready," I whispered before I left the kitchen and walked into the guest bedroom. I closed the door behind me, but I didn't lock it because I knew he would end up coming in here at some point anyway. I sat on the edge of the bed and stared at the wall in front of me, trying to process my thoughts.

What I had told Ellie was the truth. Recently, Damien and I had been getting along well. Things were lovely and we had settled into a routine in our daily lives, but our nights were anything but routine. Our nights were spent exploring each other's bodies, discovering new pleasures about the other as we went. And his comment brought me back down to Earth. After all, just like the first go round, I was preparing for this "relationship" to end as soon as we caught the culprit.

A knock on the door disturbed my train of thought. I wasn't expecting him to come in here so soon.

"Come in," I said, keeping my voice level, determined not to give too much away.

He entered the room quietly and I wouldn't have known for sure that he had come in if I hadn't smelled a hint of his cologne. I turned and saw that he'd brought two bowls of dinner with him.

"I wanted to talk."

Of course he wanted to talk, and I knew he was going to force the issue even though I didn't want to. The quicker we got this over with, the faster he would get out of the room.

"I want to apologize again for what I said. It was uncalled for and the furthest thing from the truth." He made a move to sit next to me on the bed. Part of me wanted to lean into him and be in his arms, but now wasn't a good time.

"Okay."

"That's all you're going to say? You aren't going to call me an asshole?"

"We both already know you're one so what would be the point?"

He chuckled. Our dynamic was back to normal.

"Are we good now?"

This had been the first time we truly worked through an issue that we were having instead of Damien steam-rolling over me. I felt good about his willingness to meet me halfway. We were working better together and that made me happy. I nodded before I asked, "So, how was your day?"

"Pretty good. Thought I might have to stay a bit later, but thankfully my senior staff worked it out among themselves."

"Bought another company?"

He snorted. "No, but I'm in the process of buying another piece of property in the city."

"Do you really need another house here?"

"It's not that. It's office space."

"Ah." That made more sense. We stopped talking temporarily when I lifted a forkful of the food up to my mouth. I closed my eyes and let the sensations of the food take over, transporting me to another place and time.

"This is damn good."

I cracked an eye open and looked at him. He was busy finishing a bite and putting another one in his mouth.

"Thanks." My voice wavered a bit before I stuffed my face with dinner again. An apology and recognition on the same day, let alone within the same hour? Was the world ending? Because I was not used to this type of behavior from him, but the small gesture warmed me. Or it could have just been the food. We continued eating for a few minutes before Damien cleared his throat.

"Anais."

"Yes?" I said after I finished swallowing the food in my mouth.

"You need to pack and be ready in about ninety minutes."

I did a double take. "Are you going to tell me where we're going?" I asked.

He made a noncommittal noise before he asked, "Where's the fun in that?"

"Since when do you do anything fun? Well besides going to Elevate." I asked. *Since when does he apologize, thank you, compliment you, and surprise you with something that so far sounds like something you would enjoy?*

"I'm glad you think Elevate is fun." He paused before he continued, "Maybe I'm turning over a new leaf. Pack for three to four days, and you can bring your laptop and work with you."

He knew me too well. "Can you at least tell me what the climate is?"

"Similar to here. Done?"

I nodded and he took the bowl I was holding with him out of the room. I racked my brain trying to figure out where we might be going as I walked into the guest closet and stopped. There was nothing in there except some fancier gowns that could only be worn to a big event. "What the—"

My mind raced as I left the guest room and looked out into the living area, but Damien was nowhere to be found. Even though I had been sleeping with Damien in his bedroom, I still got dressed in the guestroom. Speaking of his bedroom, I heard movement coming from there and followed it. I found him standing with his back toward the door, shirt-less. I watched as his muscles moved and the urge to run my hands down his back stopped me from saying anything that would detract from watching him.

"Is there something I can help you with?"

Of course, he knew I was standing there. He turned around to face me and threw a shirt over his head, robbing me of the view I had been enjoying.

"Where are my clothes?" I didn't even have time to process him not wearing a suit and tie, instead opting for a navy T-shirt over dark-colored jeans.

His eyes darted over to the door leading to his walk-in closet. I side-eyed him as my feet brought me over to the closet door that was already open with the light on. His clothes were on one side of the closet and someone had neatly hung mine on the other. I turned around, and he was standing in the doorway.

"Since you were sleeping in here, I thought it would be easier to have your stuff moved in here."

It was a gracious gesture, but he could have asked me if I wanted to have my things moved. Yes, it was more convenient, but I wondered if it was another way he was trying to keep me under his thumb. I felt guilty that this was where my mind went.

"Time is ticking."

Damien's voice broke through my thoughts and kicked me into action. Once I picked out my outfits, I brought the duffel bag out of the closet and placed it on the floor near the dresser. I hadn't checked the dresser in the guest room to see if my underwear was still in there, but it made sense to check here first. I opened the top drawer and found many types of lingerie in it, but this was clearly for the bedroom activities that Damien had planned. I touched a red G-string that was semitransparent.

"Only the stuff hanging in the closet was brought in here, but I had a spare drawer that could fit some of the brand-new lingerie I bought for you in it. I'll have that fixed while we are gone. You should take some of those pieces with you." He was leaning on the door frame.

"Thank you." I grabbed my duffel bag and walked toward the door, hoping that Damien would move, but he didn't. He shifted himself and stood up straight, his body taking up even more space.

"What? No insult? And here I was ready to punish you by fucking your mouth when we get there." He shrugged. Little did he know, I didn't think that was a punishment. "Finish packing because we need to go soon. Don't forget to grab a couple of pieces from that drawer."

With that, he walked out of the room.

I was on time for whatever Damien had planned, and he didn't have a conniption. I stared out of the car window. Based on the streets we were passing and my knowledge of New York City geography, it seemed as if we were moving closer to the water.

We pulled up to a stop in front of a building near the water. "Are we going on a boat?"

I could see Damien's smirk because of the lights reflecting off the hard planes of his face. "No."

I held back a retort because I didn't want to drag Rob into

our conversation. Most of the ride was in silence and I relished in that because I was still peeved at him, but I debated with myself whether it was worth asking that question. Clearly, I was wrong.

Damien got out of the car before Rob, but I waited for Rob to open my door. Once I was out of the car, Rob closed the door behind me and rushed over to help Damien.

"We only have a couple of carry-ons and our laptops. Don't worry about it. We'll see you when we get back."

Rob nodded as another man approached. I assumed he had come from inside the building we were standing in front of.

"Mr. Cross, Mrs. Cross, welcome! My name is Clay and I'd be happy to grab your bags and get you both situated ahead of your flight."

His words made me freeze in place. *Mrs. Cross? Flight?*

The only thing that pushed me forward was Damien's hand on the small of my back as he led me into the building. We were greeted by what looked to be a lounge. In one corner were colorful couches and to the right of that was a bar which, after everything that had happened tonight, might be helpful to calm my nerves.

"Can I get you anything?" Clay looked between me and Damien.

"A couple of glasses of water for both of us." Damien moved his hand from the small of my back to my waist, making sure that Clay saw it.

I rolled my eyes at his obvious show of possession, but I didn't move.

"I'll have that right out for you both."

Damien guided me to the bar stools, and we sat down.

"I can order my own drink, thank you very much."

"Water is better than alcohol. Just in case you get motion sickness."

I could admit that made sense. "Can you give me a hint now?"

He glanced at me before he pulled out his phone and said, "We're going on a helicopter." I could see he was fighting back a smile.

"Holy shit," I mumbled. "You're really not going to tell me where we are going? Could we have driven there?"

The smirk was back on his face. "We could have, but this is better. It was easier to take a helicopter than to have to sit in traffic or go through an airport. So, we're flying."

It didn't take long for Clay to get us our waters and for our ride to arrive to drive us to the helipad not too far from the waiting area we were in. The process was quick, and soon we were getting on the helicopter. When the helicopter took off, I had a chance to look at New York City's skyline from this different viewpoint. The city lit up in the night was stunning, and once we moved past it, I focused on where we could be going.

I assumed it had to be close because otherwise he would have had us fly on a private jet. My thoughts were confirmed when the helicopter landed about thirty minutes after we took off. Once we had unbuckled all of our safety equipment and stepped off of the helicopter, we were greeted by a woman who introduced herself to us as Kim at what I assumed was another lounge.

"Welcome to the Hamptons!"

I gasped and gripped Damien's left arm. "Are we going to see my parents?"

I think this was the first time I saw Damien share a smile with me that took up his entire face. "That is what you wanted, right?"

"Um, hell yes!" I exclaimed, almost launching myself at him. Instead, I grabbed him by the lapels of his brown jacket and placed a hard kiss on his lips.

"I can't believe it!" Tears welled up in my eyes.

"Are you crying?"

"Yes, but they're happy tears. Oh, I can't believe this," I repeated. "Thank you. Thank you. Thank you!"

Kim started walking in front of us as another gentleman came out of the building and went to the aircraft to grab our carry-ons.

"I'm so happy you pulled this off. It was so hard trying to deal with everything without them being nearby. This was incredibly sweet. Thank you."

I followed Damien to a fancy sports car and I half expected Rob to appear out of thin air ready to take us to our destination. As Damien slipped behind the wheel, he exuded more power than usual.

Once we were on the road to see my parents, my mind wandered back to being referred to as Mrs. Cross. It had been the first time since the engagement announcement that someone had said that, even if it was by mistake, and I wondered what it would be like to be married to Damien. When talk of the fake engagement had started, getting married to him seemed like the worst thing in the world. Now, the idea didn't seem so bad, but I needed to remind myself that I had to stay on my A game because there was always a catch.

23

DAMIEN

"Well, this is a fancy car."

"Aston Martin DBS," I said as I started the car, enjoying the power that was now beneath my fingertips. The car still had that fresh new car smell because I didn't drive it as much as I would have liked.

"Aston Martin is one of the cars that James Bond drives, right?"

"It is."

"Well then, it fits you perfectly."

I glanced at Anais out of the corner of my eye and although I wanted to stare at her smile for a while longer, I turned my attention back to the road. I felt as if I'd hit the jackpot. Her smile turned into giggles that she couldn't contain. The mood had lifted considerably since earlier that night. The air between us felt different, and it wasn't because I was close enough to her to get a hint of the shampoo and conditioner that she used. I heard her rub her body against the black leather seat and all it did was remind me of the black leather dress she wore to Elevate.

"Why am I not surprised that you would rent this type of car?"

"Who said it was a rental?"

I could see her look at me out of the corner of my eye, slack jawed.

"You own this car?"

"Yes." How long was she going to continue this line of questioning?

She mumbled something under her breath about how she couldn't imagine how much it cost, and I decided not to tell her it was a few hundred thousand. It was one of the newer cars in my garage out here.

"What's with all this?"

"What do you mean?" I asked, taking another opportunity to look at her for a moment. The smile was gone, and a curious glance was in its place.

"Why are you being nice to me suddenly?"

"I can't be nice?" I asked. My grip tightened on the steering wheel as the GPS led me along the quiet roads to the house I had purchased a couple of years ago. That was also something she didn't know. I owned the home that her parents were staying in and had let them use it rent free. Ilaria had worked out the rent with who she thought was a property manager, but it ended up being Melissa who sent all of the paperwork to me. Not a cent was deducted from their account.

"I'm sure you can, but outside of your family, you're not. So why?"

Should I tell her it was because I was attempting to listen to her more and I knew this is what she wanted so I made it happen?

No, where would the fun be in that? I'd wait until she realized what this was all about. Things were getting better, but the sooner she came to terms with the fact that she was mine, the better.

"I assume you're capable of being nice, but—" Her words stopped abruptly before she took a deep breath and continued. "I can't help but to think that you're playing one of your games."

"I don't play games, Spitfire. I do what I say I'm going to do and what I say is final." I could see that she was understanding this, but there was still work to be done. "You have a hard time listening to the things I say, and that's because of your desire to defy me at every turn."

That made her lips twitch again before she turned to look at the window. There wasn't much to see given that it was dark outside, but I rather she did that versus us having another argument.

"Do we need to get our stories straight before we see my parents?"

Her voice broke my concentration temporarily. "What is there to keep straight? If we stick to the basics, everything should be fine. We met again at the gala and started dating. We kept it a secret until I asked you to marry me. The end."

"That makes sense." This might have been the first time she had agreed with me outside of the bedroom, and I couldn't deny that it felt good. But I also enjoyed when she let me know that she wasn't pleased about something. It showed me she could take it as well as she received it, and it would do her well when it came to living her life with me. "I just hate lying to them."

Her words made my stomach drop. It was clear she was

still operating under the assumption that this whole arrange-ment was ending soon.

"I have a small update for you about who sent that gun to your office."

Her head whipped around toward me. "What did you learn?"

"The surveillance cameras caught the package being dropped off."

"How? You wouldn't have access to that unless...wait, do you own the building I work in?"

I scoffed. *I would tell her about me going after it when we were closer to a sale date.* "No. If I did, it would be in better shape and have better security features. Kingston has ways of getting around certain technology blocks. That doesn't matter. What does matter is that we are finding more leads and getting closer to uncovering who this person is. Here's his photo."

She gasped. "This is the man with the very raspy voice that hit me with his shoulder! I have no idea who he is, though, but he keeps popping up randomly."

"I didn't recognize him either."

"We should probably show it to my parents too. They might recognize him."

I nodded. "That's fine."

"I'm willing to bet he's the one that shot my father."

"There's a chance that he did, but we don't know for sure."

"True."

I drew my gaze to hers as I checked to see her reaction before I turned my eyes back to the windshield. Based on her eyes widening, I knew I'd shocked her. Interesting, because I thought she wanted it to end. At least, that was what she kept telling me.

"I'm happy that the engagement has distracted people enough that the press hasn't bothered to dig into what happened to my father."

"Well, that was the whole point of it, right?" I asked dryly. I shook my head but didn't turn to look at her. *After all, I paid for the press to be distracted.*

"Yeah, but I still don't know what the benefit of us being engaged is for you. In fact, I would say it would hurt your reputation with whatever woman comes after me." The fight to keep my face neutral raged on inside of me. I didn't want another woman replacing her, and it made me angry to even discuss it.

"Trust me, my reputation is not in tatters due to us being engaged."

She mumbled something I didn't catch.

"Can you repeat that again?"

"Okay, I believe you."

My head jerked at her admission. I hadn't expected to have an ounce of her trust, yet some was there. I knew taking her to see her parents was something she wanted so I took Broderick's advice and brought it all together. *Damn, he was right.*

I had told myself that traveling to the Hamptons would help her see what I meant by being mine and the life she could have and the one that we could build and lead together. Also, getting out of the city would do us both a bit of good and so far it was starting out on the right foot.

We continued the rest of the way in silence, although it wasn't awkward. Anais pulled out her phone and was busy in her own world as I drove. My mind wandered and I tried to think of what else I could do to make her see I was trying to make her happy.

Once we pulled up to my estate, I said, "Welcome to my home."

"This is where my parents are?" Anais gasped in amazement. "Wait, you own this one too?"

"I do."

"Why didn't we just come here when your house was broken into?"

"Because I knew you didn't want to be alone, and I thought you and my mother would get along well."

She stared at me for a moment before looking down at her hands. She looked back up and at the building in front of her. "This is stunning. This house is very you."

"That somewhat sounds like an insult."

"Not at all. It's the modern vibe that seems to run through all your homes."

That was true. The architecture of the house drew me to it when my Realtor mentioned that the property was available. It had the similar floor-to-ceiling windows I loved in my other homes. I had to renovate it to fit my style, having the outside painted with black and gray with a touch of white, but the location couldn't be beat. The property's seclusion and privacy were another reason why I bought the place. Having access to the beach was key, although I didn't really get out here enough to enjoy it. The view from my window when I visited was stunning, but nowhere near as beautiful as the sight before me.

Before I could say anything, the front door opened, and one of the guards stationed to watch over the Monroes walked out and headed toward us. I stepped out of the car and once he saw who I was, he greeted me with a handshake.

"Mr. Cross."

"Brendan." He sometimes took over shifts at Elevate as well.

I walked over to open the door for Anais, but didn't give her much room to get out, causing her body to brush up against mine. Her eyes made their way up to mine as she said, "Thank you."

"You're welcome."

She looked like she wanted to say something else, but she didn't, so I took a small step back and walked away from her to retrieve our bags from the trunk while she grabbed her laptop bag. I locked the car door and the two of us made our way to the front door where Brendan was currently standing. He moved out the way, giving us room to walk inside the house and close the door.

"What's all of this commotion—" The words died on Ilaria's lips as she stared at us, open-mouthed.

"Hey, Mom."

That was enough to knock her out of her shell shock. "Anais. Oh, my sweet child."

The two ran to each other, much like they had when I'd brought Anais to the hospital after my team made sure she was safe. When they put their arms around one another, their tears this time were much happier. It brought back memories of when my mother greeted me after the fire. My mother, of course, wasn't happy that Charlotte had died, but she had been relieved that I hadn't perished along with her. I'll never forget the look on my mother's face when I walked across the threshold, right behind my father. That look had haunted me until Charlotte's memory overtook it.

"How's everything going?"

"Wonderful. Your father's making improvements daily and is resting right now. Everyone who comes to check on him has been absolutely wonderful and I believe being closer to the ocean and in this beautiful location has helped put him in a better mindset as well. I'm so happy that you could come." She pulled Anais into a hug again.

"I'm happy to be here. In fact, it was a bit of a surprise. Damien didn't tell me where we were going." The two women finally seemed to remember that I was still in the room.

Ilaria turned to me and said, "I don't know how we could ever repay you for all of this."

"Don't worry about it; it wasn't a problem. It's been worthwhile." My gaze landed on Anais, letting her know exactly who I was talking about.

24

ANAIS

The next morning, I stood outside the room but couldn't bring myself to knock on the door. The person on the other side was going to be angry, and there wasn't much I could do about it.

I had made my choice.

I had made my decision.

Yet, it had hurt him in the process even though I was doing it to save him.

At least, that was what I told myself.

I knew I couldn't tell him the real reason why I had done what I did when it came to Damien, but fixing things between us was high on my list of priorities because the strain between us was killing me. I stopped biting the corner of my lip once I realized I was doing it. My stomach dropped when I took a small step closer to the door. I took a couple of deep breaths before my fist tapped on the wooden door.

"Come in." His voice sounded stronger than it had the last time we had a video call.

I slowly opened the door and stepped inside before I closed it behind me.

"Hey, Dad."

"Hi, sweetheart." He looked up from the book he was reading, his reading glasses resting on his nose. He placed the book on the side table and pushed the glasses up into his short salt-and-pepper hair.

So far, so good. I was expecting hostility, given what the conversations had been like on our video calls, so this was a welcome surprise. He was sitting up in bed and patted the spot next to him, and I sat down.

"I'm sorry I didn't get to talk to you much last night."

"That's okay. I'm just happy that you're here."

"Even though I broke the news to you about my engagement the way I did?" I wanted to rip the Band-Aid off now.

"Anais, I trust you to make your own decisions because I love you and know that you have a good head on your shoulders. Based on my interactions with Damien and from what I've heard, I thought you could do better than him, but hell, I would probably think that you could no matter who you chose to be your partner."

I could understand that. He wanted the best for me, as any good father would.

"Is this something you really want to do?"

I nodded. "I wouldn't have accepted his proposal if I wasn't sure." The lie fell from my mouth without hesitation. I was getting good at it.

My father coughed and then said, "So Damien is doing all of this?"

"All of what?" I knew what he was talking about but wanted him to spell it out.

"Allowing us to stay here, my medical bills..." His voice faded as he grimaced, and I didn't know if it was because of his injury or because he was uncomfortable with this topic.

"Yes, he said he was taking care of all of it. Can I get you something? You look like you're in pain."

"I'm fine, I'm fine." He adjusted his body and that seemed to help. "Did he ever mention why he's doing all of this? I'm sure it's not out of the goodness of his heart."

A few weeks ago, I would have said the same thing, but now, this felt different. I smiled and said, "He's doing it because we're engaged, and he has the means to take care of the things that mean something to me." I couldn't bring myself to take the lie far enough to say he was doing it because he loved me.

"You mean a lot to him then."

"I hope so. After all, he asked me to marry him."

He seemed to accept that answer. "I want you to be happy and if Damien makes you happy, so be it."

"Thanks, Dad. I would hug you, but I'm worried about your leg..."

Dad smiled. "I still have one good side. Come here."

I turned around and gently laid my head on his shoulder. He squeezed my hand and somehow I knew everything would be all right between us, but I wasn't so sure about where things would end up with Damien.

～

"Honey, have you started thinking about your wedding?"

My mother's question shook me from my daydream. It

was a few hours after I had spoken to my father, and he was currently upstairs resting.

"Uh not really." I glanced at the ring on my finger, before looking at Damien.

He was sitting across the room in another chair, pretending he couldn't hear my mom's question. He had his laptop on his lap and was typing away, so maybe he was working. I wanted to tell him that since it was Saturday, he shouldn't be working, but it didn't surprise me he was. I could understand it, given that I had worked long hours and weekends as well. At least that sometimes happened before Damien came into my life. I turned my attention back to my mother.

"Well, I found some wedding magazines the last time I was out. Do you want to look through them and talk about what you're envisioning for your big day? It might be fun."

I looked over at Damien and found him staring back at me, laptop and whatever he was doing on it forgotten. I assumed he was watching to see what my answer would be. "Uh—yeah. Sure, Mom. That would be great."

The smile that lit up my mother's face was one that I hadn't seen for a while and that made the lie worth it, although I still felt guilty. She walked over to the kitchen counter and grabbed what looked to be five magazines and hurried back over to me and sat down, her smile even wider.

I tried my best to hold it together, but I couldn't. Tears threatened to fall from my eyes while my mom talked about a beautiful pink bouquet that she saw on one page. I glanced up at Damien and found him still looking at me, his expression unreadable. That was the icing on this cake, making it all too much to bear right now.

"Hey, Mom?" I asked.

"Yes, sweetie?"

"I'm going to go to the bathroom. I have a headache, but I'll be right back."

"We can look at this later. Is there anything I can do? There might be something you could take here." She glanced at Damien before turning her attention back to me.

"Oh, no. I'll find it. Thanks, though." I stood up and didn't peek in Damien's direction before I headed up the stairs and into the bedroom that he and I were sharing. I was thankful that we could still sleep in the largest guest room during our stay in the Hamptons with a private bath. I closed the door behind me and sat down on the edge of the bathtub and cried. No matter how hard I tried, there was nothing I could do to stop the tears.

Everything that I had gone through over the last few weeks was coming to a head. Normally, I would have been surprised to hear the bathroom door open without a knock, but having lived with Damien, I had grown to expect it.

"Can you please give me a moment to myself?" I asked. My words came out barely above a whisper, and the trembling of my lip didn't help the delivery sound any stronger either.

"No," he said and joined me on the edge of the tub. "What made you so upset?"

I didn't answer for a beat because I was too busy trying to calm myself down. He stood up and it took two small steps before he was standing in front of me. He held his hand out and once my smaller hand was enclosed in his bigger one, he pulled me into a standing position.

"Tell me what's wrong." This time he wasn't asking; he was demanding.

I thought about lying to him as well, but I knew that was pointless because I would only avoid the inevitable. "I'm tired of lying to everyone. I'm tired of being in this situation. I'm just tired."

I paused, debating my next sentence while Damien didn't say a word. Feeling braver, I took a deep breath and continued. "Look, I know that this hasn't been fairy tales and roses and that isn't what I expected given how all of this started. But I know that neither of us wants this. You saw how happy my mom was about planning a wedding. It gave her hope that things will get better because my father is on the mend and now she has a wedding to look forward to. When we tell the world that this engagement is over, it's going to pull the rug out from underneath her. It would be the third time in recent months that she's had to deal with some sort of bad news. Now I know in the grand scheme of things, we are still fortunate. I just don't want to be the person who causes my mom pain."

Saying the words out loud helped relieve some of my pent-up frustration. It temporarily halted my tears, and the burden that I had been carrying around felt lighter.

"How do you know I don't want to get married?"

"Damien, please. The quotes you've given to the press over the years, and I'm pretty sure you've also told me you don't do relationships."

When he didn't reply, I knew I was right, and the realization still felt like a punch to the gut. Although I had told myself not to fall for him, that was what was happening and once this threat was over, he would be out of my life. I needed to, once again, start preparing for what life would look like after Damien Cross was gone.

"Anais, my goal was never to hurt you."

"No, your goal was to own me. And you do. I've told you before that you've forced me to be with you, whether it's from me being unable to protect my family, to throwing together this fake engagement scheme. The power balance has been one-sided this entire time." I gestured to the two of us, and whatever we were.

"You're wrong. You've had more power over me than you could ever know. That's why I wanted you to be mine. When you realize this, that is when everything will make sense."

I had more power over him than I could ever know? I didn't have time to analyze this because he placed his finger under my chin and lifted my head so that I was looking him dead in the eye, giving him a better opportunity to look at my tear-stained face. He wiped the tears from my face and eyes before he walked out of the bathroom, leaving me alone.

When I entered the bathroom, I had wanted to be alone with my thoughts and to cry in peace, and then he had barged in, interrupting the privacy that I'd craved. So why did I long for him to come back?

25

DAMIEN

For the rest of the day, I made sure to give Anais the space that she wanted. Later that night, I gently closed the door behind me and walked further into the room. The only light that guided me came from the window that looked out over the water.

I gazed at the outline of her body as I removed my clothes. I admitted to myself that I wanted to keep her by my side, no matter how much of a selfish bastard it made me. When I was down to my boxer briefs, I slid between the covers, hoping to not disturb Anais. I threw an arm around her waist, but I hadn't expected her to turn around to face me. Naked.

"I was waiting for you," she said, answering my question before I could ask it. That was just before her lips landed on mine. The words caused my cock to harden and there was no way she couldn't feel it on her abdomen. I flipped her onto her back, hovering over her like a predator that had caught its prey.

"You know you're going to have to tone down the volume

on your moans tonight, right? Unless you want your parents to know what I'm doing to you."

All she did was nod, and I wondered if she didn't trust herself to let out a groan right then and there.

Our kissing soon turned into a make-out session. Feeling her nipples become small pebbles against my skin forced a low growl to leave my lips during a slight break in our kissing before my mouth attacked hers again.

Instead of worshipping her breasts before I made my way down to her pussy, I moved my fingers down to her treasure trove, not surprised in the slightest by what I found.

"You're that wet for me, baby? Already?"

"Mm-hmm. What are you going to do about it?"

"I can think of quite a few things."

I laid a hard kiss on her mouth before a finger made it past her other lips and into her warm and wet center. She released a breath she had been holding in appreciation as my finger moved in and out of her.

"You know what I think?"

"What?" Her question was a breathless whisper.

"I think you can handle another."

She responded with a whimper when another finger joined in on the fun. Watching her eyes close in ecstasy as I played with her cunt would never get old.

The sounds leaving her lips increased in frequency and intensity the faster my fingers worked her up into a frenzy. Her hands clenched the sheets as her head swung back and forth before her eyes met mine in the soft moonlight. This was what I wanted. I wanted this forever.

My fingers had a mind of their own and I groaned when I

felt her becoming wetter. Until she reached the end of her rope.

Her pussy convulsed around my fingers, causing her entire body to tremble. I didn't stop my motions until I milked every bit of her orgasm.

When I was sure I had, I put my tongue on her nipples as my fingers played with her now sensitive clitoris. I wanted to make sure she was ready to go when I was ready to put my dick inside of her.

"Be careful with how loud you're moaning," I said. The volume of groans had once again increased. Although she looked like she didn't give a damn who heard right now, I knew she would be mortified if her parents heard us.

I stopped licking her tits. "I want to give your tits more attention, and my cock needs to be in you. Put your fingers on that pussy for me."

She did as she was told, and I got up and found a condom in the bedside drawer. I quickly sheathed my dick before I turned to face her. Her eyes were closed, and she was biting her lip with her hair splayed all over her pillow. The moon cast a soft glow over the perfect picture her body painted as she was pleasuring herself.

I sat down on the corner of the bed and looked over. "Anais, come here."

She slowly opened her eyes and swung her legs off of the edge of the bed. She took the couple of steps before she climbed into my lap and sunk her wet pussy on top of my dick. There was a mutual groan as she adjusted herself. "Ride me, Spitfire."

And ride me she did. The view this gave me was spectacular. I could see her moving up and down on my cock. My hands landed on her waist to give me something to hang onto. She was setting the pace as I was letting her run the show.

Her head flew back, causing her long dark strands to form somewhat of a cape behind her. Watching her bring herself back up to another peak was mesmerizing. I caught one of her nipples in my mouth and she let out a gasp. It sent even more blood to my groin.

"I'm getting close." Her words came out rushed and I knew I was getting close too.

She careened over the brink and I soon followed. I held onto her for a moment, embracing the connection that we just had.

"Wait up for me anytime you want if that's the welcome I get."

Anais tried to push her hair out of her face and stared back at me. "Did you just make a joke?"

"I guess I did."

26

ANAIS

nother evening, another event that I had to go to with Damien. A few days ago, we had returned to New York City and I felt recharged after spending time with my parents. They hoped to return home soon, and Dad could still continue any treatments that he needed here. I would be grateful to have them closer to me again, so that I could help when necessary instead of having to travel to get to them or talk over a video call.

"You still hate these things, don't you?" Damien asked as we walked further into the hotel where a fundraiser for a local politician was being held.

"Yeah, how did you know?" I could talk about social media and marketing until my cheeks got tired but going to events with people who had more money than I could imagine made me want to shrink and hide.

"I watch you. I noticed when your eyes darted toward the entrance, trying to make sure that you had an escape route. You seemed breathless when we walked up the stairs and we both know you're in excellent shape." The heat in his eyes and his expression told me he wasn't talking about my cardio routine. Not shocking. "You also looked as if you were giving yourself a pep talk to convince yourself everything's fine."

His perception of me was a little unnerving, but not unexpected. After all, keen perception was probably how Damien figured out the best way to outmaneuver his competitors and his enemies. Was that how he still felt about me? Was I still something that needed to be conquered? I refused to ask because I was afraid of the answer. Before we could move further into the building, Damien pulled me aside.

"I don't know what makes you doubt that you belong in this room but fuck that and whoever has made you feel this way will have to answer to me." The venom in his voice told me he was ready to kill whoever had caused me to doubt myself. "You have every right to be here."

"Because I'm on your arm?"

"No, because you have shown and proven tirelessly how much you work to support your job, your family, and the others around you. That is worth more than any money in the world. Don't let anyone ever tell you any differently."

His words moved me more than I could say. Of course, I knew he spoke the truth in regard to my own feelings deep down, but to have someone else acknowledge those things about me, to know they understood everything that I did, was immeasurable. It touched me in a way that no one else ever had. The only response I could give was to nod because I didn't trust my voice not to crack if I spoke.

He ran the back of his hand across my cheek, his gaze boring into mine with a tenderness that I didn't expect. The gesture caused my heart to flip and the feelings I had for him to take an even stronger hold on me. As much as I denied wanting to fall for him, wanting to be with him, this dangerous man was very close to owning not only my body, but also my heart and soul.

A throat cleared from off to our left. "Mr. Cross?" someone murmured, attempting to draw our attention their way.

Damien gave me a regretful look, as if he hadn't wanted the interruption, but knew now wasn't the time. We turned to face the speaker.

The woman looked sorry she'd disturbed us, but she was just doing her job. "Right this way." She gestured for us to follow her.

Damien placed my hand on his arm, and we followed the woman into the event. She left us at the door and my gaze took in the room. Fancily dressed people chatted in various groups around the large ballroom.

Our first stop was to get a drink—a glass of wine for me, a bottle of beer for him. Once that mission was accomplished, the small talk with other people began. For the most part, it was just networking. Damien moved his hand to the small of my back. That simple move gave me a sense of security that I hadn't felt when I first walked into the room, despite the fact that I'd had my hand on his arm as we entered. His hand on my back made me feel protected, like he was paying attention and would step in if I needed him to, but that he was willing to let me shine as well.

We strolled around the room and he introduced me to some people he knew, some of whom I exchanged business cards with. I hoped this would lead to an increase in clientele for Monroe Media Agency.

An older woman in a brown dress approached us and

Damien smiled as his hand moved to my waist. "Gretchen, it's good to see you."

"Damien, it's been a while, you look good." She leaned in and kissed his cheek, then her eyes strayed over to me.

"Gretchen Jones, I'd like you to meet my fiancée, Anais Monroe. Anais, Gretchen is a friend of the family. She's the CEO of Savory Perfumes."

"It's a pleasure to meet you," I said, shaking her hand and trying to keep my stomach from hopping out of my body. Savory Perfumes was a huge company and owned many of the biggest perfume brands in the world.

"Anais is the social media director for Monroe Media Agency, maybe you've heard of it?" There was an uplifting note in his voice, like he was proud of me and what I did, and it warmed my heart again.

"I have, you do good work over there."

I spoke to her about the company and some of the things we were working on, feeling assured about my ability to convert her to a client.

"Do you have a card? I would love to see what you can pitch to my board of directors."

"I do," I replied, pulling a new card from my purse with a smile and handing it over.

"We'll definitely be in touch. It was lovely meeting you, Anais, and congratulations again." She gestured to my left hand with a grin. Her reaction was one that we had been getting for most of the night because the ring was a show-stopper.

"Thank you, it has been wonderful meeting you as well. I'll be looking forward to your call. I already have some great ideas to pitch to your board." Anais smiled confidently as she shook Gretchen's hand.

"It was great seeing you again, Damien. I need to catch up with Selena."

"I'm sure she'd enjoy that."

Gretchen gave us a little smile and finger wave as she left us to join another group, and I expelled a heavy breath as my shoulders sagged in relief. I was confident in my abilities but being on and attempting to not appear nervous took its toll on me. However, having just the possibility of gaining a new client made me ecstatic.

What took me by surprise was that when Damien introduced me to someone who might be interested in Monroe Media Agency, he took a step back and let me drive the conversation. It allowed me to show off my skills and talents and to increase my clientele.

I leaned into Damien's side, smiling. His fingers on my waist tightened a little in a pleasant way as his gaze met mine. "Can we take a small break from meeting people? I love getting to talk about the agency but it's a little overwhelming and I'm getting tired."

"And hungry. You haven't eaten in a while. Lucy's meal is waiting for us when we get back home."

His hand on my back guided me over to the table filled with the typical high-end fare. He filled a plate with caviar and lobster stuffed mushrooms for me, and then filled another for himself. As I took a bite, he said, "We'll leave in a few minutes."

I looked up at him, seeing the heat in his gaze as his focus was on my lips. "Why?" I asked, but secretly I was thankful as I had been ready to leave about twenty minutes earlier.

"Because you need to eat more than just this, and I have a few ideas about dessert."

His intense gaze told me that while dinner might be about eating food, dessert was probably about eating me, and I felt my cheeks heat at his implication.

"Mr. Cross."

I heard a familiar voice just as I was wiping the crumbs from my lips and attempting to keep a lid on the blush threatening to creep up on my cheeks. It wasn't from embarrassment, however; it was because I couldn't wait for him to take me home as well.

Home.

Now this person was potentially standing in the way of our quick exit. I turned and saw Jon from the "working dinner" that Damien had brought me to weeks ago. Damien placed his hand on my waist, his grip firm but not painful. It was easy for me to tell that his cool demeanor on the surface was anything but on the inside. I had to wonder about it. I knew Jon was an asshole, but Damien's reaction to his appearance seemed to be more than mere annoyance at his presence.

"Jon." His tone was full of hostility.

"It's wonderful to see you again," he said holding out his hand to Damien.

Damien glanced at it for a moment, and just as Jon's smile was about to slip, he went ahead and gripped his hand, shaking it.

Jon turned to me, like he was going to offer me his hand as well, but I just smiled tightly. I saw him give me a once-over, clearly not having learned his lesson from the last time we met. I shifted my eyes to Damien and watched his face harden. There was a storm brewing in his blue gaze as a muscle twitched in his jaw. Jon's confidence was laughable.

"Is there anything I can do for you, Jon?" Warning was laced through Damien's words and I knew he was a ticking bomb ready to explode. It was only a matter of time.

"I was just coming over to say hello and wondered where we stood in our negotiations. I've been trying to reach you, but you've been avoiding me."

A smirk popped up on Damien's face that looked lethal as his grip on my waist tightened slightly. If he hadn't been holding me, I might have been tempted to take a step away from him myself.

Damien's eyes narrowed. "Oh, I thought Will might have told you. There is no deal."

Jon slowly turned red, embarrassed by the change in events. I didn't blame him because even I was taken back by Damien's tone, and he wasn't talking to me.

"Ah, excuse me." A light cough stopped him from speaking for a beat. "I wasn't informed. May I ask why? I was under the impression that our dinner went well."

This man must have a death wish because there's no way he was questioning anything that Damien said or did. No one did that—well, except me.

"When you disrespected my fiancée, the negotiations were over," he growled in a low voice, stepping a bit closer to Jon. If there was any questioning about what he meant, his frightening tone made everything crystal clear. "Even now, you continue to undress her with your eyes with no shame, so fuck you. You need me, but I don't need you."

"So, you're willing to hurt business relations all for a piece of ass?"

My eyes widened at his words. This man clearly didn't value his life. Damien shifted so that I was slightly behind him and his fingers curled into fists. I knew I needed to do something to keep him from hurting Jon and causing a scene in front of all these high society people. I calmly took a step and turned my body to face his and placed my hand on his shirt, just above his heart and gazed up at him, reminding him of where we were. I was worried he was going to strangle the clueless man in front of us, and no one could afford to have that on the front page of a tabloid.

The only clues I had that he understood my actions was a slight twitch of his eye and a nod. His hands returned to my waist when I turned around and was safely back at his side, but his stormy gaze moved back to Jon.

"You have forty-eight hours to leave New York City. I suggest that if you ever want to do business or hold a job again, that you apologize to Anais, but you'll never work in this town again. The only reason you aren't picking your teeth off the ground right now is because Anais is right here. If I don't hear that you've left town in forty-eight hours, I'll make sure to haunt you for the rest of your life here. You can tell Will I said that. He'll see you as the worthless associate that you've become."

Jon was visibly shaking. It could have been from anger or fear. Or maybe it was both. He turned to me and I could see that he was biting back a sneer. "I apologize. I shouldn't have said what I said." That told me his shaking was more from anger than anything.

"Damien, we should leave." My words were calm and even, but inside I was shaking, terrified that he was going to act on the feelings I could see lurking in his eyes.

"You're right, we should." His harsh tone told me that he was beyond livid.

Damien looked at him once more before reaching over to grab my hand and together we walked away from Jon and toward coat check. Damien said nothing as he reached into his pocket and grabbed his phone. When he was done typing, he looked up at me and asked, "Are you okay with us taking a pit stop before we head home?"

"Sure. Why?"

"I promise it won't take more than half an hour." It wasn't lost on me that he hadn't answered my question.

WE DROVE around the city and before I knew it, the large buildings that made it easy to recognize my hometown were in the distance as we came across a more secluded area.

"Damien, you said it wouldn't take longer than thirty minutes. I'm starving."

"We're almost there." There was an edge to his tone, like he wasn't himself. Or maybe he was, but harder and harsher.

True to his word, the SUV came to a stop a few minutes later in front of a rundown warehouse that looked to have been abandoned a long time ago. There was barely even any lighting in the area, giving it an almost haunted look with the one flickering street light. It went without saying that I couldn't wait to leave.

Damien caught my gaze, he looked determined, but his words were gentle as he spoke to me. "Anais, I want you to stay here with Rob okay?"

Questions popped into my head but none of them made

it to my lips as I nodded. Damien's gaze intensified for a moment as he stroked my cheek with his thumb before he kissed me. I could still taste him on my lips as I watched Damien leave the vehicle. When I heard the locks engage, I looked in the rearview mirror and found Rob looking at me before he turned to look straight ahead. *Why did he lock me in here? What is going on?*

There was a small light flickering in a broken window of the warehouse. Before I could examine it further, another dark colored car drove up and two men exited the car. One guy reached into the back seat and brought out another person, who looked to have a dark colored hood on his head. My eyes widened and I covered my mouth, fear pooling in my stomach as I watched them jerk the man forward. They entered the warehouse as well and then all was silent.

My eyes darted back to Rob. "Can you tell me what is going on?" My words came out much calmer than I was actually feeling.

"It wouldn't be wise, Miss." His words were even with no emotion behind them, causing my stomach to drop further.

Time moved at a snail's pace until...it didn't. I heard two loud bangs and some more commotion, causing me to jump in my seat. My heart pounded in my chest and before I could process screaming, I saw someone exit the warehouse. Under the flickering light of a street light, I caught a glimpse of the face of the man who had turned my life on its head. Yet now I couldn't imagine what life would be like without him. I exhaled loudly, without realizing that I was holding my breath in.

Rob unlocked the vehicle and Damien slid into the backseat next to me. Once he was in the car, Rob pulled away, hopefully taking us home.

I glanced at Damien and found him looking straight ahead. I waited a beat to see if he would break the silence, but he didn't. I took a few deep breaths as I did my best to control my heart rate, but I could feel adrenaline creeping in. I could only imagine what he was feeling.

"Damien, what happened back there? What was that bang? It sounded like gunshots."

"It was." He seemed calm, but his breathing was still heavy.

I reached over and grabbed his hand, squeezing gently. His hand shook slightly, and he had a wild look in his eye. It was clear that his behavior was from anger. "Are you hurt?"

He shook his head but stayed silent.

"Did you hurt someone?" My tone was gentle but worry had a hold on me and I couldn't shake it.

It was then that Damien turned to me and when his gaze landed on me, I felt the brutal force of the inferno behind his eyes. I knew it wasn't directed at me, but I was afraid for the person who had put that look in his eyes. "I killed Jon Moretti."

"You did what?!" I screamed and dropped his hand as both of mine flew to cover my mouth. I'd suspected he'd shot whoever it was in the hood, but I didn't think he'd killed them. "Why would you do that? I thought you told him he had forty-eight hours to get out of town?"

"I changed my mind. He continued to disrespect you, and no one disrespects what's mine. I should have killed him after that dinner."

"Damien, I—"

"He fucked with what's mine and paid the price. When news of his death hits the streets, that should be a warning for all not to mess with what's mine." His eyes blazed, as if daring me to be pissed off at him over it.

I recalled the information that I saw in Jon's folder in Damien's office. "But he works for Will? Aren't they a part of the Vitale family? Did you just start a war with the mafia over me?"

I replayed Damien's words in my mind multiple times, but I didn't have the reaction I thought I would. I closed my eyes and deep down I knew that him killing Jon wasn't a shock. He kept testing Damien and all that I'd heard and now knew about Damien told me that what happened tonight wasn't out of the realm of possibility. What concerned me more was that Damien might have started a confrontation with the mafia that could have been avoided. I feared for what Will's reaction might be and what Damien's retaliation might end up being. The blood that would be shed over this didn't have to happen, but this was now the inevitable.

It didn't help that Damien let my question hang in the air as his eyes were once again focused on looking straight ahead as we rode through New York City's streets.

27

DAMIEN

A nais avoided looking at me on our way back to the penthouse. She'd been much calmer than I expected after I admitted to killing a man after he mistreated her. I would do it again in a heartbeat.

I could have probably eased into telling her what I had done instead of leaving her shell-shocked. That was my mistake.

"Talk to me, Anais."

"Nothing. I'm fine."

I knew it was a lie. "You're not fine."

She turned to me and looked me straight in the eyes and said, "Nothing. There was just a lot of excitement back there."

"Do you have any more questions?"

"Why did you tell the truth about what happened back there? You could have played it off if you wanted to." Her words were barely a whisper, but she never let her eyes move from mine.

It was my turn to lean over and grab her hand, lifting it to my lips briefly. "Because I want you to see everything that my life entails. Yes, things can be glamorous, but that is also a part of my life too."

"Was that the first time you killed someone?"

My lips twitched. She'd asked the question without fear. "No."

She nodded and the weight I was carrying lightened a fraction. "Should we be concerned about the mafia now?"

"You won't have to worry about it." I looked over her and saw that she was doing the exact opposite. "Did any of that scare you?"

"I'd be lying if I said no. More so because I wasn't expecting it, but I'm not going to lose sleep over Jon."

"Good. If anyone has an issue with you, they will answer to me." I paused before I changed the subject. "Speaking of sleep, are you sleepy? Still hungry?"

"No," she said before a yawn escaped her lips.

"Sure about that?"

That got a small smile to appear on her face. "I guess I am. Didn't realize I was until just now."

"Well, at least tomorrow's Friday. One more day and then we can sleep-in."

"You? Sleep in? That's a rarity."

That was accurate. In the time we had been sleeping in the same bed together, I had still been in bed when she woke up maybe twice. "Let's grab brunch somewhere in the city this weekend. I think we've both had enough of the fancy dinners for a while."

I remembered overhearing her tell Ellie that I hadn't taken her out on a date, and it sounded as if that hadn't been the first time they'd spoken about it. She must not have expected my words because her eyes lit up with excitement.

In the dull light from the streetlights that flickered through the car's windows I could see a smile was forming and soon it took over her entire face.

"That sounds like a great idea."

"I need to make up for that shitty work dinner that I brought you to. Pick any place that you want to go to, and I'll make it happen."

I watched as the smile on her face grew wider. I was proud of myself for having put it there.

"Does Thirteen Park Avenue serve brunch? I deserve a do-over there."

"I don't see why not." I pulled out my phone and emailed Melissa, telling her to check with the restaurant tomorrow and if they did, tell them to pull out all the stops for a Saturday brunch.

"I'd love to go there if they do."

As I placed my phone back in my pocket, Rob pulled up in front of our building. He walked around to let Anais out while I opened my door. We were walking past the front desk when the staffer on duty stopped us.

"Ms. Monroe?" I knew I had seen her before, but I had never caught her name. Her name tag said Lydia. We both turned to face her, and I wondered why she would call Anais's name instead of mine.

"Something was delivered for you a couple of hours ago. Let me go grab it."

My guard went up as I watched the woman walk into the back. "Did you order something?"

"No," she replied. "I don't think my parents would have sent me anything here."

I grabbed my phone out of my pocket and sent a text to

Kingston.

Me: *Anais received a flower delivery and neither one of us know who it's from. It might be nothing but wanted to give you a heads-up in case we need to meet.*

Kingston: *I'll come over anyway. I've got some more information on the gun/other package Anais received.*

Me: *Okay.*

Kingston: *I should be there in fifteen.*

When I placed my phone back in my pocket, Lydia appeared again, holding a vase of sunflowers.

"Oh!" Anais said before stepping forward. "These are pretty. Are you sure you didn't send me flowers?"

I didn't respond because I couldn't get my mouth to form words. When she took her green eyes off the vase and looked at me, I spoke. "No, I definitely wouldn't have sent you sunflowers." I didn't go any further because I didn't want the staffer who was looking at us curiously to hear any more. I didn't want her to hear that these flowers brought back memories I had hoped were buried, and I didn't know how to feel now that I knew they weren't. The last time I gave a woman sunflowers, she ended up dead.

I asked Lydia to hand them over to me and Anais and I made our way upstairs to the apartment. As I placed the flowers on the kitchen counter, I could smell the dinner that Lucy left in the oven for us, but any thoughts of eating it had vanished once I saw these flowers. I grabbed a glass of water for her and a whiskey neat for me. I hadn't expected to have anything else to drink tonight, but it didn't matter now. Nothing else did. My mind was buzzing as we waited for Kingston to arrive.

I watched as she paced back and forth, her mind clearly

in a similar state to my own. She walked over to the flowers and started inspecting them. "I don't see a card with a note or anything."

That's because the flowers didn't need one. Even if I didn't know who sent it, I knew what it was related to.

"This is all so creepy and I'm tired of it."

"I know." I didn't say much else because I knew just how creepy it was going to get. Those flowers hadn't been sent to Anais by mistake.

"We'll figure this out." Anais's determined words helped clear the fog that surrounded my brain since we entered the penthouse. There was no way I could have predicted that tonight would turn out like this.

A knock on the door stopped me from having to say anything more to Anais. Kingston had arrived. After I moved out of the way to let him in, he went over and examined the flowers. "I'm no expert, but these flowers look fine."

"I don't care. I want them examined."

"I'll call around to a couple of florists in the area to see if they made a delivery here. Hopefully gives us a lead."

"There is one thing I do know. The flowers themselves were a message for me."

Anais stopped pacing and stared at me, saying nothing. Kingston's eyes moved between Anais and me before he too settled on me.

"What do you mean?" That was the first time Anais had spoken since Kingston had arrived.

"These were Charlotte's favorite flowers. There's no way I would have bought them for you."

28

ANAIS

I walked over to Damien and placed a hand on his back. I rubbed that hand up and down his back. "Who would do such a thing?"

"We need to start digging. I need you to find all of Charlotte's associates. Family, friends, her first-grade teacher, et cetera. Anyone who might have blamed me for her death." His words came out firm and authoritative, much different from the man who seemed to be on the verge of collapsing into himself just before Kingston had arrived.

I didn't know if my rubbing his back was helping in any way, but I continued doing it.

"If this is at all related to what happened with James, we need to know. If it is connected, I suspect they didn't shoot him because of anything he'd done. I think it was a way to get my attention."

I swallowed hard. This had to be the longest night of my life. If I had been shocked when Damien told me he murdered Jon and mentioned these flowers being his ex-girlfriend's favorite, it was nothing compared to what I felt right now, but I knew I didn't have the luxury of being able to collapse now. I stood firm and tall, trying to support Damien as much as I could.

"Kingston, you had some more information on the gun."

When Kingston began talking about the gun, my ears perked up. He confirmed the gun was stolen, but they were able to get footage of the person they believed stole it.

When Kingston tossed a photo on the table, I gasped.

I nodded. "So, it's official the raspy voiced man isn't just the messenger. I think we can confidently say he's my father's shooter at this point."

Damien cursed and ran a hand through his hair.

I frowned. "Too bad my parents didn't recognize him."

"How is he connected to your dead ex-girlfriend?" Kingston asked.

"That could be anyone's guess."

I tried to stop my mind from reading too much into this, but thoughts of how my association with Damien was more than likely the reason that my father had been shot. Who even knew if the shot that was taken was supposed to be fired at me.

I shook my head. This was not the time to sit here and blame myself for things beyond my control. What I could do was help Damien and Kingston catch this asshole. "Okay, what can I do to help?"

"For now, I think the best course of action is to maintain the status quo. Don't go anywhere without security. I'm going to install more security features on this floor and in the building, but it's going to take a couple of days to get everything up and running."

"You own this building too?"

"Is that shocking?"

"So, has Edward given you any trouble?" I asked.

"No, not really, but you know it's only a matter of time before he starts calling again. He takes a small break while you're out, but his sixth sense starts tingling when you're back and the calls start coming if he can't reach you."

I chuckled at what one of my coworkers, Rachel, insisted would be the case at some point soon. "You're probably right. Listen, I'm going to let you go get some work done and get back to it myself."

"Okay, catch up with you later."

I had pulled myself together enough to work the day after those sunflowers had ripped my life apart once more. I had a lot to catch up on since my father had been shot, but I was happy to have something that was bringing some normalcy back into my life and I needed the distraction. It would be helpful to go into the office to talk to people like Vicki and Jake, but I knew that it wouldn't happen for a while yet, given where things currently stood.

I'd briefly talked to Damien before he'd left for work and he'd told me that between what Kingston knew and what had been told to my father, the police had confirmed that the gun dropped off at my job was indeed the gun that had shot my father, though they weren't able to lift any fingerprints from it. Kingston and Damien gave the police the images that they had of "raspy voice" and they were also trying to track him down. It seemed as if he might be the key to unlocking this puzzle if we could find him. Or hell, there was a good chance that he would find me instead.

My stomach growled and it made me think about both lunch and dinner. I grabbed my phone from its resting place on the coffee table and sent him a message.

Me: *I'm in the mood to cook tonight. Is there anything that you would want to eat?*

Before I had the opportunity to put my phone down, I saw he was typing a message back, so I waited. I unmuted the music that I had running in the background that I had turned off during the call with my coworkers.

Damien: *Whatever you make will be good. Why don't you go and put that toy in your pussy and then we can have some fun when I get home.*

I was annoyed with his response, yet his words turned me into a pile of mush. There was no way I was going to be able to get through the workday with that toy anywhere near my mound.

Me: *I'll think about it.*

Damien: *What's there to think about? Do I need to remind you that I control your pleasure? You know what happens when I have to remind you.*

I rolled my eyes and tossed the phone down on the couch beside me. Although I debated putting the vibrator in, there was no way I was going to do it now given the demands he had just made. Eh, I was on the clock now, but I had no issue slipping it in closer to when he would be coming home for dinner. I didn't respond to his text message and instead took a moment to grab a glass of water and drink some of it before I pulled my computer back on my lap and went back to work. I was just finishing up answering a message to Jake when there was a knock on the door.

I glanced at the door before finishing my sentence. Whoever was on the other side knocked again.

With a sigh, I muted the music that was playing in my browser again and placed my computer on the cushion next to me and looked at the clock. It was 11:37 a.m.

I got up and looked through the peephole and opened the door.

"Where is Kingston?" I asked when Carter appeared at my door. If he was doing one of Kingston's daily checks, he was early. It took me a second to realize how rude I sounded, and I said, "Sorry, I didn't mean it that way. I just wasn't expecting to see you."

"That's fine, Ms. Monroe. Something else came up that he had to attend to, and he asked me to escort you to Damien's office."

"When did Damien say I needed to go to his office?" Was this why he wanted me to put the toy in? To be primed and ready for him to take me? Why hadn't he mentioned it when he texted me?

"I think it might be related to his birthday."

Birthday? Damien hadn't mentioned his birthday was coming up. Part of me wanted to stay here as a way to say screw him for not letting me know it was coming up, but I knew I might regret it if I did. After a quick debate with myself, I decided to go and write it off as my lunch break.

"Okay. Just give me a moment to change and I'll be down in a minute."

Carter nodded and I headed the bedroom before deciding the jeans I had on were fine. I changed from my t-shirt into a blouse and added a blazer. I quickly brushed my hair and debated whether I should throw it into a ponytail and decided not to but placed a hair tie on my wrist just in case I changed my mind. After messing with my hair for a little while longer, I decided that was the best it was going to get on that front. I slipped some black pumps on and thought I looked pretty put together for someone who had little notice that they were leaving the house. I tossed my makeup bag into my purse and headed out to the living area.

"Okay, I'm ready."

"Excellent. Let's go."

As I looked at Carter, a slightly uneasy feeling flowed through me due to his eagerness. Carter walked out of my apartment before me, and I turned around to lock the door behind me. When I turned back around, my eyes widened as Carter raised his hands to hit me with something that I didn't have time to identify. Before I could react, I felt the force of something hitting me, and all went black.

29

DAMIEN

"Have you heard from Anais today?" I asked Rob as I got into the SUV and slammed the door behind me. I couldn't wait to get back home and tell her that I was pretty confident I would be closing the deal on her office building. Of course contracts needed to be worked out, but I made the owner an offer she couldn't refuse, and she jumped at the chance. Now I could share the news with Anais.

Rob shook his head. "She hasn't asked to leave today."

I nodded, feeling satisfied with that answer. She did mention wanting to cook dinner tonight, so I wondered if she had asked anyone to get her any groceries. Maybe it could be something that we could do together since I was getting home a little early and it would be nice to do something low-key. I hadn't realized how domesticated we had become until I rushed to get back to her whenever I could slip away early. Even at work, my mind would drift to her, causing me to become somewhat distracted, although it hadn't hurt business.

I looked through my text messages and realized that I had told her to put the vibrator in her pussy earlier. I shook my head at myself, wondering how I had forgotten, and decided this was a prime moment to tease her about what I had planned tonight. I dug into my pocket and discreetly pressed the button, but nothing happened. Something was interfering with the signal, but it was more than likely because of her not turning her phone on. I couldn't fight the smirk from appearing on my face. I knew she was going to give me hell for demanding that, and I couldn't wait. Forever my Spitfire.

Rob navigated the SUV through New York City rush hour traffic like the professional that he was, and he pulled up to the front door in no time. I grabbed my briefcase just as he pulled to a stop. My smirk turned into a grin. I couldn't wait to get upstairs to Anais.

"Don't worry about getting my door. I got it," I said. "Oh, and by the way, why don't you take the night off?"

He looked at me through the rearview mirror. "Are you serious?"

"When do I ever joke? Go have fun," I said before I stepped out of the car. I closed the door and entered.

"Good evening, Mr. Cross," said Lydia.

"Good evening to you too," I said as I headed toward the elevator. I flashed my badge that allowed me to get to the floor where my penthouse was. It took a second before the elevator moved and I watched as the numbers moved up one by one. The long ride to my front door made me wonder if it was worth moving back to my other home in NoHo to avoid this climb to the top. I checked my watch, realizing I was being impatient because I really wanted to get to Anais as soon as possible.

My heart pounded when my front door was in my view. Just a few more seconds until I could kiss Anais. I turned my key to unlock a door and when I pushed the door open, I knew something was wrong. It was dark, not yet pitch black because the windows let some light in, but it made little sense to have no lights on in the apartment with the sun well on its way to setting. Had Anais fallen asleep or slipped past Kingston without me knowing? Where was Kingston anyway? Had I heard from him at all today? Rob had been with me most of the day, so she wouldn't have had our private mode of transportation.

"Anais?" I called.

No response. "Anais?" I asked louder, hoping that she might have taken a nap in our bedroom. Still, I heard nothing.

I flicked the light switch closest to me, illuminating the living area. Nothing looked disturbed or abnormal. I closed the door and dropped my briefcase. I walked past the living area and into the bedrooms, the bathrooms, and my office. There was no one in there. My searching turned frantic as adrenaline took over. "Anais!"

I ended up back in the living area and just as I was about to pull out my phone, I noticed something I hadn't seen when I walked in. There was a white piece of paper on my countertop in the kitchen. I debated whether I should pick it up in case there were fingerprints on it. Then again, maybe Anais had left the note, but I feared the worst. When I got closer, it was clear the note wasn't from Anais because there was a miniature sunflower resting on it.

.   .   .

Dear Damien,

    You should have listened all those years ago, but since you didn't, now you'll pay the price.

    See you soon.

    Charlotte

I CLENCHED my fist and made a silent vow. I would have Anais back in my arms if it was the last thing I did.

STEEL EMPIRE

BLURB

Our bond is steel.

We began to rebuild what we had,
    Because I'm determined to make things right.
    Someone is out to ruin me,
    And they're using Anais to do it.
    Danger threatened to take her from me forever.
    But what they don't know,
    Is when someone threatens what is mine,
    There will be hell to pay.

PLAYLIST

Stronger (What Doesn't Kill You) - Kelly Clarkson
Confident - Demi Lovato
you should see me in a crown - Billie Eilish
Battle Symphony - Linkin Park
How to Save a Life - The Fray
Locked out of Heaven - Bruno Mars
It Ends Tonight - The All-American Rejects
Good Girls Go Bad - Cobra Starship, Leighton Meester
Death of a Bachelor - Panic! At The Disco
End Game - Taylor Swift, Ed Sheeran, Future
Safe and Sound - Capital Cities
Clovers. - JoJo

The playlist can be found on Spotify.

1

DAMIEN

The demons that haunted my nightmares were supposed to remain there.

Yet, they had materialized into the real world and stole what was mine. There wasn't much I feared, but my life had been turned upside down twice in recent weeks.

When Kingston alerted me that there was an incident involving Anais and her father and that his team was rushing in, my heart felt as if it were being strangled. It took precious moments for me to reach Rob and head down to the car because there was no way I would stay at my office waiting for word on what happened to Anais. Every second that passed without word made my mind race, wondering if the moment she walked out of my parents' home would be the last time I saw her. After I was told that although James had been shot, Anais was fine and they were transporting her to a safe house, I felt as if I could breathe again.

Once it was confirmed that Kingston had Anais and she was safe, I knew that everything was going to be fine. I trusted

Kingston with my life, and I knew that he would do everything in his power to make sure that Anais was okay.

The slight tremble of my hand as I pulled at my tie told me my feelings about this were completely different. The item of clothing now felt as if it were restricting my breathing, a change from just before I entered my home. The headache that was starting to form would not deter me from what had now become my only purpose: saving her.

Someone kidnapped her and I would drag whoever did this through the bowels of hell to get her back. This was a war and there wasn't a chance that I would lose.

I pulled my phone out again and clicked a single button to redial the number that I practically had memorized due to how many times I had seen it in the last hour, but I got the same thing every time: Anais's voicemail. I called both Kingston's and Carter's phones and got the same result. *Where the fuck is everyone?*

I cussed at myself for not working faster. The extra security measures that were supposed to be in place weren't due to be installed until Monday. *I'm failing her.*

My phone ringing brought me out of the spiraling that my mind was determined to take. "Damien."

"Mr. Cross?"

"Yes?"

"I just emailed you all of the security footage that we had from today. Is there anything else I can get for you?"

At least someone is responding. "That will be all for now. Thank you."

As I hung up and placed my phone down on the counter in front of me it rang, making me jump slightly. My brief hope that it was Anais was dashed when I looked at the caller ID.

"Where are you?" I couldn't stop the agitation in my voice because I knew time waited for no one.

"I'm almost at your place. I swung by on the way from New Jersey and picked up Broderick and Gage. We should be there in fifteen."

My fury increased with every word Kingston said. "Good. And be prepared to explain why you were in New Jersey and not here protecting Anais." I hung up the phone, not giving him a chance to respond. I could have been more understanding, but I didn't give a fuck. I wanted answers and I wanted them now.

Anais. Everything in me circled around thoughts of her. How I made a vow to fix things with her and show her the life we could lead together. Yet, someone was determined to stop that from happening.

If the unthinkable happened at the end of all of this, the biggest regret I would always carry with me was not having told Anais I loved her. My stomach almost revolted at the thought. A light cough left my mouth as I tried to contain my emotions, the silence of the suite almost too much to bear.

My eyes drifted back to the piece of paper sitting on my kitchen counter. This short letter was signed by a woman who I thought was dead. It did cross my mind that it could be someone playing a practical joke. After all, the letter was typed, not handwritten, so it would be hard to tell if this came from Charlotte herself.

But the sunflower that came with it was a trigger. Hell, the sunflowers from the day before tore through my mind as if a bomb had detonated. I felt as if I had seen a ghost when they were delivered to Anais. That should have been a sign that this wasn't anything to be taken for granted, but our intel had taken too long to make any connections before disaster hit. Where the hell was Carter?

The whiskey in my cabinet was tempting, begging me to give in to its lure, but I refused. Nothing would distract me from getting Anais back where she belonged: here with me.

Hindsight slapped me in the face and had its way of making one feel foolish. I had spent most of my time thinking that all of this was the result of a bad transaction that James Monroe had made. But I was wrong. Guilt rushed through my mind because I now knew that the person who had taken Anais had done it to hurt me.

As I grabbed my laptop to check the security footage, I thought of all the ways that this could have been prevented. My past was finally catching up with me and I needed to know who this was and what their motives were.

Images from the night of the fire flashed through my mind as I tried to focus on the task at hand. There was no way that Charlotte could have survived the fire. Who would try to play this fucked-up game? Whoever it was, they weren't going to get away with it.

A shot of adrenaline pulsed through my veins as my eyes scoured the video in front of me, trying to see if I could spot anything that might provide a clue for us to go on. But before I pressed play, I had a feeling I would find nothing. If the kidnapper was smart, they would have done the same thing that Anais had when she slipped out. The garage provided a perfect opportunity to leave unnoticed.

Unless my eyes were lying to me, my assumptions were correct. I didn't see anything on the video that would give even a sliver of a hint as to what happened to Anais. Unless someone had eyes on the penthouse, very few people knew about the blind spot in the garage, which forced me to consider Carter as the prime suspect. His lack of response meant that either he was incapacitated in some way, or he was the one who had kidnapped Anais.

Could this be Will's response to my killing Jon? That wasn't out of the realm of possibility but for him to have carried this out so quickly would have meant that he already had someone following me for a while. Plus, I knew this wasn't really his style. While I was prepared to face whatever he did after I killed one of his men, I suspected that he would let it be known that he had done it instead of playing mind games like this. Why would he pretend that his dead sister was alive?

That was the first time in a long time that I thought about Will and Charlotte as siblings. I ran a hand through my hair, walked over to the letter, and read it once more. I lived my life doing what I wanted whenever I wanted, no matter the cost. *What did Charlotte warn me about all those years ago that I didn't adhere to?*

I looked at my phone, but saw nothing on the screen indicating any changes to the situation I found myself in. I walked into my office and opened a drawer I knew all too well. Inside was a medium-sized black box that I pulled out and placed on my work surface. Once I put my thumb on the track pad and heard the lock disengage, I lifted the top of the case open and took out my pistol. I double-checked that the safety was on before I grabbed my holster and put it on my waistband. I hoped I wouldn't have to use it, but I was prepared to. Nothing was stopping me from getting Anais back in my arms.

Adrenaline raced through me as I walked back into the living area. I glanced at the note on the counter, but my head swerved when I heard a knock at my door. I walked over and flipped the lock before I swung open the door. I wasn't shocked to find Broderick, Gage, and Kingston on the other side. "We need to figure this out. If you have any intel, speak now," I said, not giving anyone else a moment to respond. "I'm determined to get Anais home as soon as possible."

I didn't expect my brothers to have any answers since they hadn't been at my side or with Anais these past few days the way Kingston had. The three men walked into the penthouse and my brothers sat down on the couch. Images of how Anais loved to curl up on the cushion closest to the window flashed through my mind. It was one of the many places in here that I knew I would always find Anais's presence, whether it was because of the scent of her shampoo or her leaving a book behind. Kingston walked over to the kitchen counter, dropped the bag that he had brought with him, and picked up the letter. I waited a beat before I cleared my throat and he looked up.

"We don't have time to waste," I said to Kingston. "What forced you to leave Anais here? And where the hell is Carter?" My anger was rising to the surface, but I did my best to restrain it. Keeping a cool head right now would be best for everyone.

Kingston flinched slightly before squaring his shoulders, ready for battle. Deep down, I knew there had to be a good reason why he hadn't been with Anais, but I also knew I wasn't going to like the answer. Especially since the end resulted in her being who knows where. A part of me was afraid, but I wouldn't admit to it.

"Our deal when we first talked about me protecting Anais was that if I were called away for anything, someone else on her detail would take over until I came back. That was the case today."

I leaned back on the kitchen counter and folded my arms. Where was this going?

"I was called away to New Jersey this morning, due to an emergency at one of the satellite offices. We thought it might have been a hack and I needed to be on site to make sure that the protocols that we had in place were being followed and none of our data leaked. So, I asked for Carter to be the one to come up and check on Anais and the suite. We didn't think this was related to you at all and my trip was supposed to be relatively quick. The plan was that I would be around to do the next shift before you got home, but I was further delayed by some other issues that came up as a result of the mayhem this 'hack' caused. This happened on my watch and I take full responsibility. You know I'll be standing right by your side to get her back."

I looked around the room and watched as the twins nodded after Kingston finished speaking. The deep breath that left my lungs was a result of me choking up and trying to quell my rage. The urge to punch my fist through the wall was there, but it wouldn't get us anywhere, and I knew that my family would stop at nothing to rectify this situation. "Where is Carter now? He was the last person to see Anais." I paused and my eyes were on Kingston. "What do you mean a hack?"

Kingston nodded and ran a hand through his dark blond

hair. "Turns out the hackers didn't actually steal any information, nor did they really try to. It was just enough to get everyone's attention and to keep us spinning our wheels for a few hours. That is also getting sorted back at the office. We are trying to figure out how they were able to pull that off, but that's for me to worry about since we have more pressing matters here. I ran a scan to see if I could track both Carter's work cell phone and his personal one, and they both seemed to be turned off, but my team will continue to ping both of those phones along with Anais's to see if either of them are turned back on. We're also doing another deep dive into Carter's background. I'm sorry, man."

"You followed the plans we had in place in case an emergency came up. We didn't know that someone on the team would go rogue. I think I was the last person to hear from her, at least out of everyone in this room."

I checked my phone for messages from her and I noticed Gage moving out of the corner of my eye. When I looked up, I saw that he had grabbed Anais's laptop and was walking over to Kingston. "This might provide some answers about what she was doing if she was working just before Carter showed up."

Why didn't I think of that? "That makes sense. That fucker...when I get my hands on him, he's dead." I meant that with every fiber of my being.

Gage handed the laptop to Kingston, who brought it to the kitchen counter. His hands flew across the keyboard. "Can you hand me that bag on the floor? It has my laptop in it." Gage bent down and handed him the bag. I looked over Kingston's shoulder and found him already on her computer.

"How did you know the password?"

"She had muted a video that was playing and since it was the top window open, her laptop never went to sleep. Saved us a bit of time from having to try to figure out her password."

Broderick walked over to see what Kingston was doing and the three of us looked on as our cousin worked some magic on Anais's laptop, hoping for a lead.

"Is that a group chat?" Broderick asked, pointing to a page near the corner of the screen.

Kingston tilted his head. "It looks like she was in a chat with a few of her coworkers. The only names I recognize are Vicki and Jake. The last message she sent was at 11:33 a.m. and she had a meeting on her calendar that ended just before that. Carter was supposed to check on her around noon, so this leads me to believe she was taken between 11:35 and noon."

His words further fed my anger, yet a sense of dread crept into my mind. She had been gone for hours and none of us had been the wiser. I should have checked in on her, but I had been so focused on closing the deal to buy her office building that I hadn't thought to text her after our midmorning messages. "Yeah, she works tirelessly so I can't imagine her not responding to any messages if everything had been okay." I looked over and checked the clock on the wall. "Carter and whomever else he is working with or for currently have about a six-and-a-half-hour head start on us."

Broderick raised an eyebrow at me. "Are you sure that he's working with someone else?"

I slightly nod. "Based on the attention that was given to making it seem as if Charlotte was alive, I would say so. How would he know about her? Either he did his research, or someone informed him about what happened all those years ago."

Gage and Broderick shared a look. Only they knew what the other was thinking. Some things never changed.

I sighed and looked at Kingston. "Did you find anything else?"

"I'm working on it," Kingston replied. Then he made a noise that sounded like he was hesitant to share it. He switched to his laptop for a moment before turning back to Anais's.

"What's wrong?"

"I might have some information that could help us track her down."

"Any information is good since we don't have much to go on at this point. I want all the information that your team has on Anais, myself, Carter, and anything anyone can tell us about Carter as soon as possible. Even if someone on your team thinks that something is pointless, I want it. I want to have everything in place because questions are going to start coming up and I will need to talk to her parents." I muttered a cuss word. "Once I tell them, they are probably going to want to go to the police, which may or may not be helpful depending on who orchestrated this. In my opinion, whoever did this was sending a message to me specifically and the less we tell the authorities, the better."

Someone took the woman I couldn't get enough of because of me, and it was due to something Charlotte told me during the brief time that we had dated. The letter from "Charlotte" proved that and I didn't have time to sit here and think about what she told me back in high school. What I did know was that no one ever took or disrespected what was mine and survived. I could wait on the police to investigate, but I liked taking matters into my own hands.

Ding.

The sudden noise came from Kingston's laptop and he shifted his body to look at the screen.

"Here are all of Charlotte's known living associates. I also pulled a list of people we looked into when we were looking at Carter." We rushed over to his computer and read it from over his shoulder.

"Okay," I said, scanning Charlotte's file before my eyes darted to Carter's. I wasn't shocked to see a couple of the names on Charlotte's list, because I had met several of them during the time that we dated. Carter's was a different matter. "Wait a minute. Jacob Doherty? She has a co-worker named Jake..."

I turned so that I could look at Anais's computer again. "I'm sure there was a Jacob or a Jake that popped up in the group chat conversation that Anais was having before she was taken?"

Kingston's, Broderick's, and Gage's gazes moved to Carter's file. Kingston's finger was hovering over the trackpad before he clicked on Jacob's name.

There it was.

He worked at Monroe Media Agency and to make matters worse he was a subordinate of Anais's. That more than likely meant over the time they had worked together, a sense of trust and mutual respect developed between the two. Jake temporarily lived with Carter when he first moved to the city years ago. I was willing to bet this penthouse that because of their connection and Jake's position at Monroe Media, Carter had recruited him to help him get closer to Anais in the workplace. *Fuck.*

"Anais told me that Jake threw Edward, a representative of one of Monroe Media Agency's clients, out of the office. Saying that while he preferred to talk to Anais, he had become increasingly more erratic since her father's shooting. As I mentioned before, I checked into it, but found nothing that would make me think that he had anything to do with this. What if all of that was bullshit and he threw the client's name out there to throw her, and therefore us, off the scent?"

"Would also explain the delivery of the gun to her office." I grabbed the letter from "Charlotte" and said, "Looks like we need to pay Jake a visit."

2

DAMIEN

"**A**nything there?" I said, checking to see if Kingston was able to spot anyone in the apartment that we were looking into. I was ready to storm in there like I owned the place. Hell, after this was all said and done, I might own it.

"No. Based on the evidence we have, Jake lives alone."

I knew double-checking things before we went in there made sense even if my patience was wearing thin. The longer we sat here staring at this fucker's window, the longer it took for us to get to Anais.

"All right let's go," I said, hitting the button to unlock the car door.

Kingston locked it again with a quick click. This might be the one time where having automated locks was detrimental.

"Wait." Kingston's voice stopped me. "Let's wait one more minute to make sure before we go in there like *Rambo*."

I knew what he was saying made sense. He was very particular about how he did things in his work and personal life, so I knew he wanted to be thorough. I also knew that he took Carter being the culprit extremely seriously because he was one of his men. "This better be the quickest minute of your life."

Kingston shook off my comment with a shrug. "Carter's not going to have a life worth living, but you need to let me do my job." Kingston glanced at me before turning his attention back to the window.

I looked through the rear-view mirror and found the twins staring intently out the window, not wanting to get in the middle of whatever Kingston and I were doing. I also didn't want to mention to anyone in the car that I had no intention of letting Carter live to see another day after I got my hands on him, but we'd deal with that when the time came. I swear if a hair on her head was missing, I'd—

"Damien." My thoughts stopped when I turned to Kingston again. "Let's go."

I unlocked the passenger side door and left the first barrier that was blocking me from releasing my rage onto Jake's face. It took everything for me to not sprint across the street up to Apartment 3B and snap his neck. Based on what I saw on the outside, it wouldn't be that hard. The building needed to be completely renovated or it needed to be torn down and rebuilt. It wasn't hard to see that the worn-down structure was dingy even at night. The light hanging just above the door didn't have a light bulb in it and the light flickering just beyond the front door was in desperate need of repair. The fact that any owner would allow this building to get into such a state was despicable.

It didn't take long for us to make it up to his apartment. The janky lock on the front door of the apartment building was easy to open and us breaking and entering meant nothing to me.

I wondered if our heavy footsteps would have been a warning to him as we marched up the stairs, but it turned out that someone else in the building was either having a party or just playing very loud music. That would make things considerably easier because I knew this might get loud.

We stood outside for a moment and a quick head nod with Kingston, Broderick, and Gage confirmed that we were all ready. My fist pounded on the door and it creaked under the weight of my hand. I wondered how much effort it would take to rip it off its hinges. Broderick placed a hand on my shoulder when my fists pounded on the door too many times. I waited several seconds to see if we could hear anything, but all we heard was the loud music coming from the floor below. I waited for a brief pause in the music before lifting my fist and pounding again.

"Jake. We know you're in there. And if you don't want this door to be taken off the hinges, open. Up." My bellowing echoed in the hallway yet there was still no response.

"All right. The only way he hasn't heard us is if he's taking a shit," I said.

"We saw someone's shadow move back and forth across the window before we came up here. Someone's home," Gage said.

Broderick looked at the door, examining its sturdiness. "I think we could take this down." Before any of us could move the door swung open and it took me a millisecond to recover. Jake's eyes widened as he saw that there were four pissed-off men standing outside of his apartment and when his gaze landed on me, his eyes grew even larger. He backed up with his hands up.

"Listen, I didn't do anything. I have no idea why you're here. I've been just minding my business, dude."

The tremble in his voice annoyed me yet was satisfying. We made our way into his apartment and Kingston closed the door behind us. One glance around proved that the apartment was just as shitty on the inside as it was on the outside. Jake didn't help matters given how messy he kept his space. The fact that anyone could get away with this was mind blowing. When all of this was over, I made a note to myself to ask Melissa to report the state of this apartment to the city. Although Jake was on my shit list, that didn't mean the rest of the tenants deserved to suffer.

My dry chuckle made him jump. *Good.* "Why do I get the suspicion that you aren't just minding your business?" I said, mimicking the quivering that I heard in his voice. My eyes moved around the room, trying to see if I could spot Anais anywhere. "Stay here."

I searched from room to room but came up empty. Kingston, Broderick, and Gage followed suit when I returned. They tore through his apartment in a New York minute because that was all we had. When we came up empty-handed, I walked back over to Jake and levied a heavy glare at him. I folded my arms across my chest and stared at him.

"Where is Anais?"

"Who?"

I grabbed him by his shirt, lifted him up, and threw him against the wall. I could hear several stitches on his T-shirt ripping as I did. "Where is Anais Monroe? Don't act stupid with me," I said, making sure to enunciate each word perfectly, so there was no risk of misinterpreting.

He took a hard gulp and said, "I don't know who you're talking about."

"If you value your life, you won't want to fuck around with me right now. Where. Is. She?" I maneuvered so that my left arm was holding him up against the wall. I kept pressure on his neck and my body slightly shook because of the anger that was about to boil over. I could feel my sanity slipping through my fingers and it was only a matter of time before I was about to break. "Tell the truth."

His eyes moved down to my right fist, which was clenching. It should have served as a warning, but he didn't take heed to it. "I told you the truth. I don't know who Anais is."

That did it. The feeling of my right fist crushing his nose brought power and some pain but just hearing the crunch was satisfying. Gage tossed a paper towel at him, granting him more grace than I could muster in my pinky finger. I wanted to make his nose bleed even more. I held back and let him drop to the floor like a sack of potatoes.

"Ouch—Yes!" He tried his best to contain the blood and the nasally tinge to his voice that was both grating and satisfying. "I know Anais. She's my boss."

"Where is she?"

"What do you, uh, mean where is she? Last time I saw her was when there was a big deal over a package being delivered to the office and she was there. The l-last time I ran into her was when she was talking to Vicki after a meeting." His stammering was getting on my nerves. "I mentioned to her something about one of our clients who no matter how hard we tried always wanted to talk to her instead of someone else."

"And that's when you tried to throw this client under the bus and told Anais that his actions were escalating."

Jake didn't deny anything this time.

"Now if I have to repeat myself again and ask about Anais..."

"What do you know about Charlotte DePalma?" Broderick's question cut through the tension that was building in the room like a heated blade.

That question hit a nerve. Jake let out a curse, but it was mostly muffled by the blood spewing from his nose. "I've only briefly heard about her. Haven't seen or talked to her. Stop touching that!"

Gage stopped looking through the papers on Jake's desk. He sent a smirk over to Jake before he went back to searching through papers. That's when the light bulb went on in Jake's head. "Listen, I had nothing to do with any of this. M-my job was to spend the last few months keeping tabs on Anais and report anything I found to Carter. He was doing something similar, I assume, for whoever hired him. Carter was my contact, but I heard him mention something about reporting to his boss. Oh, I also was given a box and told to deliver it to Anais at the office. Never saw the guy who gave it to me before in my life."

And there is the confirmation we need. "So, your job was to stalk her and you're the reason why that gun popped up at Monroe Media Agency," I said before I shared a look with Gage.

His eyes darted toward Gage again before returning to me. "I wouldn't—" The words died on his lips. "Can I have a towel, please?"

Broderick came out of the bathroom, towel in hand. He

stared at Jake, almost daring him to do something before tossing a towel at him. The twins shared a look between each other.

Jake drew the towel up to his nose. "I think I need to go to the hospital."

"Don't care. How did you stalk Anais?"

"I might have followed her a few times and took pictures outside of her apartment window."

I saw red. "You fucking asshole!" I pulled my fist back, ready to land another hit, and he flinched back in response before attempting to cower.

"Damien, he's not worth it," Broderick said, saving Jake from another punch to his already busted face.

"Listen, I'm also the one that brought the box into Monroe Media Agency, but I didn't know what was in it. I swear that's all I did. Hey, I reported whatever I found to Carter by text message. I'll give you the number he gave me, and I'll also write down the address where I took photos of Anais. Carter gave me the key to an apartment, and it made things easier." He took a deep breath and visibly relaxed. "I'll give you everything and I swear I was never told about her disappearing. I only did this for some extra cash."

So, Jake was kept on a need-to-know basis. Smart, just in case he leaked any information. I took a step back, giving him an opportunity to get the things that he offered. He had nowhere to go but out the window, which would be a pretty steep drop. That was only if he made it past all four of us.

Jake walked over to a desk and flipped open a notebook. "It's around here somewhere," he muttered, as he moved on from the notebook and dug into one of his desk drawers.

"If you're trying to do something funny and pull out a

weapon, you'll be dead before you can blink." And I meant it. The fear I saw in his eyes was unmistakable when he briefly looked at me before returning to searching. My gut told me that he wasn't going to attempt to escape this situation, but I prepared myself just in case.

"Ah, here it is," he said, pulling out a torn piece of paper that clearly had seen better days. He turned it over and scribbled something down on it before handing it to me. I saw the phone number and the address and handed it to Kingston. "I need to go see someone about my nose. Fuck."

I ignored him. "Kingston, is this number registered to Cross Sentinel?"

"I'm almost positive it's not, but I'll double-check. Maybe we can pick up a signal from it." Kingston looked at me before looking at Jake and said, "I'll make a phone call and meet you in the car." He walked out with the piece of paper in hand.

I turned my attention back to Jake, who was holding out a key that I placed in my pocket. "If you hear from Carter at any point, you call me. If you tell anyone else what transpired here tonight, you're going to end up in the Hudson. Got me?" He nodded his head. "Definitely have your nose looked at, but you're lucky that's all that happened. You should probably start searching for a new job too."

With that, Broderick, Gage, and I filed out of Jake's tiny apartment and soon found ourselves entering Kingston's SUV. As we closed the doors, Kingston was wrapping up a phone call.

"So, Carter must have had a burner phone because just as I thought, that number didn't belong to us."

"Kingston, any updates on a signal from all of Carter's phones or Anais's?"

"Still nothing. Looks like the burner phone is off as well." Kingston pulled out of the parking spot and drove down the street. "I already put the apartment address that Jake gave us into the GPS. It shouldn't take us too long to get there."

I looked at the map on Kingston's screen and recognized the streets. "Hidden Tavern is on that corner. I think this building is near Anais's old apartment."

3

ANAIS

I could feel something wet falling on my face. *Am I outside? Is it drizzling? I can only hope that this is water.* I wanted to know what it was, but it took too much energy to open my eyes. It felt as if my body was being weighed down by something, pulling me further and further into the depths of the unknown. Visions of water surrounded me from all angles as I tried to fight, but nothing I did was helping to propel me in the opposite direction.

I yanked hard and felt something move, but there was no change. I tried again in an effort to potentially free myself. Nothing. I couldn't tell if I had imagined that I had moved or if I had made the motion. That was when I felt something hit me on my forehead. Then again and again.

Liquid? But I'm already surrounded by it. How can I feel drops of liquid on my face when I'm in the middle of the ocean battling to survive?

Yet the drops continued. I shifted and wiggled my fingers. The slight fidgeting led me to feel a cool hardness under my fingertips. *Am I on land? I think I'm lying on something hard.*

Coldness crept in as the pressure to keep my eyes closed eased yet opening them wasn't an option. Or so my body was telling me. The smell of mildew and something else I couldn't place filtered through my nostrils. A hazy feeling took over me as I tried to awaken my mind and body.

My eyes flickered when another drop landed on my forehead. *Where am I?*

A dull throbbing in my head took hold, yet, for some reason, I still couldn't open my eyes. I pulled all of my focus and energy away from identifying my surroundings by touch, smell, and hearing toward opening my eyes. A sudden noise that wasn't too far from me made me jump and adrenaline forced an eye open. However, I couldn't keep it open because the pain was intensifying and what felt like a jackhammer had made my head its home. *Am I alone?*

How I wished I weren't alone and instead back in Damien's arms. I held back a sob as a picture of Damien flashed through my mind. Would I ever see him again? Our relationship was reaching new heights and I could feel our partnership getting stronger. The vulnerability he displayed after he killed Jon, and the day the sunflowers were delivered, were just small snippets of the trust that had developed between us. Now, all of that was up in the air. The rush of emotion that I felt when I admitted to myself that I loved him hit me like a boulder and I fought the urge to cry.

I wondered if I had imagined the noise that I heard just a couple of minutes before. I thought about speaking to see if someone was there and could help me but keeping silent won over as I didn't want to alert anyone that I was awake and trying to pull myself together. Anything that might give my adversary the upper hand. I suppressed a groan and finally, I was able to open one of my eyes into a tiny slit and keep it open.

I was in what looked to be a dark room. My wobbly sight tried to focus on something but couldn't. The blurriness increased due to the blistering pain that was radiating through my skull. Unfortunately, that wasn't the only pain I was feeling. My body ached as if I'd just lost a fight. *What happened to me?*

I tried to force myself to open up my other eye, but it still felt too heavy. It was time to try something else. I slightly wiggled my feet, both seemed to be just fine, but when I tried to move my hands more, I froze. It hurt to move them and they were being restrained behind my back.

I heard another noise come from a corner of the room that I had no chance in hell of seeing. If I thought the first noise might have been a fluke, this one proved that I wasn't alone. Fear jolted my mind and body into action, and instinct called for me to flail my limbs to see if I could get up, but I refrained. Instead, I channelled my energy to slowly opening my other eye, allowing me to see my environment better. Part of me wanted to scream out for help, but fright kept a choke-hold on my vocal cords. I still had to squint both of my eyes, but at least I was able to use both of them.

What came into focus was the fact that I was in a small dark room. My first thought was that it had to be a basement given the lack of light and windows from what I could see. There were shadows in the distance that I couldn't make out and who knew what lurked in them. It differed from the plain room that Damien's men dragged me to right after my father was shot. The mildew and moldy smells were becoming suffocating, and the muskiness of the room increased not only my desire to figure out where I was but also the fear that was driving my heart to race.

My eyes opened a smidge wider as some of the memories flowed back into my consciousness. I remember being in Damien's penthouse and Carter coming up to the suite to tell me that Damien requested that I travel to his office to attend something related to his birthday. After I pulled myself together, I left the penthouse, but didn't pay attention to Carter as I locked the door. Then everything went black.

I should have known something was up, because Damien hadn't mentioned his birthday before he left the house. I blindly trusted Carter, who was supposed to protect me, and I shouldn't have.

I know I had been hit with something pretty heavy due to the headache I was sporting, unless it was from impact elsewhere. I wondered if I had a concussion, but those thoughts were cut short when I heard another noise from somewhere behind me. I tried to roll onto my back, but it was difficult given the placement of my hands.

These fucking zip ties again. If I never saw another one again if I got out of here, it would be too soon. I struggled against my bonds, secretly hoping, and praying that I would miraculously be free, but nothing happened.

Carter. Yes, we started out on the wrong foot after he led the team that snatched me out of harm's way and treated me more harshly than needed. I never would have thought that he would kidnap me and throw me back into peril. When I shifted my position, I almost cried out in pain. This time not from the throbbing in my head, but from an ache in my abdomen. It felt like I had been kicked there.

My brain struggled to figure out what his connection was

to the raspy-voiced man, but I hadn't a clue. I closed my eyes once more as the pounding in my head took over. *I need to get out of here.*

After several deep breaths, I opened my eyes again, hoping and praying that there was something I missed. Something that might aid me in getting out of here. Nothing but pitch blackness greeted me in return.

That was until I heard a slight commotion again. My stomach was in my throat as one word fell from my lips.

"Hello?"

4

DAMIEN

Kingston was right. We arrived in no time to an apartment building that looked almost identical to Anais's. When we opened the door, I shook my head, taking it all in. There was so much shit in the apartment that I knew it would take us a while to get through it all. Kingston must have reached the same conclusion because his hand immediately went for his phone and soon, he was calling for some members of his team to come to the apartment to do a more thorough search than we could do in the limited time we had. Every precious second wasted meant that Anais's life was in more danger.

The apartment was more of a studio. Carter and whoever he was working with had made sure to leave a mess. I flicked the switch, and a dullish light lit the room. The room was almost bare, from its off-white walls to the wooden floors that had seen better days. There was an almost-deflated air mattress in the room along with some food wrappers. Someone had lived here at least part-time.

"You've got to be kidding me," I said to no one in particular as I looked around the room. "It's clear he didn't have any time to clean anything out, so there might be something here. Just who knows what because of all of the shit we'll have to dig through."

"This might be a dead end."

I almost growled at Broderick, but he was right. This was looking more and more like a dead end.

"I won't rest until we find her."

"I know."

"There are some scraps left around so maybe something is here to tell us where he took Anais," said Kingston, interrupting my conversation with Broderick.

I hoped he was right.

"I'm going to stand guard at the door right here and keep watch."

I nodded at Broderick and the rest of us started digging through the papers and other items that we found. It was clear that someone had left in a hurry. If this space was indeed Carter's, I hoped that him kidnapping Anais wasn't a well-thought-out plan and that he had made a few mistakes that we could find.

"Someone's coming."

"Can you see who they are?"

"No. It's too dark."

A crash at the door caused both Kingston and me to draw our weapons. Broderick took a few steps back to line up with us before the intruders came in. I wish I could say I was surprised to see Will and his men standing before me, but I wasn't. It was only a matter of time before he would appear, and he couldn't have had worse timing. I also wasn't surprised that the two men that followed him into the room had their weapons drawn as well.

"What are you doing here, Will?"

"I think you know why I'm here."

I took a step toward him, ready for battle. "Where is Anais?"

Will held up his hands, while his guys behind him strengthened the hold they had on their guns. "What do you mean where is Anais?"

"This is not the time to fuck around with me. Where is she?"

"I have no idea what you're talking about. I'm here about Jon. Someone told me they saw him go into a warehouse the other night and not come back out. Your cousin over there owns said warehouse so it doesn't take much to put together what happened. I've had eyes on you ever since."

"You knew he had it coming. You should be thanking me."

Will shrugged. "He might have, but he was still a member of the Vitale family and it's up to us to take out our own trash. You should have just come and talked to me."

I adjusted my stance, my finger firmly on the trigger. "I know the Vitale family also does their damnedest to protect their women. I was protecting mine. He had plenty of warning to stop his behavior and refused." I knew I didn't have to explain myself to Will, but I didn't want to kill him. This standoff was causing me to lose even more time. The longer we had to stand here and deal with this, the more danger Anais was in. "We can hash this out at another time."

"But I want to 'hash' this out right now."

"Will, I don't have the time to deal with this—"

"Is it because your fiancée is missing?"

My shoulders tensed as his words floated around the room, but I didn't respond.

"Looks like one of the big dogs has suddenly become extremely vulnerable. What a perfect time to use this to my advantage."

I glanced at Gage, who was standing to my left. I could see that he was itching to make a move but I didn't know if he was armed because Kingston and I were the only ones who drew our weapons. "Did you take Anais?"

Will scoffed. "You would have known if I had. I don't exactly shrink off and hide from my actions. But now you must answer for what you've done to Jon. Family above all else, right? Put the gun down."

"Don't do it, Damien." Broderick's voice seemed a million miles away as I stared down the three men in front of me. Would putting my gun down get us out of here faster? I was also risking my life and the lives of my family if I did what Will asked.

"Put the gun down." His words came out low, almost daring me to disobey.

"Don't listen to him!"

My thoughts were at war with one another as I struggled to rise above the madness that had been a result of my own doing. I was the one who brought Anais into this; I was the one who killed Jon. And Will did have the upper hand here. But there was one card I hadn't played yet, and I knew once I did, that it would flip everything.

"Anais received sunflowers yesterday."

Will's eyebrow rose. "And what does that have to do with anything? Did she have a secret admirer, ready to swoop in once you threw her to the wolves?"

I kept a cool head, although it was tempting to rise to the bait that Will had just thrown out there. "No. But when I arrived home this evening and found that Anais was missing, I did find a note that was left behind. The note was signed with Charlotte's name."

I could see when my words registered in his mind. "Damien, I didn't think you would stoop so fucking low to lie about—"

"I'm not lying. Pull the piece of paper out of my back pocket."

Will shared a look with his guardsmen before walking around and coming toward me. Kingston and I still had our guns trained on the men in front of us who were ready to answer any gunfire with a response of their own. I knew I was giving Will an opportunity to assault me, but it was a risk I was willing to take. Anything that might lead to this stalemate ending and giving us an opportunity to get out of here and deal with the people we needed to deal with.

Will snatched the piece of paper out of my back pocket before taking a large step back from me. I held back the sigh of relief that was on my lips because he hadn't thrown a cheap shot in order to get me to drop my gun.

"You're telling the truth, but this has to be a lie. We both know that Charlotte is dead."

Will walked back into my field of vision and I could see that some of the confidence that he walked in here with had diminished.

"I don't know what this means yet but somehow, Charlotte is connected to Anais's disappearance and—"

"SHUT UP!" Will's words were raw and emotional. Something that I hadn't seen since the day of Charlotte's funeral. It was easy to hear his labored breathing in the silence of the room.

When it seemed that he wouldn't be saying anything else, I spoke up. "I know I'm the last person you want to deal with right now and you want revenge because I killed one of your guys. But if there is a shot that we can save my fiancée and your sister, we need to do this."

Will's eyes hadn't left the piece of paper, but he didn't say anything after I made my proposal. I started to wonder if he had gone into shock.

"Boss? What do you want us to do?" The man standing over Will's left shoulder spoke, asking the question we all wanted to hear the answer to.

"If you can promise me that we can find out about what happened to Charlotte and how she's tied into this, I'll spare your life."

"Deal," I said. "Now have your men drop their weapons and we'll drop ours." I allowed the words to pass over my lips, not knowing if I was telling the truth or not.

I could feel the power dynamic in the room shift as Will considered my words. He looked at the men standing over his shoulder and gestured for them to lower their guns. It took a moment for each man to comply, but once they did, Kingston and I followed suit.

"What can we do to help?"

What Will said was like music to my ears. "We need help digging through all of this stuff. We are looking for something that might give us a hint as to where Anais might be. If Charlotte is alive and involved in any of this at all, my gut tells me we will find out once we find Anais."

Will nodded his head. "But don't forget what I said. If this is a wild goose chase, I'm shooting you myself."

"Do you think I would lie about something like this?"

Will took two steps toward me and we were only standing about a foot apart. "No. But I know that people get desperate when they are backed into a corner. And that's where you are."

With a nod of his head, he gestured for his men to follow him and as the men walked around me, I put my gun away. The studio apartment didn't hold much in the way of furniture. Aside from the air mattress there was an old desk in the corner, and I headed over to it. Everyone spread out and looked through all of the crap that Carter and any of his accomplices left behind.

"Kingston," I said without looking up from the task at hand. "When are your men supposed to get here?"

"Not for another twenty to thirty minutes or so."

I wanted to be out of here by the time they arrived, with our next location in hand. Having them in here with us would only cause even more confusion and there was no way all of us would be able to fit in this small space. It was already a struggle with the seven of us here.

I was scanning through the papers in my hand when Gage said, "I found something."

I never knew those three words would cause my heart to careen out of control, but I bolted over to him and everyone else followed me. I looked at the pieces of paper in his hands. They were receipts from a hardware store and a grocery store in Gray, New Jersey. "It might be a long shot, but it might be a lead. Looks like he might have been preparing for something."

Normally I wouldn't have automatically assumed that someone stopping in a store in a random town would mean that they were staying there. But since this was the only lead we had, and that grocery list looked particularly long, it was worth a shot.

"Are you coming along?" My gaze left the receipts and drifted toward Will.

"Yes."

5

ANAIS

"Hello?" I asked, repeating what I said because I didn't get an answer the first time. My voice was nothing more than a croak. I decided to switch tactics because I needed to find out what was making noise in that dark abyss. I heard some rifling in the distance and panic set in. Was there a creature down here with me? After all they wouldn't be able to respond in words to me...

"Hi," came a soft voice laced with a hint of scratchiness, but full of relief.

My heart raced as I tried to make sense of it all. Fogginess clouded my mind as I tried to piece together the information I had. Who was this person and how were they involved in all of this?

"Who are you?" I asked, not wanting to trust that they were a prisoner like me.

"My name is Jenna." Her voice sounded a little stronger, but hesitant. "I thought you were dead."

"I feel that way if that's any consolation."

I could hear more movement and a few seconds later a

figure appeared. A woman with lighter colored hair that reached a few inches past her shoulders leaned down in front of me. I pulled away from her, weary that she might hurt me instead of help.

"Where are we?" The scratchiness in my throat became more prevalent.

"No clue. I woke up down here just like you did except when I did it, there was no one here."

I muttered a curse and closed my eyes tight, before opening them back up. Unless this was a ploy to get me to trust her, I could confirm that she was in the same predicament as me. "Great."

"It's so nice to have someone else here, as bad as that sounds," she said. "Are you feeling okay?"

I groaned and tried to swallow. The dryness in my throat was making me uncomfortable, but it ranked low on the scale of things that were fucked up about this entire situation. "I understand what you mean. I might have a concussion. Blazing headache and my vision is still a bit blurry although it seems to be clearing up. Body is hurting too." I closed my eyes and tried to swallow once more.

"I heard him bring you in here and I did my best to check up on you when he left, but you wouldn't wake up. There wasn't much I could do with my hands tied behind my back."

I nodded and thankful that she had looked after me. Yet, I immediately regretted the decision to move my head. I hissed and winced.

"Be careful," she said before she plopped down on the ground next to me. It was clear she was in better shape to move around than I was.

I took a deep breath and let it out. "How long have you been here?"

"Um, I'm not sure. There are no windows in here. If I had to guess maybe a day or so."

"And I just got here according to your calculations."

"That's right."

"Then today is February 4th."

I heard her gasp and suck in a breath. "I've been here for two days."

I felt bad for her, but a small glimmer of hope popped into my mind. "Would anyone know that you're missing? Maybe someone called the cops and alerted them that you didn't go to work?"

I saw Jenna shift slightly. "Potentially, but more than likely it will be a while before they discover I'm missing."

Just as quickly, those hopes were dashed and I could only hope that by now, Damien was looking for me.

"It felt as if we traveled for hours before he brought me here. Of course, that could be wrong."

That was understandable, especially if she had been kidnapped in a similar manner to me. "Where do you live?"

"Small town in Pennsylvania. Not too far from Philly."

The east coast of the United States was pretty large, but I wanted to bet Carter and whoever else he might have been working with stashed us not too far from New York City or Philadelphia.

"I live in NYC so maybe we aren't too far from either place." I was trying to sit up and not having much luck.

"That's where I'm from originally. Oh, let me help," Jenna said as she let me use her body as leverage to help me sit up against the wall about six inches away.

I leaned my head back on the wall, the motions that we just made taking a lot of energy. After a few deep breaths, I felt comfortable opening my eyes again.

"Have you been able to find a way out? Would it be something we might be able to achieve together? If Carter is alone, we might be able to outmaneuver him."

"Is that his name? And no. It's useless to scream. When I first got here, I screamed off and on until my voice went hoarse. I tried it again just before he brought you down here, but to no avail."

Ah, that explained the soft yet roughness of her voice. Sitting up allowed me to get a better visual of the room. I wondered if we were underground. That would explain the lack of windows.

"I never got a chance to ask you if anyone would be looking for you?" Her voice grew with the same hopefulness that I had just moments before.

"Ah, yes. My parents will start questioning things within the next day or so since I call them a few times a week. My best friend will also start panicking because we text at least once a day. I also wouldn't be surprised if my fiancé was looking for me right now."

"Fiancé? At least you have someone to look to when we get out of here."

I didn't correct her because of course I couldn't tell her that my relationship with Damien was fake. I assumed at the very least he would want to rescue me because he didn't want to have to deal with being a prime suspect in a kidnapping investigation. I moved my fingers and that was when I realized that something was missing. "Shit."

"What's wrong?"

"My ring is missing. I either lost it when Carter kidnapped me, or he snatched it."

"I'm sorry."

I didn't tell her how much I despised it anyway, but not having it hurt me more than I was willing to admit. Since Damien was the one who gave it to me, I was willing to overlook the issues I had with it. That shook me.

"Anyway, the best bet is that my fiancé, Damien, will be the quickest to start searching for me."

Jenna joined me in lying back against the wall. "I knew a Damien once."

"Oh really?" My heart leaped into my throat. It couldn't be possible that we knew the same Damien, right? New York City was huge and I'm sure there were a ton of Damiens within the city limits. "What's his last name?"

I asked the question, not sure if I wanted to know the answer. I held my breath as I waited to hear her response.

"Cross. His name is Damien Cross."

6

DAMIEN

"Did you send any more of your men to protect Anais's parents?" I needed to reach out to my father to warn him as well.

Kingston nodded. "Sent that message when I was waiting for you all to leave Jake's apartment."

"And I just texted Dad about what was going on. They are on high alert as well," Broderick chimed in from the backseat.

Well at least I don't have to worry about that.

The ringing of my phone dragged my attention away and the caller ID showed that it was an unknown number with a New Jersey area code. I answered without even thinking, hoping that maybe it was Anais calling from another number. "Anais?"

"Is this Damien?" The female voice wasn't the one I was longing to hear.

"Yes. Who is this?" I didn't have time for games. At least I wasn't driving so this phone call wasn't hindering that.

"Hi, this is Ellie. I called to see if Anais was with you? She and I were supposed to talk this evening, but she never called me."

I sat up a little straighter, causing the seat belt to pull a little tighter. I paused before responding, trying to decide how I was going to word what I wanted to say. "Anais has been kidnapped." Any finesse that I wanted to have was long gone. Being blunt and getting straight to the point was the goal here. The quicker this conversation went, the better.

"What! Did you just say that she has been—" she said. Her voice became more high-pitched. "Wasn't it your job to protect her?"

Hearing someone else say the words that I had been using to beat myself up over the last few hours added to the sucker punch feeling that I was currently nursing. Everything she said was correct and once again thoughts of how I failed Anais flooded my brain.

"Listen, Damien, I shouldn't have said that. I assume that you wouldn't want anything—"

"You're damn right I wouldn't want anything to happen to her."

I heard what sounded like a sniffle before Ellie said, "Have you heard anything from Anais or the person who kidnapped her? Are there any r-ransom demands?"

"I haven't heard anything." Wouldn't now have been an ideal time to contact me about paying for her return? Maybe Carter and whomever he was working for weren't after money.

"So, we don't know if she's dead or alive." Her voice cracked at the end of her statement and it was easy to tell she was barely hanging on.

"Ellie, I'm going to get her back. I promise you this."

I heard some shuffling in the background before Ellie sighed on the other end of the line. "I know you will. Is there anything I can do to help?"

"As of right now, no. If Anais or someone else contacts you about her, call me immediately."

"O-okay." There was a brief pause on the other end of the line and then she continued, "Now I'm thankful that we didn't try to move me back to the city yet. Nick mentioned that it might be a few more days before it made sense for me to come back."

At the mention of her bodyguard's name, I looked up from my phone and turned to Kingston. Kingston nodded, confirming the information that Ellie shared.

Yet another thing I didn't know about Anais. Ellie's comment caused a new round of thoughts to pop into my head. Was it possible that Carter told someone else about his plans even if he was being vague about it?

"Who is Carter closest to, Kingston?"

"I assume he would be closer to a few of the guys on the team because he's been with us for a couple of years." He stopped and glanced out of the sideview mirror before he continued. "Maybe Nick. He has a knack for making friends with anyone. He's who we sent to watch Ellie."

"I'll ask Ellie to grab him." *This might be another break for us.* "Hey, Ellie?"

Her sniffling continued and I could tell she was attempting to calm herself down.

"Yeah?" Her voice was shaky, and I wondered if she would be able to hold it together for much longer.

"Is Nick near you now?"

"No. He's probably sitting in my parents' living room. I

had wondered why he decided to set up shop there a couple of hours ago, but it was because of all of this I assume," she mumbled as I heard a commotion in the background before Ellie said, "Here's Nick."

I put the phone on speaker and set it on the console.

"Okay, Nick. Kingston here. How close are you to Carter?"

"We talk on occasion. Have grabbed a couple of beers here and there when we were off the clock."

"Do you know anything about whether or not he had some sort of property close by? Within driving distance of New York City?"

"Yes. He mentioned having a place in Jersey. Some sort of cabin that he would go to when he had time off. He didn't refer to it as a vacation spot, just that he had a place where he could stay when he wanted to lay low. His goal is to retire and eventually move to an island and be away from the world."

Chances were that he didn't take Anais anywhere near an island, but I wanted to double-check one thing. "Did he ever mention where the cabin was?"

"Yes. Sorry, I'm blanking. It was something unusual. Not Orange, New Jersey..."

"Gray?"

"That's it."

"Address?"

"Not one that I know of. I also don't know if the property is in his name or not."

Kingston cleared his throat. "Nick, I'm sending backup your way just in case Carter or any associates of his try to cause any more shit."

"But I have a handle on everything—"

"Carter is considered armed and dangerous. He has

nothing to lose, and I don't want to lose anyone else. Copy that?"

"Yes."

I was thankful that we were already on our way to Gray. We didn't have an address, but at least we had an area. Maybe we might be able to talk to someone there and get directions.

Kingston placed more pressure on the gas, and we sped off to New Jersey, to a town that might be where Anais was being held captive.

7

ANAIS

W as it the concussion or did she really just say that she knew Damien Cross?

"How do you know him?"

"We dated a lifetime ago."

I raised an eyebrow. "How long is a lifetime?" My heart started racing as I waited for her answer.

"Our senior year of high school. We hadn't been dating for long, before something tragic happened, pulling us apart."

"You're Charlotte." I could barely see Jenna look down at her lap, her hair covering her face. I almost expected her to deny the claim, but she didn't. She sniffled and I continued, "Damien thinks you're dead."

"No one has called me Charlotte in well over a decade. And most people do think I'm gone." Another sniffle ended her sentence.

I wished I could have handed her a tissue, but I didn't have one and our hands were tied. The tone of her voice made the story sound believable, but I was still studious.

Here was a woman that was supposed to be dead for years due to a house fire, yet now I was supposed to believe that she was alive and well? I saw how much Damien was affected by her "death" and if she was telling the truth, I wished she would have told him that she was alive. At the very least, I knew I should be nice to her just in case she was involved in my kidnapping and maybe that would be enough to buy me time.

"Is it okay if I call you Charlotte?"

"Yes, I would like that."

"What happened? And how did you get here?"

"Since you know my real name, I assume Damien told you about what happened that night."

"Yes, he told me his version of events, but I want to hear from you."

"The whole thing was a setup."

"Wait, what?"

"I was forced to lure Damien there."

"Wait—What? Why would anyone want to kill Damien? He was only in high school."

"The long and short of it is that it all started with our parents. Martin Cross and my father, Harvey, were associates and did business together until my father died. One of my older brothers, Vincent, always blamed Martin for my father's death."

That's when it clicked. "And by killing Damien that was his way of getting back at him."

"Right. I just did as I was told. Well, sort of." She sighed again. "Vincent lost it when our father killed himself and with Will away at the time Vincent was my only guardian. Vincent was in and out of trouble as a teen and Dad always bailed him out. With him being the oldest child they were extremely close so when Dad passed I was shocked that he took it harder than both Will and me. Once the dust settled, he hatched this plan where I would start dating Damien and that later turned into the trip up to our vacation home in upstate New York. He threatened to kill me if I didn't do what he wanted."

Charlotte took a deep breath and continued, "A few days before heading upstate, I decided there was no way I could kill Damien and I came up with a plan. I gave Vincent the signal when I knew Damien was downstairs, hoping that it would give Damien an opportunity to get away because he was on the first floor instead of the second. I left my phone in the bedroom and tip-toed across the hall to the guest room with a small bag that I'd packed. I'd hoped and prayed that he would survive as I climbed through one of the windows in a guest bedroom and took off into the forest. I knew there was a chance that Vincent might kill me, so I kept going. I called the police from my burner phone and ditched it while I was travelling through the woods. I eventually made it to civilization and was able to disappear. I kept tabs on the news and everyone had assumed I died in the fire and I thought Vincent had too. I bought a fake identity and changed my name and moved to a small town in Pennsylvania. I've been hiding in plain sight until Carter tracked me down, which makes me think that Vincent just let me go."

Her voice broke and she sniffled again.

"Are we completely sure that Carter works for Vincent? I don't know much about Will other than the evening I met him."

Charlotte nodded. "He probably kidnapped me to kill me

but harming you would be the way to get back at him." She paused and although I had several questions running through my mind, I gave her the moment to herself. "He hasn't mentioned Vincent, but I assume that would be the only person who would want to track me down, especially now that I know your connection to Damien." She sniffled again. "Vincent is very thorough and has friends in high places in addition the power that he wields. I assume I'm a loose end and it's only a matter of time before he kills me, especially since I disobeyed his orders. Since Carter hasn't killed either one of us, I assume he's holding out until he can get us to Vincent."

"Does Carter have a schedule for when he comes down here? I assume he brings you food and lets you use the bathroom."

She nodded. "He does, but I couldn't tell you when he comes down."

"That's right, you can't tell because we don't have phones, nor can we see outside... Well, I think we need to have a plan for when he comes for a visit."

NEITHER SHE NOR I knew when Carter was going to come down, but when he did, I pretended to still be out of it. I heard the basement door open with a loud creak and an overhead light turned on. I could see that it lit the room up considerably through my closed eyelids. I wasn't sure where Charlotte had decided to go because she was out of my field of vision, but I had hoped that she had done what she said she was going to do, while I sat in a corner, looking feeble and weak.

"Figure out a way to eat this. We'll be leaving here in a few hours."

I could hear him getting close to me and almost jumped out of my skin when I felt him pull my hair back. He placed his fingers on my neck and mumbled, "Still alive."

I cracked open one eye, glad that my hair was somewhat masking my face and the small vision problem I had earlier was doing better. Just as he was about to place a plate of something in front of me, his body lurched forward. That's when I knew that Charlotte had stuck to the plan.

Charlotte rammed him hard from behind, sending him head-first into the concrete wall, but she didn't stop there. As he fell to the cold stone floor, she kicked him hard in his groin, twice, then stomped on his head, all before he knew what hit him.

It all seemed to happen in slow motion. Once she had him down and hopefully out for a few minutes, she ran over to me, and stood by me, ready to help if she could as I struggled to my feet. I knew I was wasting precious seconds, but my head was still throbbing from that knock on the forehead he'd given me.

Carter groaned as he started to come to, and I knew we needed to get out of there or he'd probably kill us.

"We need to go now!" I rushed with her toward the stairs.

The stairs weren't very steep, but they were difficult to climb with our arms secured behind our backs and my injury. As soon as we reached the top, I kicked the door closed behind us. I took a second to grip the knob and turn the lock. It took me longer than normal with my hands behind my back, but I finally managed it. I wasn't sure if it would hold if he decided to throw his weight against it, but hopefully, it would give us enough time to figure out how to get out of the zip ties.

Glancing about the room we now stood in, we could see that he must have been living up here for a while. There were beer cans and empty pizza boxes littering the coffee table and floor of the living room. Through the doorway, I could see a pile of dishes in the kitchen sink, and an overflowing garbage can that was starting to stink.

"Do you see a weapon or something that we can use to untie our hands?" Charlotte asked.

"We should check the kitchen. Maybe there's a knife or something in there."

We passed through the opening into the small kitchen. It really was tiny, just a sink, fridge, oven, and a small countertop with two drawers and a cabinet below.

"I'll try the drawers." Charlotte backed up toward one of the drawers and used her tied hands to open it.

"Hurry, I think he's on the stairs, Charlotte!" I urged her, but I wasn't sure where he was at the moment. I glanced over my shoulder back toward the living room, praying we'd be faster than Carter.

I moved over toward her and glanced in the drawer, adrenaline pumped through my body and thanked everything I could think of when my eyes landed on a pair of scissors.

"We can use those scissors to cut these off, can you grab them?" I asked. "Never mind. Yank the drawer out, move out of the way, and let the drawer fall. That'll be faster I think."

She did and down went the drawer along with all of its contents.

I winced as we both dropped to the ground and I grabbed the scissors first. Once we were back to back, I used my left hand to feel where her fingers were, I found the small space between her hands where the zip tie held her wrists together. I slipped my fingers into the finger-holes and opened the scissors and just as I made contact with the plastic of the tie, I heard Carter slam his shoulder into the basement door and I jumped, losing my grip on the tie. "Okay, we need to try to line up so that I can cut you free."

"Okay," she said.

It took a little bit more maneuvering than I had planned as Carter's body could be heard ramming into the door again.

"Shit!" I swore, dropping the scissors. Scrabbling, I stretched to pick up the scissors once more. "We're close, just need to line it up properly again."

I stared over my shoulder and almost shouted out when we got Charlotte's binds positioned with the blades of the scissors.

"I think you've got it lined up."

"Okay, it's going to take a bit of chopping because these things are dull. I'm trying not to hurt you."

"Don't worry about that," she said, even though I know she didn't mean it. A pounding on the basement door made her yelp, which caused me to jump.

"Try to ignore him." My breath was coming out in short spurts as Charlotte tried to help by rubbing her hands back and forth against the scissors as I tried to cut the plastic. Of course, the scissors had to be dull because that was just my luck. "Almost got it."

She then yanked on the zip tie. I turned around and looked at her wrists and noticed they were turning red from the strain she was putting on them. When we whittled away another piece of the zip tie, it took one final tug and Charlotte was free.

"Yes!" She didn't even take a moment to nurse her red wrists before she took the scissors out of my hands and began to work on my zip tie.

When we heard the basement door burst open, I yelled, "Oh no! Just go."

"But—"

"Just go!" I screamed, my voice still hoarse. "Take the scissors with you!" I knew there was a slim chance that I would be able to get free if she left the scissors here, but leaving another weapon at Carter's disposal wasn't wise.

Charlotte grabbed the scissors and scrambled to her feet. She ran toward the back door and yanked it open.

"Come back here, you bitch," Carter said. His lips curled into a sneer as he took a step toward her.

"Go!" I yelled at Charlotte. She spared one glance at me before she took off running.

"Well, too bad she left you behind. You're the bigger prize anyway."

8

DAMIEN

All I could think about was probable scenarios that might have happened to Anais and what state she might be in. My mood drifted from rage to sorrow because I was the one who put her in this situation. I tapped my phone, which was resting in the center console, and wondered if now was the right time to call Anais's parents to let them know that their only child was in grave danger. I felt someone clasp their hand around my shoulder, and I turned around and found Broderick leaning forward from his seat in the row behind me.

"Everything is going to be fine. Anais is strong and we're going to get her back."

I wanted to believe that, but there was more going on than just that. It was the feeling that I now knew that the reason she was in this predicament was because of me. I also had no doubt that we would get her back, I just didn't know what shape she would be in when we did.

And that caused the rage in me to build further. Yes, I was furious at Carter, but I was also pissed at myself. I hadn't done enough to protect her and that thought nearly killed me. There was more I could have done. Not knowing whether she was alive or dead caused turmoil to roll through my body.

She's alive. She's going to be okay. As I told myself these words, I wasn't sure if I really believed them. Flashbacks to what happened to Charlotte played in my mind. I remembered how much I had hoped and prayed that by some miracle she had made it out of that burning house alive. When I was at her funeral about a week or so later, guilt surged through me and continued over the years. My feelings for her had turned from sharing times of happiness in the months that we were together to anticipating that her memory would terrorize me once I fell asleep.

I was surprised that by now, Carter hadn't tried to contact either me or Anais's parents demanding conditions of her release. That told me that there was more at play here than we were currently aware.

As the SUV sped down the road, causing the streetlights to be nothing more than a blur, I vowed to make sure I didn't make the same mistakes again.

WE MADE it to New Jersey in record time, but the drive for me had been brutal. Thanks to the lack of traffic on the street and Kingston's superb driving skills, we were now five minutes outside of Gray, New Jersey. It still felt as if we weren't getting there fast enough. Every second that passed meant that her life was on the line, and who knew when Carter might cut the cord?

The thought of losing her made me want to break

through a thousand brick walls. My thoughts came crashing down when Kingston swerved, trying to avoid something that I had missed while I had been caught up in my own head.

"What the fuck?" I said as he swerved to get back on the road and then slammed on the brakes. "Is everyone all right?"

I looked back at my brothers and through the back windshield toward Will's oncoming SUV as it pulled to a stop behind us. Turning forward, I looked to see what Kingston had swerved to miss. A woman ran toward us, waving her arms above her head. My heart stopped, but it soon became apparent that it wasn't Anais.

"What the hell, Kingston!" Broderick yelled from the backseat.

I didn't get a good look at her as she ran over to the driver's side window.

"Please help," she said, trying to catch her breath. She held her hand out, pointing down the road and said, "Me and another woman were kidnapped, and I was able to get free but she's still with him."

"She must be talking about Anais!" My heart pounded in my chest as I tried to undo the seat belt, but my hands were shaking as rage filled me. I was going to kill the fucker if he had hurt one beautiful strand of hair on her head. As I got free of the belt, I pulled my gun and opened the door. The woman couldn't have been running for long. I would find where the fucker was keeping Anais and then I would beat the shit out of him.

I followed where the woman had pointed down the road, and a couple of minutes later, I came across a narrow dirt road that showed footprints from where the woman had been running. I followed it to a cabin that was surrounded by trees.

Had she not pointed it out, I doubted we would have found it so easily.

The cabin looked a bit run-down, but someone was in the process of fixing it up based on the tools located outside. There was a light on the main level, and I hoped, given that it looked to be a relatively small home, it might be easy to locate Anais. Unless he moved her when that woman ran off. I took the safety off my gun and decided to take a look around the cabin. Silently, I moved through the trees, checking it out. When I reached the back, I could see the door was standing open. I headed toward it, quietly so I wouldn't draw Carter's attention. Thankfully, the stairs of the porch didn't shift or make too much noise under my weight. I looked through the kitchen window to see if I could see him or anything that would tell me what I was walking into.

A quick look showed me Carter was standing in the kitchen and I quickly ducked down. If I went in the open back door, he'd be right there, and I wanted to take him by surprise. I moved back down the stairs and went around to the front of the house. If the front door was locked, I wouldn't have a choice but to use the back door, but it was worth it to take him by surprise.

I grabbed the knob and twisted and thankfully it opened quietly. I took a step through the door and closed my eyes for a split second when the floor groaned under my weight. I took a step through the door and closed my eyes for a split second when the floor groaned under my weight. I paused for a moment to see if anyone had been alerted to my arrival. No one came so I stepped farther inside and looked to my left and to my right.

Carter was standing in front of the kitchen counter with Anais at his feet.

Fuck! How did I not see her on the floor when I looked through the window?

The stars had aligned because Carter's back was to me, but Anais's back was up against the cabinets with her head limp, chin on her chest.

I thought I knew what fear was when I hadn't known her fate, but when I saw her like that and she didn't move immediately, real, terrifying fear slammed into me making it hard to breathe. I couldn't tell if she was alive. My heart clenched and I saw nothing but red.

Another second passed and I heard Carter murmuring to himself, yet he didn't look over to the door. Then something drew my attention, a movement, and my eyes were drawn back to Anais, and found her staring back at me. She was alive. The fear left me, but the rage intensified as I watched her eyes widen. I put a finger to my lips to let her know not to alert Carter as I slowly moved toward them.

But something must have given me away, some slight sound or creak of the floor, because suddenly Carter turned around, whipping what looked to be a weapon out toward me. I acted on instinct and shot him in the arm holding the weapon. His knife fell to the ground with a clack and Carter moaned in pain. I kicked the knife further away and dragged him from the kitchen by his hair, closer to the front door.

Carter grunted, but I didn't care that I was hurting the fucker. He didn't know what pain was, but he would by the time I was done with him. For now, I slammed the butt of my gun into his head and knocked him out, letting him drop to the floor. He'd be out for a while, at least long enough for

Kingston to arrive and cart him off. I dashed over to Anais and dropped to my knees in front of her, setting my weapon down at my side within easy reach.

"I'm so glad to see you," she said. Her voice was hoarse and sounded like music to my ears.

"The feeling is mutual."

"Can you...untie me?" I leaned over and saw that her hands were tied behind her back with a zip tie that had scuff marks as if someone had tried to cut it open. I noted that this time around, her wrists weren't as bruised as they were when I tried to save her from sharing the same fate as her father. When I thought about how Carter had done that too, rage filled me once again.

"Did you find—"

Her words were cut off when Kingston came rushing into the cabin with his gun drawn. He surveyed the scene before he walked up to Carter and said, "You have a lot of explaining do, asshole." He turned to us. "Are you two all right?"

"Yeah, we're fine. Do we have a knife in the car? I don't want to use Carter's weapon of choice."

"We might. We definitely have something to cut that with in my bag."

"Sounds good." I stood up and put my gun away but didn't take my eyes off of Anais. I couldn't believe that we found her, and she seemed relatively unharmed. The fear that had a chokehold over me earlier was fading away and relief was taking its place. I bent down to pick up Anais, cradling her as if she were a doll made of glass, and carried her outside.

"I'm so glad to see you," she said.

"You said that already."

"It bears repeating."

I snorted. "That I understand, Spitfire." I looked down at her and noticed a glassy look in her eyes. "You're going to see a doctor."

"Not going to argue with you. My head is throbbing and my body hurts."

"Rest for now. I'm taking care of everything."

"Okay."

With each step I took toward the SUVs parked on a dirt road leading to the cabin, the further away we moved from how quickly I came to losing her.

We were about halfway to the SUV when another one drove up. There were no lights on or sirens blaring so I assumed it wasn't the authorities.

"There's my team," Kingston said from behind me. I glanced over my shoulder and found him walking out of the cabin with Carter, who was still moaning in pain. "Shut up."

"Ow."

"We'll get him back to the warehouse and interrogate him, you'll want to be there, I assume?" At my nod, Kingston glanced over at Will's SUV. "When we get everything settled, you're going to want to hear the rest of the story."

I didn't reply; my attention was focused on making sure that Anais was safely in our SUV. Broderick was in the driver's seat and Gage was sitting in the front seat staring out the windshield like a deer in headlights. I rushed past the driver's side door and opened the back door.

"Damien—wait."

I froze. Those two words sent an ice-cold shiver down my spine. The voice couldn't be real. It was impossible because that voice belonged to someone that I knew was long dead.

My heartbeat slowed and I slowly turned around as two people came toward me. Will I recognized immediately, but the other... the other had to be an apparition because I'd watched her die in a house fire. She looked different now, different hair color, older, but still there was no mistaking her.

"Charlotte?" Her name came out in a harsh whisper as I stared at her.

The trance that Charlotte had over me for a brief moment was broken when Anais moaned in my arms. I needed to make sure that she was okay because she was my priority now. I turned back to the SUV. "Broderick, can you call a doctor or nurse? Have them meet us at the penthouse."

"You got it. I know just who to call."

My eyes drifted back to Charlotte, who was definitely not a ghost or a figment of my imagination.

"Is everything cool with us now?" My gaze didn't shift from Charlotte, but it was Will who spoke.

"You're not going to believe this, but Charlotte is pretty sure our older brother, Vincent, is behind this."

9

ANAIS

"Damien?" My voice sounded rough to my own ears.

"I'm here." He sounded nearby, but I couldn't tell how close.

Determination forced me to open my eyes. I squinted as my eyes tried to adjust. I found Damien sitting in a chair a couple of feet away, with his head in his hands.

"Are you okay?"

Damien looked up at my question and walked over and sat down next to me on the bed. I shifted over slightly to give him more room but winced.

"Don't move."

"I won't do it again because it hurt."

"Grace should be here soon, but you can rest until she gets here."

I stopped myself from nodding my head, instead taking a moment to look at Damien. The soft light from the lamp on the bedside table cast a warm glow in the room. Damien brought me into the bedroom that had once been his but was now ours.

The light also revealed just how much tonight had taken a toll on Damien. From his wrinkled clothes, his hair sticking up in every direction, and the redness that could be found in his gaze.

"I could have lost you tonight."

His voice stopped me from observing his appearance and when I looked up at him, I couldn't stop the wetness that was forming in the corners of my eyes. The slight quiver as he said the words was almost my undoing.

How close I had been to death tonight could be anyone's guess. What I did know was that everything that transpired tonight would stay with me for the rest of life.

"I'm not going to let another moment go by without telling you that I love you."

His words would also stay with me for eternity and beyond. The tears fell from my eyes as I whispered, "I love you too."

His head slowly moved down toward mine, his eyes focusing on my lips. "I'm worried about pulling you into my arms, since we don't know what your injuries are yet. But there is one thing I can do."

His lips came to rest on mine.

"Ms. Monroe?"

I could hear someone calling, but I didn't want to wake up. My eyelids felt heavier than I could ever remember them feeling.

"Ms. Monroe?"

The voice was a bit louder, and I tried harder to open my eyes. Once I was able to open them into tiny slits, I could see a sliver of my surroundings. I couldn't get a good visual of where I was, but I knew there were a few people in the room based on the murmurs I heard in the background. I blinked hard. That seemed to work because I was able to open my eyes wider and catch a glimpse of what was going on in the room. I found myself in our bedroom in the penthouse.

"Hi," I said, my voice barely above a whisper. Someone rushed to my side and when I looked up, I found Damien.

"Anais, how are you feeling?"

"Mostly tired. Head still hurts but I'll take that over the somewhat blurry vision I experienced in the cabin and my body is sore." Tears welled up in my eyes as I relived my experiences over the last twenty-four hours. Who knew what Carter would have done once he moved Charlotte and me? I wondered what happened to her.

Damien grabbed my hand, and I took the opportunity to glance around the room and I found Damien, Broderick, and a blonde woman who I had never met before. When my eyes landed on her, she spoke.

"Hi, I'm Grace. I'm going to take a look at you to see how things are going. We want to make sure you don't need to go to the hospital."

I froze at the word *hospital* and Damien must have felt me tense up. "She's not going to the hospital," he said.

"She will if it means saving her life. Concussions can be tricky. If everything checks out, I'll be happy for her to stay here and you can let me know if she develops any more symptoms. If her symptoms get worse, you need to rush to the emergency room."

Damien didn't have a response. Broderick walked up and put a hand on Grace's shoulder and said, "Damien, you know she's right. You asked me to call a doctor or a nurse and I called the best doctor I knew." Grace and Broderick glanced at each other before looking back at me. *What's up with them?*

"Let me examine her and I'll let you know what I think."

Damien moved out of the way, allowing Grace to move closer to me. Broderick stepped out of the room, but Damien refused, instead deciding to sit in as Grace started her assessment.

The examination didn't take too long, and Grace took a small step back and said, "So far it looks like Anais is doing as well as could be expected so she can stay here. For the next twenty-four hours, you'll need to make sure she doesn't sleep more than a few hours at a time. No television, phone, or laptop for at least a week, I'd prefer two, but I understand you may need to use your phone and laptop for work, so I'll suggest keeping it to no more than an hour a day. I'll come back and check on her in a few days to make sure that she is improving. Resting is key here." Grace looked at me and then back at Damien. "If you notice anything like vomiting, slurred speech, or if a severe headache isn't getting better let me know and bring her into the emergency room. Sometimes symptoms of a concussion don't show for a few days."

Damien nodded. "Thanks for coming."

"It wasn't any trouble. Happy to help."

Grace turned her attention to the door and opened it. Broderick appeared and asked, "Is everything okay?"

Grace nodded.

"Good. Are you still coming over with Hunter to get pizza and watch basketball on Sunday?"

"Since I'm off, I wouldn't miss it."

"Let me walk you out." With that Broderick and Grace left the room.

"What was that—"

"Anais, don't worry about it. We need to focus on you getting well."

"But what about Charlotte?"

Damien's eyes froze over. "She's okay. We can talk more about that later."

GROGGINESS FLOATED over me like a heavy blanket as I tried to wake up the next morning. I vaguely remembered being woken up multiple times last night by Damien. I groaned as I started to feel my muscles working again. Flashbacks of the events at the cabin slammed into me. I thought I had been lucky enough to escape them while I was dreaming, but it seemed my luck ran out as the weight of those memories crushed me while I was awake. Parts of last night were a blur. The feeling that I was going to die in that basement was very much real. I had wondered if I would ever see my parents or Ellie again.

I heard a noise come from another corner of the room and I turned my head slightly. I found Damien typing on his computer in a comfortable-looking black chair that was closest to the side of the bed that I was lying on. I'd worried about not seeing him again either.

The images of the chaos when Charlotte and I tried to

escape and when she finally did flooded back to the surface. I wondered where Charlotte was as I moved again, trying to get comfortable and ease the thoughts of the trauma I had experienced over the last twenty-four hours out of my brain.

Damien either heard me or saw me move because he looked over. He placed the laptop at his feet and came over to me, still the picture of perfection and control.

"Hey, how are you doing?"

"Better. I think." I moved to sit up in bed. My voice sounded better, and my headache had lessened, showing me that I was healing from this ordeal. At least, physically.

"Don't move too much. Doctor's orders." Damien placed a firm hand on my shoulder, slowing my pace before moving to fluff my pillows and then helping me sit up.

"So, this gives you even more reason to be bossy."

"When have I ever needed an excuse?"

That made me snort. He sat down next to me on the bed and tucked a piece of my hair behind my ear. The soft gesture sent a warmth through my body that I hadn't felt since Damien lifted me out of the disaster area that had been the cabin. Now that I was more lucid, there were questions that I wanted answered that I was tired of avoiding.

"What's going to happen to Carter?"

"Don't worry about him. He will be taken care of."

I chose my next words wisely because I knew that it was opening another can of worms. "Then I assume you talked to Charlotte. She's fine, right?"

He stiffened at the mention of her. I was hesitant to ask about her again, but she was an integral part of what was going on. "She's going to be fine. You were by far in worse condition than she was. She's under Will's protection now. Kingston offered a couple of his men, but Will declined."

"How many people work for Kingston?" I blurted the question out and left Damien chuckling.

"I'm not sure, but he has a whole operation that he has built from the ground up. Tried to recruit Broderick, Gage, and me, but we decided to offer funds for the initial investment instead. The rest is history."

"And as far as we know, Carter was the only one who slipped through the cracks? I don't want Charlotte to be harmed."

"Yes. Kingston's team has been working day and night to make sure that Carter was the only rogue team member and so far, that is looking to be the case. You seem to be pretty attached to Charlotte's well-being."

"I am." I took in a deep breath before I continued. "She saved my life."

"I know, and for that, I will forever be grateful."

"I think it would be wise if you two spoke as well." Based on what she told me, I thought her words might help ease some of the pain that Damien had been dealing with years after the fire.

"That is not up for discussion."

I wasn't shocked by his words. I was shocked that he let this conversation continue for as long as it had. I couldn't stop the yawn that passed my lips.

"You are overexerting yourself."

"No I'm not. I'm not doing anything but talking."

Damien gave me a pointed glare.

"Well, it seems that we know that chances are that Charlotte's brother is the one behind all of this."

Damien nodded. "That hasn't been confirmed, but we'll find out more information about that soon. Charlotte mentioned something about it to Broderick and Gage when she confirmed her identity."

His words had a strong whiff of danger and apprehension. He let his brothers handle the woman whose memory had haunted him for years instead of doing it himself. I assumed part of that was due to him taking care of me, but I wondered if he was avoiding her on purpose. I wanted to tell him that I thought it was important that they spoke, but I didn't want to push him any further.

"How long have I been out?"

"Well, it's about 3:00 p.m."

That meant I had been sleeping on and off for about eight hours.

"Have you been waking me up every couple of hours?"

Damien nodded. That meant that he hadn't been able to rest much at all either. "You should get some more rest."

"I think a bath might help relax me and make it more likely that I'd fall asleep." I also wanted to take the opportunity to remove the grime as well.

Damien stood up. "We can make that work. I'll go run a bath."

"Thank you."

It felt weird to have him wait on me, but I didn't read too much into that. I slowly took the covers off of me in an abundance of caution, because I didn't know how my body would feel or how well I could currently move due to the concussion or any sore muscles and bruises I had.

"Hey, don't move too fast," Damien said as he walked out of the bathroom and spotted the position that I was in. He helped me up and took me to the bathroom where I saw myself in the mirror for the first time.

"Well, I look horrible." The bruising on my forehead said as much and I tried to mentally prepare myself for what I would find once I rid myself of all of my clothes.

Damien sat me down on the edge of the tub before he responded. "You are and always will be beautiful. The most beautiful and elegant person that has ever entered my life. Inside and out. And the people that did this to you will now answer to me."

The finality in his words was what made me stay quiet and I turned my attention to the tub that was quickly filling up with warm water. When it was at the perfect depth, Damien reached over and turned it off.

"You know, I didn't even realize you changed my clothes." He had put me in some of his clothes that were a loose fit on me.

"I knew the clothes that you had on weren't going to be comfortable for you to rest in. How much help do you need?"

"Thank you. I can definitely get my shirt off, but the pants might be a little difficult," I said, making moves to taking my shirt off. That was when a memory clicked. "Oh my God. I didn't tell you that I think either Carter stole the engagement ring, or it got lost when he was bringing me to the cabin."

"Don't worry about it."

"It seems to me there are a whole lot of things I shouldn't be worried about that I'm actually worrying about."

"You hated it anyway."

I was speechless, but what he said was true. The ring wasn't what I had envisioned, and I was upset that I didn't have any input in its selection even if it was for a fake engagement. I decided to focus on getting in the tub. It took longer than normal for me to take my clothes off, but it hadn't been as a result of me staring at the bruises that had formed on my body.

Damien's eyes lingered on my naked body before he spoke.

"I didn't see all of these last night," he murmured before helping to lower me into the tub. After he did that, he walked toward the door and dimmed the lights so that there was a nice warm glow.

"Where are you going?"

"To change the bedsheets. I'll come back in soon to bring you back to bed."

"You aren't going to have someone come over and do it for you?"

Damien bent down on one knee and smirked at me. "You don't think I know how to change the sheets on a bed?"

"I—uh."

"It keeps me humble." He didn't say anything else before he left, and I found myself laughing. It felt good to laugh out loud.

I don't know how long I soaked in the tub, but a soft knock brought me out of the daydream I was in. Had this been the first time Damien ever knocked before entering a room I was in? "Come in."

Damien strolled into the room. "Are you done with your bath?"

"I am."

Damien helped me stand up before grabbing a towel off of the warming rack and wrapping me up in it. He stood by me as I walked back into his bedroom and found a freshly made bed, some of my cosmetics, and another set of Damien's sweatpants and a T-shirt that I didn't even know he had. I could have cried from happiness, but I swallowed those tears.

"Thank you," I whispered as I sat down on the bed.

As I got ready for bed, Damien said, "Your parents and Ellie are on their way back to New York City to be with you."

"That's great. I miss them."

"I know you do."

"I'm starting to feel a little more tired."

"That's fine. Go to sleep and then when you wake up, they will be here."

He helped me get into bed and I mumbled something in agreement, but I couldn't even remember what I said. My mind drifted to sweet dreams that I hoped wouldn't be interrupted by the nightmare I had just lived.

THE NEXT TIME I woke up, I heard chattering in the living room. It was dark outside, making it harder to recognize what time it was, but I assumed it was the evening of the same day. It took a few moments for me to will myself to reach over to turn on the lamp on the bedside table near me.

It was there that I found my purse and grabbed it off the bedside table. I looked to see if all my things were inside. When I picked up my phone, I heard a light knock on the door.

"Come in," I said, feeling weird telling someone to come into Damien's bedroom. Speaking of Damien, he was the one who had knocked and greeted me with a small smile.

"Did you sleep well?"

"I think so. Are my parents and Ellie here?"

Damien nodded. "And they'll be staying in the building for a little while to be closer to you."

That brought a smile to my face. "Yes! I want to go see them," I said as I whipped off the covers.

"How about they come in here?"

"But you don't like people being in your bedroom."

He shrugged. "Some things change." He wasn't wrong about that either. "I'll bring them in here and then I'll have to head out. There are guards at the door making sure that no one enters or leaves without my permission."

"Where are you going?" I asked.

"I have some business to take care of, but it shouldn't take too long."

I started to ask what he meant but stopped myself when I heard my mom say Damien's name. Damien turned around and waved them in and soon my parents and Ellie came rushing over to me.

"Oh, my baby," Mom said as she softly pulled me into my arms. "My baby. How are you feeling?"

"Hi, Mom. I'm doing better."

Dad came over and although he looked better, I could see that he still looked worse for wear. My eyes bounced between my parents and realized that neither one of them had slept much since I assume Damien had told them I had been injured. Now, how much he had told them was up for debate and I knew I had to be careful what I said.

Ellie sat down at the foot of the bed and gave me a small smile. It felt great to see her again too. Damien pulled up two black chairs that he kept in the sitting area of his room up to the bed, giving my parents a place to sit.

They both did and Dad looked up at Damien before sticking his hand out. "Thank you for saving my daughter's life."

When Damien reached out and shook his hand in return, I could see the mutual understanding passing between the two.

"Anais—" Mom was ready to rapidly fire off some questions, but Dad turned and placed a hand on her knee.

"Don't give Anais the third degree just yet. I'm sure she's exhausted from everything that happened."

I knew how hard it was for Mom not to say anything and my gaze floated to Damien, who was making his way out the room.

"Damien, be careful out there."

He responded without turning around. "I always am."

10

DAMIEN

"I can't wait to get my hands on that fucker," I said as I sped down the street.

I glanced over at Kingston, who was busy on his phone doing who knows what. Broderick was sitting quietly in the back but Gage said something had come up, although he had wanted to join in on the "fun" that was going to be had. Kingston's team came in and cleared Carter's apartment and the cabin he kept in New Jersey with ease over the course of the last day and a half or so.

I asked Will if he wanted to join, but he left what was going to happen to Carter up to me. I had hoped to talk to Charlotte before I saw Carter again, but she was still recovering. I also needed to talk to Will about Vincent, whom I'd never met or seen before, but his main priority was tending to his sister.

"Couldn't we get Rob to drive? Driving a little wild over there."

I glared at Broderick through the rear-view mirror, who in turn smirked. "I felt like driving tonight. Be happy that I haven't thrown your ass in the river." I turned my attention to Kingston. "Did your guys find anything at his place or in the cabin? Maybe something pointing to Vincent?"

"Still looking through everything, but so far no. It might be easier to force him to talk when we get there."

The desire to show Carter that he didn't fuck with what was mine would be rectified momentarily. I tightened my hands. "Did you find anything about where Vincent is?"

Kingston shook his head. "No one knows where he is. All signs point to him skipping town although we both know he didn't." He cleared his throat. "Is everything okay with you?"

"Why?"

"You make it a point of always maintaining control, yet I can feel you about to spin out of control on this one. You're holding on to the steering wheel so tight, that I wouldn't be surprised if it cracked under the pressure."

I glanced at him, feeling the tension building in the car. "I'm still in control."

"You just had to rescue the woman you love after she was kidnapped and then found out that the girlfriend you thought was dead is anything but. That would fuck anyone up."

"Love?"

I saw Kingston look up from his phone out of the corner of my eye.

"Anyone can see it. You're not doing a good job of hiding it. It's either that or you're getting soft."

"He's right." And there was Broderick chiming in from the back.

"We are not going to talk about this now or ever."

Broderick grunted, but it was too late. He was already in my crosshairs.

"Don't you have enough things to worry about? Especially when it comes to a certain doctor that we all know?"

"Shut up, man," he said.

"Got him," Kingston said. The unexpected comment forced us all to chuckle, a much-needed change from the dark mood that had taken over the SUV since we started our journey.

Once more silence overtook the vehicle as I headed toward an abandoned warehouse in Staten Island. A low fog covered the streets as we drove along with the GPS guiding us to our destination. The closer we got to the warehouse the more abandoned the streets surrounding it were. The number of people and cars in the area decreased the farther we went until my GPS told me that the building was up ahead. I parked the SUV in front of a warehouse that looked to be deserted on the outside, but that was done by design.

We stepped out of the car and went to a huge building with graffiti on it. There was a dull light shining through one of the windows, but other than that it looked as if there was no one around. The perfect place to carry out the activities that were about to take place.

Kingston walked up to the building first and knocked on the door before establishing who we were. When the door opened, it confirmed what I knew all along: what was occurring inside this warehouse was a completely different animal. Inside, the building was buzzing with activity. The warehouse was bigger than I realized on the inside and was designed like a high-tech office filled to the brim with computers. A quick estimation told me that there were about twice as many computers as there were people. For those members of the team who didn't come into the office full-time, maybe? We trusted Kingston with how he ran his business, but I didn't realize he was doing all of this.

One man walked over and shook Kingston's hand and pointed to a door on the right. "Down there."

Kingston opened a door and a set of stairs greeted us. How ironic was it that Carter had been thrown into a basement as well? Rage and adrenaline pumped through me as Kingston, Broderick, and I descended the stairs, and I couldn't help but smirk at the sight before me. There sat Carter, in the middle of a room with a couple of bright lights illuminating the place. His arms were tied behind his back. A couple of men were standing several yards behind him and I knew they were ready to finish Carter if he tried anything.

"About time you bastards turned on the lights in here."

"Good evening, Carter. Doesn't feel great being stuck in a room in total darkness, does it?" Kingston said as he approached the man in the chair. His dirty, bloody, gray shirt was ripped at the sleeve to make room for the bandage that was wrapped around his arm. Satisfaction surged through me at seeing the wound that I caused. I hoped it hurt like a son of a bitch. I was happy that he looked like shit, but he should be pleased he was alive.

"Fuck you," he said.

"That's not how you should talk to the person who holds your life in their hands, is it? Where is Vincent?" I didn't recognize my own voice as the sinister words hung in the air.

"I don't know who the hell you are talking about," he said.

His eyes darted between Kingston, Broderick, and me told me that either he was worried about what would happen to him or he was lying. I decided that it was both and I walked up to him with my fists clenched. I gave him a small smirk before I threw the first punch. The crunch of bones under my hand made the sting of impact worth it. This was gratifying, more so than when I killed Jon. Why had I stopped taking care of these types of things and let Kingston's squad handle them?

He laughed as blood poured from his mouth. "I bet you wouldn't do that if I had my hands untied, bastard. No way you could've done that had we been on equal ground."

I snorted because I knew he was full of shit. "Now where is Vincent?"

This time Kingston joined in on the fun and threw another punch. That one led to one of Carter's teeth flying out of his mouth. Then, he spit out another.

"I loosened it for you," I said.

Kingston gave me a sarcastic chuckle and I glanced at Broderick, who was now rolling up his sleeves, clearly preparing to jump in at any moment.

"Tell us where Vincent is."

"You're all fucking insane."

"That's the sincerest compliment you could have ever given us," I said as I took a step to my left and squeezed the arm where I shot Carter. His scream of pain was elevated once more when Broderick got in on the action. But still he said nothing.

I released his arm from my grasp. Kingston strolled over to me and out of the corner of my eye, I saw him reach out his hand. I opened mine and he placed a pistol in it. I checked the gun before I took a step back, held it up, and aimed and yet there was no response from him. A smirk appeared on my face just before I shot him in the foot.

"Ah! Okay! Okay! Fuck, I'll talk, you sick son of a bitch. I'll tell you what I know if it stops you assholes from beating on me." His words came out muffled due to the damage we inflicted on him.

I took a step back and shrugged, dropping my arms to my sides. "Fine. Spill."

"I don't know where Vincent is. I swear. All of our transactions took place either over burner phones or in public spaces."

"When was the last time you saw him?"

Carter swallowed hard. "The night Anais snuck out and went to Hidden Tavern. I was standing outside when she left the penthouse's garage. I alerted Vincent, who staged everything else at Hidden Tavern. It was one of his hangouts."

And this was why Dave, the private investigator who worked for Cross Industries, was one of the best in the business. If he'd had a little more time to put two and two together...

"It was happenstance that I ended up working for Vincent. He put out feelers for someone to join him on this job just as I was getting my feet wet at Cross Sentinel, but I don't know how long he was tracking you all. The plan was to hurt you the way your father hurt his, and to kidnap his sister, whom he knew was alive the entire time, and bring her back here to face what he viewed as treacherous behavior. He was still pissed that she hadn't done what she was supposed to do when it came to killing you and he wanted her to pay."

"So, you've been tracking me for years."

Carter nodded. "And who knows how long Vincent has

been but if there was one thing that I learned about working with him is that he's patient. So, while you think you've won since you've captured me, you are highly mistaken. Vincent is still walking these streets and will wait to strike."

I thought it was funny how he thought he was still in any position to threaten me, but I continued my questioning. "How did Anais get pulled into this?"

"She fell into this because of the deal you struck with her father." Carter paused to spit out some more blood. "We started tracking anyone that you did business with and it wasn't hard to guess that if you caught sight of her, you would have wanted to claim her. I mean, who wouldn't?"

Broderick's arm stopped me from fucking Carter's face up more before I could think to move on him.

"Once we confirmed your intentions the rest was easy because I was already on the inside. My job was just to deliver Anais and Charlotte to him. I didn't know what he planned on doing with them once I delivered them because that was the end of my job. At first, he wanted me to hold out because he assumed you didn't care about her just like the other women you slept with, but that turned out to be false. When Anais stuck around and lasted longer than the rest, we started planning our move and when you guys broke up, I was placed on her security detail. And then the shooting brought you two back together, closer than ever."

I hated to admit that I believed him. I took a step forward, refusing to look at Kingston or Broderick because I knew they would have smug looks on their faces, but I addressed Kingston first, although I was staring at Carter. "We need to find everything on Vincent as soon as possible."

"Already on it."

"Tell me this, why did you leave that note from Charlotte?"

"To fuck with you. I actually came up with that idea myself to cause you to spin out of control. We knew there was no way you could have moved on from that night unscathed."

"But it failed because—"

Carter interrupted me, "You know what we couldn't figure out though? We couldn't figure out why Anais was different from the other women that floated in and out of your life. I mean other than being smoking hot—"

He stopped because I took a step forward and bent down to look Carter right in the face. "You have a death wish and I'm happy to grant it."

"Either you're going to kill me, or Vincent is. There's no way that I'm making it out of this alive. I didn't deliver the women in the timeframe he wanted. I'm as good as dead, but so are you."

"You think that Vincent is going to avenge your death? Laughable. I'm glad you came to the same realization that you're a dead man no matter what."

"Whoa." Carter's deer-in-headlights look was the first real emotion he had shown all night outside of when pain was inflicted on him.

"You thought I was going to give Vincent the pleasure of killing you? After all you did to what is mine?" I scoffed. "I only agreed to stop beating on you. Thanks for all of the information."

Carter shook briefly before his expression turned stoic, accepting his fate. All of this could have been avoided if he had done the right thing by not taking the job of Vincent's lackey. Or even if he would've told Kingston the plan, he might've saved his own life. I could let Kingston's men take over, but where would the fun be in that? He needed to pay for the turmoil he had inflicted on Anais and her family. I made a promise to myself to protect her at all costs, and this was the first step into rectifying it.

He tangled with the devil and it was time to pay the price. I pulled the trigger, finally feeling satisfied.

11

ANAIS

I was still awake when Damien returned, and I smiled at him when he walked through the front door. My parents and Ellie left about thirty minutes ago after I had made my way to the living room to turn on some music in an effort to take my mind off of everything.

"Everything all right?" I carefully looked him over. He didn't seem to be bleeding anywhere. Or so I thought until I noticed his right hand. "Let me see it," I said as he walked closer to me on the couch.

"You should be in bed."

"Yes, I know, but I'm resting by sitting on the couch. And no, I didn't walk here by myself, Ellie helped me get settled here. By the way, thank you for renting out a couple of apartments in the building for them to stay in the short term."

"They help you and you care about them, so I'm making sure they are nearby. It also helps with security concerns. Did Lucy come by with meals?"

"She did. I had one of the dinners she left, and it was delicious. I know you're attempting to change the subject."

I thought I was the one who always tried to deflect. The closer he came to me, the more I could feel the energy leaping off of him. His hand slightly shook before he put it down at his side. Damien removed his coat and tossed it over the back of the chair. Had I ever seen him not keep things neat?

"Everything is fine. Things have been taken care of or are in the process of being taken care of."

"Where is Carter now?"

"Somewhere he won't bother you again."

I reached over and grabbed Damien's uninjured hand. "Stop trying to shield me from this. Where is Carter?"

My tone was unwavering, and I deserved to know an answer. Damien raked a hand through his hair before he looked at me. When our eyes connected, I could still see the fury in his. "He's in hell, which is where he belongs for hurting you both physically and emotionally. He gave us some information that helped fill in some gaps, but not all of them."

That confirms that Jon and Carter are both dead and I couldn't give a damn. Fuck them. Damien's hand clenched the back of the couch, his knuckles turning white, and I sighed. "What else aren't you telling me, Damien?"

"You're safer than you were with Carter on the loose, but the person who hired him is still out there."

"Raspy-voice man. Vincent DePalma, I mean. How could I forget his name?"

Damien picked up my hand and started rubbing small circles into my palm. "The quicker we find him, the better. He also has a lot to answer for. Along with my father."

That led to a double take. "What does your father have to do with this?"

"Vincent is doing all of this to avenge his father's death, which he thinks my father was involved in. Now, we need to get the bottom of this. And the quicker we do, the better."

"Damien." He looked at me and said nothing, waiting for me to continue. Thoughts were swirling through my mind about telling him how much I missed him while he was gone, even with my family here, but I cleared my throat and said, "Definitely. I understand that."

"You know what else I think you'll also understand?"

"What's that?"

"That once you're fully healed, I'm going to put you over my knee and spank that ass until it's a pretty pink color and then I'm going to take you from behind, which I know we will both enjoy."

I let him change the subject this time because he instilled his trust in me. It was the first time that I felt as if he viewed me as a partner versus another person who he could just tell what to do. He wasn't wrong about that. I would never tell him this, but I missed being with him. Our relationship hadn't started off on the right foot, but I looked forward to us connecting with one another in multiple ways in the bedroom and outside of it.

"Damien, come to bed so you can finally get some rest."

"Are you now giving the orders around here?"

"Looks like it."

I WAS RUNNING toward the light; my salvation seemed to be in reach. My arms and legs propelled my body forward and I could see that I was getting closer and closer. That was until hands grabbed at me, pulling me in the opposite direction. I refused to be deterred and fought against the forces that were trying to yank me toward the darkness. I wasn't going back there.

It seemed the more I struggled, the harder it was to move, but I knew this couldn't stop me. It wouldn't stop me.

That was until I heard a gunshot. The loud blast made me stop moving and consequently, the hands that were holding me back fell by the wayside. Why had they let go?

I looked behind me but saw nothing but darkness. My gaze drifted around me until it landed on my stomach where I found blood seeping through the white T-shirt that I hadn't realized I was wearing. Panic surged through my veins as I placed my hands on the hole in my abdomen. The pressure that I was applying on the wound wasn't doing anything because blood slipped through my fingers. I looked up and found someone running toward me just as I dropped to my knees, feeling light-headed and losing energy from blood loss and from having fought against what was holding me back.

A shadowy figure appeared in the light up ahead and the person took off running toward me. As I was falling to the ground, I saw Damien's face appear before me.

I woke up with tears in my eyes, looking around the cool, dark room. I felt my chest before my hands ended up on my cheeks and I tried to calm my racing heart. A glance down at my stomach confirmed that nothing was there but the tank top I had fallen asleep in the night before.

Having a nightmare a few nights after I'd been kidnapped wasn't surprising. While my body aches and concussion symptoms lessen, it seemed as if my fears took over my dreams and turned them into nightmares. I took a moment to take a breath before removing the covers off of my body. I found a sweatshirt that I threw over one of the black chairs in the bedroom. Once I felt some sense of security, I walked toward the bedroom door, hoping to find the person who should have been sleeping beside me.

I opened the door and snuck down the hall where I heard Damien talking to someone in his office with the door opened a smidge.

"Nothing yet?" Damien didn't say anything back right away as he listened to the person on the other end. I waited to see if he would say something else to give me a hint about what he was talking about. Who the hell would he be talking to at this time of night?

I took a step closer to see if maybe I could pick up on anything the other person was saying. Nothing.

"We'll check in tomorrow." When he hung up the phone, I opened his office door and he glanced at me. "You don't ever do what you're supposed to do."

"Shouldn't you be doing the same?"

"Work never sleeps."

"That didn't sound like work."

"It's nothing for you to worry about. Let's get you back to bed." He stood up and walked over to me. "You've been crying. What's wrong?"

"Just had a bad dream. I'm fine."

He pulled me into his arms and a few more tears fell from my eyes. Having someone know what you needed before you realize it was life changing for me. To have someone know you well enough and to love you, faults and all, was a magical experience. I appreciated him not asking me what happened in the dream right now because I was afraid to relive it.

"You know there's another way that we can take your mind off of that nightmare."

His words opened up something inside of me that told me I was ready for whatever he had planned. He helped me remove my sweatshirt and I knew that without a doubt, I was in for a pleasurable ride.

"Oh, really?" My voice came out as a breathless whisper. The heat in his eyes gave me a hint as to what he was referring to. "Finally going on a date to Thirteen Park Avenue? I'm still waiting on that by the way."

Damien chuckled. "No. This would be...closer to home. Much closer."

Him calling this place our home made my heart swell. "What did you have in mind?"

The light in his eyes darkened before his lips descended onto mine. The touch of his lips was almost my undoing. I felt as if it had been so long since the last time we kissed with such heat and passion. I knew that he was treating me like a delicate flower after Carter kidnapped me, and I was happy to see that the passion and desire had been building up inside of him just like it had been in me. It was time to unleash all of this pent-up energy.

"You don't know how fond I am of you wearing these cute skimpy pajamas to bed." He left small kisses on my lips after every third word.

"No, you never mentioned it."

"That was my mistake. It's time to rectify that."

I reached for his pajama pants, but he stopped me. "Not tonight, Spitfire. This was just for you. Sit down."

His words made my hands stop midair. Curious about what he had planned, I sat down on the couch, my body shivering at the sharp contrast between my hot skin and the coolness of the leather cushion. Damien followed suit and before I could blink, his lips were on mine. His kisses started out soft before they became hungrier, as if he needed to get closer to me than he already was.

The kiss turned feverish in its intensity and I didn't know the placement of his hands until they were on my breasts. Heat traveled through my body and landed in the place where I wanted him to pay the most attention to. When he broke our kiss, I longed for him to come back because I wanted to feel the weight of his lips on my own.

Damien slowly made his way from my lips to my jaw to my neck to my chest. He left a trail of light kisses in his wake. He continued lightly massaging my breasts through my tank top and my desire for him continued to grow.

He moved his head and whispered into my ear, "How wet are you for me?"

His breath lightly tickled the shell of my ear and I shuddered. "I'm dripping."

"No surprises there since it's been a while. You know what to do. Spread 'em."

His demand sent another surge through me. Without needing any convincing, I opened my legs, ready to receive whatever he was going to give me. He moved off the couch and kneeled in front of me. I felt like a queen on her throne as I watched through heavy eyes what he was going to do next.

"This pussy is mine."

I nodded my head, not sure if he saw me, and not caring,

to be frank. I didn't trust my mouth to form any words while I eagerly tried to anticipate his next move. His fingertips moved toward my pajama shorts, caressing the fabric of my waistband. I could feel his touch through the pants, but I needed more.

As if he heard my thoughts, he pulled at the fabric. "Lift your bottom."

I did as he asked and soon my shorts and underwear descended down my legs. He tossed them over his shoulder, neither one of us caring where they landed. My body dropped back down onto the cushion and the contrast between the temperature of my skin and the couch felt like a cool reprieve this time. That didn't last long, however.

It wasn't long before Damien was staring at my aching, wet pussy. "Move your bottom forward."

I did as he said, and I felt the light touch of his finger draw up and down my folds.

"You weren't lying."

Before I could say anything, his mouth descended on me and a huge moan left my lips, finally happy to have him where I ached for him most. Who needed food when he was acting as if I was his last meal?

He shifted his body, causing my legs to widen in order to accommodate him, and the extra room must have been what he needed because he began to devour me. The rhythm he was keeping with his tongue was bringing me closer and closer to a peak that I hadn't reached in what felt like forever, and when he added one finger, and then two, I cried out.

"You're getting close."

All I could do was nod my head. I looked down at him and found him looking back at me with such intensity that between having his gaze on me and his fingers stroking me at just the right pace, I came undone, letting out a long-awaited release. The smirk on Damien's face told me that he was pleased with the outcome.

He stood up and placed his middle finger in his mouth, sucking my juices off it before he said, "I just can't get enough of your taste."

I wondered if I could have another orgasm just from his words.

When I caught my breath, I reached for his pants once more before he stepped out of my reach.

"Spitfire, I told you this was strictly for you. If you put your mouth on me, it won't just end there. And I want you at your best when it's time for me to fuck you again."

THE NEXT MORNING, Grace stopped by to check in on me. She performed a brief examination but focused more on asking me questions once she sat down in the black chair, just across from the couch I was lying on.

"I see Damien went back to work. I was surprised to see Kingston standing at the door when I was brought up."

I snorted. "He's been having a couple of in-person meetings here and there, but he should be home in about an hour or so. It feels weird to have him around so often nowadays."

Grace nodded before getting down to business. "How are you doing?"

"Not too bad. A small headache, some tiredness and soreness, but I assume it's my body healing."

"That it is. And it seems that you're getting around better."

That was true. I had opened the door myself to let her in and had been resting on the couch before she arrived.

"Fantastic. Keep an eye on any changes, but you look good to me. I still want you to avoid doing strenuous activities and continue to get as much rest as you can."

Resting might drive me up the wall, but I knew how vital it was to my recovery, so whatever it took. Plus, it wasn't like I couldn't go downstairs and see my parents and Ellie if I wanted to.

"You'll be back up and running in no time, but I repeat, take it easy as much as possible. Based on what I've heard about you, I assume you really want to go back to work."

I was willing to still be out for a couple more days, but once I felt as if I was back to normal, I knew the desire to work would return. "I don't want to overdo it and potentially end up in a worse position."

"That's the right attitude to have. If you need anything, you have my card right there on your bedside table, and Damien knows how to get in touch with me."

I debated with myself about whether or not to ask the thing that had been on the tip of my tongue since I met her. I knew it was somewhat inappropriate but when you have a lot of time to sit back and just think of random things while you're supposed to be resting, it stirs in your brain.

"I can't remember if I told you this before but thank you for coming on such short notice the night of the attack."

Grace smiled at me. "It was my pleasure. Broderick seemed a little panicked when he called me, and I was happy to assist."

There was my opening. "How do you and Broderick know

each other?" I tried to be as vague as possible as a way to not alert her to the fact that I was digging for information.

"Broderick and my brother have been best friends for..." She paused for a moment. "Has it been twenty-five years? Maybe? Sorry, it's hard to keep track."

"That's okay. It happens to me as well. That's a long time."

Grace smiled. "Yeah, he's been annoying me for about that long, but he's a good guy. The number of things I could tell you about him...well, we would be here all day. I've got him out of so much stuff over the years...usually due to Gage or my brother, Hunter, dragging him along."

I chuckled, and based on what I knew of them, this wasn't at all shocking. "I'm sure they both could make life quite entertaining."

"Oh, that's for sure. I'm not so sure how Selena made it with all three of them running her house into the ground. Then adding Hunter or Kingston into the mix and, well, you know what I mean."

I grinned and nodded before I winced slightly, wishing I hadn't moved.

"Are you okay?"

"Yes, just shouldn't have nodded that aggressively." I waved my hand. "Don't worry about me, I'm fine."

"Okay. You need to get more rest, and I'm going to get out of here, but it was nice seeing you and I hope we get to see each other again real soon."

"Thank you so much for everything."

"Not a problem." Grace stood up and shook my hand before leaving the apartment, closing the door behind her.

12

DAMIEN

I was lying in bed watching as Anais slept peacefully beside me. Both of us had forgotten to close the curtains, but now the moonlight provided the perfect lighting and backdrop for me to watch my sleeping beauty. I woke up when my arm fell asleep underneath her head, and although my brain was yelling at me to move, I refused. Lying here beside her, stroking her arm up and down, I resisted the urge to wake her in hopes that she would continue to rest.

I longed to take her body again, but I knew that she was healing from the wounds that had developed both physically and mentally. I replayed the moments that we spent together at Elevate in my mind, but it wasn't just due to the sex being phenomenal. It was because of what our relationship had developed into that made the moments where we enjoyed each other's bodies even more incredible. Our relationship grew so quickly that I knew I would do anything for her, including kill, and I had. I wondered if this was the same feeling that my parents had for one another.

Mine. That was the only thing I could think of when I

looked at her. I had done my part to keep my feelings at bay. To remain unattached in every sense of the word besides a roll in the sack had always been the goal when it came to women. But this was different. She was different. What we had was different. If the time during which she was stolen from me taught me one thing, it was that life was precious, and so was my time with her. It could have all been gone in the blink of an eye if Vincent had gotten the opportunity to have her in his grasp.

I saw the expression on Anais's face when she told me that her engagement ring was missing. What she didn't know was that I was relieved it was gone too. Yes, it had cost a small fortune, but it could be replaced. She couldn't. I knew how much she hated that ring, and the ring represented a lie that we were perpetuating to the world. That was over.

"I'm going to fix all of this," I whispered, a vow only I could hear. A few ideas appeared in my head, but first I needed to have a conversation with my father.

The prickliness in my arm won and I moved one of my limbs to get out from underneath her. I turned to throw my other arm over her waist, molding my body to fit hers. As I was about to doze off back to sleep, I felt Anais shiver against me. It was then that I realized that a thin layer of sweat had broken out on her back.

A low groan escaped her lips. I sat up, but kept my arm on her waist, hoping that it would provide a sense of comfort that could transcend to the dreams I suspected she was having.

"No." Her voice was just above a whisper, the end of the word sounding more like she was moaning in pain.

"Anais," I said low, hoping to wake her up from the

turmoil she was embroiled in. It didn't work and she whipped her body out from underneath my arm, catching me temporarily off guard. She had flipped over onto her back and the jerkiness of her body made me think that she was either trying to fight or run away from someone in her sleep.

"Anais," I said louder. Still she didn't wake up and tossed once more. "Anais," I repeated and gently shook her awake.

I watched as her eyes popped open, yet she wasn't truly with me for another couple of seconds. Her gaze searched the dark room and when they landed on me, she visibly relaxed.

"Damien." That one word seemed to help slow her rapidly beating heart and she turned her body to lean into mine. I hugged her, gently stroking her back in hopes that she wouldn't have too much trouble falling back to sleep.

"Bad dream again?" I asked although I knew the answer. It seemed as if the nightmares that I faced had been transferred to her. And all of this was because of me.

"Yes, I was dreaming that I was running away from Carter. He caught me but I don't know what happened because you woke me up. Thank you."

"It's not a problem. You know I'm always here for you."

She pulled back and wiped the sleep from her eyes and looked back at me before she said, "Looks like we both have demons that we fight when sleep is supposed to come."

"True," I said. "Mine seem to have faded since we found out that Charlotte was alive."

"Yes, and I'm glad. I noticed you weren't waking up in the middle of the night."

"And you're going to make it past this too." I pulled her into my arms again and brushed my fingers through her hair. I heard her sigh softly and I hoped that was a sign that the terror she had faced in her dreams would become dormant once again so that she could fall back to sleep.

"I know."

"Damien! Did I miss Melissa calling to schedule a meeting with Mr. Cross?"

"You didn't." The next morning, I showed up to Dad's office unannounced on purpose. I didn't tell him anything other than Anais being safe on purpose. This conversation needed to happen in person, and I was willing to wait.

Ellen, my father's long-time assistant, stood up and stared at me, her eyes wide and mouth open. No one stormed into Martin Cross's office and definitely not one of his sons. I wanted to take him by surprise, in hopes that he would do what I wanted him to do: tell the truth. No more hiding behind burying the past and talks of never speaking of this again. He might not have known everything, he knew more than he was letting on, including why Vincent blamed him for his father's death. I wanted answers and I wanted them now.

"Let me see if Mr. Cross is available."

"No need," I said, before brushing past her and knocking on my father's closed office door." Before he could say come in, I waltzed into his office and shut the door behind me.

"To what do I owe this pleasure, Damien? I wasn't expecting you today." Dad placed his pen down and gave me a small smile.

"Can we talk for a minute?"

"Of course, son. I have some time before my next meeting. What do you want to talk about?"

"I want to talk about that night. The night of the fire. I know there's more to the story that you aren't telling me, and I demand to know everything."

Dad's face turned cold. "Why? That's in the past and we buried that."

"No. You buried it and I didn't say anything about it even though I continued to suffer with the aftermath of this for years."

Dad leaned back in his chair with his arms crossed. "Do you want to take a seat before this conversation continues?"

"No. Speaking of things being buried, it seems that things don't stay that way because Charlotte is alive."

Dad sat up with a start, placing his hands on his desk. "Charlotte is what?"

"She's alive. I saw her with my own two eyes." I moved away from the door and walked closer to my father's desk. "There's a lot that you need to be filled in on that I've been keeping quiet while we get things sorted, and it revolves around you and the DePalmas."

"We've both been keeping things from each other, it seems." He said it matter-of-factly.

I agreed, except the secrets that I had been keeping were only a few days old versus his, which were well over a decade. I waited for him to say something else, but he didn't. He almost looked to be in a daze, a reaction I'd never seen on his face.

He snapped out of it and directed his gaze to me. "Charlotte is alive?"

I nodded. "If I hadn't seen her, I wouldn't have believed it either."

"How did you find out?" Dad stood up from his chair and walked toward me. He placed a hand on my shoulder.

"When Anais was kidnapped and met Charlotte while they both were in captivity."

I watched as the information registered. "Is she also okay? Why didn't you call me?"

Why hadn't I? Honestly, I hadn't thought of it. Things were moving so fast with trying to save Anais that it didn't give me an opportunity to tell him while we were on the move. Then I spent most of the last few days making sure that Anais had everything she needed and more.

"Dad, I was taking care of things. That's why I took off or have been working sparse hours from home."

"I thought it was just to take care of Anais, not that all of this other mess was entangled in this. I can't remember the last time when you took off completely. No emails, no meetings from home."

That was accurate. Work didn't matter as much to me right now when the center of my world had been thrown into harm's way.

"We needed to take some time to ourselves as well as get a bunch of things sorted. Charlotte helped save Anais's life, Dad."

I don't know if I've ever seen my father look so shocked.

"That wouldn't be the first time she saved someone's life."

My eyes narrowed as I scanned my father. He looked at the wall to the right of my head before looking back at me. "Care to elaborate?"

Dad looked at me before his eyes glanced at a small table

behind his desk. I knew he was looking at the family photos that he placed there years ago. He sighed and I could see that he was trying to figure out how to approach the situation at hand. I'd seen the same look on his face during many meetings just as he was about to speak. But I spoke first, voicing one of the thoughts that stayed with me all of these years.

"Something I always wondered about that night is who told you that something might occur that made you drive up?"

"I received a phone call on my office line at home. Since it was the weekend, it went straight to voicemail. I ended up checking it about twenty minutes later after dinner with your mother. The voice on the message was soft, but it didn't take much for me to put together that it was Charlotte. She said that you were in danger and that I needed to get up there. I rushed to tell your mother and our house went into lockdown. We decided to send several of our guards to get your brothers, who were at a friend's house, just in case this was a direct attack on our family. I went with my driver to go and get you. We raced up there and I spotted your car when we arrived and made a split-second decision to send my driver back home, because the plan was to drive your car back."

His eyes glazed over once more, as if he was recalling the night in question. I saw a small tear forming in the corner of his eye and when he focused on me, the tear threatened to fall. I could only imagine how he felt when he arrived at the scene, when he didn't know if his first born was alive or dead. It was then that I realized the steadiness that he showcased when we were driving away from the house.

"We saw the smoke coming out of one of the windows on the top floor, but I again told my driver to leave. When he pulled off, I heard a loud bang and that's when I ran toward the house and you know the rest of what happened that night. Son, I had hoped to get her too but, by the way the fire was burning, I—I thought I was already too late. The police said the fire was accidental, but I knew better."

My gut told me something similar, which was why her memory haunted me. But there was one thing that was left unanswered. "How is Harvey involved in all of this?"

This was the first time I had said Will, Vincent, and Charlotte's father's name in years. I had no opinion of him either way because I might have seen him in passing when Dad did business with him, but that was it.

Dad turned away from me and walked back toward his desk. He looked down with his back to me before sitting back down in his office chair. "Harvey was a troubled man. Was involved in things he shouldn't have been in and I bailed him out a few times. When I refused to bail him out again, he had nowhere else to turn. I didn't save him, and he was killed because of it. I assume if Vincent is coming after you, he blames Harvey's death on me."

"And so he took it out on me. I'm sure it didn't help that I was dating his sister."

"I would think so."

"Harvey died just before the fire by his own hand. Why would Vincent wait so long to do anything?"

"If you are now his target, because you escaped the fire, then he waited for you to care about something or someone enough to strike."

I knew my dad was talking about Anais without mentioning her name. "In the end, Charlotte ended up saving not just Anais's life this time, but my life years ago. I don't know if I would have been able to make it out there if she hadn't waited or contacted you. Then if you hadn't gotten there when you did and busted down the front door…"

"Yeah, I guess she did."

"And there is no way I'll ever be able to pay her back… outside of making sure her brother can't do anything to harm any of us again. It's about time we find out what hole Vincent climbed into."

13

ANAIS

"**D**o you need anything?"

I was in the kitchen preparing sugar cookies and had just placed them in the oven. It was something that I wanted to do to pass the time while I was supposed to be resting. I didn't want to aggravate my recovery and had been trying to find different activities I could do that didn't involve watching a screen.

Thinking about one particular activity brought my attention back to Damien. The question was a loaded one and I stared Damien down. There was something I wanted that Damien seemingly refused to give me. "Yes, there is something I want."

The look on my face must have given my intentions away because Damien slightly shook his head. "No."

"You don't even know what I was thinking."

"Oh, but I do. Because it's the same thing that has been on your mind for the last few days. When I'm going to fuck you next."

One would think that out of all of the things that Damien

and I had done, I wouldn't have a reason to blush anymore, yet his words made my cheeks heat up like an inferno.

"I've never said that—"

"Your eyes betray you, Spitfire. Everything will return to normal in due time."

I knew it would, but that didn't mean that the desire that still burned for him in my body was willing to wait. The time that we had apart when I left our arrangement was nothing compared to this torture. Being around him, yet not touching him intimately was a form of torture.

Damien took a step closer to me and laid a hand on my cheek. Although we lay together in bed at night and his touch brought me comfort and security, it wasn't doing everything I had come accustomed to. I missed when he would showcase how well he knew my body and just how to pleasure it. He tilted my head up and pressed a soft kiss on my lips. There was no heat, no fire.

My hand landed behind his neck and pulled him closer to me, deepening the kiss. I knew he wanted this as much as I did, yet he pulled away. I stared at his lips, wishing they were back on mine.

"I want you to be fully recovered for the activities that I have planned. Only then will we partake in them."

The urge to mock his last sentence was there but I swallowed the retort. The best course of action was to change the subject. "There have been a couple of things that have been on my mind that I've been meaning to ask you."

"Well?"

"This is embarrassing, but when is your birthday?"

"We've never talked about that, have we? July 24."

I sighed. "Now I feel even more like an idiot."

Damien raised an eyebrow at me and stared down into my eyes. "Why?"

"Carter lured me out of here the day he kidnapped me by telling me that there was something happening related to your birthday."

He wiped a piece of my hair away from my face and tucked it behind my ear. "It's not your fault. We spent most of our time together battling versus getting to know the random details about one another. That will change."

His words reassured me, and I knew that he was right. I hoped my next question wouldn't do much damage to the mood that had been created, but it needed to be asked. "Anything new about Vincent?"

Damien's jaw clenched. Clearly that subject was the wrong one. I wondered if he was going to tell me anything else.

"We still don't know where he is. He's all but vanished, but that doesn't mean that I don't have people on the ground who are trying to flush him out. Hopefully, we'll have an update soon."

His answer seemed final, as if he had just closed the door to this conversation. I nodded my head before walking out of the kitchen. Damien followed me into the living room, and I sat down on the black leather couch. I pulled my hair out of its ponytail as Damien followed my lead and sat down next to me. He gently pulled me into his side.

"Do you enjoy living here?"

His question was unexpected. I looked at him for a moment, studying his face as I tried to come up with an answer. "Why wouldn't I?"

"That's not an answer."

I knew it wasn't, but I wanted to take a more measured approach. "I have everything I could ever want here, Damien."

A small smile tugged at his lips. "Is this your way of saying you hate living here much like you hated the engagement ring I gave you?"

My eyes widened slightly before I was able to control myself. I knew he caught my reaction, so I stopped trying to hide it.

"It's not that I don't like living here, it's just not me. Everything that's here besides the clothes that I brought with me or the wardrobe that you bought for me isn't mine. Yes, I'm able to do certain activities that I love here, but nothing here reflects my personality. Plus, I feel so far away from the bustle of New York City." I grabbed Damien's hand and continued, "Once again, it's not that I don't appreciate being able to live in a penthouse, but I associate living here to living in an ivory tower, so far away from the world. I know that this was done to protect me, but I was also kidnapped from here. So, it doesn't really matter where we are. I did like living in your mansion in NoHo as long as I have the ability to make it more me."

"What? Don't you like the black leather couch, the dark furniture, and the big-screen TV on the wall?"

I chuckled. "It's not bad, but there could be a little bit more color in here and in the NoHo mansion, if I'm being honest."

Damien was tossing the idea around in his head. "Well, let's see what we can do about changing things up a bit and what moving back to the mansion would look like. It might not be immediate, but we should be able to make it happen."

I reached over and gave Damien a big hug. When I pulled away, he placed a finger under my chin, lifting my head, and my gaze met his. Without a second thought, he leaned over and kissed me, causing fireworks to shoot off behind my closed eyes. The kiss wasn't as heated as I would have preferred, but nonetheless, it was magical.

When we broke apart. Damien rested his forehead on mine as we slowly caught our breath.

"I think we're getting this compromising thing down pat," I said.

Damien pulled away a tad, but I could still see the sparkle in his eyes. "It's only because I've agreed with most of the things you said. I'm making no promises about things we actually disagree on."

I playfully rolled my eyes. "Well, I'm glad about that."

After a beat, Damien cleared his throat and said, "There's something I've been meaning to tell you."

My stomach dropped for a moment. What could he have been keeping from me? "Go on."

"So, I mentioned that I was acquiring some office space before Carter kidnapped you."

I vaguely remembered him mentioning it, but I nodded my head, encouraging him to continue.

"The deal is looking pretty solid, so I wanted to share it with you."

"That's great news!" I was still somewhat confused about the whole thing because it was rare if ever that Damien went into more detail about one of his acquisitions. "What are you going to move into that office space? Starting another company? Taking over an already established one?"

"As of now, neither of the above."

I raised an eyebrow at him. "Is the building worth that much that it makes sense to buy it outright instead of taking over a company that was already there, move one into the building, or start a new business there?"

"The value of the building didn't matter. I bought it so I can protect the most precious thing in this world to me."

"What's that?"

"You."

I ran what Damien said again through my mind before I responded. "You bought my office building?"

Damien nodded. "I knew there was no way that I would be able to keep you at home or locked up in this 'ivory tower' so I'm doing my best to protect you when you're going to be out and about."

"But Damien, once Vincent is caught—"

"Anais, you will always be in danger because you are associated with me. I have enemies in New York City, hell, probably all over the world waiting for an opportunity to strike without a second thought. It's important to me that I keep you safe and right now the security in your building is atrocious. That's how we think Vincent was able to bring a gun in a box to Jake, who then planted it in your office before Vicki collected your mail?"

Damien had a great point. There was nothing in the form of security that would protect me at the office. "Did you even try to talk to the owners?"

"I did. We were lucky enough and got a screenshot of Vincent dropping the gun off. The owners were hardly cooperative with the investigation and would only give a small amount of information to the police. I took matters into my own hands and made them an offer that they couldn't refuse."

I was floored by what Damien had just said. I knew he would take steps to protect me, but I wasn't prepared for him to spend what had to equal millions, if not billions, of dollars to buy an office building and then retrofit it to be more secure so I would have a safe place to go to work. Not only would he be helping to ensure the security of just me but as a result everyone in that building would have a safer working environment.

"And when the time comes, we can add a daycare in the building. Or hell, one can be added to Cross Tower for that matter."

"What? Why?"

"So, when we have kids, they'll be close by and we won't have to worry about anyone we don't want getting hold of them."

"You want kids?" My eyes went wide. We hadn't spoken about it before and I wasn't sure he wanted them.

"With you, yes."

"I don't know what to say." I stared at him in amazement. "Thank you."

"Those words are all I need outside of you telling me that you love me."

I gave him a small grin. "I love you."

He stepped up to me and pressed his lips upon mine.

14

DAMIEN

"Are you sure this is the place Dave said we should go?"

I looked down the street before I glanced at Broderick and asked, "Do you think I would bring us here if it wasn't?" Broderick shrugged so I continued. "According to Dave's intel, Vincent was here a couple days ago. I don't know if he'll show here again tonight, but it wouldn't hurt for us to scope the place out. Also, it wouldn't hurt to show our faces because you never know who might see us and tell him we were looking for him."

"Good plan, then."

"Sometimes I have those." I smirked at Broderick before turning to knock on a door. We were standing outside of a well-worn door in a shady part of town. I heard what sounded like a scraping noise a second after I knocked. My eyes caught a glimpse of a camera in my peripheral vision. I knew that someone was watching.

A few more seconds passed before the door opened up a

smidge. No one said anything, but it was clear that someone was standing just behind the entrance. It was another moment before the door opened up all the way, creaking on its hinges. The man standing on the other side of the door sized both Broderick and me up before he spoke.

"What business do you have here, Mr. Cross?"

The man standing in front of us definitely got his job in part due to his ability to intimidate based on his stature alone. The gentleman wore a black suit that almost looked too tight for his frame due to his muscles bulging against the fabric, almost daring it to hold on for dear life.

"None. We just came here to have a drink, that's all."

The man continued to look us up and down probably trying to determine whether or not we were lying. After giving it another thought, he moved to the side, allowing us to step through the entryway.

Broderick and I entered a dimly lit hallway. The security guard closed the door and moved around us before he walked down the long and narrow hallway. Broderick and I shared a glance before we followed him. It wasn't long until we reached another door at the end of the hallway. Without a word, the guard opened the door and walked through it. We entered into what looked to be a seedy version of a nightclub.

The moment we stepped through the door all eyes were on us. People were trying to figure out why in the world Damien and Broderick Cross would be at this establishment when we had our own club in the same city. I made sure to make eye contact with several of the patrons, hoping that any of them would tell Vincent that we showed up at his stomping grounds. I knew that word would travel and that someone here more than likely knew what he was up to.

"Well, here you are. Don't start any trouble." If the guard's words hadn't conveyed his message, the tone of his voice accomplished it.

"Wouldn't dream of it." That was only partially true. If I did see Vincent here tonight, there was no telling what would happen. But something told me that wouldn't be the case. I wouldn't be surprised if he received a warning the moment that I stepped foot into the club. I also would make sure he knew that I was looking for him.

Broderick and I strolled over to the bar and found two stools off to the side. Before the bartender noticed us, I glanced over at the selection of liquors and noted that they didn't have some of the more expensive brands that were served at Elevate.

"Can I get you two anything?"

A female bartender was looking over at us as she took care of the water that she was grabbing for someone else.

"Two beers. That one on tap is fine." I looked at Broderick, confirming the drink I selected before turning back to the bartender.

She gave both of us a smile, her gaze lingering on Broderick a little longer than necessary.

That might be useful later.

When she walked away, I turned to Broderick and whispered, "When we are about halfway done with our drinks, I want you to ask her when the last time she saw Vincent was."

"Oh, you saw that she gave me the 'please take me out back and fuck me against the building' eyes too."

I shrugged and gave the bartender a polite smile when she returned. Once again, her eyes stayed on Broderick for a few extra seconds before she went to serve someone else.

Broderick and I would quietly talk to one another as we sipped our beers while I looked around, hoping to catch even a glimpse of Vincent.

"Hey, pretty eyes, have you seen Vincent DePalma around here recently?"

Broderick took the perfect opportunity to question the bartender. We had been sitting here drinking our beers. She had come over once before to ask if we needed anything, but we both declined. When she came over a second time, Broderick pounced.

A light rosy color appeared on her cheeks as she looked back at Broderick before she looked up at the ceiling, trying to recall the last time she saw the person in question. "Um, maybe a couple of days ago? He was in here boasting about how this was his time now and that everyone would finally see what he was all about. He's been talking about how he was going to take everyone who wronged him down for months. Guess whatever thing he had planned was finally happening."

I shared a look with Broderick before I said, "Well, if you see Vincent, tell him that Damien is looking for him. And I'm not the only one."

The bartender's eyes darted from me to Broderick before landing back on me. She nodded her head and went off to check on another customer.

"Am I leaving you here so you can go after her?"

Broderick shrugged. "You mean if you didn't just scare her off? She did provide us with some information. Maybe she deserves a reward."

I snorted. "And I'm sure that you'll be the one to give it to her. Have fun." I stood up and downed the rest of my beer. I tossed a few dollars on the bar and left, my thoughts centering on getting back to Anais as soon as possible.

15

ANAIS

As the days flew by, the physical bruises were fading, but the scars that formed in my mind were still present even as I was trying to get back to my habits and schedule. I was back to working from home and loved being able to contribute to Monroe Media Agency again. Dad was also back at work, which was a relief.

After everything that occurred over the last few weeks, my father's first act when he returned to the office was firing Jake because he had wanted to do it in person instead of having Vicki do it. Last I heard Jake was leaving New York City, which was probably best for all parties involved. Deep down, I knew he was fortunate to leave with his life and if he hadn't helped Damien reach me by giving up the information to the apartment that he had taken photos of me from, he'd probably be dead next to Jon and Carter.

I still hadn't seen or heard from Charlotte. I knew that she had been moved to another undisclosed location, but where? It was definitely for safety since Vincent was still roaming the streets of NYC and was now potentially even more dangerous

than when he just had a vendetta against Damien, so I understood the need for secrecy, although I thought having both of
us talk with her might help with some of the healing that
both Damien and I needed.

While Damien, Kingston, and their men were trying to
flush Vincent from wherever he was hiding out, I took a sip of
the coffee I had just brewed, needing a small boost to get me
through the last ninety minutes of work. I was determined to
get through some of my workload after everything that had
happened.

I stretched my arms above my head as my phone rang. I
picked up the device and glanced at the screen before I
answered.

"Hey, Damien."

"Anais."

Listening to the way he said my name would never get
old. "Yes, did something happen?"

"No."

I waited for him to elaborate, but he didn't. "Damien,
something has to be wrong. You called me instead of texting."

I could hear his low chuckle on the other end of the line,
which made me tremble slightly. In his voice, it was easy to
tell that he had something up his sleeve. What it was, only he
knew.

"I want you to be ready to go in ninety minutes."

I rolled my eyes at his demand. "What are we doing?"

"We're going out on a date."

～

ROB CLOSED the car door after I sat down in the backseat.

"Anything new about Vincent?"

Kingston just shook his head but didn't look up from his phone. It was clear that the Cross men refused to explain anything.

I cleared my throat before I turned my attention to Rob. "How did you and your wife like Colorado? I don't remember if I ever asked with everything going on."

Rob smiled at me in the rear-view mirror. "She loved the time away from the city. I might have gotten a few bumps while skiing, but nothing that I couldn't handle."

"I'm glad you both had a lovely time. I can't remember the last time I'd been on a vacation that was strictly about having fun."

"Where would you go given the choice to go anywhere?"

I thought about it for a moment before I responded. "Probably somewhere almost the complete opposite of where you went. I'd love to spend time on an island, enjoying the sun and getting out of the dreary weather that New York City has had lately."

"That's true, but spring is right around the corner."

Thank goodness. I was over winter as this might have been the worst season of my life. My thoughts ventured toward all that had happened this winter. The biggest standout out of all of it was Damien. I would have categorized him as one of the worst things to ever happen to me. There was no way I could say that now. The journey that we were on together wasn't easy by a long shot. It would be easier to step away and go back to a life that didn't involve Damien at all. But that would be the cowardly approach. I now knew where I needed to be: next to Damien. Seeing how distraught he was after he rescued me and during the early hours of my recovery didn't make me think of him as weak. It took a lot of courage to be vulnerable and I believe that was when our relationship turned a metaphorical page. It made me realize how much he truly cared for me.

"Ms. Monroe? We're here."

I shook away the thoughts that had taken up most of the car ride and looked out the window. We were double-parked outside of a huge building with no signs that gave it away. Thoughts of what happened the last time I went to a restaurant popped into my mind before I was able to swipe them away. I hoped that this evening's adventure wouldn't be a replica of what occurred the last time I had gone out with Damien. Something told me it wouldn't.

Kingston walked with me up to the front doors and I was greeted by a woman in a white button-down shirt and black pants.

"Hello! Welcome to Bella River! How may I assist you?"

"I'm with Damien Cross."

"Ah, yes. Mrs. Cross, right this way."

Kingston stared at the woman with an eyebrow raised before I gave him a small wave. After I had been called Mrs. Cross on the way to see my parents when they were staying in the Hamptons, the slipup didn't seem weird to me and I didn't bother correcting her. The hostess walked inside and once the doors closed, she turned and smiled.

"I know you're going to have a good time here tonight."

"I hope I do too."

"First time here?"

"Yes, it is." I refused to admit that I had never heard of the restaurant before tonight.

"Well, I won't ruin any of the surprises that are in store.

But I do believe that you're going to have a magical experience."

I glanced up from staring at the floor. Her warm smile helped settle some of the nerves I had been feeling since I walked out of the house.

I smoothed the black coat I was wearing down as the elevator came to a stop. When the doors opened, I followed the hostess out and together she and I walked toward another set of doors that looked like it might lead outside.

"After you, Mrs. Cross." She held the door open and let me walk through first.

I found us standing on the roof of the building. I would've expected there to be more people out there, but I couldn't see any from my viewpoint. The sun was starting to set, casting a warm glow, and creating a soft, romantic vibe over the space.

"There you are." The hostess and I turned our heads and found ourselves face-to-face with Damien Cross. "I was wondering when you'd get here."

I turned to the staffer. "Thank you for bringing me up."

"Anytime, Mrs. Cross. Please let me know if either one of you need anything." With that she left us alone, and the beat of silence warmed me briefly even as a light breeze passed between us.

"I don't think I'm late."

"You aren't. I just wished you were able to come sooner."

"Or did you hope that I was late so that you could punish me later?" I took a step toward Damien with a smile.

"That wouldn't have been the worst thing in the world." Damien took a step toward me and closed the gap between us. I noticed that he had unbuttoned the top button of the white button-down he had worn earlier that day. He looked more relaxed than when he had left for work early that morning. He still wasn't back in the office full-time and I loved it. Selfishly, I've gotten Damien to myself. It allowed us to spend more time together with limited interruptions. He leaned down and greeted me with a kiss that I missed deeply. "Good evening to you too."

Damien chuckled. "Do you want something to drink?"

It was then that I realized he had his trademark whiskey in hand. He took a small step back before taking a sip. I nodded because a glass of wine sounded wonderful right now.

"Come this way. The bar is just over here."

I followed Damien's lead as we walked around a corner and I was left speechless. There was a bar with a bartender who gave me a brief smile when I came into his line of sight, but no one else was around. There was a small partially enclosed area where a table was set for two and the only light was the sunset, the candles on the table and the soft string lights that surrounded the bar. There were tons of flowers draped over the enclosed area, creating a sense of springtime, something I so desperately wished it was. A soft melody played in the background, the perfect finisher to what looked to be a masterpiece.

"This is stunning, Damien."

"I'm glad you like it. Come on, let's get you a drink and get us situated so we can start our night." I smiled up at him as he walked over to our table. When I started to slide my coat off my shoulders, I looked down at my dress and said, "This dress isn't appropriate for sitting outside in this weather."

Damien's eyes were staring at the parts of the dress that I had revealed to him when I partially removed the coat. I saw the heat rising in his eyes and my body immediately knew how to react to the attention.

"There are heaters out here but if you get cold, I have no problem asking for us to be moved inside. They should be happy to accommodate."

I took my coat off completely and placed it behind my chair before taking a small step back so he could pull the chair out. He was right and I felt warmer than I thought I would. I had doubts about whether or not this off-the-shoulder, tightly fitted blush dress would be okay for dinner on a rooftop. The dress came up to just above my knee and it had a split that reached midthigh. The tan strappy heels, the gold jewelry, and the tan purse that I chose to wear finished off the outfit. I hoped my more natural makeup brought a soft glow to my face that would be missing this time of year.

"This is all so lovely."

"Thank you. Something told me you would enjoy it because their speciality is seafood cuisine."

I smiled at Damien's attention to detail. I loved seafood and didn't have it as often as I would have liked. The last time I had it was at the fundraiser, just before Jon's murder.

It took no time for us to pick out what we wanted to eat and for me to get served the glass of wine I'd been craving since he mentioned it. We kept the conversation light and breezy, just like the soft wind I felt in this enclosed space. Our dinner was served, and we spent most of that time quietly eating and enjoying the silence that passed between us.

"This lobster tail is taking me on a journey that I didn't know I wanted or needed." I placed the last bit of lobster into my mouth before I wiped my lips. Damien took a sip of his whiskey as I turned my attention to the current melody that was playing over the speakers. "Let's dance."

"I don't dance."

"You don't dance, or you don't want to dance?"

"Both."

I snorted. "You do now, come on, Damien. Humor me. We don't have to do anything fancy, I promise."

Damien hesitated for a moment. Was this the first time I had seen him unsure about something? He pushed his chair back and stood up before he walked over to my side of the table and held his hand out. I stood up as well and allowed him to bring me into his arms as we gently swayed to the soft melody playing on the speakers.

"You know, I debated hiring live music to play here tonight."

"I'm glad you didn't. It might have been a little weird having them sit around and watch us eat and now dance. Tonight's been perfect, just the way it is." Between our slow dancing, his embrace, and his woodsy cologne, I was being lulled into a fantasy where everything was perfect, and danger wasn't lurking behind every corner. It was where Damien and I could just be ourselves with no priorities other than one another.

"I love you."

I still wasn't used to hearing him say those words, yet they warmed my soul and as his lips made their way toward mine, I whispered, "I love you too."

⁓

"YOU'VE BEEN TEASING me all night, Spitfire."

I looked around the penthouse before my eyes landed back on Damien. He had just closed the door. "How? I haven't done anything."

"The dress you chose to wear tonight hugs every single curve of your body and I can't wait to strip it off of you. Inch. By. Inch."

Goosebumps appeared on my flesh, giving a glimpse of the effect he was having on my body.

"Turn around."

I did as he said but I wasn't giving in that easy. "Why don't I make things a little easier for you?" I twirled slowly so that my back was to him and reached up, finding the zipper of the dress. I pulled it down, revealing even more skin than before, and looked at him over my shoulder. My heart was pounding with anticipation. The heat that was in his eyes earlier tonight returned with a vengeance and I knew I was in for a wild ride.

Before waiting for him to say another word, I walked out of the room and into the bedroom, adding a little extra sway to my hips as I went. If he was going to accuse me of being a tease, there was no way I wasn't going to live up to it, punishments be damned. By the time I reached the foot of the bed, I heard the bedroom door close with a resounding click.

"Do you think this is a game?"

"No, I—"

"You don't run this. I do." Damien spun me around so that I faced him, pulled me toward him, and kissed me like his life depended on it.

He paused briefly to whip his shirt off before his lips latched on to mine once more. His fingers moved across my back, looking for his end goal, and when he found it, the only noise I could hear was the zipper of my dress moving lower and lower. When the zipper reached its destination, I let the dress fall from my body, leaving me in just a bra and panties.

"Much better."

A drop of self-consciousness appeared before me as he examined my body with only my underwear covering my modesty. Most of my bruises had faded, but I knew I still had a couple that were somewhat noticeable on my skin. I let out a deep breath and cleared the worry from my mind. These were some temporary scars on my body because I survived something traumatic. And if the way Damien was looking at me was any indication, he couldn't care less.

Without breaking eye contact, he reached behind me and unsnapped my bra and it fell to the floor. "Lie down on the bed."

Without looking behind me, I sat down on the bed and before I had a chance to suck in a breath, he was on me. His lips tasted my neck before making their way to my breasts. He took his time massaging my breasts and sucking on my nipples. He alternated between which breast would get attention, so I didn't know what was coming next. He licked my left nipple once more before he looked at me and stood up.

He took a second to step back and toss a condom on the bed that he pulled out of his pocket. While he undid his pants, I took a moment to admire his bare chest, which was crafted to perfection from his neck down to his six-pack.

Damien moved back over me, his fingers going farther south. When he reached the apex of my thighs, he shifted the flimsy fabric of my thong out of the way and replaced it with his fingers. "Oh fuck, you're so wet for me."

He slowly removed my panties and I almost growled. "If

you don't stick your cock in me and fuck me within the next five seconds, I'll—"

"You'll do what, Spitfire?"

He didn't give me an opportunity to answer because I felt the head of his dick at my entrance. The anticipation was going to kill me, I was sure of it. When he finally sunk his cock into me, I sighed with relief. I'd missed this connection with him so much.

"Damien, I'm not fragile like expensive china. When I said I wanted you to fuck me, I meant it."

"Whatever the lady wants, the lady gets."

When he pushed all the way into me, my eyes closed as I took a moment to enjoy the sensations of having him inside my pussy. He picked up the tempo and I moaned as his cock was hitting all of the places that I needed him to hit. His pace continued to quicken and soon he was fucking me the way I wanted to be fucked.

"Yes, oh my..." I couldn't find the words to express how good this felt. My eyes fluttered shut. "I'm close."

"You can only come when I say so."

"What?" My eyes sprung open and landed on Damien.

"You can't come until I say so. That's payback for your little striptease earlier."

"You've got to be fucking kidding me."

"No. I'm fucking you, but I'm not kidding. Take all of this, Spitfire."

I should have known he would find a way to punish me for the stunt I pulled earlier, but I didn't know it would be right now. I focused on not orgasming as Damien moved in and out of me, his smirk telling me that he was enjoying this too much. I groaned and closed my eyes tightly as I tried to prevent what had become my body's natural instinct. This was unbearable.

"Come, Anais."

"Yes!" The word came out as a hiss as I was finally able to orgasm.

Relief and ecstasy flooded my body as I finally gave in to what my body was seeking. Damien groaned as he found his own release. He lay down on top of me and the only thing that could be heard between the two of us was our panting as we tried to catch our breaths.

"We can never go that long without sex," I said.

"You read my mind. Deal."

16

DAMIEN

"Is Charlotte going to be here? She might know something that might help."

"Will didn't say whether or not she would be."

"I hope so. She helped save my life and I want to, at the very least, thank her for that."

"Makes sense to me."

"Thanks for letting me come with you. I know you usually handle business like this on your own."

"Yes, I usually do. But I wanted to give you another peek inside of my world. Is that alright?" I said slowly. This was another way I was trying to fix things. This situation involved her directly and she should be in the room to give her opinion and make decisions.

Anais hesitated before she said, "Okay." I could see the skepticism in her eyes. She would soon learn how serious I was about making things right. I held open the wooden brown door and allowed Anais to walk in first. A woman sitting at a reception desk looked up at us.

"Can I help you?"

"Yes, can you tell your boss that Damien Cross and Anais Monroe are here to see him?"

"Ah. They are expecting you, just give me one moment."

The woman picked up the phone and announced our presence to the person on the other end. When she hung up, she gave us a tight smile before she spoke.

"I'll show you to the conference room."

She walked around the desk and opened a door. She walked through first and held it open for us before she started walking down a short hallway with us following behind her. The receptionist approached another brown door and gently knocked before opening it and gesturing for us to go in. I nodded my head in acknowledgment and Anais whispered a quick thank-you before we entered.

"Damien, Anais. Welcome to my office." Will stood up from the table and stuck out his hand to shake.

I returned the gesture and as he moved to shake Anais's hand, my eyes landed on the woman who seemed to be a blessing and a curse to my life. Charlotte stood up and shook my hand too and I noticed the air in the room had changed from indifference to awkwardness. Given what this conversation was going to be about, I wasn't surprised. Anais moved around me and hesitated as she stared at Charlotte, before she said, "Is it okay if we hug?"

A smile appeared on Charlotte's face. "Of course."

The two women embraced, and Will and I gave them their moment as we picked seats at the long table. Yes, Charlotte and I had a history, but they deserved to take as much time as they needed given what they had both been through. Together.

When the women broke apart, Anais said, "I owe you so much."

I stood up to walk over to Anais when her voice broke, but she looked over at me and mouthed that she was okay.

"No, you don't. We both worked together to escape, and it worked."

"It doesn't make anything you did less heroic."

"It goes both ways, Anais."

The women hugged again before taking their seats. I pulled out my handkerchief and gave it to Anais, who used it to do dab at the corners of her eyes.

Will spoke up this time. "Let's cut straight to the chase, shall we?" He leaned back in his chair, his eyes coolly assessing the situation.

"I agree."

"How are you doing, Anais?"

I lightly cleared my throat, daring him to say something else. Anais placed her hand on my knee, and I could read the warning in her eyes. "She's not what this discussion is about."

I knew many people didn't threaten Will, but I couldn't care less. I was just as dangerous as he was, if not even more so. He couldn't run his operations without me, so it was best if he stayed on my good side.

"I can speak for myself, Damien. I'm fine, Will. Thanks for asking. How are you, Charlotte?"

"Better."

"Do you have any updates on Vincent?"

Will shook his head. "He knows he's a dead man when I find him."

Of course, Will didn't know his location. That would

make things too easy. "You don't have anyone tracking him? He can't be this hard to find."

"Well, have you found him yet?"

He did have a point. "No, but he wasn't doing legwork for any of my businesses either."

Will rubbed a hand across his chin. "Vincent hasn't worked for the Vitale family in years. He disappeared years ago and to be honest, I fully expected to get a call at some point that his body had been found. With everything going on now, I've had my men trying to find him and we've been able to find a trail of breadcrumbs that has painted somewhat of a picture of what he's been doing over the years. Apparently, he's been building relationships with other organizations in the city, doing odds and ends for them in exchange for favors and their silence about his whereabouts. Explains the capital he was able to gather in order to do everything he's done so far. He doesn't hang around his usual haunts and hasn't been answering calls from anyone. The only people he might be willing to try to find are you or Charlotte at this point."

That thought crossed my mind. If he had gone as far as to hire someone to kidnap his sister after she spent years in hiding and came after what was mine, he had to have been planning this for a while. But what was his ultimate goal? Did he still want to get back at me? Kill Charlotte for disobeying him years ago? I had no doubt that he was planning something to strike back. It was just a question of what and when. And how could we get him before someone else got hurt?

I set those thoughts aside for the time being because we had some other issues that needed to be resolved.

"Charlotte, you and I have some things to discuss."

She nodded. "I know. What can I answer for you?"

"Although I assume I know the answer, I still want to hear it from you. Why did you pretend to be dead for all of these years? Were you hiding from Vincent?"

Charlotte looked at her brother before she looked down at her hands. "What was the thing I told you before the fire?"

An image of Charlotte at eighteen flashed through my mind. We had sat down on the couch in our home for the weekend about to tear into some pizza when she stopped from eating. "You told me that I needed to be careful, and I asked you why and you said you just had a bad feeling."

"That's because I knew Vincent was going to do something that weekend. I knew because he recruited me to bring you up there to burn you alive."

I tightly gripped the arms of the chair that I was sitting in to avoid jumping out of my seat. "He did what?"

Charlotte sighed. "Vincent was convinced that your father led my father to kill himself. I overheard Vincent talking to someone on the phone about the situation shortly after we started dating. The gist I got from it was that my father owed Martin a lot of money because he lost some of the merchandise Martin was supposed to buy from him. Martin wasn't willing to forgive the debt and that caused my father to spiral until he ended it all. Vincent caught me, called me into his office, and it was like a light bulb went off in his head and he concocted this plan that I was supposed to help him carry out in order to get revenge for our father's death. Vincent told me I was as good as dead to him if I didn't help, and how dare I ruin Dad's legacy."

Charlotte took a moment and looked over at Will again, who nodded. "So I did it, I invited you up for the weekend and immediately regretted it. I debated going to the police but knew that if Vincent knew it was me who ratted, he would have me killed. I wanted to warn you that Vincent was acting deranged and wanted you dead, but I worried about what the end result of that would be for me too. A few hours before the house was supposed to go up in flames, I called your father and told him to come and get you and when you went downstairs for a drink of water, I signaled to Vincent before I climbed out of the window and I ran. I prayed that your father got to you in time and I just ran. It was cowardly I know, but—"

"But what choice did you have? We were still in high school and you did your best to warn someone who could do something about it. You saved my life as well."

Tears formed in Charlotte's eyes. "You wouldn't have been up there if it weren't for me."

"You ended up saving both of our lives, although I'm sure yours changed dramatically when you ran."

Charlotte nodded. "I debated calling Will, but I didn't want to drag him into all of this either, so I took off and never looked back."

This was the first time I felt at peace with what happened that night. Charlotte's explanation made sense and I could easily tell that she was caught between two terrible outcomes and had done her best to forge her own path ahead. Her efforts worked until Vincent started causing trouble years later.

"Thanks for giving an explanation, Charlotte."

She gave me a small smile before I turned to Will. "We'll head out, but if you find anything, you'll contact me."

I saw the smirk appear on Will's face before he could remove it. "Is that an order?"

"Your words, not mine. I'll be in touch." I stood up from the chair and walked toward the guard standing by the door.

"Damien."

I paused and turned to look over my shoulder at the man sitting behind the great big desk that almost reminded me of my father's at my childhood home.

"If you find Vincent before I do, I want him back. Dead or alive."

"Deal."

"I FEEL like we're getting closer to Vincent, yet we still have a ways to go. Turns out he went rogue, and Will doesn't know where he is either. I think he got the message about what happened to Carter loud and clear and ran. Will is looking for him too." My leg bounced up and down at my desk while I chatted on the phone hours after the meeting with Will and Charlotte after Anais went to bed. She was drained from the meeting earlier today.

"I'm not surprised. We're digging through some of the devices we found at Carter's apartment and the cabin to see if that would give us any leads. We are also digging into both of their backgrounds to see if anything pops."

"Are you working with Dave?" I mentioned the name of the person we usually called on to find everything there was to find about someone.

"Yes. Uncle Martin authorized it."

"You didn't tell me you spoke to my father."

"Must have slipped my mind. He knows everything now. Might be helpful to dig up any known associates of Harvey as well. They might be helping Vincent now."

That might be helpful. Anything that could get us closer to him would be key. I knew that if Will found him before I did, I wouldn't get a chance at him. I would be happy to deliver his body to them once I was finished with him, so we had to find him first.

"Did they have anything to say about us finding him? I'm not keeping it quiet that I'm hunting him down."

"No one is stepping on anyone's toes here. Will understands why you'd be going after him. He fucked with what was yours and he doesn't care as long as the end result is the same."

"Let me know if you hear anything else."

"You got it."

I hung up the phone and stared at my computer screen. *Where do we go from here?*

Thoughts of how to lure Vincent out circled in my mind but I kept coming back to the only thing that seemed like a sure deal: when he was going to strike again.

17

DAMIEN

I finished typing an email to Melissa when my phone buzzed on my desk. Who would be calling at this time of night?

I had slipped out of bed while Anais slept in hopes of getting some work that might make me tired enough to fall asleep beside her. I looked over at the caller ID and closed my eyes. Why was he calling me when we had already met earlier today? I took a deep breath and answered the phone. "Damien."

"He killed a couple of my men. I thought he might attack because he probably thought I was involved due to Charlotte."

"Son of a bitch." I ran a hand through my hair, making even more messy than it was before. I made a note to check in with Dad after this just in case Vincent tried to go after him because it seemed as if his target on me was shifting. "How did it happen, Will?"

"He, or someone he must be working with, snuck and

attacked them while they were out on a run for me. This fucker has to pay and I'm growing impatient."

"I know. Any word on his whereabouts?"

"No. You know I would've reached out to you if I heard anything."

"Would you have though? I think you wouldn't have hesitated to kill me over Jon's disappearance just a week ago, even though he was an asshole. You'd have taken me out without even a blink of the eye."

"Touché," Will said before taking a deep breath. "There has to be more we can do to get to him. I don't know how long I can patiently wait for something in this case before we find him. Brother or not, I will not allow for there to be more fucking blood spilled unless it's his. This needs to end."

I rubbed my hands across my face, mentally going through the information that has been gathered. What were we all missing? This man couldn't have that many resources to be able to hide for this length of time. "I've already stepped things up a notch by going to his old stomping grounds and I've talked with some people I know have done business with him. In other words, he has to know I'm looking for him. Let's give it a few days to see if my inquiring pisses him off enough and causes him to resurface."

"Okay and I'll see what I can do on my end."

THE NEXT MORNING, I couldn't help but smile. Anais had no idea what was coming. It was time for us to do something for her and that was a promise that I took seriously.

My urge to get her out from the city was intense due to

Vincent still being on the run. I decided to take her away for a bit while I waited to see if Vincent would appear. Since I didn't know how long it would take, secretly getting away for a bit would be fun and rejuvenating, something I thought Anais desperately needed. When we returned, it would be time to enact a new plan if mine didn't work. I was determined that everyone in this situation wouldn't live in fear any longer, particularly Anais and Charlotte.

Now it was time to take Anais's mind off this. I made a few arrangements myself and had Melissa finish up the rest. I tossed a card in front of Anais while she was sitting on the couch.

"What's this?" she asked as she looked down at the white cardstock and flipped it around in her hands.

"I didn't know you had trouble reading."

I watched as she rolled her eyes, making a note to myself that she would pay for that later. She finally read the card and then it slipped from her hands and fell to the floor.

"We're going to St. Barts?"

"Oh, so you do know how to read," I said, folding my arms over my chest. I tried to contain my happiness over her being excited, but I couldn't. This was the happiest she had been in weeks and it was me that put that smile on her face.

"When do we leave?"

"Tomorrow morning."

She sat forward and the shock was still evident on her face. If she stayed like that long enough, I would have no issue putting my cock in her mouth.

Anais hopped off the couch and into my arms. I was somewhat worried, about what that movement might hurt her head, but she seemed fine as her bright smile flashing back at me.

"How did you know? Did Rob tell you?"

"I don't divulge my secrets."

Anais laughed. "I don't know how I could thank you for this. There is nothing I would be able to do that would ever compare."

"Don't think that way...but there are several ways I can think of you might be able to make it up to me."

ONCE WE WERE SETTLED and up in the air, Anais turned to me and said, "You know one thing I've never done?"

"Gone to St. Barts?"

"Besides that."

"What?"

"Joined the mile-high club."

I raised an eyebrow at her. "Is this your way of dropping a hint?"

"I'm glad you got it. Plus, I already know you have a bed and everything in the back of this jet. This is practically a hotel with wings."

I nodded, agreeing with her assessment. She turned back around and smiled at me. I couldn't help myself and tucked a piece of hair behind her ear and laid a kiss on her lips.

"Get up. We're going to start the initiation process and I can't wait to have your pussy in my face. I want you to go to the bedroom and remove all your clothes. You'll have less than a minute."

Anais glanced toward the front of the plane, probably

looking to see if the flight attendant was nearby. She unbuckled her seat belt and quickly walked toward the back room. I counted to twenty slowly before I joined her.

"Lean over the bed."

Watching her stand there with her ass up in the air teased me and made my cock twitch as I thought of all the things that I could do to her from that position.

"I thought you wanted to eat my pussy?"

"There are a lot of things I want to do to you, but I've decided to get to the pussy eating later. I want to worship this ass for now." I removed my clothes and tossed a condom on the bed. I watched her for a moment then moved closer to her and ran a finger up and down her slit. "Fuck...you're dripping already."

"Tell me something I don't know."

I slapped her ass after her sarcastic comment. It didn't have its intended effect because she was still smirking at me. So, I slapped her ass again, this time choosing the other butt cheek. A moan left her lips, encouraging me to take things up a notch.

"You're enjoying this, aren't you?" I finished my question with another slap on that ass that soon turned into another slap. "I haven't done my due diligence in appreciating this masterpiece."

I laid soft kisses on her back as I gently massaged the flesh I just tormented. When I made my way back down to her cunt, a low groan flew out of my mouth. "You're even wetter than before."

"I want your cock inside me."

"Is that right?" My cock grew harder at her words, begging to be inside of her pussy immediately.

She eagerly nodded her head and when she looked at me over her shoulder, it wasn't hard to tell that she was already halfway there. As I removed the condom wrapper, Anais shook her head.

"What's wrong?"

"Forget the condom. I've been on birth control this entire time."

I raised an eyebrow. "That would have been something to tell me months ago."

"You didn't ask and we don't need it. I'm clean."

"As am I." I flipped her over, lining up our bodies. I teased her entrance with my cock for a few seconds before I guided myself into her cunt. The sensations that I felt without the condom were like night and day and I wondered why we hadn't done it sooner.

Anais shivered when I was fully seated in her. I leaned down to kiss her square on the lips before I started moving my hips. The sounds that left her were like music to my ears and I picked up the pace.

"Yes!" she said, and I could see her losing control.

The wanton-look in her eyes shone through just before her eyes closed. I felt my own release building as I reached down to play with her nipples. We continued at this rapid pace, both of us enjoying one another and seeking salvation on the other end. When I felt her pussy tighten around my cock, I knew her release was imminent. With one final scream, she arched her back and we both let go. Heavy breathing was the only thing that surrounded us as we stared into each other's eyes.

When our breathing slowed down, I said, "Welcome to the mile-high club. I hope you enjoy your stay."

18

ANAIS

I sat in the car and watched in awe as we passed some of the sites that St. Barts had to offer on the way to where we would be staying. I couldn't believe I was here. I couldn't remove the smile from my face as our personal chauffeur took us to our home away from home. I couldn't wait to frolic around in the water at one of the beaches on the island. When I took my eyes off what was going on outside of my window for a moment, they landed on Damien, who was staring at me.

"What? Is there something on my face?"

"No. I'm just watching you."

"That's not creepy at all," I said with a smile before turning my attention back to the window. I was shocked that we were in St. Barts on our first official vacation with one another. Hell, I never thought we would have ever gone anywhere after our deal was up because I didn't want to. Yet here we were, about to enjoy a few days in the Caribbean sun.

"I'm surprised you didn't take me to a private island that you owned or something."

"That's for the next trip."

"Did you just tell a joke? I can't believe it."

Damien shook his head at me before looking back down at his phone, I assume checking in on some of the things that were going on at his office. The view in front of me was already one of the most beautiful things I had ever seen, and it was all flying past me too fast for me to appreciate it. I hoped that the place where we would be staying had a stunning view that I could just stare at for hours if I wanted to.

I smiled. Who was I kidding? Damien Cross always booked the best of the best. And that's just what I saw as we were coming up to the grounds that I assumed we would be staying at for the next few days. There was enough space to fit at least twelve people given the number of bedrooms. That worked out well for us because we had a couple of guards who traveled with us and would be staying here. The private chauffeur, chef, and butler were an added bonus to go along with the private access to the beach. I was dying to try the spa that was located in the basement. Plus getting back into the spirit of working out regularly wouldn't be a bad idea and the fully equipped gym provided enough incentive.

Our security detail came downstairs and chatted with us briefly about securing the villa. When I saw our butler for our stay bringing in the last of our bags, I excused myself and walked over to him.

"Thank you so much for helping us bring our stuff inside."

"It was a pleasure."

Damien appeared by my side and placed an arm around my waist. "We can handle the bags from here."

I turned and found Damien looking at me just as the gentleman turned to leave us to ourselves.

"What?" I looked back at the retreating man before turning to Damien. "I was just thanking him for helping us with our stuff."

"That's unnecessary."

"Green is not your best color."

It took him a second to understand what I meant. "I'm hardly jealous. I was just letting him know that his services were no longer needed."

"You know, you didn't show much of your jealous side when we were back in New York. Well outside of that moment just before we traveled to the Hamptons."

"Things happen. Times change. Speaking of change, we should get changed."

He was right. The clothes we had on were for colder weather in New York.

"Well, if you don't mind bringing our bags up now that you declined the help, I can find something to change into." With that, I spun on my heel and turned to pick out which bedroom we would be staying in on the upper level. I knew I would pay for my little stunt later and I was looking forward to it.

The villa was decorated in bright yet soothing colors creating a relaxing vibe. It was easy to see that the décor was inspired by the country we were in. I was already mentally making plans to return, and I hadn't even been here for half a day yet. I heard some noises behind me and turned to see Damien bringing in my bags.

"Thank you." I walked over and brought his face down to me and laid a sensual kiss on his lips.

"For?"

"Bringing me here and for bringing up my bags."

He smiled briefly before walking toward the doorway. "Do you want anything to eat?"

"I would love a little something. The other thing I would like is some company while I take a shower. You know if you're not too busy conquering another company."

Damien looked at me with a dark gleam in his eye. "It just so happens that my schedule is completely free for the next few days other than fucking you. Get in the bathroom, Spitfire."

"Do we ever have to go back?" I asked, floating along in the infinity pools at the villa Damien rented out. The two guards that were here with us were seated on a couple of lounge chairs nearby but were doing anything but relaxing. I could see them scanning the perimeter every chance they got. With Vincent still at large, Damien thought it was better to be safe than sorry, although even he doubted Vincent would do anything in St. Barts. Damien thought that if Vincent would want to put on a show, and he'd do it in New York City to showcase his power and get the most media attention. Who knew if he would actually admit to the crime but he would revel in media attention surrounding it. Avenging his father's death would be all that he would need.

"We do but not for a little while."

"Well, I'm enjoying this very much. Excellent thoughts and planning on your part." I could see some crinkling at the corners of his eyes, which let me know that he had enjoyed that compliment. The sun was shining brightly, and we were lying under a deep blue sky. It was a picture-perfect moment. And I swore I had only seen such vivid beauty in paintings.

The sound of Damien's phone ringing brought us both out of the moment of bliss that we were feeling. He swam over to the edge of the pool and pulled himself out. He grabbed a towel to wipe himself off before he picked up his phone.

"Kingston sent a text." He walked over to the pool and placed the phone just out of reach.

"I'm going to call him back and put it on speaker phone so we can all hear what he needs to say."

"And I'm going to stay right here, basking in the sun in paradise no matter what he says."

He shook his head and called Kingston back.

"I hope I didn't interrupt anything."

I thought about telling him that he had interrupted some quiet time that I was enjoying spending with Damien, but I didn't.

"Don't worry about it. Anais and your team members are here too. What's up with the 'call me asap' text?"

Kingston got straight to the point. "Vincent has resurfaced. Dave has been helping us tail him."

"What do we have on him? Do we know where he is? Do you think it's time to bring someone in to take him out?"

"Yeah, he crossed into our territory and tried to get into Elevate last night. We confirmed it this morning and I called you immediately."

"Are you serious? By the way, hi, Kingston," I chimed in from my spot in the pool.

"Hello. Yes, it confirms that he is still in the city and

maybe he thought you might be there? Who knows? It also shows that he doesn't give a fuck about anything if he thought he was going to get into Elevate and do whatever he had planned."

"Without a doubt."

"Do you want me to step up security at all of your properties in the city and send a couple more folks to St. Barts?"

I watched as Damien thought about Kingston's proposal. "To me it makes sense, at least for now. If he's brazen enough to come to Elevate, which is heavily guarded, who knows what else he is trying to pull?"

Damien nodded. "Anais is right. We'll step up security and then evaluate once we are back in the city."

"Sounds good," Kingston said.

"The plan is working. I should have an update for you within the hour. Hell, it might have been the reason Vincent resurfaced to begin with."

I raised an eyebrow at Damien. What was he talking about and why was he being purposely vague about it?

"Okay. Thanks for the update. If anything else comes up, let me know." Damien turned to look at me. "I'd do anything to keep her safe."

"I know that. We've all seen how much she has changed you. For the better, I might add."

"I'll talk to you soon."

"Have a good one."

Damien hung up the phone and tossed it on one of the lounge chairs.

"Well, that's a way to bring the mood down. What plan are you doing?"

Damon looked at me before looking out at the pool.

"Kingston and I, along with his team, are working together to find a way to lure Vincent out of hiding and this might be showing that our efforts are working. Anyway, enough about this. Do you want one of those fruity drinks you are in love with?"

"Yes, a piña colada would be great." Why did I get the feeling that there was something he wasn't telling me?

19

ANAIS

I sighed and leaned my head back on the edge of the bathtub, allowing the warm jets to soothe my aching muscles. This included the tenderness between my thighs after Damien gave me his all just a couple of short hours ago as a gentle reminder of what he could do to me. I made a note to myself to get some sort of spa session in before I left the island.

Ellie's words about not becoming addicted to him floated to the surface. I knew I was long past that, however. He had ruined me for any other men who might come along in the future and I could say without hesitation I didn't want anyone else.

But I still felt as if a ticking time bomb was waiting to go off with the potential to take everything that I had worked so hard to build down with it.

What was I thinking, falling in love with Damien Cross? Although he was still demanding, I could easily see that things were getting better. He listened to me more and tried to understand my opinions about certain things. Although at times, he would still say a comment that came across as a demand and that was supposed to be the be-all and end-all. When he did that and I didn't agree, a debate would ensue, and I was perfectly happy with that.

I thought back to some of the fun that we'd had in St. Barts whether it was lounging on the beach, visiting some of the local sites, or getting Damien to try new fruity drinks. Damien rented a catamaran to take us to a small private island where we enjoyed snorkeling, an activity I'd never done before. We got to enjoy swimming with the sea turtles and other tropical fish, and it quickly became one of the best memories I'd ever had. The scrumptious breakfast and lunch that we had catered by a private chef capped off a beautiful day.

I also couldn't forget about the sexcapades we were getting into while on the island as well. We'd taken our time exploring every inch of our bodies over multiple surfaces in this villa and I enjoyed every minute of it. I knew Damien knew how to make my body sing but being in paradise was an additional aphrodisiac.

I glanced down at myself, happy with the glowing, tanner skin I was sporting due to my time in the sun. When the water started to cool down, I stood up and took my time stepping out of the tub and drying myself off. I took even more time moisturizing and throwing a robe over my naked body before I opened the door to leave the bathroom.

It was there that I was greeted with several bouquets of red tulips and roses sitting on the dresser in the bedroom. I knew for a fact they weren't there when I got into the tub and a quick look around confirmed that I was alone. Where had Damien gone? I picked them up and smelled them. They were beautiful and their color reminded me of the red roofs we saw in Gustavia when we went exploring yesterday.

I smelled the flowers once more before putting them back and turned around to find another surprise for me on the bed. A long silky cream-colored dress was lying on the bed next to a white square note.

Put this on and come into the living room.

"Damien, what are you up to?" I muttered to myself before I put the dress on. It reminded me of the silky navy dress that I had worn when I met Jon for the first time at that business dinner. I put on some light makeup and took my hair out of the braid I had placed it in after I washed my hair and before I soaked in the spa tub letting the soft dark waves kiss my shoulders. I walked out into the living room and smiled when I saw Damien sitting on the edge of the couch.

"Hey," I said softly.

He looked up at me with an unreadable expression on his face. He didn't say anything as he stood up and walked over to me. He held his hand out and I placed my hand in his as he guided me to the stairs.

"What's going on?"

"Watch your step."

Flower petals were laid on the floor, creating a path leading to the main floor of the villa.

Nerves bubbled under the surface when he still didn't elaborate. "Damien, what is all of this?"

"Me making up for lost time."

"Wait, what are—"

I was speechless. The main floor had been completely transformed since I had gone upstairs to shower and then soak in the tub. The overhead lights were low, and the living area was lit up by candles with flower petals on the floor and sparsely spread out on the dining room table. Light music played in the background and the glass door was open into the backyard, allowing for a soft breeze to enter, turning into a complete romantic oasis. The furniture had been rearranged to make the room look more open concept.

"What's wrong?"

"Nothing. Everything is perfect."

A sweet smile appeared for a brief second on his face. "Good. I thought we deserved to have a date night while in paradise. I thought about pulling something together on the beach, but you were complaining about the sand and—"

I couldn't stop the grin that wanted to burst out immediately. "No, I wasn't!"

Damien gave me a knowing smirk before he led me over to the dining room table. "Hungry? I thought something lighter might be appropriate because you mentioned you weren't hungry before going upstairs."

The staff at the resort had put together an enormous feast for two people. Instead of having one big meal, there were a lot of appetizers, but enough of them to make up a full meal. If this was what Damien called light...

I grabbed as much food as I wanted and walked over to the couch as I waited for Damien. He soon joined me with food in hand before he left again to get our drinks. Once he was back, we chatted and ate the food in front of us, just like any regular couple would.

Damien cleared his throat and turned to me. "This would be of interest to you. Cross Industries is thinking of starting a new social media network."

My head nearly spun off my neck at his comment. "You're

what? How come you've never mentioned it before? That's incredible!"

"It was a work in progress for a while and I wanted to wait until we had a mock-up before sharing the news."

"Mock-up, huh? Well, grab it, please! I can't wait to see it."

"I'll pull it up on the big screen here. I'm sure some of the images will be familiar to you."

That was when I saw that he brought his laptop down and had it already hooked up to the television. *He is really prepared for anything.* I crossed my legs as the presentation started and was amazed by the sight before me. The crisp colors, the layout of the website, and so much more were pulled together nicely.

I looked over at him and asked, "When is this going to go live?"

"Maybe in the next year or so. Keep watching."

I flipped my eyes back over to the screen and saw that in order to show the website's layout, a fake profile was made featuring photos of me and some of us. Some I recognized from events that we attended, but others I hadn't realized that Damien even took. I glanced at him again when he came over and sat down next to me and smiled as he took my hand into his.

"Our relationship started off rocky to say the least, and I've thought about how much of a selfish prick I was when it came to you." His words made me swallow hard. "Anais, there are so many reasons why you should have run as fast as you could away from me. There are so many reasons why I should have let you go time and time again. You deserve to live a happy and wonderful life and I debated whether or not I can be the one that can give it to you."

"Damien, I agree and it's taking me some time to realize where I want to be and that's with you. This isn't because you're holding a contract over my head or anything like that. I appreciate what we've grown into no matter how we began."

"We've been through a lot together in the short time that we've known each other, and I'm determined to show you how much I love you and wash away any thoughts that you have that this engagement isn't real. I'm doing things differently this time. Marry me."

I chuckled. "When most people propose to someone else, they ask the person versus make a demand."

"That's not my style but I can try it out right now. Anais, will you marry me?" Damien held out a small black box and opened it.

"Oh my—" Any other words died on my lips because the ring in front of me left me stunned beyond belief. "When did you get this? Did you ever find out what happened to the other ring?"

Damien shook his head. "Forget the other ring. I heard this was more along the lines of what you wanted."

All I could do was nod as I stared at the beautiful piece of jewelry in front of me. The ring was much smaller than the one he originally gave me and instead of a huge diamond on the band, he'd replaced it with an emerald. Tears formed in my eyes as they darted between staring at the ring and the man in front of me.

"Yes, yes, I will marry you!" The tears were soon a victim of gravity and there was nothing that could stop their downward trajectory. This was the story I couldn't wait to tell our children ten years down the line. This was the moment I craved with the man I desired more than anyone before.

Damien placed the beautiful ring on my finger, and I took a moment to stare at it before I found myself staring into his beautiful blue eyes. He softly wiped each tear that was falling from my face before he pulled me in for a mind-altering kiss.

His lips moved toward my neck before he said, "Bedroom now."

There was the Neanderthal coming out to play. I grinned when an idea popped into my head. I quickly stood up and took off running toward the stairs. I grabbed the fabric of my dress, pulling it up so I didn't trip.

Damien didn't follow behind me immediately, so I ran past the bedroom we were sleeping in to another one that was unoccupied.

Damien didn't leave me alone for long. "Spitfire, I'm going to fuck you wherever I find you."

My heart thundered in my chest, excitement building as I heard him enter the bedroom next to where I was. I slid farther into the room, hoping to hide from him just a little bit longer. That only bought me several seconds. Soon he was in the doorway, stalking toward me.

"There you are." Damien had already removed his clothes and was holding his dick. *Always prepared.*

"Here I am."

He took another step toward me and I took a step back. The pattern continued and my pulse quickened with each move we made. In the dull light, his feelings were flashing in his eyes like neon lights. He was ready to claim me as his once more. I felt my back hit the wall. There was nowhere else to go, nowhere else to hide.

Damien ran a finger along the thin straps holding my dress on me. "This will have to go. Lift your arms."

"But—" I looked out the window before looking back at him, knowing there might be a chance that we could be seen.

"The only person you need to worry about seeing you naked tonight is me."

That was when he pulled the silky dress over my head, leaving me completely bare to him. His eyes perused my body before he started his attack on me again. Every lick and nibble was meant to drive me wild.

My gaze didn't waver once they met his again as I did as he asked, and the dress was tossed to the side like yesterday's trash. He took both of my hands in one of his and held them against the wall. Still, I kept my eyes on him, refusing to be intimidated.

"You didn't put anything on underneath the dress. Excellent." One hand held my hands on the wall as the other moved down my body to my pussy. "That chase made you wet for me, didn't it?"

"Maybe." I let the word lazily roll off my tongue.

"Are you ready? We can take it slower later."

"Yes, please." My voice came out in a breathless whisper.

"Your arms will stay up in that position until I tell you when you can move them."

I nod quickly, hoping that would get Damien to move faster toward our goal. Damien slowly moved his hand from my pussy and toward my calf and lifted my leg around his waist. He did the same with my other leg and I growled in frustration.

"Getting impatient, Spitfire?"

I almost didn't hear his question due to him moving my body so that my pussy lined up with his cock. Without a second thought, Damien entered me completely and I moaned because he didn't stop until he was completely inside of me.

"Fuck, how is it that I already want you again and we haven't fucked yet?"

"Our bodies are addicted to one another, that's why." My words stopped abruptly due to him slamming into me again. And again. And again. The wall was allowing Damien to fuck me from a different angle, and it felt glorious. The only thing that could be heard between us was our heavy breathing and our bodies becoming one.

I could feel the sweat gathering on my back as Damien pounded into me.

"Do you want to come?" Damien's words came out as more of a series of grunts, but I understood him just the same.

"Yes, oh God, yes!" I said and felt my body begin to shake against his. As I rode the wave of my orgasm, he continued thrusting into me.

"Anais..." Damien groaned as he too found his release. Both of us stared at each other without making any moves to break our connection anytime soon.

"Is Cross Industries really creating another social media platform?"

Damien chuckled. "There have been talks, but I don't have any concrete information. What I do have is another smaller surprise for you."

I lifted my head slightly, which had been lying on Damien's chest, to get a better look at him. It had been about thirty minutes since we properly celebrated our engagement and we had somehow made it to the bedroom we were staying in. "What's that?"

"We're moving back into the mansion. In fact, we should be all moved back in by the time we step foot back in NYC."

I sat up and looked at him in disbelief. There would be no more hiding out in the home in the sky unless I wanted to.

"Thank you," I whispered and leaned over to kiss him softly on the lips. I could feel him growing harder under my leg that was thrown across his body. He deepened the kiss and flipped me on my back.

"Ready for another round?" Damien asked.

"Always."

ANAIS

"So, this is where Damien lives when he's not at the penthouse. And now it's your home."

"Wow, I forgot you haven't seen this place yet." Being back in the place I renamed as the NoHo Mansion felt wonderful. We had more space, and I couldn't wait to add pops of color to the place to make it fit a blend of styles versus strictly Damien's. I was drawing from some of the colors and vibrancy that we saw while we were in St. Barts, determined to bring some of paradise home. We had been back in the city for several days and I was already ready to return to the island.

As I showed Ellie around the home, I made a mental note of things I wanted to change or update. I also couldn't stop myself from thinking about changing at least one into a nursery, but that would be a while yet. I wanted Damien to myself for a little while longer before the pattering of baby feet in this home.

One thing I wasn't expecting to be weird that was, was now having access to the main bedroom on the top floor. The

room that had been a source of contention early in our relationship was now accessible to me whenever I wanted. It was
another room on my list that needed pops of color. I also
hoped subtle changes would remove memories of the nightmares that Damien experienced alone. Thankfully, neither
one of us were having many nightmares these days.

"Speaking of him, where is Damien?"

"He went into the office when we met up for lunch to get a
few things done that he hadn't had time to work on this week."

Ellie nodded, shifting the box she was holding and looked
around my newly claimed living room. She had come over to
check out my new engagement ring and to help me start
making small changes to the NoHo Mansion. "Pretty sure I
could fit the apartment in the living room alone."

That triggered a light bulb moment. "We should talk
about that. With me moving in with Damien, what are you
going to do? How can I help?"

Ellie smiled and said, "Damien offered to let me rent the
apartment I've been staying in for a discounted rate. Said I
could do it as long as I was friends with you, so now you'll
never get rid of me."

I couldn't stop the giggles that left my mouth. "Never
imagined I would be able to anyway."

A knock on the door stopped us both from talking. I
glanced at Ellie before I walked closer to the front. Damien
installed an all-new security system including cameras and
other accessories while we were in St. Barts, in order to
ensure that he was doing everything to protect me.

"Kingston."

I double-checked that it was indeed him although I recognized his voice before opening the door. We gave each other small smiles before I brought him into the living room where Ellie laid eyes on him.

Her mouth fell open for a split second before she said, "I remember you! You were giving me hell when Anais and I went to Elevate."

Kingston shrugged before crossing his arms. "I have no recollection of that."

"You are so full of—"

"Hey now. You guys need to cut it out because chances are you'll be seeing a lot more of each other." I couldn't say that I didn't find this amusing. Ellie almost looked as if she was going to take off her shoe and aim it at his head while Kingston viewed her coolly, yet a small smile played on his lips. *This is interesting.*

"Damien's going to be home a little late and he couldn't reach you."

Really? It's the weekend and he isn't supposed to be in the office anyway. I pulled out my phone from my back pocket and sure enough, found a text message from Damien stating the same thing.

Damien: *Going to be home later than planned tonight.*

Me: *Sorry I missed this message. Kingston came in and mentioned it. See you when you get home.*

When I put my phone back in my pocket, I looked up to find Ellie glaring at Kingston.

"Have you always been a prick? Or was this behavior saved just for me."

Kingston shrugged. "Just for you."

I could see that Ellie was about to snap back and I

jumped in before she could. "Okay, enough, you two. Kingston, I'll let you know if I need anything else."

Kingston nodded his head and turned to leave but was stopped by Ellie's voice.

"Do you really need a coin to get into the sex club?"

Kingston looked over his shoulder, right at Ellie. "No." And with that, he walked out as quickly as he entered.

"That man is infuriating."

I nodded my head. "And to make matters worse, he hasn't seen one episode of *Friends*. Who does that?"

Ellie raised an eyebrow at me but didn't ask questions. I was thankful that she hadn't. Before I knew it, we were settled on the couch watching a romantic comedy. About halfway through the movie, Ellie needed to get a drink from the kitchen so I paused the movie so she wouldn't miss any of it.

"Things almost feel back to normal," I said as I waited for her to come back from the kitchen. "Granted things have changed, but they are also still the same. Like look, we're watching a movie in the early evening."

"Yep, except it's in a mansion that is probably worth more than anything I will ever own in my life."

I rolled my eyes and shook my head, but she continued.

"Things have changed a lot. Who would have thought you'd be engaged to one of the most notorious bachelors in New York City? Especially after I warned you not to get addicted...although I would say I think he's as equally addicted to you if not more."

"You never know what could happen. Get over here so we can finish this movie."

"I'm coming, I'm coming."

While I waited for Ellie to get back, I checked my phone

again but there were no new notifications. I sent a text message to Damien, asking for an update on when he would arrive home.

Me: *Are you coming home soon?*

Damien: *It'll be a little while yet, but hopefully soon.*

Me: *Okay see you then.*

Once Ellie was seated again, I unpaused the movie and we finished watching it. A glance outside confirmed that it was evening as Ellie stood up to stretch. "I should probably call Nick so that we can head back to my apartment."

As Ellie did that, I checked my phone again but there was nothing from Damien.

"Nick should be outside so I'm going to go."

I put my phone back in my pocket and walked Ellie to the door. I gave her a big hug before opening the door.

"Tell Damien I said hi and that he really did a good job with this engagement ring."

I smiled. "He did, didn't he? I'll let him know."

Kingston came to the front door and Ellie served him with a glare before walking down to the car that Nick was waiting in. With a small wave, I watched as Ellie drove away.

I turned to Kingston and said, "Can we go to Cross Tower? Maybe me showing up there will be enough to get him to leave his stuff at work."

"Sure."

"Also don't tell him. It can be a surprise."

I could see Kingston weighing the choices and he said, "I don't see why not."

"Perfect. I'm ready when you and Rob are."

21

DAMIEN

"Mr. Cross."

"Yes?" I said as I looked up at Melissa, who was standing in the doorway.

"Do you need anything before I head out?"

"No. I've got everything else. Thanks for coming in on your day off. Have a good night."

Melissa lingered for a second before she left, closing the door behind her. I continued reading the briefings that I received while I was out on vacation, trying to get ahead on discussions that were occurring on Monday.

A quick glance at my computer screen told me that an hour had passed since Melissa had left and I was still sitting here answering emails and reading reports. I checked my phone and noticed that I missed a message from Anais when a knock on my office door left me puzzled. *Who is here this late on a Saturday?*

"Who is it?"

"Cleaning."

"Come in."

Just as I said the words, I reminded myself that it was the weekend and that there usually wasn't any member of the cleaning crew here now.

Someone wearing dark clothes, a baseball cap, and dragging a large garbage can opened the door. With my foot, I slowly opened my bottom drawer, not wanting to take any chances having entered an unknown situation.

"It's about time that we met each other in person, Mr. Cross."

I stood up from my chair. "I see you finally got my message, Vincent."

The man in front of me chuckled but it was clear he didn't find what I said funny. He moved farther into the room. "I'm here to collect what is owed to me."

"What? My death?"

"Precisely. I wanted to make you hurt as much as your father made me hurt, but there's been a change in plans."

"Due to the botched kidnapping?"

Vincent shrugged. "Sometimes it's easier to do things yourself. I'll make sure that the job is done right this time. Why don't you take a seat?"

"I'd rather stand."

Vincent pulled a revolver out of his pocket. I raised my hands and he gestured with the gun for me to take a seat. I hesitated before sitting in the chair and I stole a glance at my gun that I started carrying with me after Anais's kidnapping.

"You're going to pay for what happened to my father. Martin Cross is going to understand the pain of losing his own flesh and blood."

"What? Because my father didn't want to bail yours out again?"

"He could have saved his life."

"Not based on what we now know. Your father owed a lot of people money and it was only a matter of time before they came to collect."

"Liar!" Vincent roared and I saw a vein in his forehead that looked like it might burst at any moment. Until he suddenly calmed down. "You are just trying to rile me up. I'm going to enjoy the little game that I have planned."

Although the look in his eyes told me what I was thinking was a bad idea, I decided to try to reason with him. There was a low chance that I would be able to grab my gun in time to protect myself in case he decided to fire. "I know you've been harboring these feelings for a long time, but I swear, my father wasn't responsible for Harvey's death. I have the records that show how my father tried to help yours and—"

"Hey Damien, I wanted to...what the hell?"

My greatest fear became a reality, when I saw Anais's bright smile as she stood in my office doorway.

"It's nice to officially meet you, Anais. How funny it is that we keep bumping into each other." The sinister voice forced Anais's eyes to bounce between me and him.

"I can't say the feeling is mutual and I wouldn't call stalking bumping into each other."

Vincent smirked and glanced back at me and then back at her. "Well, it's nice that you could join us. I was just about to have a conversation with your fiancé before I killed him. Congrats on making everything official, by the way. Saw the ring on social media a couple of days ago."

"What are you doing here, Anais?"

"I had the same question."

"Fuck you." I glared at Vincent, not caring that he was holding a gun directed at me.

"I wanted to surprise you." Anais stuttered over the last word.

"Well, it's nice that you could join us. As I said, I was just about to have a conversation with your fiancé before I killed him."

I could feel Anais watching me before she moved farther into the room. She stood several feet away from me, creating a triangle between the three of us. "Let her go."

"No. Because that would defeat the purpose of the game I want to play. Russian roulette, and it will be starring the two of you. There are six bullets in this gun, five are blanks and one isn't. Which one of you wants to go first?"

My eyes met Anais and I could see the tears already falling from her eyes. Once again, because of me, she was in a predicament that she shouldn't be in. "I will."

"Damien, no." Her voice trembled and I watched as the tears became a steady stream.

"Fire the gun at me."

"No, because that is what you want. Anais is up first."

Because I didn't doubt that he would shoot her first, I leaned down and reached for my gun in my drawer. Before I could grab it, Vincent noticed and pulled the trigger with no hesitation and I slightly jumped at the loud bang, but that's all there was. That gunshot should have been loud enough to alert someone if they were in the vicinity.

Vincent's expression turned demented when he faced Anais. "Looks like you're up next."

There was a stare down between Anais and Vincent for a moment before she turned to me and mouthed, *I love you.* Terror shook me to my core as I watched her turn around and face the man who could be her murderer. Instinct kicked in, and I knew I couldn't let this happen. I thought about going for my gun again, but there was no way to guarantee I would reach it this time. There was also a chance that he would just shoot Anais anyway.

"Shoot me again."

"Damien, please don't."

"If anyone should die tonight out of the two of us, it should be me."

"No."

Before Vincent could choose who to shoot, I darted over to her pushing her out of the way in case it was a live round. When the gun went off, Anais screamed as we both hit the ground, me pulling her on top of me so I took the brunt of the fall. Our bodies ended up closer to the desk, something I was grateful for. Our moment didn't last long because I didn't trust that he wouldn't try to shoot us both while we were down on the floor, so I jumped back up and pulled Anais with me. I made sure she was behind me as I put my body between hers and Vincent's gun.

"Damien, it looks like you're up next and you know I have no problem killing you."

I stood firm as he pulled the trigger again. Shot number three rang out and once again, it was a blank.

Vincent smiled and fired shot number four without announcing it. I heard Anais gasp behind me, and she placed a hand on my back, the touch was trembling with fear.

"Looks like we're down to two remaining shots. Which one could it be?"

A noise near the door distracted Vincent, who turned to look. It was a split-second decision that I had to make, and pushed Anais behind the desk. I grabbed the gun and jumped up, quickly weighing my options before I pulled the trigger. Anais screamed again and Vincent's body hit the floor with a loud thud.

With Vincent's body out of the way, I could see Kingston in the doorway with his gun drawn. Relief filled my body as I realized it was only him and that he had probably done something to cause the distraction.

I looked at Anais and whispered to her, "Are you okay?" I could tell she wasn't as tears fell from her eyes.

She nodded her head, and I took a moment to scan her body with my eyes and hands, making sure that she actually was okay. Then, I pulled her into my arms, enjoying the feel of her body intertwined with mine.

"Everything is fine now, I promise."

After we embraced for several more minutes, my attention was dragged to Kingston who was staring at Vincent's dead body. "What the fuck took you so long?"

"We were downstairs in the car so things were a little muffled. I got suspicious when I hadn't heard anything from Anais. Looks like Uncle Martin needs to overhaul security here because there is no way Vincent should have been able to get up here."

"I'll be sure to let him know."

Kingston walked over to his body and kicked the gun out of the way. He bent down to check to see if there was a pulse.

He looked up at me and said, "He's dead. Looks like both of our shots hit him."

The words I had been waiting to hear since I found out about Vincent were one of the top three things I had ever heard. It was finally over.

"We need to call Will and fill him in. We have a special delivery to make."

22

DAMIEN

I pulled the SUV into a parking garage, in a spot that wasn't well lit by lights. There were no other cars around, but we were expecting at least one to pick up the package we had.

"I'm glad to have this off of our hands." I reached into my pocket and pulled my phone out.

Me: *We're downstairs.*

I looked at Kingston and said, "Drop off should be any minute."

He laid his head on the headrest of the passenger seat. "I'm glad."

"Tired? I thought you worked all of the time?"

"After this shit? A vacation is calling my name."

I snorted. "I would think that is well deserved."

"Yeah, I should take a break before either you or your brothers get into some more shit and call me."

There was a knock on the window closest to me and I turned to look out of it. There I found the man of the hour.

"About time you joined us."

"You better have some good news."

Will's ability to skip the bullshit was one of his greater qualities. "And if I told you I did?"

Will stood up and looked at me. "He's dead?"

I nodded. "I brought him just like I said I would. He's in the trunk."

Will took a step back and Kingston and I got out of the vehicle. A slight breeze filtered through the garage as we walked to the back of the SUV and I popped the trunk. Will waited as Kingston unzipped the body bag and took a look inside it. With a slight nod of his head, Kingston closed the body bag back up and Will stared off into the distance. Kingston walked back toward the passenger side of the car, giving Will and I an opportunity to talk alone.

He was silent for a moment before he said, "You know, I never thought I would be relieved that my brother was dead. Part of me wishes I would have been the one to put the bullet in him."

I thought about my relationship with my own brothers and his statement hit me hard. Having one of my brothers do what Vincent did would be an enormous betrayal, one that I wasn't sure if I would ever get over.

"At least Charlotte doesn't have to live in fear anymore."

Will looked back at me for a second before turning to look off into the distance. "Charlotte will always have to look over her shoulder due to her connection to me, much like Anais will have to because of you. We can do our best to protect the ones we love but that threat is always there, hiding just under the surface. And I'll never forgive myself for failing her."

"How'd you fail her?"

"If I had been here after our father died, she wouldn't have gotten caught up in Vincent's shit. I would have made sure of it. But I was off dealing with my own stuff and I thought everything would be fine here. I was wrong and I'll live with that for the rest of my life."

"You couldn't have known."

Will shook his head and I could see that my words didn't have their intended effect on him. He still blamed himself for what happened.

"Speaking of Charlotte, she's gone."

I narrowed my eyes at Will. "What do you mean she's gone?"

"She left the city again. Of course, this time I know where she went, but out of the abundance of caution and her privacy, I'm keeping it quiet. Being kidnapped and dragged back to New York in addition to everything else that happened...it would be a lot for anyone but even more so for someone who has had to look over her shoulder every time she went somewhere or did anything for over a decade. So, I let my baby sister go again. If it gives her happiness and peace, that's what I want her to have." He slowly turned and faced me again.

I held out my hand. "Everything is settled between us now?"

Will stared at my hand before shaking it. "It is."

"I'm sure we'll be in touch."

"I'm sure we will."

23

ANAIS

ONE MONTH LATER

T his red dress looked fantastic on me, but it would be better served on the floor, I thought as I examined the dress from all angles in the mirror. The lacy bodice was mostly see-through, only hiding my nipples before it flared into an A-line skirt that was also sheer. I put on the short red skirt that came with the ensemble under the sheer garment to keep some of my body covered. It was a bit dramatic for an evening at Elevate, but I was in a celebratory mood and this dress called out to me when I picked it up a couple of hours ago. I wore my hair down and added a red lipstick, knowing that it was only a matter of time before this whole look would be ruined anyway.

I grabbed a long black coat and threw it over my arm. It would help give the illusion that I was more covered than I was and only Damien and I knew what I was really wearing underneath.

It was still revealing, yet I felt more empowered than I had in a very long time. I felt as if I was the queen of this kingdom and I had so much power at my fingertips. I regularly brought one of the most powerful men in New York City to his knees and he enjoyed it. I gave myself one final look over and walked toward the elevator. I had no intention of walking down the stairs in these sky-high heels even if the mansion was nowhere near as tall as the penthouse.

Things had quieted down since Damien killed Vincent. We cut the amount of security that my parents, Ellie, and I needed, and life had gone back to some semblance of normal. I decided to go to therapy after the events that took place to have someone to talk to and work through the trauma that I'd dealt with over the last few months. It was one of the best decisions I could make for myself and I was happy I did it.

Damien did end up closing the deal on my office building and I was soon back walking the halls of Monroe Media Agency. It felt good to be working among my coworkers again and to have that social interaction while we were doing our best for our clients. Once word got out about the threat to Damien and me and the aftermath of Vincent's death, business was booming for us. At least something good came out of this treacherous shit show.

When the elevator reached the main level, I walked toward his office where I knew he would be this evening. When I reached the doorway, he didn't look up, even though I assumed he sensed my presence and heard my heels on the floor.

"Ahem."

Damien looked up from the document and saw me standing in the doorway, my outfit on full display. He raised an eyebrow, daring me to continue.

"Take me to Elevate."

"Since when do I take orders for you?" He leaned back in his office chair, lazily taking all of me in. "When did you get this outfit?"

"Sometime within the last month or so but that's none of your concern. I want to go back."

He stood up. "But it is my business seeing as how I—"

"Control my pleasure, I know. An adventure at Elevate would be pleasurable for both of us."

"You know if we go there, we're going to turn it up a bit."

I nodded. "I'm looking forward to it." I turned around to give him an eyeful of the dress. His eyes swallowed me whole and I was willing to bet that he wanted to take me up against the wall right here. In order to prevent that from happening, I turned on my heel and walked down the hallway.

When he followed me into the living room, I noticed he'd unbuttoned the top button of his white shirt. "Are you sure you want to go to Elevate? We could have plenty of fun right here."

"I'm positive. This dress deserves to be stared at."

"As long as all they're looking at is the dress and not the body wearing it. That belongs to me and to me alone."

"That just so happens to be fine by me, Mr. Cross."

"I'm glad we could agree on this subject, Ms. Monroe. No compromising necessary."

"Do you trust me?" Damien asked as I was sitting down on the bed in the room, my dress flowing around me. When we arrived downstairs, Damien picked up a box and led me into this room.

"Of course, what kind of question is that?"

He smiled for a brief moment at my answer before placing the box on the bed next to me and opening it. When he turned around to show me, I gasped.

"You want to blindfold me?"

"Is that a problem?"

"No, Damien." The confidence in my voice thrilled me.

"I also might have a couple other items that will make this more pleasurable. If anything becomes a problem for you, tell me immediately." When I nodded my head he said, "Then let's get started, shall we?"

Damien opted for a non-themed room this time around and it looked like any other bedroom except for the giant mirror on the ceiling. I wondered if he had any plans for it.

"Strip."

That one word made me quiver with desire as I stood up and stared him down while I removed my garments. When I was stark naked in front of him, he gestured for me to sit down on the bed.

"Lie down on your back, legs spread out in front of you."

When I did as he asked, Damien handed me the blindfold and I put it on myself. With the blindfold, this was turning into a completely different experience. With the loss of my eyesight, my other senses strengthened, and I could feel my wetness growing in anticipation for what he had planned.

There was silence in the room, and I waited with bated breath to see if I could hear anything that would clue me into what Damien was doing. Silence was the only thing that greeted me.

"Damien?" I whispered after the silence became too much for me to handle.

"I'm here, Spitfire."

He was here all right. He said the words right in my ear and I felt a shift on the bed due to his added weight.

"I want you to keep your arms above your head until I tell you that you can move them."

I smirked and asked, "And if I don't?" Sassiness dripped from my words and it wasn't too long before he gave an appropriate response.

A nice, firm swat on the ass. I sighed, missing the feeling of that type of contact on my skin. I was tempted to disobey him again to see what he would do, but there was time for that later. "Okay, I won't move."

"Good girl."

His weight shifted once more, and I briefly felt skin-to-skin contact. Had he taken off his clothes too?

I gasped when something light touched my skin. The item brushed along my chest, making sure to pay special attention to my nipples.

"Is that a feather?"

"It is."

I'd never would have thought that the light touch of a feather would have me withering but here I was, trying to guess where he might touch me again. The feather took one final dusting over my nipples before disappearing.

"Good job on not moving your hands." I felt his hands move down my body with the softest of touches, almost reminiscent of the feather that was on my skin just seconds ago. His fingers stopped at my pussy where he lazily dragged a finger up and down my seam. "It looks as if you enjoyed that very much. Let's see if you can do as good of a job with this."

It was a few moments before I felt something cool waiting at my entrance. "What's that?"

Instead of answering, Damien turned it on, and I moaned so loud that it sounded foreign to my own ears. It was a vibrator, but the sensations made any thoughts in my mind vanish. This vibrator was bigger than the one I had used before and it was definitely an example of when bigger is better.

When I felt him tweak one of my nipples, my hips nearly bucked off the bed. I heard a faint dark chuckle over the noise of the vibrator as I felt the beginning of the end start. My body shuddered as an orgasm took over, making me lose all control. My groans and gasps didn't stop Damien's assault on me. He kept the vibrator turned on as I rode out my orgasm.

Suddenly the vibrations stopped, and Damien rubbed my sensitive clit. How I kept my hands in place, I'd never know.

"You don't know how beautiful you just looked as I watched you come hard. But now it's time for you to see it for yourself."

The blindfold was taken off my eyes and it took me a moment to adjust to the light. My eyes found Damien's and saw the look of love gleaming from them. He bent down to kiss me before he positioned himself at my pussy and guided his cock inside of me. He groaned as he pumped into me.

"Look up. I want you to watch yourself as I make you come. You may move your arms."

My eyes slowly moved from him up to the ceiling where I got a front row seat to watching our own personal show live. I watched as he pumped his dick in and out of me, creating an even more intimate connection as our bodies found a rhythm that was just for us. Being able to watch ourselves perform such a sensual and primal act was the most erotic thing I had ever seen. And then Damien's eyes met mine in the mirror. Watching the look on his face as his thrust met one of mine painted a beautiful scene of our love.

I could feel another orgasm building within me just as Damien sped up the pace, telling me that he was getting closer to the edge as well. I bit my lip when I saw him briefly close his eyes as he continued fucking me.

"I'm going to come," he announced as he looked down at me, but my eyes were fixated on the mirror above.

I shouted first as my release charged through me and not once did Damien stop his motions until he joined me on the other side of his orgasm.

Sweat and heavy breathing were shared between us before I said, "That was extraordinary. I'm just in awe."

"And to think that this is just the beginning, Spitfire." He wiped away one lonely happy tear that fell from my eye.

"I love you."

"And I love you too."

EPILOGUE

ANAIS

"Think your mother is having enough fun with this?"

"Oh, this?" Damien snorted. "She's just getting started. This is why I said we should just tell her how we envisioned it and she will take it from there."

"You were right...again."

"I'm still not used to hearing that."

I flipped my hair over my shoulder. "Good. Don't."

Damien reached down and patted my butt. Even though the pat was light, and my gown stood between him touching me, I was thinking about the moments we spent the night before and how I couldn't wait to get out of here to do it all over again.

"Stop looking like that."

I turned to Damien. "Looking like what?"

"Like you want me to bend you over right now and welcome our guests with a real show."

I chuckled. "That would be quite the show."

"Oscar worthy, although it wouldn't be acting."

"Damien, there you are." Selena Cross floated into the room wearing a beautiful gray dress. Not a hair was out of place and she looked at ease even with all of the craziness that was currently going on. Since she was running the show with a team of planners, that might have helped. "Martin is looking for you. He's in the office."

He turned to me and placed a kiss on my lips. His mother patted him on the shoulder just before he gave what could be described as a small smile before he walked away.

"I wanted to come over and say congratulations and welcome to the family." She opened her arms and I stepped into her embrace.

"Thank you, although not quite yet. We need to take our vows."

"I consider you part of the family." She pulled away and looked at my gown. "This is absolutely stunning." The strapless eggplant-colored dress that I was wearing tonight was fitted to my body like a second skin. I accessorized with other purple items and decided to wear my hair up in a low bun for the night.

"And I love yours."

"Thank you, I picked it out just for this evening. I thought it would be on the safer end and wouldn't clash in any of the family photos."

That's right. There probably would be a lot of photos taken and a lot of people here. The thought made my stomach twist a couple of times, but I tamped it down by thinking about how all of this would be over soon.

The Cross estate had been completely transformed into a spring oasis that was stunning. Soft cream-colored flowers, many of them roses and tulips, were all over the home and the layout of the home was converted to fit what had to be at least one hundred people here tonight. I wasn't looking forward to it.

"Damien mentioned that you weren't too crazy about all of the attention."

I shrugged. "It's not my forte, but I know some of it comes with the territory of being with Damien, so I'll deal. Plus, it might mean more business for Monroe Media Agency, which would be a great thing."

"Another reason why you and my son are a great match." Her words confused me, and I must have been wearing it on my face because she chuckled before she said, "You both think strategically and balance each other well. I knew that when you came and stayed with us for a few days, and I watched how you two interacted. I hoped things would lead down to this path with you two getting married, but I didn't want to push. Now here we are."

"Now here we are," I whispered and gave her a small smile. "Thank you."

"You're welcome."

"Okay, Mom. I want some more time with my fiancée."

"All right, even though you've had plenty of time with her. Given the fact that you guys have just come back from vacation again."

That was true. Damien had taken me to Paris after I mentioned wanting to go. It was somewhat of a working vacation because we both held business meetings while there. But once work was done, we spent the rest of the time enjoying one another.

When Bernard opened the front door, Broderick and

Gage walked in. It was fascinating to look at all four Cross men in their suits prepared for the night's events.

"If you all aren't a dapper bunch?"

"Dapper? Really, Mom?"

I snickered at Gage's response.

Selena patted him on the arm and said, "We should get ready because our guests will start arriving in a few minutes."

Damien grabbed my hand and gave me a gentle squeeze before he rubbed my knuckles. I smiled up at him, happy to have his company to get through this night. True to Selena's word, people started arriving a few minutes after we separated.

My parents were one of the first to arrive and when they reached me, they gave me a big hug. Dad was doing much better and was almost back to being one hundred percent. Mom was doing well too, and Dad was planning on taking her on vacation in a couple of weeks to give not just both of them an opportunity to relax, but to thank her for everything that she did when he was recovering from getting shot.

"You look beautiful, sweetheart." Mom held both hands on my arms and she took a piece of my hair that had gone astray and placed it behind my ear. It was a habit she developed when I was a toddler, and she did it on occasion even though I was an adult. As a teenager, it annoyed me, but now I realized she was only trying to help.

"Your mother is right. You look stunning." He leaned over and placed a kiss on my cheek. He then turned to Damien and shook his hand. "It's nice to see you."

I appreciated Dad being polite although I don't know if he had completely warmed up to Damien as of yet. I felt bad for telling him that little white lie about whether or not Damien and I were involved, but I was happy to see that he seemed to be moving past it.

The four of us quietly talked until I heard my name from across the room. I turned and found Ellie walking up to me. When she reached me, she gave me a tight hug before grabbing my left hand. "I still can't believe you're engaged!" She dropped my hand and pulled me into her arms for a quick hug.

I chuckled. "You say that every time we see each other in person."

"I know but I still can't believe it. Is this the part where I threaten Damien?"

"I would suggest not doing that, Ms. Winters."

I wondered if I was the only one who knew he was joking based on the looks on my parents' and Ellie's faces. "He's kidding."

The sigh of relief that everyone released made me nudge Damien. He looked at me but said nothing.

"Hi Anais and Damien."

Our attention was diverted once more when Grace walked up to us, greeting us. I quickly introduced her to Ellie and my parents. After that was done, the group started to have a round of small talk. I looked around to see if someone in particular had spotted who had just arrived. *Bingo.* Broderick's attention was completely on Grace, even as his twin was talking to him. It was a few seconds before Broderick noticed me looking at him but it didn't matter anyway because he just shrugged and turned his attention back to Gage.

"Interesting," I muttered.

"What's interesting?" Damien whispered in my ear.

"Nothing, nothing important." I turned to face him,

pulling him closer to me by his lapels. "Let's enjoy this night that was put together in honor of us."

"Oh. So, are you finally saying you're mine?"

"No." I paused. "I'm finally saying that *you* are mine."

Damien shook his head and gave me a kiss on my lips. It held promises of what was to come later tonight once we were alone. He grabbed my hand and pulled me through the crowd until we reached a makeshift stage. First, he helped me up and then he followed suit. Broderick, who was standing on this side of the room, handed Damien a microphone but Martin Cross got up on the stage with another microphone in hand.

"Excuse me." Martin waited a beat before he continued. "First I want to thank everyone for coming to celebrate my son Damien and his fiancée, Anais."

A round of applause could be heard in all corners of the room, making me want to slink away, but I refused. I belonged here. This party was to celebrate my upcoming nuptials with Damien. And dammit, I was doing just that.

"I also want to thank my wife, Selena, and Anais's mother, Ilaria, and the wonderful staff here to help pull all this together." The room clapped once more. "Now, I want to introduce my oldest son, Damien."

I tried to control the rush of emotions that I could feel creeping up my face as Damien held out his hand for me and together, we walked toward the center of the stage. "Thanks, Dad." He smiled at his dad before squeezing my hand.

I took several deep breaths as the crowd quieted down and Damien turned to me.

"First I want to thank everyone for coming out this evening. It means a lot that you're here to celebrate us. I never knew what it meant to love someone. I did my best to avoid anything related to a significant other or finding a partner for life. Until I met Anais, I thought I had everything even though there was always a nagging feeling in the back of my mind. She was what I was missing." He smiled at me. "It was always you. Thank you for changing my life for the better and I can't wait to make you my wife. And if anyone knows me well enough, you know how impatient I am so don't be shocked if we get married tomorrow morning."

A light chuckle rippled through the crowd. It was clear that Damien was telling a joke...right?

SOMETIME LATER, I was washing my hands in the bathroom after fixing up my makeup. Taking so many photos and talking to so many people had taken its toll on the state of my face, so a quick touch-up was required. As I was getting ready to walk out the door and rejoin the party, a voice made me stop.

"Stop being an asshole. I don't have to explain myself to you."

"When you are standing there flirting with that fucker, the hell you do."

"What business is it of yours who I flirt with? What has gotten into you?"

"It became my business when you—Grace. Grace!"

I thought it was Broderick who screamed her name. *What is that about?*

I waited a few more seconds before I walked out of my hiding place once I thought the coast might be clear.

"There you are."

I turned and found my husband-to-be with a soft smile playing on his lips.

"My trip to the bathroom took a little longer than usual."

"Did it have anything to do with Broderick and Grace? I saw them standing nearby when I walked out to find you."

"Maybe." I sang the word in a whimsical voice that made Damien chuckle.

"Whatever is going on between them is none of your concern."

"Speak for yourself. Now that I'm not getting kidnapped or shot at, I have plenty of time to worry about what is going on with the people around me."

He leaned over to give me a kiss before he whispered in my ear, "And I can't wait to punish you for that smart mouth later."

I smiled back at him because I knew it wouldn't be much of a punishment since I would enjoy it.

Instead of a replying to Damien, I looked down the hall. Something told me that the danger the Cross Family had faced was only just beginning.

THANK you for reading Steel Empire! While Anais and Damien's trilogy is complete, the Broken Cross series continues with Shadow Empire, Broderick and Grace's book. Keep reading to find a sneak peek of it!

SHADOW EMPIRE BLURB

What lurks in the shadows...

I was in the wrong place at the wrong time
When Broderick Cross saved me from an untimely fate.
I hated him with every fiber of my being,
And I know he won't touch me because I'm his best friend's sister.
Or that's what I thought.
But even with danger knocking on my door,
The one I need protection from is him.

SNEAK PEEK OF SHADOW EMPIRE
GRACE

I hated that son of a bitch, with every inch of my being. Could I believe I was thinking this about Broderick now? No, but his behavior had put me on edge.

Our eyes met as soon as I entered the bar. Not even the darkness of the environment could prevent the stare down that occurred. His blue eyes clashed with mine and warning bells sounded in my mind.

It was the first time I had seen Broderick in person since we last spoke at Damien and Anais's engagement celebration. It wasn't a shock for me to be invited due to my relationship with the Cross family and I was glad to attend and celebrate the happy couple. Seeing some familiar faces was usually great, especially when you're attending an event alone. I was hoping to enjoy a night off when I didn't have anything going on, but of course Broderick Cross showed up to this party as well.

Broderick had been in my life for as long as I could remember. I was seen as just the younger sister who followed them around when we were children. That faded as we got older, and I'd seen Broderick more while I was in high school and in college.

Normally, our relationship was on good terms. It wasn't unheard of that I would watch football with him and my brother when I was free. That was all ruined the night he tried to take control over who I could and couldn't speak to. I rolled my eyes and turned away, choosing to fall deeper into the crowded bar, hoping to blend in and find my brother at the same time.

I shouldn't have been surprised. My brother was hosting the party, so the chances of Broderick attending were high. The only way it would have been higher was if Hunter had asked to host the party at Elevate. After all, the two of them had been thick as thieves for decades. Deep down I knew there was a good chance that he would show up, but I also didn't want to miss out on an evening of fun all because Broderick had decided to be a prick several weeks ago.

My work schedule sometimes meant long hours, and while my job was mostly rewarding, it had its drawbacks too. Tonight, I had an opportunity to relax and here he was attempting to insert himself into my night after I told him to get lost the last time that I saw him.

While I was at Damien and Anais's engagement party, I struck up a conversation with a man in attendance. The conversation was friendly at best and Broderick came over fuming. The whole incident was very dramatic, and I was still pissed about it. Never in the time that I'd known Broderick had he ever pulled the stunt he did that night, and I wasn't sure what made him snap and the bottom line was that I didn't need Broderick fighting battles for me. Not now, not ever.

I pulled at the dark denim jacket that I had thrown on over my low-cut black shirt and jeans with black flats. The perfect outfit for me for this spring evening. I tucked a piece of my blonde hair behind my ear and smiled at the bartender when I approached. I ordered a light beer and received it immediately, basking in the fact that I didn't have to pay due to my brother having an open bar.

"There's my favorite little sister."

I smiled at the moniker. "I'm your only little sister," I said as I turned around. There standing behind me was my older brother, IPA in hand, ready to be the life of the party.

"I'm glad you could make it."

"Same, but I wouldn't miss your promotion celebration for the world. I'm so proud of you."

I leaned in to hug him and when I looked over his shoulder, I saw the only person who was currently on my shit list.

"Hey, man, congrats again on the promotion."

Broderick came around Hunter's left side while I stood on his right. It took everything in me not to roll my eyes. I waved my brother off when one of his friends called his name and all that was left were two piercing blue eyes staring back at me.

"Grace."

I let out a deep breath. "I don't want to talk to you."

"Tough shit. I want to talk to you."

He had some damn nerve. I leaned over and whispered to him, "I'm not talking to you about anything related to my personal life because it is none of your concern. Better yet, I don't want to talk to you at all. So leave."

That didn't do anything to deter him. "Hellion, if you want to experience Elevate up close and personal, all you have to do is ask. Not entertain the idea of some asshole in a cheap three-piece suit taking you there."

My mood soured. Broderick had the audacity to say these things, but I refused to sit here and tolerate it. I took another swig of my beer before I put it back down on the bar and turned to him. "Who knew how much of an asshole you could be? Wait, don't answer that. Have a good night."

I hoped the bite in my tone told him that I wanted him to have anything but. I made my way through the crowd and found my brother.

"Listen, Hunt, something came up and I need to head out," I whispered in his ear.

"Already?" The look of disappointment made me feel like shit, but I knew if I stayed, Broderick would be watching me like a hawk all night, which was disturbing, whereas my own brother wouldn't do this. I also didn't trust myself not to snap at him again. Hunter opened his arms and I stepped into his embrace. "Do you want me to walk you to the subway?"

I shook my head. "No. Don't miss out on your own party because of me. I might decide to take a cab. I'll call you later."

"You better."

I gave him one last smile before I strolled toward the door. Just before I reached it, I looked up and found Broderick staring back at me from another corner of the room. He lifted his beer in a mock salute, and I gave him my one-finger one in return. Two could play this immaturity game.

I pulled out my phone to call a car and saw that the wait time was way longer than I wanted to deal with. I adjusted my jacket over my body, applied a coat of lip gloss, and put my phone back in my purse before I wandered down the street. I had walked a couple of buildings away from the bar before I heard a low groan coming from my left. When I looked, I found a dimly lit alleyway, but I saw nothing in the darkness.

Is someone over there? Where did that noise come from?

Although fear swam through my mind, I knew I had to do something. That was when I saw someone leaning against a brick wall and it was clear that they were hurting in some way. As I started to walk into the alley, another figure appeared from the shadows and walked up to the person and the next thing I heard was a croak. The figure backed away from the person, who slowly slid down the brick wall.

Did...did I just see someone get stabbed?

A scream bubbled below the surface, and I knew if it erupted from my mouth I would draw the attention of the person still in the alleyway. Before I could emit any sound or run away, I felt a hand slip over my lips, and another around my waist as I was dragged away from the opening of the alley. That something felt warm against my lips. Since I still had the ability to fight, there was no way I was going down without one. I fought against my attacker, and I heard a grunt before someone said, "Grace, cut it out."

Broderick?

"Let me go!" I screamed, but it was mostly muffled by what I now knew to be Broderick's hand.

He continued pulling me back until he whispered in my ear, "I'm going to remove my hand, but you have to promise not to scream."

I nodded my head quickly and he did as he said he would. As he wiped his hand, removing the remnants of my lip gloss from it, I said, "Broderick, I might be able to save his life, let me go."

"Do you want to save your own? Be quiet and follow me."

Shadow Empire is available now!

ABOUT THE AUTHOR

Bri loves a good romance, especially ones that involve a hot anti-hero. That is why she likes to turn the dial up a notch with her own writing. Her Broken Cross series is her debut dark romance series.

She spends most of her time hanging out with her family, plotting her next novel, or reading books by other romance authors.

briblackwood.com

ALSO BY BRI BLACKWOOD

Broken Cross Series

Sinners Empire (Prequel)

Savage Empire

Scarred Empire

Steel Empire

Shadow Empire

Secret Empire

Stolen Empire

Brentson University Series

Devious Game

The Billionaire Trilogy

The Billionaire's Auction